"The print equ_____ _wn. High praise, indeed. A biza___ _____ _____ _astic that really, really works. *The Stand By Me*–cum–*The Outsiders* feel . . . is real, and honest . . . perfectly unique. A grown-up, odd, compelling journey through adolescence, and heartache, and of course, Neverland. Fascinating and completely engrossing."

—The 11th Hour

"[Golden's] novels capture the charming mystique that permeates New England, to which he adds a shuddering dose of the occult." —*Boston* magazine

"I defy anyone to read a few scenes and not be swept up. Golden's imagination was working overtime when he crafted a way to blend this coming-of-age story with not just a bona fide childhood classic, but Gaelic mythology as well. Golden keeps those pages flying by, without forgetting to bring it full circle and give your heart a tweak or two in the very end."

—Brian Hodge, author of *Wild Horses*

"A clever and touching dark fantasy novel [that is] magic to read. As dark, and as mature, as any good fairy tale is at heart." —Gothic.net

And the Novels of Christopher Golden

Strangewood

"Christopher Golden gradually brings into being a world of haunted and perilous fantasy that, while moving into greater solidity, never loses touch with its painful, sweet, embattled human context . . . a beautiful and wildly inventive hymn to the most salvific human capacity: imagination. A notable achievement."

—Bram Stoker Award–winning author Peter Straub

"If Clive Barker had gone *Through the Looking Glass*, he might have come up with something as imaginative and compelling as *Strangewood*. It's been a long time since I've read such an original novel."

—*New York Times* bestselling author Kevin J. Anderson

continued . . .

Praise for Christopher Golden
and His *Shadow Saga*

"Harrowing, humorous, overflowing with plot contortions . . . abundantly entertaining . . . a writer who cares passionately about the stuff of horror."
—Douglas E. Winter, editor of *Revelations*

"Fast and furious, funny and original!"
—Joe R. Lansdale, author of *Captains Outrageous*

"Just when you thought nothing new could be done with the vampire mythos, [Golden] comes along and shows us otherwise." —Ray Garton, author of *Live Girls*

"An imaginative storyteller whose writing is both chilling and suspenseful." —Philip Nutman, author of *Wet Work*

"Filled with action, sweep, and dark mythology."
—Rex Miller, author of *Slob*

"A breathtaking story . . . a brilliant epic."
—*Dark News* (Paris)

"An intriguing adult mystery, not for the faint of heart."
—*Murder Under Cover, Inc.*

"Passionate . . . excellent . . . [a] brilliant vampire novel in a blizzard of bloody tooth bites this year."
—*LitNews* and *Dark Channel*

"Golden has created a new myth . . . worthy of the praise it has already received, and more." —*Eclipse Magazine*

"A fast-paced action thriller that will hold the reader's attention from the first page to the last." —*The Talisman*

"Sort of M. R. James meets Godzilla."
—Mike Mignola, creator of *Hellboy*

Straight On 'Til Morning

Christopher Golden

With a New Introduction by the Author
and a Bonus Short Story, "Runaway"

A ROC BOOK

ROC
Published by New American Library, a division of
Penguin Group (USA) Inc., 375 Hudson Street,
New York, New York 10014, USA
Penguin Group (Canada), 90 Eglinton Avenue East, Suite 700, Toronto,
Ontario M4P 2Y3, Canada (a division of Pearson Penguin Canada Inc.)
Penguin Books Ltd., 80 Strand, London WC2R 0RL, England
Penguin Ireland, 25 St. Stephen's Green, Dublin 2,
Ireland (a division of Penguin Books Ltd.)
Penguin Group (Australia), 250 Camberwell Road, Camberwell, Victoria 3124,
Australia (a division of Pearson Australia Group Pty. Ltd.)
Penguin Books India Pvt. Ltd., 11 Community Centre, Panchsheel Park,
New Delhi - 110 017, India
Penguin Group (NZ), cnr Airborne and Rosedale Roads, Albany,
Auckland 1310, New Zealand (a division of Pearson New Zealand Ltd.)
Penguin Books (South Africa) (Pty.) Ltd., 24 Sturdee Avenue,
Rosebank, Johannesburg 2196, South Africa

Penguin Books Ltd., Registered Offices:
80 Strand, London WC2R 0RL, England

Published by Roc, an imprint of New American Library, a division of Penguin
Putnam Inc. Previously published in a Signet mass market edition.

First Roc Printing, September 2006
10 9 8 7 6 5 4 3 2 1

PUBLISHER'S NOTE
This is a work of fiction. Names, characters, places, and incidents either are
the product of the author's imagination or are used fictitiously, and any resem-
blance to actual persons, living or dead, business establishments, events, or
locales is entirely coincidental.

The publisher does not have any control over and does not assume any
responsibility for author or third-party Web sites or their content.

For my brother Jamie.
How much do *you* remember?

and

For Barbara English.
The first girl I ever loved.

Author's Note
and
Acknowledgments

This novel is a work of fiction . . . mostly.

Every writer I know cannot help but include elements of his or her life, memories, pet theories, philosophies and frames of reference in their work. Sometimes characters are created from whole cloth, but at others, they are amalgams of people you've known throughout your life, including yourself. Some of the characters in *Straight on 'til Morning* are extreme examples of the latter.

It should be noted, however, that none of the characters herein are meant to precisely reproduce any actual, living person. That is not what fiction is about. Any attempt to do such a thing would have been misguided, and altered the story as I needed to tell it.

This is a work of fiction. I've said that, I know, but it bears repeating. The characters are fictional, though they may seem familiar to some. Tommy Carlson, for instance, is based on two close childhood friends of mine, though one significantly more than the other. Neither one of them, however, would behave the way Tommy does in the following pages.

It's fiction.

On the other hand—(you knew that was coming, didn't you?)—many of the events in *Straight on 'til Morning* actually happened. I think you'd be surprised to find out how many. They didn't happen in the order I present them, and certain circumstances have been changed, but though it's all fiction, the first half of this novel is also, in some fundamental way, *true*. More true, even, than if I had tried to recount the actual events with their actual participants.

I'd like to thank my agent, Lori Perkins, and my editor, Laura Anne Gilman. As always, grateful, endless praise for the loving patience of my wife, Connie, and the love of my crazy boys, Nicholas and Daniel. For support and friendship, thanks to Tom Sniegoski. Thanks to my mother, Roberta Golden Poulos, for making all the adventures possible.

Finally, a very fond thank-you to June Jewell, Kerry Brusco, Steve Crain, John Rice, and my big brother, Jamie Golden, for setting off into the woods with me in the first place. Your cooperation and enthusiasm made this all possible.

Introduction

Coming of age.

A shred of truth: writers don't generally sit down and think to themselves, "I'm going to write a coming-of-age story." Other sorts of novels do have their origins in such thoughts. "I'm going to write a vampire novel that challenges the conceits of organized religion" or "I'm going to write a novel focused on how we are all the sum of our experiences, and how the fear of losing our memories is one of the most terrifying of all."

I've done both of those, and such thoughts were, by and large, at their genesis.

But for me, and I'd wager for many other writers as well, the coming-of-age story does not begin in quite the same way. It happens more organically. Perhaps I'm being naive, but somehow I doubt that when Stephen King came up with the idea for his landmark novella *The Body* (which would become the film *Stand by Me*), he began that process by deciding to write a coming-of-age story. Instead, I imagine him thinking to himself that he'd like to do a story about a group of kids and their adventures in a landscape very similar to the one in which he had been a child. I imagine him wanting to give new life to that moment of his own past, but also to tell the story of these boys, and of something grim that they encounter that changes them forever.

I could be wrong, of course. Maybe I'd lose that wager. But I doubt it. Coming-of-age stories, it seems to me, are nearly always about *the story* and *the moment*. At some point along the way, of course, the author most certainly realizes what he or she is writing and that instead of being about the moment that defines the era in which it is set, it is about the moment at which things *change*.

But I suspect that most of these stories do not start that way.

When I set out to write *Straight on 'til Morning*, I was not focused on the bittersweet nature of such tales, and such endings. Had I given it a moment's thought, in fact, I doubt I would have written it at all. Some of the greatest stories ever written in dark fantasy and horror have been coming-of-age stories. King's *The Body*. Bradbury's *Something Wicked This Way Comes*. Robert R. McCammon's *Boy's Life*. Dan Simmons' *Summer of Night*.

I would be an outrageous liar if I claimed that these stories did not influence me, but I forged ahead without thinking, without truly being aware that I was striking out into similar territory. It was the story, you see, that led me into that strange yet familiar territory, and by the time it occurred to me, I had no choice but to go on, if only to see how it would end. I make no comparison, of course. Only a fool would dare. Even to attempt to cover similar territory is daunting enough.

When I set out to write *Straight on 'til Morning*, I had read a lot of wonderful stories set in the childhood of the fifties and sixties . . . and not a single one that reflected my own experiences growing up in the seventies and eighties. Much as I love King's story "Sometimes They Come Back," it speaks of a different time, like the songs of Billy Joel and the novels of S. E. Hinton.

So, yes, I wanted to re-create the era of my own youth. But first and foremost, I had a story to tell . . . a story about a girl.

I had girlfriends in junior high, in that junior high girlfriend kind of way. There existed in some of those encounters an intensity unique to being in the seventh or eighth grade. Part of being that certain age, of discovering so much about the world and yourself, is the feeling you get that your emotions are as boundless as the universe.

But even if I said "I love you" then, and meant it with every iota of my being, there was a hollowness to the sentiment. At that age the heart of a young boy is like the Earth when it was still a ball of fiery magma constantly changing, shifting and churning, still trying to figure out what it will become.

Yet in my heart, in those years, one thing never changed. I went about my days and nights, hung out with my friends, professed undying love to girlfriends, but in the back of my mind there was always one girl.

Bobbi English.

There's no point in me going on at length about what I felt for Bobbi English growing up. It's all right here in these pages. She was one of my closest friends and I secretly loved her from the time I was ten until I was fourteen or fifteen. Secretly, because Bobbi was more than a year older than I was, which was a big deal at the time. I could simply not imagine that she'd have any interest in me other than as her friend and sometimes sidekick, but back then, that was enough.

You'll find the rest of the story in the pages that follow. Not all of the events herein are true, of course. There are monsters in these pages, and myths and strange, legendary places, and there's magic as well. But nearly everything that happens in the first half of the novel really did happen. The caveat at the beginning of the book extrapolates a bit more on that point.

For now we'll just say this: *Straight on 'til Morning* is a coming-of-age story. No denying that, now. But in all the ways that matter, it's *my* coming-of-age story. The characters in the book, even the bad guys, are based on real people. Friends who knew my brother and me in those days and who've read the novel are endlessly amused by the portrayal of Kevin and Jesse Murphy simply because it's so true.

I'd venture to say that in some ways, the portrayal is even more true than the truth. If you have a hard time understanding that, then I'm not sure I can explain it. The essence of who we were back then, it's all in here.

A couple notes on the story itself.

First, it turns on a dime. Consider that fair warning. More than one reviewer compared its structure to *From Dusk 'til Dawn*. Take that as you will. The point of bringing it up is simply that you ought to be aware that as quiet and nostalgic as the coming-of-age elements are in the first half of the story, you should not be lulled into a false sense of security. Yes, it's a coming-of-age story, but it is also very much a dark fantasy novel. There are two journeys within these pages, one very personal and one surreal and wild, as the title should indicate.

Don't say you weren't warned.

Second, one of the most amusing comments I've seen about *Straight on 'til Morning*—one that has been noted several times by readers of the book—is that there's too much profanity within these pages, that thirteen-year-old kids fresh out of junior high don't actually speak this way. To those readers, I have only this to say:

You don't know what the fuck you're talking about. ☺

The characters in *Straight on 'til Morning* have filthy mouths because when I was thirteen, everyone I knew spoke that way. A sentence wasn't complete if it didn't have a swear in it. I'm well aware that not everyone grew up cussing like a truck driver but that was my experience.

Enough of this shit, as Kevin Murphy might say. We've got quite a journey ahead, one that will alter the lives of the Murphy brothers and their friends forever. Come along. . . .

—Christopher Golden
Bradford, Massachusetts
December 4, 2005

Straight
On 'Til
Morning

Prologue

In the summer of 1981, not long after his fourteenth birthday, Kevin Murphy learned that he wasn't bulletproof. Up until that point, he believed, like all children believe, that the world, even the universe, revolved around him. The neighborhood around Fox Run Drive and Londonderry Lane was his. The friends he spent the early part of that long ago summer with were, at least to Kevin's mind, just along for the ride. Like George Reeves in the old black-and-white *Superman* show he watched in reruns on channel fifty-six, Kevin was bulletproof.

Indestructible.

By summer's end, he would know differently. By summer's end, nothing would be the same. Much later in life, Kevin knew that it was that hot July in 1981 when he had learned the hardest lesson of all: The world did not revolve around him. The universe would continue on toward infinity with nary a pause to reflect upon any tragedy that might befall him.

As the years passed into decades, the memory of that summer blurred and faded. How much of what he recalled had really happened and how much was his own fancy he could not say with any certainty, even less as time went on. And the less he could remember of those events, the more they haunted him.

They haunt him still.

But on a cool night, the last week of June, all that unwelcome knowledge was still yet to come. The world existed just for Kevin, and that was very fine indeed.

Book One: Fantasy Girl

1

On the last Friday in June—the twenty-sixth, to be exact—Kevin Murphy sat on the slate stoop in front of his house, reading a book and listening to the little radio he'd brought outside with him.

It had been a perfect day, about eighty, with a cool breeze that made the leaves flutter on the three good oak climbing trees in his front yard. Kevin had spent the afternoon playing touch football with his brother, Jesse, and some of the kids in the neighborhood. The score had gotten up pretty high, but it wasn't like they could really count anything, what with the roster of each team changing so often over the course of the afternoon.

Eventually, though, dinnertime came around and the game ended. Kevin and Jesse had gone home and ordered pizza delivery, then paid with a check their mother had left them for that purpose. Aileen Murphy was a real estate agent, and she often had to work late. But pizza was fine with the Murphy brothers.

The front of the house was shaded now, and it was cool enough when the breeze swept across the lawn that Kevin shivered a bit. He was so wrapped up in the book he was reading, however, that he barely noticed. It was a mystery novel, only it wasn't like other mysteries. The detective in this one was a black-belt midget circus star. Kevin had read it twice already.

There was a crackle of static on the radio, and then WAAF started playing "Fantasy Girl," by .38 Special. All the stations were playing that song. Kevin knew he should have been sick of it by now, but he started bopping along to it anyway.

Distracted by the music, he slipped a finger in the book to mark his page, and looked around. Donny Marazik's jacked-up van was parked in front of the Herndons' across the street, and Kevin marveled at the thing. It had a huge cooling unit on top, and tires almost as tall as he was. He and Jesse could sit Indian style under the van and not bump their heads. There were no cars at the Goldman house, next to the Herndons'. A Forsale sign jutted at an odd angle from the ground, bowed by the high winds the previous night. Back in May, Mr. Goldman had a heart attack and died, right there in the driveway.

It was kind of creepy.

As he looked at the closed-up face of the Goldman house, Kevin saw something moving out of the corner of his eye. He glanced over to see Jack Ross walking toward him, cutting through the late Mr. Goldman's backyard. The Rosses lived on Londonderry Lane, which bisected with Fox Run Drive—where the Murphys lived—just a few houses down. The strip of lawn between the Murphys' front door across the street on to the Goldmans' property, and through the Rosses' backyard, was worn yellow by their passing over the years.

Jack didn't quicken his pace at all as he approached. Nor was he ever likely to do so. Jack Ross had just turned fourteen, but he had a way about him, a kind of silence and a coolness to his blue eyes, that reminded Kevin of Clint Eastwood in all those spaghetti westerns. In a group, Jack would always hang back, just observing. He'd shrug his shoulders as an answer. But Kevin had seen him get mad a couple of times. It wasn't pretty.

"Hey," Jack mumbled as he walked the last few steps toward the Murphys' front stoop. " 'Sup?"

"Waiting for Tommy," Kevin replied. "We're walking down to Diana's. I guess Carolyn and April are gonna be there, too. You should come."

Jack tossed his long brown hair back and glanced

away. "Nah. Just gonna hang out with Jesse tonight. 'Sides, if April wanted me to come, she coulda called."

"You guys fighting?" Kevin asked, concerned. He'd been the one to introduce Jack to April, and he didn't want things to go badly for them.

Jack just shrugged.

"Jesse's taking a shower," Kevin told him.

With a roll of his eyes, Jack yanked open the Murphys' screen door. "He's always in the fucking shower." He went in. A moment later, he called up to Jesse. "Hey, dickhead! Let's go!"

Kevin chuckled. He knew that if Jack didn't want to go with him, it was probably because either he or Jesse had scored a bag of weed. As far as Kevin was concerned, they could have it. If April was his girlfriend, he wouldn't choose to get stoned instead of hanging out with her. But, then, that was probably why, even though he and Kevin were the same age, Jack would usually rather hang with Jesse, who was two years older. They had more in common.

He had just dipped into his book again when the screen door popped open, nearly slamming into his back. Annoyed, Kevin stood up and turned around, glaring at his brother.

At fifteen, Jesse Murphy was about the same height as his little brother, but brawnier. Kevin had dark hair and deep brown eyes as opposed to the blue eyes Jesse had inherited from their mother. Neither of them looked as young as they were. Kevin—who had been skinny all his life—had suddenly become broad shouldered the previous winter. But Jesse just looked tougher. Jesse, who had always been the more imposing of the two, had long hair and a buck knife on his belt, and a Harley Davidson wallet on a chain that stuck out of his back pocket. He smoked Marlboros like each might be the last one made before the factory shut down.

"What time did Ma say she was coming home?" Jesse asked.

"Like seven, I guess," Kevin muttered.

"Leave her a note, will you? Tell her I went out with Jack and I'll be back around eleven."

Kevin scowled. "You can't write? Leave her a note yourself. I'm leaving as soon as Tommy gets here."

"Why are you being an asshole?" Jesse asked, frowning.

"Why are you?" Kevin retorted.

Jesse popped a butt into his mouth and lit it with a bic. He took a long drag, then glanced over his shoulder at Jack.

"Come on," he said.

The two set off across the lawn, then turned up the sloping hill of Fox Run Drive. At the top of the street was a forest that was part of a state park. There were a million things to do in those woods. Drinking beer and getting high, however, had recently replaced building tree forts and playing soldier at the top of the list. Not that the latter two were off the list completely. Only bumped down a few notches.

For his part, Kevin would rather take his girlfriend up there and play "truth or dare." Beer was all right, but drugs just took too much effort, cost too much money, and distracted from the only goals that mattered to him: the whole girlfriend thing, and going to the movies.

When they were gone, Kevin went back to his book. He'd barely read three pages when he heard the whistle that the Murphy brothers and everyone in their group used to call out to one another. Kevin responded with that same, telltale whistle, and a moment later he heard the light footsteps of his best friend, Tommy Carlson, as Tommy came round from the backyard.

They'd been friends since the first grade, though it was hard for anyone to see why. Though he looked like a strong breeze might snap him in two, with wispy, white-blond hair that made him look almost ghostly, Tommy was a fanatic about sports; both watching, and playing. Kevin, on the other hand, could barely remember which sport the Boston Celtics played, never mind what the team's lineup might be.

Still, there was no one Kevin Murphy would rather have in his corner. If he was in trouble, he knew he could always call on Tommy. That was what it meant to be friends, as far as he was concerned. In a bad spot, Tommy would watch his back, and Kevin would do the same for him.

"What's up?" Tommy asked.

Kevin showed him the cover of the book.

Tommy grinned. "Man, you read the weirdest shit."

"Least I know how to read," Kevin replied fondly.

"You ready to go? I told Diana we'd be there at seven-thirty."

"How did Tommy Carlson get so pussy whipped?" Kevin asked, shaking his head in mock sorrow.

"If you'd ever seen a pussy, you wouldn't even ask that question," Tommy told him knowingly.

Kevin just laughed.

It was more than a three-mile walk to Diana's house, which was on a narrow side street that ran parallel to Route Nine. Once upon a time, the distance had seemed huge, but in the past year, they had traversed that stretch of road so many times it seemed insignificant now. During the school year, it hadn't been unusual for them to get off the bus at Diana's stop, walk home in time for dinner, and—if it was a Friday—walk back that night to hang out.

Now, though, it was summer, and they were free. No bus rides, no school bells. It might have been less than three months, but that last Friday in June, high school seemed very far away indeed.

The evening wore on, the sun casting shadows which spread greedily as one of the longest days of the year came to a close. They walked along Pleasant Street, past the school where Kevin had attended kindergarten, then turned at Temple. At the bridge that spanned the Massachusetts Turnpike, they hocked huge gobs of spit down at passing cars, and Kevin dared Tommy to drop his pants and moon the highway below. Tommy refused, and Kevin wasn't about to do such a thing himself.

At least, not before dark.

Not long thereafter they were turning onto Haskell Road. Diana's house was a blue-and-white split level, a lot like the Murphys', but smaller. Diana had two older sisters, both almost as beautiful as she was. They weren't around much, but Kevin figured that was probably for the best. Being around too many of the Abbott sisters at any one time was likely to turn any guy into a babbling idiot.

It was strange, in a way, that the two guys should spend so much time with Diana. Diana had only been at St. Margaret's School with them since the beginning of seventh grade, and she was both beautiful and confident. Her skin was pale and her features fine: deep brown eyes and a mischievous, knowing grin. Her dark hair was cut in a stylish bob, a boyish look that was offset—even overturned—by her curves. Diana had matured early.

Only weeks before Kevin had asked Carolyn out, he and Tommy had both become infatuated with Diana. In that way that boys have, however, they had agreed that they wouldn't allow her to come between them. Both of them would pursue her, and may the best man win. Diana just liked Tommy better. He was much more laid-back than Kevin; much less serious. Diana liked that.

Kevin talked too much, and he knew it. He was also a bit too enthusiastic about trying to help people, to tell them how they could fix their problems. He simply couldn't help himself.

In his secret heart, he'd regretted Diana's decision only for the most selfish of reasons: the rest of his friends' parents were all still married, but hers were divorced. It would have been nice to have someone he could feel comfortable talking to about his dad. Sean Murphy drank too much, had never been faithful a single day to his wife, and wasn't around very much even before the divorce, but Kevin missed him just the same.

Jesse didn't want to talk about it. Not at all.

Tommy and Diana turned out to be a great couple. Not only that, but their getting together started a chain reaction that made it all feel like destiny. Once they had started dating, everything seemed to come together. April Harrington, whom Kevin had known since the first grade, had told him that *her* best friend, Carolyn, really liked him. The three girls and two guys had hung out together for months after that, and then Kevin introduced April to Jack Ross.

A convenient six-pack was formed.

Now, though, things were changing. They'd graduated eighth grade and high school lay dead ahead. The relationship between Jack and April had obviously begun to wither, and things with Kevin and Carolyn were pretty stormy too. He was looking forward to seeing her tonight, but he knew that could change at any moment.

It was the strangest thing. One minute, Kevin would be so angry with her—for smoking, or flirting with someone else—and the next, he'd just want to hold on tight. Kevin loved her, at least a little. But he was afraid that part of the reason they couldn't stay broken up was because Carolyn seemed so delicate. He didn't know how to keep from shattering her, or if he was willing to work hard enough to learn.

Still, when Tommy went up the cement steps in front of the Abbotts' house, hand on the rusty, black wrought-iron railing, and pressed the doorbell, a slow grin spread across Kevin's features. Carolyn Kaminksi was his girlfriend. He was happy just to be there.

A few seconds went by. Tommy glanced back at Kevin.

"Ring again."

Tommy didn't. Instead, he opened the storm door, and knocked three times. From inside, they heard Diana's high, sweet voice. Then the door opened, and she offered them that mischievous smile. Kevin almost didn't notice. Diana wore a lime green tube top and very short shorts. She pulled Tommy to her for a deep kiss.

"All right, get a room," Kevin sighed, glancing past them, trying to spot Carolyn.

"I already *have* a room," Diana said, as she pulled Tommy into the house.

Kevin was a little irked that Carolyn hadn't come to the door, but he didn't speak up. He didn't want to start anything. Diana led the two guys down the stairs and into the den. April and Carolyn sat on the ratty pull-out couch drinking Löwenbrau from those too-cute little seven-ounce bottles that came in eight packs and singing along to Springsteen on the stereo.

"Hey guys," April said happily as they walked in.

"A," Tommy replied. "What's up, Carolyn?"

Carolyn said nothing. She wouldn't even look at Kevin. At length, she took a swig of beer and very pointedly glanced at Tommy instead.

"Hi, Tom."

Kevin groaned and sat down heavily in the ugly orange beanbag chair next to the couch. He looked at April.

"What the fuck did I do now?" he asked.

April shrugged apologetically, a tiny ghost of a smile at the corners of her mouth. Kevin had known April for years. She always seemed unsettled, her eyes far away, as though she had somewhere to be but could not recall exactly how to get there. In some way he could never explain, he understood that feeling, understood April. He trusted her. She was practical, logical, with a good heart. Carolyn had a good heart as well, but she was a little short on the other two.

With a sigh, Kevin slid off the beanbag onto his knees on the floor. He scooted over in front of Carolyn and got up in her face so she'd have to look at him.

"What's the problem?" he asked harshly. "Aren't you sick of fighting yet?"

"Of course I am," Carolyn replied, eyes narrowed with pain. Her lip quivered and she pushed an errant strand of hair behind her ear, then glanced up at him defiantly. "You think I like this shit?"

"Then what?" Kevin asked.

He was uncomfortably aware that the others were all there, watching, waiting; aware of the ticking of the moon-and-stars clock by the door, and the way the moisture had bowed the wood paneling; aware, perhaps most of all, of the way Carolyn dropped her gaze, causing her long brown hair to fall across her face, covering one eye and casting her features in shadow. It was usually very sexy. At the moment, it was only frustrating.

"You were supposed to call me this morning," she said.

Kevin would have laughed if it hadn't been for the hurt in her voice.

"I talked to April this morning," he replied patiently. "Tommy talked to Diana. We all knew wc were meeting here tonight. I'm sorry. I didn't think it was a big deal."

"It was a big deal to me."

Carolyn turned those wide, sad eyes up to him. Kevin held her hands in his own, and straightened up to kiss her on the forehead, and then on the lips. She responded, and when the kiss ended, their faces remained close, foreheads pressed together, holding the space between them as intimately as they could. Carolyn smiled. She had a wonderful smile. Her best feature, Kevin had once told her. Followed in a close second by her enormous breasts. That part he kept to himself.

"Excellent," Tommy announced. "How 'bout the boys get a brew now?"

"In the fridge. Come on," Diana said, dragging Tommy upstairs. She glanced back into the den. "Kev?"

"It wouldn't kill me," Kevin replied.

When they'd gone up to the kitchen, Kevin managed to plop himself down on the couch between Carolyn and April. He threw an arm around each of them. April wore cutoff jean shorts and a thin, blue cotton top with narrow straps. Carolyn's wardrobe was a mix of the other two girls'—she wore a purple tube top and cutoff jeans—

and it had occurred to Kevin more than once that the three of them probably shared all their clothes so much that their wardrobes had pretty much become one anyway.

Scrunched between them, he kissed first April and then Carolyn on the head. "See, this is my favorite spot in the world," he declared.

A moment later, Tommy and Diana returned with the midget Löwenbraus. As the frisky couple fell together in a tangle on the beanbag chair, Kevin opened his beer and took a long swig.

"We should have gone to the movies tonight," he told them. "There's dog shit on TV."

"I think we can think of ways to keep busy," Tommy said, and turned to look lasciviously at Diana.

Carolyn ran her fingers through Kevin's hair. "I'll second that."

Kevin frowned. "Guys, that'd be pretty rude, don't you think?" he asked, then glanced at April. "Unless we're all in the mood for a little swapping."

April grinned. "At which point Jack would kick your ass. Not that it wouldn't be fun."

Carolyn whacked Kevin in the arm. "Maybe you missed that you're talking to my best friend?"

"I've known April much longer than you have, Carrie. Wouldn't be the first time we kissed. Sixth grade spin-the-bottle memories still keep me up at night."

Tommy cackled. "I'll bet they do."

"That's not funny," Carolyn said grumpily.

"He's just kidding, Car," April reassured her.

Kevin looked at his girlfriend and shook his head. "You've gotta relax. We're all friends here."

Carolyn seemed almost embarrassed then. She shrugged. "What can I say? I'm the jealous type."

"Yeah, well obviously Jack isn't," April said. "Or he'd be here. Where the fuck is he, anyway?"

Kevin swallowed. He didn't want to hurt April, but he wasn't going to lie for Jack, either.

"Hanging out with Jesse," he told her. "I have no idea what's up with him. You guys fighting?"

April leaned into him on one side, and Carolyn did the same on the other.

"It's pretty hard to be fighting when you never see each other. I mean, I talked to him this morning, and he said like, two words," April said, exasperated.

"It's Jack," Tommy said, wiping beer from his lips. "He never says more than two words."

April shrugged. Kevin decided not to pursue it any further. If she wanted to talk about whatever was, or wasn't, happening between her and Jack, she knew Kevin was there for her.

"So, what do you guys want to do?" Carolyn asked. "We could just hang out and listen to music, but maybe we could play a game or something instead."

"Naked Twister?" Kevin joked.

"I don't think so," April replied, one eyebrow raised.

"Well," Diana said slowly. "We could play strip poker."

They played only until the first person had to shed all of his clothes. Tommy lost. It was a close game, though. Diana and April were both down to their panties when it was all done. Carolyn had managed to keep her bra on as well, and Kevin actually still wore his pants, though nothing else. He was glad, though. Sitting there, after four or five seven-ounce Lowenbraus, he had a hard time focusing on the cards instead of the girls' nudity, and as a result, held his hands in a strategic position, blocking anyone's view of his crotch.

It was nearly ten, and Diana's mom was due back by eleven. The girls were sleeping over, but the guys had to leave. Carolyn had had too much to drink, and she was swaying as she came over to Kevin and put her arms around him, locking her hands behind his waist. She kissed him deeply and ground herself against him. Hungrily, he returned her kiss. The beer had gotten to him, too, and he didn't pay any attention to April now.

At least, not until she lit up.

Kevin glanced over and saw her taking a long drag on a Marlboro Light, even as she tucked the box of cigarettes back into her purse.

Her purse.

Thing was, it wasn't April's purse at all. It was Carolyn's.

"What the fuck?" Kevin snapped, and glared down at his girlfriend, who went stiff in his arms. "Are those butts yours?"

Realizing her mistake, April fumbled to come to Carolyn's defense. "They're *mine*," she said. "I just didn't want my parents to find them in my pocketbook."

"Bullshit," Kevin said. "Your parents know you smoke." He backed away from Carolyn, looking at her and shaking his head. "Is it so goddamn hard? One little thing I ask you. Don't smoke. I mean, what, cigarettes are more important to you than I am?"

Instead of trying to make excuses, she got angry. "I tried to quit. I couldn't. You want to break up with me over it. I think that's really stupid. So I smoke. April smokes, and you don't give her shit."

"I *do* give her shit!" Kevin barked. "But she isn't my girlfriend."

"So, I'm supposed to obey you or something?" Carolyn glared at him defiantly.

"It isn't that," he said sadly. "It's just disgusting, okay? Kissing you after you've smoked, even seeing you smoke, it's just—"

"When did you see me smoke? Did you notice when you kissed me? No. I haven't had a cigarette since right after lunch."

Kevin let out a long breath. "You know what? We had a cool night. I'm not gonna fight about this with you." He waved at April and Diana and gestured for Tommy to come along.

"You're just going to leave, right now? In the middle of a fight?" Carolyn asked, horrified, as she walked after him.

"Fight's over," he said. "I want to be with you, but I don't want you to smoke. That's your choice to make."

"And if I keep smoking you break up with me?" she said angrily. "That fucking sucks. That's crazy. Jesus, Kevin, I don't think you love me at all."

Kevin didn't respond to that. Instead, he looked at Diana, mumbled a thank-you, and pushed out the door. Half a minute later, Tommy followed.

It was cold for June, and Kevin wished he had brought a jacket. When he and Tommy had set off after dinner for the three-mile walk to Diana's house, he hadn't expected it to get so cold. Kevin figured the temperature had dropped twenty degrees, easy, since dinner. He shivered lightly as they turned toward home.

Kevin was still fuming after his fight with Carolyn, and Tommy wasn't saying much. They were both feeling the beer more than they wanted to let on. Traffic breezed by as they strode along the sidewalk with drunken confidence. They swayed a bit, but not too much, and neither one of them had gotten sick. That was good.

Kevin found the taste of beer pretty nasty, but he wasn't about to confess that to anyone. Besides, he figured the buzz more than made up for the taste. Drinking was new to all of them, but they were wasting no time in becoming better acquainted with it.

A while later, as they turned off Pleasant Street and onto Fox Run, Kevin was walking with his shoulders hunched, trying to keep warm.

"You cold?" Tommy asked.

"It's a little nippy," Kevin admitted.

"Should've had another beer," Tommy told him sagely.

"No shit."

That was easy for Tommy to say, though. He'd had the smarts to wear his denim jacket. Kevin, on the other hand, had only a baseball-style concert shirt. Kevin stuffed his hands in his pockets as they trudged up the hill. Tommy noticed, and grinned.

"Pussy."

"Fuck off," Kevin replied happily. "But since you brought it up, how *are* things going with Diana? She seemed pretty frisky tonight."

Tommy didn't really respond to that. "She's something, that's for sure. Too bad you and Carolyn can't seem to keep it together," Tommy added. "Maybe you should lay off on the smoking thing."

Kevin was about to rebuke his friend, but hesitated. At length, he shrugged. "Yeah, maybe," he mumbled. "It's just nasty, you know? If she loves me so much, I don't get why she doesn't just quit."

"If you love her so much, why is it so important?"

Surprised, Kevin looked over at Tommy, studying his friend's blue eyes, now lined with red from too much beer. Tommy Carlson had never been much for romance. Sure, he was in deep with Diana, but the whole puppy-dog, flowers and candy thing had never been part of his repertoire. On the other hand, Kevin was a hopeless romantic, though it occurred to him that nobody would be able to tell that if they'd heard him arguing with Carolyn.

"Maybe I don't," Kevin finally replied.

They walked on in silence for half a minute. Though it was clear above and the stars shone in the sky, the trees that surrounded the houses on either side of the road seemed to shut out the moon and stars. A breeze kicked up and rustled through the leaves, making the dragging branches of a weeping willow seem to reach out toward them from the darkness on the side of the road.

"Do you?" Tommy asked, sincere now. "Love her, I mean?"

Kevin smirked. "I think so. But shit, Tommy, I'm thirteen. What the fuck do I know?"

They both laughed hard at that. Ahead, a corona of light spread out from the metal dome of a streetlight that jutted from a telephone pole. The bare bulb burned inside. Without any thought, really, Kevin glanced down at the ground and spotted a flat, round stone. He had no real intention of breaking the light, mainly because he had no expectation that he would even hit it.

"Whaddaya think?" Kevin asked.

Tommy noticed the rock, glanced up at the light, more than twenty feet above. "No way."

Kevin held the stone with one finger along its sharp edge, cocked back his arm and threw it. It flew straight up and into the metal cup of the street light. It struck perfectly, sliding quickly along the inside of the cup in an arc, and dropping down the other side to tumble to the ground. But it didn't come down alone. That arc had sliced cleanly through the neck of the bulb, plunging the street below into sudden darkness. The glass sphere came down along with the rock, impossibly intact, and shattered on the pavement by their feet.

"Holy shit," Kevin breathed, a broad smile on his face. "Did you see that?"

"Never in a million years," Tommy said in amazement. "How does that happen? It came down whole. That was a million-to-one shot."

There was a brief pause as they looked at one another, grinning, and then they sprinted wildly up Fox Run Drive, away from the scene of the crime. When they stopped, breathing a little hard, Kevin found that the adrenaline rush had kicked his buzz into high gear. Oddly, he felt both more drunk, and yet somehow far more clearheaded than he had minutes before.

"Holy shit," he said again.

"You know nobody's going to believe that one," Tommy informed him.

"Hey, I have a witness."

"Who?" Tommy asked, an innocent expression on his face.

Kevin gave him the finger, and they started up the street again. They had crested the hill, and were a few houses away from Londonderry, which bisected Fox Run at a place they called, appropriately, Four Corners. Several houses beyond that was the Murphys'.

"You want to crash at my house?" Kevin asked. "I'm sure my mother wouldn't care."

Tommy considered that for a few seconds, then shook his head, just once. It looked like he might be about to say something, but whatever it might have been was interrupted by the sudden roar of an engine and the squeal of tires.

Headlights snapped on, and behind them, rubber scarred pavement as a car shot straight for them.

"Jeez—move!" Kevin screamed.

He slapped his hand on Tommy's back, propelling him forward. They ran full tilt onto the Olsens' yard, and the steel beast behind them tore up the grass as it bumped up over the curb in pursuit.

"Get the fuck away from us you assholes!" Tommy shrieked as he ran.

Kevin didn't have the focus to yell at them. He was running for his life, an image of the car he'd only barely seen already haunting him. A glistening metal grill. Huge tires. Dark, tinted windows that made it look like there was nobody behind the wheel.

The car's horn blared and Kevin's heart seemed to stop beating for a moment. As though he had plunged, suddenly, beneath the surface of the ocean, he found he could no longer hear.

Ahead of him, Tommy dodged behind a thick willow tree, and Kevin followed.

When they turned to glance back, the car was already returning to the pavement, engine revving, tires laying a patch of black rubber. The driver had turned out the headlights again, plunging the vehicle into such darkness that they couldn't even tell what kind of car it was.

"You son of a bitch!" Tommy called out furiously. "What the hell's wrong with you?"

Kevin didn't say a word. Couldn't say a word, as he watched the black car disappear into the dark.

Heart beating once more, too fast, breath rasping in his chest, he fought down the horrible taste that had risen in the back of his throat. It was a little like beer, a little like tinfoil, a little like tears; it was the taste of profound, almost primitive fear. Kevin had never felt such fear in his entire life.

He didn't like it. Not one bit.

2

For several minutes after the car had driven off, the world was different. The air seemed charged with a kind of electricity, an energy composed of infinite possibility. Kevin gazed about him, looking at the trees and the stars, at the houses all around, some with lights inside, others eerily dark. He had the feeling, just then, that anything might happen. Someone—some bastard—had tried to run him and Tommy over.

Not played at it. It was important to him that he not lose track of that. The guy behind the wheel of that car, already taking on a kind of nightmarish every-car quality in his head, hadn't been fooling around, trying to scare a couple of punks as a gag. If they hadn't run when they did, hadn't dodged, they'd be smeared across the grill of that car now.

"Jesus," Kevin whispered.

"Lot of good he did us," Tommy replied angrily.

"Hey, we're still here aren't we?"

Tommy had no response to that. He shook his head, nostrils flaring, turning his fear into anger in a way that made Kevin envious. Sure, he was angry, but the fear lingered.

As they walked away from Four Corners and toward Kevin's house, the streetlight at the intersection behind him—a light that had been dark—suddenly flickered to life once again. Kevin turned to stare at it.

"That's weird."

Tommy nodded, glancing curiously at the telephone pole, and the light mounted at the top. Then he sort of grunted and turned back up Fox Run Drive. Kevin lingered a moment, frowning as he looked at the light, waiting for it to flicker and go out again. It happened sometimes, he knew. If a bulb was loose, or dying, a light could go off and on with a little jostling from the wind or a slamming door. Something like that.

But the streetlight burned clear and bright.

"Fucking assholes," Tommy said, as though Kevin might argue the point. "Like to get my hands on that jerk when he wasn't in his car."

Kevin cast a dubious sidelong glance at his friend. Tommy didn't notice, which was good, since the look on Kevin's face said a lot of things Tommy probably wouldn't have liked.

You're full of shit was one of them. So was *you're fourteen years old and skinny enough to snap in the first high wind; I wouldn't go picking fights with homicidal fuckers who are at least old enough to drive a damn car.*

On the other hand, a part of Kevin completely agreed with the sentiment. He wouldn't have minded getting his hands on the jerk in the car, either, particularly if he got the jump on him and had a nice, solid Louisville Slugger in his hands.

But that was fantasy. He knew that much. Not only would he likely get his ass trounced, maybe end up in the hospital, if he ever did something that crazy, but odds were he was never going to see the guy again anyway. Even if he did see him, he sure as hell wouldn't be able to recognize him.

In his mind's eye, he saw that darkened windshield again, black and yet somehow clear at the same time, nothing inside but meanness and ghosts.

Kevin shivered.

What the hell put that idea in my head?

He shook it off and caught up with Tommy, who was several paces ahead of him now. Farther up the street, Kevin could see his house, and the blue glow of his mother's window that told him she had the television on. Not that the TV meant she was awake. Most nights,

Mrs. Murphy fell asleep in front of the tube and ended up turning it off sometime in the early morning. Outside of work, and her wandering sons, it was all she had to keep her company.

"Y'know," Kevin said, "maybe you really should stay over. Your parents would be cool with it. I mean, your dad's probably still awake. You could call and say you're crashing here, if you want to."

Tommy scowled. "What, 'cause of that?" He cocked his thumb over his shoulder, in the direction of Four Corners. "He's long gone. Besides, I'm cutting through backyards."

"Still," Kevin replied, and shrugged. "Just an idea."

"Nah. But thanks."

Together, they started across the Standishes' lawn. They were an older couple who lived next door to the Murphys, and Kevin had always liked them. They didn't treat teenagers like they were all criminals, the way some of the older people in the neighborhood did.

It wasn't until they were actually on the Murphys' lawn, maybe thirty feet from Kevin's front door, that he noticed the small figure sitting on the stoop. It took Kevin a moment to realize that it was Nicole French, and the realization startled him.

But, then, seeing Nikki always startled him.

The light from the lantern above the door illuminated her wavy red hair, and cast her face in shadows. Only as he and Tommy came within a few yards of her did Kevin realize that Nikki was crying. Which was crazy, of course. The sun might go supernova, there might be a volcanic eruption in Boston, peace on earth, or a World Series win for the Red Sox, but Nikki French never cried.

Kevin cast a quick glance at Tommy and gestured to him to hang back a second. Heart filled with wildly conflicting emotions—his thrill at seeing her, his pain at seeing her crying—Kevin went to Nikki and crouched before her.

"Hey," he whispered. "You all right?"

Nikki raised her head, revealing her eyes to him. Mascara striped her cheeks. Tears slipped along those tracks. In that moment, Kevin could see her heart, could see the pain there, the real Nicole, a fifteen-year-old girl who needed very desperately for someone to care, and had come here to find that person. To find him.

Then Nikki laughed. "Does it look like I'm all right?"

Kevin flushed, embarrassed. "No, I mean, sorry. I just . . . what happened?"

Behind Kevin, Tommy cleared his throat. "Listen, Kev, I've gotta get home. I'll talk to you tomorrow, okay? We going to the trestle?"

"Yeah, sure," Kevin replied, without turning, eyes still on Nikki, heart still afraid for her. After a moment, though, he dimly remembered the car, and the danger he and Tommy had been in. He turned and gave Tommy a hard look. "You watch out on the way home, all right?"

Tommy made a dismissive face. "I'd like that shithead to come back," he sneered.

It was a guy thing.

"Take it easy, Tommy," Nikki said suddenly.

"Yeah, you too."

The second Tommy disappeared around the side of the house, heading through backyards on the trek home, Kevin had completely forgotten about him again, his attention entirely on Nikki. It had been several weeks since he'd seen her, even around the neighborhood. That was pretty much par for the course anytime she got a new boyfriend. But it didn't stop Kevin from thinking about her.

In truth, there wasn't much that could stop Kevin from thinking about Nikki. Carolyn was his girlfriend, sure. But what he felt for Nikki was something else completely. There was a place for her inside him, a little niche where the image of her, the thought of her, lived and breathed and ached even when she wasn't around.

Yet he didn't talk about her to his friends, and certainly not to his brother. There was real life, and then there was what he felt for Nikki French.

I'm such an idiot, he thought, as he watched her chew her lip in silence. It was far from the first time he'd had such a thought. That kind of self-doubt reverberated through his mind almost constantly. Embarrassed, he hoped that his feelings didn't show on his face.

It was silly. His friends would have ragged on him if he ever tried to explain how he felt about her. The only time he was tempted to reveal the truth of it was when she was around. How many times had he wanted to tell her, and wimped out? Dozens. Maybe hundreds. She always had a boyfriend, and even when she didn't, Kevin had a girlfriend, and that just wouldn't be right. Plus, she was fifteen months older than he was.

Still, none of those were the real reason he had never expressed his feelings to her. Those hesitations would have been easily surmounted if not for one outstanding, crippling factor.

Deep down, he suspected that if he asked her out, Nikki would laugh.

Kevin thought that might kill him.

Now here she was, doing the impossible. Here she was, sitting on the stoop in front of his house late at night, crying. Nikki was crying, and Kevin was thinking of himself. Crying, and Kevin was worried what his friends would think if they knew how much he worshipped her. He was just squatting there, watching mutely.

Idiot, Kevin told himself again.

"Hey, hey," he said, finally finding his voice. "Not like I'm not happy to see you, Nikki, but, y'know, was there anything in particular you wanted to talk about?"

She looked up at him with those green eyes again and attempted a small smile through her tears.

"You told me he was a fuckin' prick, Kevin. I should've listened," Nikki said at last, a hint of pained self-amusement in her voice, along with the profanity.

Kevin sat down on the stoop beside her, hands in his

lap. He looked at her with feigned surprise. "Fucking prick? I guess I was the soul of eloquence, as always. Or are you just improvising?"

"Prick. Cocksucker. Asshole," Nikki rattled off. "Pick one, that's Matt. He's been screwing this girl in our class. She's a total slut. Sandy told me about it, and when I asked him about it, he just totally shrugged like it was no big deal."

"Asshole," Kevin said under his breath.

It wasn't a continuation of the humor. His anger at Matt was very, very real. Here was yet another guy who had everything. He was going to be a high school senior in the fall. Nikki would be a sophomore, but she always dated older guys. She was smart and funny and tough and absolutely gorgeous, though she argued with Kevin anytime he tried to tell her she was pretty. He didn't care what she said. Nikki had red hair with blond highlights, green eyes, and a smile so devious she nearly had horns. There was a twinkle in her eye and a strut in her walk that had entranced him the first time he'd ever seen her.

When she had a boyfriend, she gave him all her attention.

Matt Gray had all of that, and he didn't care. Instead, he'd blown Nikki off, hurt her.

Kevin could have strangled him.

Then, suddenly, all thoughts of violence were wiped from his mind. Nikki let out a heartbroken sob that was unlike anything he'd ever heard from her. She had really cared about Matt, *the bastard*.

Nikki turned toward Kevin, lifted her arms, and leaned into him. As he slipped his arm around her and Nikki laid her head on his shoulder, shaking a bit with her tears, Kevin stopped breathing. He didn't dare. The smell of her hair, where he pressed his face against it, would be too much for him. He thought that his heart might have stopped as well. Somewhere in the dim recesses of his mind, he knew that his feelings were horribly unfair to Carolyn.

But he also knew, at last, that he didn't really love Carolyn. Sometimes, he didn't even like her. It made him feel like a total jerk, realizing that, but there wasn't much he could do about it. Except break up with her; something he'd been putting off for a while.

Too long.

"Oh, God, Kevin, it hurts," Nikki whispered, voice breaking.

She cried quietly then, all the tough, cynical veneer stripped away. Just a girl, hurting. A girl he loved.

Yet he couldn't say it. Didn't dare speak the words. And so, instead, he just held her, and tried not to breathe, and whispered comforting words that he barely heard himself. He wanted to offer her solace, wanted her to smile again, and laugh, and cuss a blue streak, as she so often did.

But for the moment, holding her safe against him, Kevin felt something akin to bliss. This was, in some ways, what he'd dreamed of.

"It's all right," he whispered again, and almost added the words he most wanted to speak.

Almost.

Coward, he thought.

Suddenly he was seized by a determination. He was thirteen, still, and Nikki was fifteen. But in three weeks, on the fifteenth of July, he would turn fourteen.

On his birthday he would tell her.

Courage stoked by this decision, he kissed the top of her head. Nikki cried a little harder then, and he held her more tightly and kissed her once more. But that was all.

On my birthday, he thought.

3

It was suicidal.

Kevin stood on the wood and steel mesh of the train trestle that stretched across part of the Framingham reservoir and looked down anxiously at the water, its surface rippled by the breeze. The sun shone down hard, and he felt it baking his skin. It was hot, in the high nineties at least, and he knew the water would be a blessed relief.

If only it weren't so far down.

The sky was a perfect, clear blue, the texture of tissue paper, the sun a white rip in its fabric. Its light sparkled brightly off the ripples below, as though they were shards of jagged glass. The reservoir itself was dark and deep. Somewhere in its depths—or so the local folklore said—there were shopping carts and a refrigerator or two. But those were hardly worth worrying about.

Cars, though, that was something else.

Kevin couldn't stare down at the water as he was doing now and not think of the cars, or rather, the stories about the cars that were supposed to have been dumped off the trestle into the depths below. Broken windows. Maybe a hood or a trunk jutting up toward the surface. Probably a bunch of bullshit; he was old enough to know that. But if it wasn't bullshit, what then?

Jump wrong, land wrong—and "wrong" was only defined by good or bad fortune—and he could break a leg, slice himself open, maybe snap his spine. It was crazy to jump.

Suicidal.

None of which had ever stopped anyone from doing it. The worst they had ever seen happen to anyone at the trestle was the time Eric Pirkle had sliced his foot open on something, and shit, that was nothing. The danger was little more than an added thrill, even to a kid as normally savvy as Kevin.

He glanced up at Tommy, who stood beside him and grinned maniacally. "You know this is stupid, don't you?"

Tommy chuckled. " 'Course it is."

A little ways along the track, where the trestle met solid ground, Jesse and Jack sat smoking a joint. Diana and April each had a sweating can of Budweiser from the cooler they'd taken turns hauling—as surreptitiously as possible—all the way from home. They'd had to walk through woods and around the edges of the reservoir most of the way to avoid the chance of anyone stopping them. All so they could drink beer that tasted like the dentist had been at work in your mouth with the drill and that nasty stuff they packed into fillings.

Now it was just after one o'clock. They'd built a small fire and roasted hot dogs on sticks, eaten a bunch of Cheetos and stuff Jack had snatched from his house. That was lunch.

The beer was dessert.

"Come on, you pussies!" Jesse croaked, exhaling a small cloud of marijuana smoke. "Just fuckin' jump. Not like you haven't done it before."

Which was true, Kevin admitted to himself. But it had been a couple of weeks since the last time, and every jump from the trestle was a leap of faith. Tommy had taken a hit off the joint to loosen up, but Kevin passed.

"Come on! Fuckin' jump!" Jesse shouted amiably from the dam.

Kevin blew his friend a kiss, and Tommy laughed.

"I'm not jumping," Kevin said suddenly, feigning anxiety. "I can't swim, Butch."

"Whaddaya mean you can't swim?" Tommy retorted, in his best Paul Newman. A barely passable Paul Newman, in truth. They'd watched *Butch Cassidy and the Sundance Kid* together on Channel thirty-eight only a few weeks earlier, and loved it.

"Whoa-oa-oa-oa . . ." Kevin began.

Tommy picked up on it and together, laughing, they leaped from the safety of the train tracks and out over the reservoir. Into open space. The hot breeze rippled across the water. Somewhere beneath them, in the dark, Kevin thought he saw a bit of metal gleaming. A second later, they splashed down, side by side, both of them holding out their arms, creating as much resistance as they could. Once underwater, they were already pulling for the open air.

It wouldn't do to go too deep. No way to know what was down there.

Water sprayed from Kevin's hair as he shook his head to get his ears clear, whooping with exhilaration. As he swam toward the land, and the steep incline back up to the train tracks, he wore a crazy grin on his face. His heart was pumping; he felt incredible, like he could fly if only he put his mind to it.

Side by side, he and Tommy scrambled up the dirt and stone and scrub incline that would take them back to the train tracks up top.

"Another go?" Kevin asked.

"Beer first, for courage," Tommy replied.

As they crested the rise, only a few yards from where Diana and April sat, arguing amiably about something or other—someone or other, more like—there came a mighty whoop. Kevin turned around to see Jack plummeting straight down into the water, blade straight, slicing the surface without an ounce of fear as to what might wait below.

"Shit," Kevin whispered to himself. Then he glanced at the girls. "That's fucking stupid. What the hell's the matter with him?"

April shrugged. "He doesn't think there's anything down there."

"He's probably right," Diana added. "I mean, one of

us would be dead by now if there was really a car or something down there."

Behind them, Jesse roared and leaped from the trestle. He was more careful than Jack had been, and Kevin was glad to see it. Much as he and his brother might fight sometimes, he didn't want Jesse getting hurt. He also didn't want to have to explain it to their mother. That was all she would need, after all she'd been through with their father over the years.

When Kevin turned back toward the others, Tommy passed him a Budweiser, dripping ice water from the cooler. It was so cold at first—small bits of ice melting in the little rim around the top of the can—that he had to switch hands a couple of times and wipe the ice water off on his cutoffs. With a grimace, he cracked it open and took a long swig.

"Hey. Spare a cold one?"

He nearly choked, beer dripping down his chin. Embarrassed, Kevin wiped the back of his hand across his mouth and turned to look up angrily at the four guys who had appeared so suddenly on the train tracks behind them.

They were older. That was the first thing he noticed. Not as old as twenty, but definitely seventeen, eighteen. The one who'd spoken—and who even now was watching them with an amused smirk on his face—was tall and thin and good-looking in an almost pretty way. His face was all pale angles, and his eyes were a startling blue so bright and clear they almost shone. His straight black hair was shoulder length, and fell across his face so that he had to toss his head back.

The other three obviously deferred to him, even in the way that they hung back, watching him as if for a cue. One, a short but gangly guy whose hair was very long and stringy, looked enough like him to be a younger brother, the runt of the litter. A weasel. He looked mean, that one. Kevin thought that the second he laid eyes on the guy.

The other two were an odd combination. The one on

the left was the muscle, no doubt, but with the orange-yellow fuzz that was all that was left of his hair after a crew cut, and the long orange lashes on his eyes, he looked almost like an albino. On the right stood a doughy-faced guy with sad eyes and thick, wild hair. He was sullen, his expression pulled into the kind of pout that would never leave his face.

Kevin wasn't the kind of person to make snap judgments, but he didn't like any of them. Not for a second. *Trouble,* he thought.

He was right.

"Jesus, what'd you guys, walk on tiptoe out here?" April asked gruffly, ignoring the guy's question. "You shouldn't sneak up on people like that."

The pretty boy laughed, and a second later, as if waiting for his permission, the other guys followed suit. Their laughter seemed forced, and it sounded to Kevin like a warning.

"We parked up behind the Red Coach Grill and walked down," the pretty boy told them. "Didn't mean to spook you. Just here for a swim, same as you."

Of course they were, Kevin thought. Nothing else to do out here. They all wore cutoffs and T-shirts, ratty sneakers without socks. Except for the orange albino. He didn't have any shoes on at all.

"Be our guest." Diana offered a diffident shrug, and reached into the cooler for a beer.

The pretty boy smiled a second, maybe thinking it was for him. Then Diana popped it and started sipping from the can.

"Your mother didn't teach you to share, I guess." The way pretty boy said "mother" made Kevin think of the way his own mom talked about his dad. It wasn't nice. Not at all.

Tommy tensed up. He stood, and Kevin was right behind him.

Pretty boy looked at Tommy. They *all* looked at Tommy.

"What?" pretty boy demanded. And there was more

to the word than just four letters. *Yeah, I'm fucking with you,* it said. *What are you going to do about it?*

Tommy just glared. He got like that when he was really angry, ready to go at it. Just couldn't speak. Kevin didn't have that problem.

"I think *your* mother should've taught you better manners," he said, astonished at the words even as they came out of his mouth.

Thirteen. Eighteen.

Not to mention four against two, if they didn't count the girls. Which they should have, but Kevin didn't want to. It shouldn't come to that. So four against two.

But only for a few more seconds. The amused smirk disappeared off the pretty boy's face, and a flicker of danger flashed across his eyes. He sneered.

"You've got quite a mouth on you, kid. Some days, that might score points with me. Not today."

"Kick his ass, Pete," grunted the weasel.

Kevin shot a hard look at the wiry runt, mostly to mask his fear. This was going someplace very ugly, maybe painful, and it was going there fast. In his head, though, he was already figuring he could maybe take the weasel if it had to go down.

Which was when the orange albino pushed through the other guys and poked him in the chest, finger jabbing at Kevin's bare breastbone.

"You look familiar, puke. We seen you before?"

Feeling as though he might throw up, Kevin tried to think of something to say. The girls stood up and moved around behind him and Tommy. Kevin was silent. It was Tommy who slapped the big guy's hand away.

"We'd remember a freak like you," Tommy said, grinning.

Kevin knew that grin, too. It was a we're-fucked-so-we-might-as-well-go-with-it grin. He'd seen the look before and it did not bode well. Tommy thought things were about to get nasty. Kevin figured he was right, but wasn't as resigned to it.

The orange albino closed in on Tommy, staring down

at him, square jaw, square head, like he was made of concrete.

"Ain't you an uppity little prick," he said.

"Back the fuck off!" Kevin shouted, his eyes flicking to the one they'd called Pete. But Pete the pretty boy's face was impassive.

The orange albino hit Tommy hard in the gut. Tommy sucked in air and doubled over but didn't go down. The big guy was going to hit him again, even as Tommy struggled to come back at him.

Which was when Jack and Jesse came up over the rise.

"Hey!" Jesse shouted.

The albino glanced his way. Tommy took that moment to clean the big bastard's clock. The blow sent him staggering backward. He looked up in a fuming rage, nostrils flaring, like he was a bull ready to charge.

"Curt, that's enough," Pcte said, rolling his eyes and tossing his hair away from his face again, like nothing at all was happening.

Kevin held his breath. Jack and Jesse came up next to him, then Jesse moved forward, right up into Pete's face. Somehow, he had sensed by instinct, just as Kevin had, which of them was the leader. The pretty boy was easily three years older, but even at fifteen, Jesse was bigger than Pete.

"Somebody here got a problem?" Jesse asked reasonably.

"Your friends wouldn't share their beer," Pete replied, just as reasonably.

"That's because it isn't their beer to share. It's mine."

Pete smiled. "Cool. Can you spare one?"

Jesse's eyes narrowed. Kevin saw it happen. The reasonable tone in his brother's voice had been just him playing it cool. But inside, he knew Jesse felt anything but cool. Water dripped down Jesse's body, a few drops still on his face, but he ignored it.

"Your buddy here just punched my friend. Probably got, what, sixty pounds and four or five years on him. Only a pussy would do something like that. You want a beer from us, the only way you're gonna get it is having it kicked up your ass."

Pete's eyes widened, like Jesse'd just showed him pictures of his sister naked. His jaw clenched, but he didn't make a move.

He didn't have to.

The orange albino—Curt—gave Jesse a hard shove, then cocked back a fist. The girls screamed at all of them. Tommy launched himself at Curt and took the big guy down hard on the dirt beside the train tracks. The doughy-faced kid moved in, and Jesse moved into a fighting stance.

"Come on," Jesse urged dough-face.

Kevin watched Pete, who hadn't made a move at all. The anger had not left his expression, but he didn't seem like he was ready to fight.

"Some brave guys you are," Kevin told him. "Even if you kick our asses, who you gonna brag to? Oh, we beat on these kids the other day. Thirteen, fourteen, fifteen. Yeah, that's something to be proud of."

Pete ignored him.

Dough-face went after Jesse, who clocked him a good one. The weasel started moving for Kevin, but Jack was there first. Jack, with his gunfighter eyes and his quiet way. He grabbed the weasel by the front of his shirt.

"Don't even," he said.

The weasel kicked Jack hard in the balls. Jack let out a piercing scream that froze everybody. April went to him where he lay on the tracks. Kevin thought maybe Jack had hit his head on the metal rail to boot. It didn't matter. Jack pushed April gently away, lips curled back from his teeth in a rictus of pain. There was spittle on his chin.

Everybody stared at him, even Curt and Tommy, who'd stopped fighting long enough to take in the moment.

The weasel leaped. Jack threw a quick jab, but he dodged under Jack's fist and hit him hard in the side, then again, too fast, in the jaw. Jack staggered back, still hunched a bit from the pain in his balls. The weasel moved in and grabbed Jack's shoulders, kneed him in the stomach, and then they were right next to Kevin.

Kevin reached out and grabbed the weasel by the hair and hauled his head back as hard as he could. The weasel screamed, and Kevin liked the sound of it. A lot. Jack swore so loudly and savagely that spit flew from his mouth, and he swept in on the greasy runt.

He'd hit the gangly kid three or four times before Pete finally acted. The pretty boy stepped in and, using the flat of his hand, popped Jack in the chest, slamming him backward hard enough to knock him off his feet. He was stronger than he looked. Kevin shoved the weasel to the tracks and backed off, even as Jesse and Tommy moved cautiously over so that the two groups were set against one another.

Kevin could barely breathe. He felt the breeze blowing past, and the sun beating down on him. His cutoffs were still wet and stiff and uncomfortable. The soles of his bare feet stung from the rough ground and splinters from the railroad ties. The sounds of traffic filtered down from Route Nine not that far off.

But none of that felt real to him. Instead, he felt like he was in a bubble, a kind of invisible web that stretched from him to his brother to Tommy to Jack to Diana to April. There was a weird energy to it. That was reality. Everything else was just flimsy and unreal, like the painted sets of a stage show.

Us, he thought. *Us against them.*

And *they* looked ready to kill. The electric crackle of menace radiated out of them, even dough-face. They were the kind of guys who wouldn't be happy to win a fight. Once it started, they'd want to hurt someone. Hospital hurt.

Again, Kevin studied Pete's face. The ghostly pale blue of his eyes had faded even more, almost like there was nothing there at all except maybe ice. The effect was so startling that Kevin blinked and looked at him more closely. But then it was gone. His eyes were still spookily clear, like blue crystal, but they were just eyes.

Suddenly, Pete turned his gaze on Kevin, who was tempted to take a step back, but somehow managed to hold his ground.

"Apologize," Pete instructed.

"Me?"

Everyone looked at Kevin. He couldn't see them all, but he felt them gazing at him. Jack was breathing heavily through his nose, still trying to overcome the pain in his balls.

"Don't do it, Kevin," he grunted.

"Shut the fuck up, Jack," Diana said suddenly. She moved up next to Tommy and he slipped his arm around her. "Go ahead, Kevin. It doesn't matter. Whatever it takes to get these guys out of here. What the hell? Bunch of kids probably seniors or older beating up freshmen. If that's how they get their jollies. Just do it."

Kevin wanted to. When he opened his mouth, he meant for the right words to come out. But what he meant wasn't what he said.

"I don't know. Seems we did pretty good for a bunch of kids." He fixed his gaze on Pete's crystal-blue eyes. "I think you should just fuck off on out of here. I mean, even if you kick the hell out of us, that'll bring the cops into it. And who do you think's gonna end up on the shit end of *that* stick?"

Somehow, Kevin kept the terror out of his face. No mean feat, considering the look Pete gave him then.

Then, suddenly, it was over. The bubble burst, and reality came flooding back in. Birds sang somewhere, and the reservoir water lapped at the shore. Traffic whizzed by. The tangible fear, the imminent knowledge of danger and pain was simply gone.

Pete laughed and shook his head. Looked at Kevin.

"You've got balls, kid."

He turned and started walking back the way they'd come, toward the parking lot behind the Red Coach Grill, which was just a ways up the tracks. The others hesitated a moment, surprised and sulky, but then they followed.

The Murphy brothers stood side by side, their friends around them, and watched the others go. Pete stopped on the tracks about thirty yards away and turned to look at them all again.

"You're lucky, you know," he said. It wasn't boasting, wasn't threatening. It was stated as simple fact. "Lucky the sun's out. If we'd caught you out at night, this would have gone much differently. Watch out, kid. Keep looking over your shoulder, all of you. This is over, but only for now."

Despite himself, Kevin shuddered.

Pete started to go, but the weasel hung back, staring at April. "I don't know, Pete. Do we have to go?" His smile was filthy. "You seem sweet, babe. Maybe I oughta pop your cherry."

"Fuck you," April snapped.

But that wasn't enough. Kevin, Jesse and Tommy all started moving toward Pete and his cronies. It was instinctive, nothing more than that. The weasel had just crossed a line, and they couldn't just stand there. Already, Kevin felt himself tensing.

Jack was way ahead of them.

"C'mere, you asshole," he snarled, advancing faster than the others.

Pete laughed then. It was a surprisingly girlish giggle, and it had a kind of musical quality, like someone hacking a violin to pieces with a hatchet.

Then he astonished Kevin by turning, shoving the weasel ahead of him, and sprinting away from them on the tracks. His friends ran, too. They all took off as fast as they could manage.

"Jack, let it go—" Jesse started to say.

It was too late. Jack was screaming, swearing, and tearing off after them. April yelled for him to stop, but he wouldn't.

"Ah, shit," Tommy muttered.

Then all six of them were running, trying like hell to

catch up with the four older guys. Kevin could hear Pete's crazy giggle floating back to him, and he almost stopped. But he couldn't.

What was coming could not be prevented.

It was perhaps one hundred yards to the narrow, wooded path that led out to the parking lot behind the Red Coach Grill. Though Jack was sprinting, and the others hustling along behind him, they didn't stand a chance of catching up with Pete and his gang. The older kids were simply faster.

By the time Jack ran from the path, knocking low-hanging branches out of his face, and emerged into the parking lot, Pete and his friends were already piling into their car. Kevin burst from the path behind him just in time to hear the engine roar into life. The others followed, and they started across the lot toward the car.

It was a Dodge Charger with tinted windows, painted a metallic black, with sparkles all over it so that it looked like the night sky. As they bolted across the lot toward the car, Pete put it into reverse, and the vehicle surged backward, tires squealing, heading straight for Kevin and Jesse, who had come up beside him. Kevin's eyes went wide and he couldn't move as the car rocketed back at him.

"Get out of the way!" Jesse shouted.

Kevin blinked, realized with horror that Pete really meant to hit him. Then Jesse slammed into him from the side, nearly carrying him off his feet, and Kevin was running, propelled out of harm's way by his older brother.

Pete slammed on the brakes, and looked out the open driver's window.

"We'll meet again," he said, smiling.

April and Diana spit the nastiest curses they could think of at him. Then Diana bent down and picked up a rock from the lot. She threw it at the car, but her aim was poor, and missed the rear windshield by several feet. Tommy was right behind her, though, and his aim was better.

He threw a rock that broke a taillight.

Inspired, they all began to bend down and pick up rocks.

Pete looked both furious and alarmed as he peeled out, steering the Charger out of the lot even as all six of them threw rocks. None of the others met their mark, or at least none that they noticed.

"What the fuck were you thinking, just standing there?" Jesse demanded.

Kevin glanced at him. "I don't know. Guess I didn't think he'd really hit me."

"Get a clue, Kev. You see the look on that freak's face? He's nuts. You know the type. Like Joe Burgess, wrecked two new cars in a month and his parents still bought him a third one. Stole cocaine from his brother's dealer, and his own brother kicked his ass. This prick's no different."

As he stared after the midnight-blue-painted Dodge, Kevin nodded slowly. The guy had talked crazy. Even though he and his freaky buddies had run, Kevin didn't have the idea they'd been afraid. Not at all. If they ever saw a chance to mess him or the others up, he was certain they would take it.

"At least they're gone," April said, shuddering.

Diana corrected her. "Not quite gone."

The Charger had torn up Route Nine to the nearest light, but it was in the left lane, preparing to come round and head east. The car would be all the way on the other side of the road, across the median and the guardrail, but they'd be passing right by again in a few seconds.

"Motherfuckers," Tommy muttered.

He bent to pick up a large rock that he'd dropped when the car had gotten out of range. Jack did the same.

"Guys, just let it go. Let's get out of here." April looked around the group, waiting for someone to back her up. She was nervous and tired and obviously didn't want to be there anymore.

Jesse shrugged, but made no move to grab a rock. "No way they're gonna hit anything from this distance."

April looked imploringly at Kevin, rightly thinking he was the only one who might agree with her.

"Guys, you could hit another car. You could cause an accident. Come on. There'll be tons of witnesses. Don't be stupid," he told them.

Tommy turned and glared at him. "Don't *you* be a pussy."

As he looked into Tommy's eyes, at the plastered-on grin that made his face into a mask, Kevin understood something that made him realize it was fruitless to argue. Tommy was still afraid. He was probably embarrassed about being roughed up like he'd been, not being tough enough to kick the orange albino's ass. But that wasn't why he had the rock in his hand or the nasty grin on his face. Tommy was terrified of those guys.

Kevin looked around. It was on Diana's face, too. April was scared, but she just wanted to run. Only Jack and Jesse didn't look scared, but that didn't surprise him. Neither one of them ever thought much about consequences, only about the moment.

Diana touched Tommy's hand. "Maybe she's right."

With a sigh and a roll of his eyes, Tommy dropped the rock. He and Diana kissed, and he hugged her tightly.

Across the street, the light had changed, and the Charger roared east on Route Nine. Kevin had just let out a breath, thinking maybe it was over after all. Then Jack screamed something almost unintelligible, but obviously obscene, at the top of his lungs, and hurled a rock into the air.

The stone was large and round, somewhat flat. It flew across Route Nine in an impossible arc. Kevin watched with morbid fascination as the rock soared over three lanes, then the median. Pete must have been driving at least fifty. The Charger's blacked-out windows were all closed, except for the one in the driver's door.

Kevin and his friends let out a collective gasp of astonishment as they saw what was about to happen. The rock went right in through the open window of the speeding car, and hit pretty boy Pete in the side of the face. The Charger swerved across the road, nearly side-swiping a battered Gran Torino. The brakes locked up and the car skidded to a halt in the breakdown lane.

They didn't wait around to see the rest.

"Holy shit!" Kevin muttered as he turned to run.

Diana and Tommy were the first back onto the wooded path. Kevin turned to make sure April was all right, but he needn't have worried. Jack and Jesse flanked her, rushing her toward the woods. Kevin darted under low-hanging branches, and they all ran for the train tracks. At the tracks, with the woods separating them from Route Nine on the one side, and the reservoir on the other, they turned west and took off full tilt.

"How bad you think he's hurt?" Kevin asked frantically.

"I hope he's in the fucking hospital," Tommy grunted.

"You better hope so," April told him. Then she turned to Jack. "You too, you idiot. I can't believe you made that throw, but if he isn't in the hospital, I'm sure they're coming back, right now. Figure there's a fifty-fifty chance they'll pick the right end of the tracks to wait for us."

"Shit," Jesse said suddenly. Then he yelled it. "We gotta book it. What if the cops come?" He glanced at Kevin. "Ma will kill us if the cops bring us home."

"Or worse," Kevin replied.

After that, they were all quiet, keeping to their own thoughts and fears. They hurried along the tracks until they emerged in the Framingham Industrial Park. Hustling through to the other side, they came to Pleasant Street, which was very busy. Cars whizzed by at an alarming pace, but they didn't see any cops. They couldn't run anymore, but they kept a breathless pace, even as they moved onto back roads, away from Pleasant. Another half mile of narrow neighborhood streets, and they started cutting across lawns until they came in sight of Ledgewood Road, where Tommy lived.

Fox Run Drive was only two streets away, and Kevin and Jesse both breathed deeply. They all did then.

As one, almost as though they had discussed it, the six of them stopped to rest. Tommy and Diana sat on the curb, and Jesse slid up onto a fence in front of the O'Rourkes' house.

It was Jack who broke the silence.

"Can't believe I hit him," he said gravely. "Not that I didn't want to hurt the prick, but . . ." His words trailed off, and he shrugged. He wasn't usually much for talking anyway.

Jesse chuckled. "Gotta say. It was a damn good throw."

Then, as if a switch had been thrown, they all started to laugh. The fear and tension had built up to such a level that laughter was their only option. It was filled with giddy disbelief at the accuracy of Jack's throw, and a relief that they were home, back on their own turf.

Our turf, Kevin thought.

"Know what this reminds me of?" he said. "In *The Warriors,* at the end, when they get back to Coney Island, and they know they're safe. That's what this feels like."

Safe.

4

On Sunday morning, the sky hung low and gray, ominous clouds moving ponderously overhead. With the curtains drawn in his room, and the imminent storm blanching all color from the world, it might well have been night. Several times, Kevin's eyes flickered open, but the dark outside told him there was still time to sleep, and sleep he did.

When he had woken a fourth time and could not manage to get back to sleep, he lazed in bed and wished he had a television in his room. It was obviously going to be that kind of day. Scratching his head, he looked at the clock on the nightstand and was horrified to see that it was after eleven. He hadn't slept that late in years.

It was just that kind of day.

The air was thick with humidity, and so hot as to make breathing uncomfortable. The darkly pregnant sky was ominous, menacing with the threat of rain. But no rain came. That would have been a relief.

Jesse had gone fishing early that morning, but Kevin did manage to have a quick lunch of tuna fish sandwiches with his mother before she headed off to the office. It was Sunday, the day of rest, sure. But for real estate agents, it was make or break day, no matter the weather.

After his mom left, Kevin descended into the basement of the Murphys' split-level. When he was a kid, he and Jesse had played with their Mego superhero action figures and *Planet of the Apes* play set and Evel Knievel stunt cycle down there. It was still their hangout, but these days it was where they listened to music or watched TV. Kevin found *War of the Gargantuas* on Channel thirty-eight, and settled down on the musty old red pullout couch to watch.

During the climax of the film, while the green and brown gargantuas were beating the crap out of each other, the phone rang. The first few rings, he barely registered it. Finally, though, he glanced over at the phone, which was on a table in the corner by an old piano on which nobody played anything anymore but the *Close Encounters* theme. Scowling, he got up to answer.

It was Nikki.

"Hey," Kevin said.

"What are you up to?"

He had a mental image of her suddenly: she stood before a mirror wearing cutoff overalls and a green T-shirt, running a purple hairbrush through her hair. It was the oddest sensation, almost as if he had seen her in just that way on television, and turned away a moment later, leaving the afterimage on his retinas.

"Kevin?"

"Whoa," he muttered. "Weirdest thing. I just had this, like, picture of you in my head, brushing your hair or something."

The second he said it, he knew how stupid it sounded. Worse, he thought it might sound a little too much like he was obsessing over her. Not that he wasn't, but it wasn't the kind of thing he wanted to broadcast. On the other hand, the image had been strong.

"What are you, Peeping Tom now?" Nikki asked.

Kevin blinked. "What?"

Her laugh was somehow both sweet and insinuating. "Maybe you've got some kind of hidden camera over here. I literally just put my brush down when you answered the phone."

A chilly ripple passed through Kevin, a queer counterpoint to the heat and humidity of the day.

"It's a purple brush," he said, almost against his will. The words just seemed to find themselves on his lips.

"You're wearing those cutoff overalls, the ones with the rip in the ass."

Silence.

"No way," Nikki said. "How the fuck did you know that?"

Kevin laughed nervously. He wondered, for a second, if she was having him on. But, no, the tone in her voice made it clear that she wasn't.

"No way," he echoed. "Now you're just messing with me."

"Seriously. You nailed it. What color's my shirt?"

"Green."

"Too fucking bizarre," Nikki muttered.

For a long moment, neither of them spoke. There was just open air on the line, and Kevin could hear her breathing. Listening to her breath that close to his ear, the image of her beginning to fade in his head, he felt as though he were standing right beside her. It was strange, but nice, too. Like they'd just passed—or built—something between them that had never been there before.

"Listen," she said at length, "my mother's got tomorrow off and she's got a million errands to do. I was thinking maybe we could go to Lake Cochituate. She could drop us off on the way, and pick us up when she's done."

"Yeah. Sounds cool. Who else is going?"

"Why?" Nikki asked, again with that laugh. "You need someone else?"

A million thoughts went through Kevin's mind. He found himself oddly tempted to ask what would happen if the weather was bad, and also felt a tiny twinge of guilt at the idea that he and Nikki would be going by themselves. Not that they hadn't hung out just the two of them in the past, but it was different now. He had already made the decision to break up with Carolyn, but he hadn't done it yet.

Kevin felt a little sick to his stomach, but he couldn't have explained exactly why.

"Nah," he finally said. "As long as there's a lifeguard on duty in case you decide to drown me."

Nikki laughed. "I'll call you in the morning."

Cochituate State Park was on Route Thirty, close enough to the Framingham/Wayland border that Kevin wasn't quite sure which town it was supposed to be in. The previous summer, he'd been there a bunch of times with Tommy, and once or twice when he was younger his mother had dragged him and Jesse there. But Aileen Murphy would only go to Lake Cochituate when she was desperate for sun. She preferred a real beach, some-where with salt water and waves. For the most part, so did Kevin.

But this wasn't about the beach. This was about hang-ing out with Nikki.

Her mother drove an aging Plymouth, and its engine rumbled when she put it in park to drop them off. The lot was filled with cars, and there were two brightly painted trucks blasting annoying jingles that were a com-bination of sleigh bells and radio static. One was a spar-klingly new, white ice-cream truck with every kind of push-up, cherry bomb, éclair and Italian ice known to teen America. The other was an ancient blue rolling hot-dog stand whose skin, underneath the new season's paint job, was more Bondo than metal.

As they tramped between the two big vehicles in the lot, Kevin carrying the radio and small cooler, and Nikki carrying the towels, the smell of boiling hot dogs wafted on the breeze. It wasn't yet eleven o'clock, but the odor made Kevin's stomach rumble.

A small path led through a woodsy area between the lot and the lake. Even as they set foot on it, the wind carried every sound up from the shore. A minute later, as they emerged from the trees onto the sprawl of grass that separated the woods from the short stretch of sand some had the guts to call a beach, all of those sounds were suddenly matched up to reality.

On the grass, a bunch of older people, maybe twenty,

played volleyball and drank beer, swearing at each other, the guys strutting and trying to look tough—but mostly coming off like Barney Fife sniffing and hauling up his pants.

Radios blared in competition with each other. Off to the south, a bunch of high school kids, maybe sixteen, seventeen, played frisbee. There was only one girl with them, wearing cutoffs and a bikini top that barely held in her enormous breasts. Kevin tried not to look a second time. He actually managed not to look a third.

Someone grilled hamburgers on a hibachi nearby.

The short, spiky grass was yellowed and scorched, and it hurt to walk on it with bare feet, but everyone tried to pretend it didn't bother them.

There was plenty of room to find a place to sit on the grass, but on the sand there was barely space enough between towels to make your way down to the water. Particularly around the lifeguard's chair. The guy sitting up there in his orange trunks had two jobs. Saving lives was one. The other was trying not to notice the teeny-bopper girls all doing their damnedest to get his attention.

In the water itself, there were mostly kids and their mothers, and a few packs of teenagers splashing each other. The lifeguard stood and blew his whistle at a couple of guys who had ducked under the string of white buoys and started to swim out across the lake.

"God, it's chaos," Kevin said.

"Yeah," Nikki agreed. "Gotta love it."

They spread their towels out on the crunchy grass and Nikki turned on the radio. Bob Seger was singing "Against the Wind" and Kevin knew even then that it would be a very long time before he could hear that song without thinking of Nikki, and that day on the beach.

He pulled off his shirt and sat down on the towel, and Nikki stripped off her clothes to reveal a blue-and-white-striped string bikini underneath.

Kevin grinned and whistled. Nikki gave him the finger. They spent an hour just lying there, talking. Nikki's mom had gone out on a couple of dates with an orderly from the hospital. Karen Blair, who lived up the street from Nikki, had actually gotten arrested for stealing a fifth of vodka from Pendolari's Package Store. Van Halen were coming in concert, and Nikki was dying to go. Kevin told her about what had happened at the trestle on Saturday, and Nikki said "no way" about five times.

It was nice. Really nice. Kevin just enjoyed being with her, not having to think about what to do or say; not having to consider his feelings at all, because he could pretend—just for that time—that Nikki really was his girlfriend.

About one o'clock, they got up and walked through the woods back to the parking lot to buy hot dogs from the ancient blue truck. The name "Greenie's" was stenciled on the side of the truck, but he'd never noticed it before. What he did notice was the way every guy under twenty-five looked at him with envy as he walked beside Nikki. He found himself blushing a little, but it didn't stop him from stealing a glance at her out of the corner of his eye.

When they'd ordered, and it was time to pay, she only raised her eyebrows and threw her hands in the air. "Do I look like I'm carrying money on me?"

His eyes danced over her perfect legs and flat belly, at the string bikini that left nothing to the imagination. Kevin shook his head, a silly grin on his face.

"Sure, use the whole chick thing to get free lunch," he razzed her.

"I'll pay you back, Kevin. I always do."

As they walked back along the path to the wide stretch of lawn, they were silent for a few moments, keeping their thoughts to themselves. Then Nikki chuckled, as if she'd thought of something funny, and yet too private to share.

"What?" he asked.

Nikki rolled her eyes, grinning. "My mother said the funniest thing when we were on the way to pick you up.

We were talking about the last couple of jerks I went out with, and she's, like, 'you should go out with Kevin.' "

His heart stopped. He forced a grin onto his face, a smile that said, *Isn't that absurd?* Kevin found it hard to breathe.

"Huh," he grunted, and hoped it sounded like he was amused.

Now! his mind screamed. *Tell her. Just fucking tell her how you feel!* But there was another voice in his head, reminding him that not only was he still, technically, going out with Carolyn, but that he wouldn't be fourteen for two and a half more weeks, and Nikki was already fifteen. *On my birthday,* he promised himself again.

"Well, it's not *that* crazy," he managed. "I mean, that she would think that."

"I know," Nikki admitted. "She doesn't get how close we are, y'know. I mean, you're like my best friend. It would be too weird. Never mind that it isn't like either one of us lacks for a love life."

Nikki shook her head, then started off on another tangent, but Kevin wasn't listening. He was stuck on those words: *it would be too weird.*

"Yeah," Kevin reluctantly agreed. "Plus, y'know, I'm younger than you."

Through a bite of hot dog, Nikki protested. "Kev, you're about the oldest guy I know. Trust me, it's a good thing."

Kevin grinned. They ate their lunch, went for a swim—completely ignoring that whole half-hour-after-eating rule—then packed up their stuff and went to wait for Nikki's mother to arrive. When she showed up, half an hour late, he was still grinning.

Carolyn called at dinnertime. Mrs. Murphy was working late at the office again, but Jesse made baked chicken and rice pilaf, and the boys made sure there was plenty left over for their mother to eat when she got home. While Kevin was cleaning up—his part of the dinner arrangement—the phone rang. He picked it up with wet hands, then dragged it back to the sink, coiled cord stretching to its limit.

"Hello?"

"Hey, cutie."

"Carolyn," his heart sank. "Hey."

"What's wrong?"

"Doing the dishes," he told her. "Isn't that enough? I was gonna call you tonight. What's up?"

"April and Diana and I are going to the movies. Wanna come?"

A nervous shiver ran through Kevin. He wiped his hands and stepped away from the sink, leaning against the wall by the phone. On the one hand, the last thing he wanted to do was get together with the whole group, break up with Carolyn with everyone around. On the other, though, he didn't see any way to say no without getting into a fight and dumping her right there on the phone.

While he was trying to decide which was worse, she got annoyed.

"I didn't think it was that hard a question."

"No, no, I was just reading the note my mom left again, trying to figure out what time she'll be home," he lied. "She's not around now, but let me give Tommy and Jack a call, see if one of their moms can drive us. Jesse might want to come, too."

"That's cool."

"Call you back in a little while?"

"Okay," Carolyn said, her voice taking on a little girl quality that he'd once found adorable but which now grated on him. "I love you."

"Yeah," Kevin said, heart aching with guilt. "I love you, too."

The movie theater was built right on to the edge of Shopper's World, on Route Nine, near the Natick line. They met the girls at a Papa Gino's in the mall, a stone's throw from the theater. When they walked in, the girls spotted them and waved. Kevin hung back a moment at the sight of Carolyn. But only a moment.

Tommy and Kevin slid in with the girls, while Jack and Jesse sat at another table with April. She had that distant look in her eyes, the one that said she would rather be anywhere but there. That night, Kevin thought she had good reason for it. He felt the same.

"Hi," Kevin said, forcing a smile.

Carolyn leaned across the table to kiss him. He brushed her lips with his, a sick feeling churning in his stomach. It was guilt; that much he knew. But it was also just anxiety because he knew what he was going to do but couldn't just do it. The awkwardness, and the expected screaming, would be bad enough. But waiting for it, dreading it, that was worse.

They sat with Tommy and Diana, and everybody started talking about food. They had only met at Papa Gino's to have somewhere to hang together, waiting for it to be time for the movie to start. They had all eaten dinner already, but nobody was going to say no to a slice, so it was decided they would get a couple of small pizzas to share. Kevin collected the money, and went to stand in line to order.

A few seconds later, Tommy appeared beside him.

"What's happening with you two?" he asked.

Kevin grimaced. "That obvious, huh?"

"Oh, yeah. I'm sure she's talking to Diana about it right now."

With a deep breath, he glanced over and saw that Tommy was right. The girls were talking, sneaking looks at them, and Carolyn looked upset. He knew he should do it right then, but he couldn't. It would be just too weird for everyone.

"I'm gonna break up with her," Kevin told Tommy.

"About time," Tommy muttered.

"Huh?" Kevin grunted in surprise. "What the fuck's that mean?"

"Come on. Gimme a fucking break. All you guys do

is fight. Every time you break up I figure it's the last time, and then you get together again."

"Not this time."

"Yeah," Tommy nodded. "I can pretty much tell that by the look on your face."

"I'm gonna wait till later, though," Kevin told him. "I mean, I don't want to ruin everyone's night. Also . . . I'm a little bummed about screwing all this up."

"What, you mean us? The group?" Tommy asked. "Don't worry about it. So you break up. That doesn't mean we can't all hang out. If Carolyn doesn't want to be around when we're all together, that's her problem."

Kevin allowed himself a small smile. "Thanks, man. I guess I really needed to hear that."

Tommy shrugged. "Everyone knows you've in love with Nikki French anyway."

"Fuck you," Kevin growled in protest.

But then it was his turn to order, and he never had another chance to follow up on Tommy's comment. Which was probably good, considering that it was true, and he wasn't sure he could have lied about it convincingly. He just didn't want anyone to think he was breaking up with Carolyn to ask Nikki out. Despite the timing, that really wasn't true. If he hadn't been such a wimp about it, he would have stayed broken up with Carolyn the first time they'd had a fight, and that would have been that.

He was determined that this time would be different.

Back at the table, he did his best to steer the conversation to the group, avoiding any kind of quiet moment with Carolyn. It worked, for the most part, but he noticed her looking at him oddly from time to time, her eyes kind of sad and far away.

In the theater, they held hands, but he thought it best not to kiss her at all. Carolyn didn't seem to notice, but she also made no attempt to snuggle closer, just twined her fingers loosely in his.

The movie sucked.

When it was over, they all walked together over to

the bus stop in front of Shopper's World, where Mr. Carlson was going to pick them all up. Mrs. Ross had driven them down, but she didn't like to go out that late at night, so Tommy's father had agreed to taxi them home. Diana's mother was going to pick up the girls.

The bus didn't run that late at night, so there were only a few other people there, apparently also waiting to be retrieved by parents or other chauffeurs. A couple of guys, about seventeen, dressed in ragged Kiss concert shirts were having a contest to see how far across the inside of the shelter of the station they could spit, "huck a looey," in the local parlance.

A pair of middle-aged women with shopping bags stood near the pay phones at the head of the concrete island upon which the bus stop stood. A dozen feet from them, Jack and April and the others leaned against the outside of the shelter. Tommy was the only one without a cigarette as Kevin and Carolyn approached. Tommy and Diana were hugging tightly, as were Jack and April. Jesse said something under his breath, probably giving Jack a hard time, and they all laughed.

Kevin hung back, letting Carolyn reach the others ahead of him. He felt a kind of cramp in his stomach, and his heart was racing. He wondered if his cheeks were flushed red. His tongue felt like cotton. The words wouldn't come. The *thoughts* would barely come.

He watched them all. His brother. His friends. His girlfriend. For the first time, he recognized that it had been a mistake from the very beginning, he and Carolyn. She was cute and everything, and there was something to be said for the way she kissed. But it hadn't been fair to her; not at all. Not when he had been in love with Nikki the whole time.

Carolyn hadn't ever had a chance. The two of them had never had the opportunity to be a real couple.

"Shit," Kevin said under his breath.

He looked up and saw Tommy watching him, and rolled his eyes just a little. Tommy raised his eyebrows as if to say, *get on with it, pussy.* Which was what he *would* have said if he'd dared speak out loud just then. Kevin knew he was right.

With a deep breath, he turned to look at Carolyn, who stood with Jack and April, staring back. Her eyes were narrowed and her lips pressed into thin, bloodless lines. It was the first time Kevin had really paid any attention to her all night, and now he realized that he should have done so much sooner.

Carolyn shook her head abruptly and marched across the island toward him. The two middle-aged ladies with their Jordan Marsh bags shuffled back into the phone kiosk as she passed, alarmed by her manner and her stride.

Inside the shelter, one of the Kiss fans hacked up a huge gob of spit and managed to fire it the length of the shelter, where it struck the far window, stuck, and began to slide under its own weight, leaving a snail trail down the Plexiglas.

Carolyn stood in front of Kevin, looking up at him with anguish in her eyes. Her lip quivered.

"You have something to say to me?" she demanded.

Kevin blinked, shocked. Had someone told her? *No, you idiot. She isn't stupid.*

"Ah, shit, Carolyn," he muttered. "I didn't . . . I mean, it isn't . . ."

He simply couldn't find the words. At least not fast enough for her.

"Know what?" she snapped. "Let me make it easy on you, okay?"

Carolyn began rooting through the black faux-leather purse she wore slung around her shoulder. Deep at the bottom of the bag, she found a pack of Marlboro Lights in the box. She nearly tore the cover off getting a cigarette out, and then placed it between her lips so it jutted from her mouth with an anger all its own. While she was looking away from him, Kevin saw that she had begun to cry. The tears went untended until she found the Bic lighter that had also slipped to the bottom of her pocketbook. She zipped it up and let it dangle at her side again.

Carolyn didn't look at him as she wiped at her eyes with a fist that was closed around the lighter. When she lit the Marlboro, the flame from the Bic blazed a little too high, and it might have singed her hair if she hadn't been wearing it tied back. As she drew a long breath of carcinogens into her lungs, Carolyn stared off at the white dome of the Jordan Marsh department store across the lot, unwilling to look at either Kevin or their friends, all of whom were doing their best not to notice what was happening only twenty feet away.

With another long drag on the butt, Carolyn finally turned to regard Kevin. Her gaze was steady, though her eyes were shot and rimmed with red. Her mascara had started to run just a little. She blew smoke out of the corner of her mouth.

"Happy now? It's easy, right? I smoke. There's your excuse. You won't go out with a girl who smokes, right?"

Kevin's first thought was *Nikki smokes*. All his bluster about her smoking was bullshit when it came right down to it. He had ridden her about it because he could. It was true he didn't like smoking, but if he'd wanted to be in her life badly enough, it wouldn't have mattered.

To know that would have hurt her even more.

"It isn't easy," Kevin told her, meeting her gaze steadily. "Of course it isn't easy. I do care about you. Maybe I still love you, at least a little. Probably always will. But tell me the truth: Are you happy?"

"Right now?" she asked, frowning. Her expression said it all.

"Not right now," Kevin sighed. "I mean, we fight so much. You're always getting pissed at me for stupid shit, you're completely jealous. I lose my mind when you smoke. I give you a hard time about ridiculous little things. I know I haven't been happy with that. I want to know if you are."

"I love you," Carolyn said, before she took another drag and looked away.

"That's not an answer."

"You know I'm not happy."

"I think it'd be good if we were both happy. I'd like *you* to be. And I gotta tell you, I'd like to be happy myself. I wish I could just rewind everything, and we could all just be friends, and not have this all get in the way. But we can't. No 'do-overs' here."

Carolyn kept her back to him for a long time. At length, she turned to face him. Her eyes were drier than he would have expected, and he was glad of that.

"*Can* we still be friends?" she asked. "I mean, is it going to be weird, hanging out with everyone?"

"That's pretty much up to you," Kevin told her. "I'd hate for that to happen."

"Me too," she whispered.

There was additional communication between them, but it was wordless. A moment later, Kevin moved toward her, and held her close and kissed the top of her head.

"I'm sorry," he whispered, after a minute or two.

"Me too," Carolyn replied. "You have no idea."

Her arms were wrapped around him, and he could smell the cigarette burning in her fingers. He felt a momentary temptation to say something, but then thought better of it.

By the time Tommy's dad showed, Kevin was standing with Jesse talking about the movie, and Carolyn was across the island talking to Jack and April.

It was over.

5

It was the greatest week of Kevin's life. For days, he and
Nikki were inseparable. They would talk on the phone in
the morning, and he would drift down to her house some
time before lunch. She made them tuna or ham and
cheese sandwiches and iced tea with lots of sugar and
lemon. Then they'd walk down to the reservoir and go
swimming, or sit on the front steps and just talk.

Nikki wanted to be a dancer. She'd never told Kevin
that before, and he wondered if she'd ever really told
anyone. It seemed to embarrass her a little. There were
lessons, too, and recitals—all in a special program unrelated to the high school. She didn't want anybody to
know. This was a side to her that Kevin had never even
imagined could exist: shy, self-conscious, even a little
afraid. It gave him an entirely new perspective on her.
And it made him love her more.

By Thursday, he didn't even call first before going
down to her house.

When he arrived, she was sitting on the front steps
waiting for him. The sun shone on the brick steps, and
Nikki wore cutoffs and a lemon-hued bikini top, with
sunglasses shading her eyes, and no shoes on her feet,
not even sandals. The world was hers; that was clear
from just looking at her. Yet Kevin remembered the
soft-voiced conversation about dancing, and he knew
that beneath the confident exterior was a girl with the
same hopes and fears that he himself had. That everyone
had. Not dancing, necessarily, but a dream of the future,
of being an adult and having a good life and being loved,

and the abject terror that arose at the thought that those things might not happen.

"Hi," he said quietly as he approached.

Nikki had been languishing there, behind her dark glasses, and he had assumed that she had her eyes closed. But when he spoke, she didn't flinch. Instead, that mischievous smile spread across her face and sent his heart speeding breathlessly along.

"I'm sick of tuna." Those were the first words out of her mouth.

Kevin laughed. "Okay. What'd you have in mind?"

"Want to ride bikes down to the center? We could get pizzas or subs or whatever. Maybe hit Cape Cod Ice Cream for dessert."

A little thrill ran through Kevin. It wasn't a date. He knew that. But just like that day at the beach, it felt like one. He grinned, and shrugged, as if it didn't matter to him one way or another.

"Sure."

They rode the three miles to Framingham Center on their bikes, with Nikki in the lead and Kevin not doing anything to catch up. As they dipped in and out of driveways, up and down sidewalks on their way along Pleasant Street, he enjoyed the breeze on his face and the warmth of the sun, and he tried his best not to let her catch him checking out her butt when she glanced back at him.

They locked their bikes up in front of Center Pizza. Nikki's was a green, battered ten-speed with peace signs made of black electrical tape over the reflectors. The bike had been her father's, once upon a time. Kevin's Fuji ten-speed was a metallic purple, and much newer, though the plastic tape that was wound about the handlebars had already started to unravel. The telephone pole where they locked the bikes was right outside the big bay window of the pizza place, so they could see if anyone tried to steal them. The bike was Kevin's only form of transportation and he lived in mortal terror of the possibility that someone might try to steal it.

After pizza there was ice cream, a combination both of them thought was pure bliss.

It was a nice day, sunny and breezy, maybe in the low eighties. But when they got back to Nikki's house, they went inside and turned on the ancient color television in the Frenches' living room. They sat together—Kevin at the edge of the sofa, and Nikki with her head on his lap, apparently unaware of the reaction her position elicited from him—for the balance of the afternoon.

Just being with her like that, relaxed and content, made Kevin feel good. For those hours, he could pretend that Nikki was his girlfriend, that he had confessed his love to her and she had returned it. It was pretty cowardly, even a little pathetic. He knew that. But it was nice, too. Not to mention safe.

And, he reminded himself, *it isn't like it's forever. Less than two weeks till my birthday. Then I'll tell her for real.*

Kevin's mother had promised to be home in time for dinner, so at five o'clock, he went out and rode his bike up the street, then turned down Fox Run Drive. No sign of his mother's car in the driveway, however. He sighed. Real estate was a tough business. Even at thirteen, he knew that much. But that wasn't all it was. Kevin's mom made no secret of the fact that her boss was a real slave driver. He didn't have any life of his own, just the job. He expected all his employees to behave as if they were in the same boat.

As he stored his bike in the garage, he admitted to himself that he was disappointed. It wasn't like he was a momma's boy or something. He liked hanging out with his friends and just hanging out in the neighborhood. But he would have liked to have dinner with his mother at night. That was what families were supposed to do.

The door was locked, so he had to fish out his key. That meant that Jesse wasn't home. He was on his own. With a pang, he regretted having left Nikki's at all. Her mom was always asking him to stay for dinner. Next time, he promised himself he'd do just that. For now, though, it was okay to be solo. He could just make some macaroni and cheese and read a book.

Just when the water for the macaroni had begun to boil, the phone rang. Kevin's eyes jumped ahead to the end of the paragraph he was reading, then he stuck his finger in the book, and got up to answer.

"Hello?"

"Hey." The voice was drawn and sullen.

"Jack. What's up? Hey, is Jesse with you?" he asked.

"Yeah, he's here. And you're supposed to fuckin' be here, too, man."

Kevin blinked in surprise. "Huh?" he grunted.

If it had been anyone else, they would have beaten Kevin to the realization of what, exactly, he had forgotten. But even when he was annoyed, which wasn't all that often, Jack took his time saying just about everything. He'd just begun to speak again when Kevin interrupted.

"Oh shit. It's April's birthday. The cookout. Is she pissed?"

"What do you think?" Jack drawled. "You fuckin' coming down here or not?"

"Be right there," Kevin said quickly.

He hung up the phone, turned off the stove, dumped the boiling water into the stainless-steel sink, and then ran down the stairs and slammed out the door. A second later, he hustled back to make sure it had locked behind him. He hustled across Fox Run and through the backyards to the Rosses'.

Everyone was in the backyard already. Jesse was standing by the grill, cooking burgers and dogs. Diana, Carolyn and April all sat with some other girls at a big wooden picnic table, while Tommy and Jack and a few other friends of April's threw a frisbee around the wide backyard. Jack's father had probably gotten the grill going, but otherwise he'd stay away, Kevin figured. More than a couple of extra kids around, and the old man's head started to throb. He was probably sitting in front of the television watching the news.

Mrs. Ross came out the back door as Kevin walked up. She carried a pair of heavy-looking pitchers with what looked like Kool-Aid in them—one red and one purple. But after she put them down, she headed back for the house.

This wasn't April's only birthday party, of course. Just a little thing Jack was doing for her, kind of spur of the moment. Kevin had known about it since Monday, but it had completely slipped his mind. He hadn't even bought her a present yet. Her parents were having more of a family party for her over the weekend, though, so he told himself as long as he got it to her by then, he'd be okay.

"Shit," Kevin muttered.

Carolyn was the first one to see him. She watched him for a moment as he walked briskly along the grass. Then she looked away, not even bothering to let anyone know he was coming.

Jack saw him and waved. Kevin waved back. When he walked past the grill, Jesse scowled at him.

"Bro, where the hell were *you*?"

"Just hanging out," Kevin said defensively. "You coulda reminded me earlier."

Jesse rolled his eyes. "You want a dog?"

"Not yet," Kevin said.

April looked pissed. When he walked over to the picnic table, Diana was the first one to talk to him.

"Look who decided to show up," she teased.

"Sorry I'm late," he said, as earnestly as he could manage. "I wasn't around this afternoon, and time sort of got away from me. Then my mom wasn't home from work yet, and I thought I should wait for her, and . . . I'm sorry, April."

With a roll of her eyes, April sighed. "I guess you just don't love me anymore." Then she laughed. "Don't worry about it. Seriously. Jesse said you were probably just hanging out with— "

The smile disappeared from April's face and she glanced quickly at Carolyn. Kevin felt awkward, and then was angry at himself for it. So what if he was spending time with Nikki? No matter what he might wish, it wasn't as if they were dating. They were just friends.

"I figured you'd see us down here on the way home. It's no big deal," April went on.

Kevin nodded, though he hadn't seen them at all. He felt pretty stupid, all things considered. But at least April wasn't pissed at him.

"Hell, I never understood why your parents named you April when you were born in July anyway," he said.

She gave him the finger. It was something she'd been teased about before, familiar territory, and they all laughed. Even Carolyn, which relieved some of the awkwardness Kevin had felt. Her house was all the way on the other side of town, and it felt kind of weird to have her be in the neighborhood, but not at his own house. Almost like she was intruding or something. He knew that was absurd, but he'd still feel better when she'd gone.

"Kevin!" Jack shouted.

He turned around just in time to see the wide glow-in-the-dark green frisbee soaring across the lawn. Kevin went to snatch it out of the air but even before he started moving he knew he was going to be too late. At the table, April was telling the others a story and did not notice the frisbee slicing through the air toward the back of her head.

Kevin opened his mouth to shout a warning but before he could utter a sound, April half turned and caught the frisbee inches from her face without even looking at it. With a frown, she tossed it to him. Kevin just stared for a few seconds as everyone else applauded April's miraculous catch.

"That was a hell of a catch," he told her. "You've got eyes in the back of your head."

"Frisbee is my natural element," April boasted, her frown blossoming into the grin that had broken so many hearts.

The all-American girl, Kevin thought. Which was

weird, because April never really fit the part, even though she looked it. In some ways, that made Jack her perfect mate, because most of the time he seemed even more distant than she did.

Kevin turned and whipped the frisbee across the lawn to a guy named Doug Barrows, a friend of April's from her neighborhood. Doug threw it to Jack, and the game started up all over again, this time with Kevin right in the thick of it.

Moments later, he found himself standing next to Tommy.

"Hey, what's up with you?"

Kevin tried a throw behind his back with the frisbee, but it went sailing off at a crazy angle. He looked at Tommy, who was watching him curiously.

"What do you mean? Nothing's up with me."

Tommy frowned. "You've been MIA all week. I left like three messages for you in the last two days, I stopped by on the way here and banged on the door. You pissed at me for something?"

"No, man, c'mon," Kevin said. "Nothing like that. I've just . . . I've been spending a lot of time with Nikki."

The frisbee came to Tommy, and he snatched it easily and then tossed it back toward Jack.

"Yeah. Ever since she broke up with her boyfriend, huh?" he said, a cynical, lopsided smile on his face.

"What's your point?" Kevin snapped.

"You're pitiful, Kev," Tommy said, chuckling. "You think Nikki French is going to be your girlfriend, or something? She goes through boyfriends like Kleenex, she's going to be a sophomore, and she's in public school. There's just way too much competition, buddy. Give it up."

"What the fuck do you know?" Kevin said angrily, trying to argue without anyone noticing. He grabbed the frisbee and threw it again, barely looking to see where it ended up. "Nikki's my friend. If more than that comes of it, great. You're just fuckin' jealous anyway."

"Yeah. I've got a girlfriend, Kevin. And Nikki's not my type."

Kevin sighed. "Look, man, I'm sorry I haven't been around. But you don't have to be such a dick."

Tommy had to dive to catch one, and even then, he missed badly and got grass stains all over his clothes. When he'd fetched the frisbee and shot it over to April, who had just come into the game, he moved back over to stand next to Kevin.

"Nikki's cool, Kevin. And maybe she likes you. I don't know. I'm just trying to watch out for you is all. That's what friends do. Look, do you want to go to the movies tomorrow night?"

Tomorrow was Friday, and Kevin had been hoping to get Nikki to go out with him. But he felt guilty for having almost missed April's party, and for not having returned Tommy's calls. Tommy had plenty of friends. Kevin was hardly arrogant enough to think that the guy needed him or missed him or something. But Kevin had pretty much blown him off, and that was just not cool.

"Who's going?"

"Nobody. Diana has some family thing, and I haven't asked Jack and April. I just thought maybe we could hit a flick." Tommy shrugged.

"Cool," Kevin agreed. "Come by like six-thirty and we can get my mother to drive us down. As long as she's home. If not, we can always hitch."

Early Friday, Kevin called Nikki. Her mom had the morning off, and they were going food shopping or something. Which was okay with Kevin. Jesse and Jack were getting a backyard football game up, and Kevin wanted to play. Nikki promised to come over that afternoon, though, around three.

It was closer to four when she rang the bell.

Nikki smiled happily as she entered the house. There seemed to be a weird, nervous energy about her, and she kissed his cheek as she brushed past him and headed down into the basement. Kevin blinked in surprise, stood frozen for a moment, then shook his head with a grin of his own, and followed her down.

"What's up with you, today?" he asked.

"Just in a good mood. Is that a crime?" She stretched, arms above her head, her tank top riding up to reveal the soft flesh of her belly, the fabric of the shirt taut across her breasts.

"In some states," Kevin replied, trying not to stare. "Why such a good mood?"

Nikki shrugged, the mood dissipating a little. "Just am, I guess."

They flopped down next to one another on the dingy old red pullout sofa, the television on for company as they talked. Kevin told her all about having nearly missed the birthday party the day before, though he neglected to mention that she was the cause.

"But you're going out with Tommy tonight, right? You guys'll have fun. How could anyone stay mad at you? Believe me, I've tried it."

"Yeah," Kevin agreed. "I'm pretty spectacular."

Nikki hit him.

"Hey!" Kevin protested. "Remember, you can't stay mad."

"Don't push your luck," she warned.

They both laughed.

Shortly after five, Kevin's mom came home. Kevin and Nikki stood at the bottom of the split-level's stairs to greet her, and then Aileen went up to change clothes and make some dinner. She also agreed, though not without a tired sigh, to drive Kevin and Tommy to the movies after dinner.

"You staying to eat, Nikki?" she asked.

Nikki agreed. While Kevin's mom was making dinner, he and Nikki sat in the kitchen with her, catching up. Mrs. Murphy liked Nikki. Kevin was pretty sure of that. He knew it shouldn't make a difference, but it did. His mom had never liked Carolyn much, and it would be nice to have a girlfriend who got along with his mother. Not that Nikki was his girlfriend. But he could hope.

"Kevin, before you go, don't forget to pack some things for tomorrow," his mother reminded him.

The next day was the Fourth of July, and the Murphys were going to drive down to Cape Cod to spend some time with Kevin's grandmother. He would rather have spent it with his friends at the beach or something, but didn't really mind. His grandmother was a real character, a funny, demanding old woman who had a busier social life than anyone he knew, despite the fact that his grandfather had died five years earlier. Five years exactly. The Fourth of July, 1976.

Aileen Murphy didn't want her mother to be alone that day. Kevin knew better than to argue with that. It was the right thing to do. He really didn't mind, anyway. Fourth of July on the Cape meant they'd go to the bandstand in Chatham that night to hear patriotic music and watch the fireworks above.

"I packed already."

"Going to the Cape?" Nikki asked.

Kevin nodded. "What are you up to?"

"I'll probably go to Hopkinton. It's gonna be a madhouse, but a bunch of kids from my class will be there."

Madhouse wasn't an exaggeration, Kevin thought. All summer long, Hopkinton Sate Park was a mass of partying teens, food vendors, and loud music. Independence Day would quadruple the chaos. Though he would have liked to spend that time with Nikki, Kevin really didn't mind missing out on it. Hopkinton was a zoo.

It wasn't long before Kevin's mom was serving up spaghetti with Ragu and leftover meatballs, salad and Italian bread.

"It's nothing fancy," Aileen said apologetically, "but if Kevin's going to the movies, I had to do something fast. Are you going too, Nikki?"

"Nah. Boys' night out, I guess," she said.

"They'll never learn, huh?" Mrs. Murphy said, as she cast a knowing glance at Nikki. Then she got up and began to clear the dishes, groaning a bit.

"Sitting at the desk all day makes me feel so old. I

think my muscles atrophy. I've got such knots in my neck, I could really use a good back rub."

"I know the feeling," Nikki replied, stretching again. "I was up late. Summer's just started and already I'm exhausted."

"Wait until you have to get a job," Mrs. Murphy told her.

Kevin just listened, watching Nikki. When the dishes were in the dishwasher, the two of them went back downstairs. They had twenty minutes or so before Tommy was supposed to show up, but Nikki didn't seem like she was in a rush to leave. With the television on, they sat together on the sofa again, just doing nothing. After a few minutes, Nikki stretched, a little moan escaping her lips.

"You really want that back rub?" Kevin asked.

"You offering?" Nikki asked, a tiny smile playing at the corners of her mouth. "I never turn down a back rub."

For a second, Kevin said nothing. The world had suddenly become completely surreal. Not only could he not believe that he had asked the question, he couldn't believe the response. He smiled sheepishly and shrugged.

"My mom gets pretty tense at work. I used to rub her shoulders a lot."

Nikki stood up and gestured for him to move. "Make room, then, Mr. Murphy." When he'd obeyed, she lay down on her belly on the sofa, eyes closed, that tiny smile still on her face. "Get to work."

"Your wish is my command," he replied.

Seated on the edge of the sofa beside her, Kevin began to knead the muscles in Nikki's shoulders. She moaned again, a little sound of pleasure, and seemed to sink deeper into the sofa cushions. His fingers worked her shoulders and upper arms, and the back of her neck. She shuddered a bit when he touched the nape of her neck, where her strawberry-blond hair was a darker red. Gingerly, he brushed her hair up to one side.

He had only ever dreamed of touching her in this way,

and he found his breath catching in his throat, his heart speeding up a little.

"Do my back," she said, her voice a raspy whisper.

Kevin's fingers worked their way over her shoulder blades and down her back. Nikki started to make little noises. Through her shirt, he could feel the strap of her bra.

Without any warning that it was about to happen, Kevin Murphy divided, becoming two people in the blink of an eye. Outwardly, he was just Kevin, innocent and calm. Within, his heart fluttered with near panic that swirled inside him along with the love and lust he felt for Nikki. It was almost as though he could see what his hands were doing, but no longer had any connection to them.

Certainly, he knew himself well enough to know he would never be daring enough to slide his hands under Nikki's shirt. He couldn't get a very good grip to rub her shoulders—really do it right—through the fabric. Moments later, he pulled her shirt up, scrunching it against the back of her neck. Her breasts had stopped the shirt from coming up in front, but he could see the back and sides of her tan bra, the soft roundness of her breasts inside it.

Afraid to breathe, afraid to pause or sweat or even blink, for fear that she would somehow sense his underlying motives, he continued to rub her back. Kevin's fingers scraped over the thin bra strap time and again as he kneaded her muscles. It was, without a doubt, the best back rub he had ever given. Just to touch her skin in that way, so intimately, was much more than he had ever believed would happen.

Nikki stirred. Her face, which had looked so peaceful, seemed suddenly troubled. He was tempted to apologize; was about to do it, to make a fool of himself, when she spoke again in that raspy voice.

"Move lower," she said. "Do my legs and everything. You're really good at this, Kevin."

"Thanks," he croaked, the word splintering as he spoke it. He repeated it, more firmly this time.

His hands slid across her butt, but he didn't dare stop. The back of his neck and his cheeks felt warm, as though he were doing something wrong and at any minute might be caught at it. He massaged her legs, especially her calves. Another tiny noise came from Nikki and he looked quickly at her face. Her expression was peaceful, as though she might drift off to sleep at any moment.

When his fingers trailed back up her legs, he surrendered all caution, and began to massage her butt as well, but quickly, and then went on to pay special attention to her lower back and tailbone.

"Mmm," she murmured. "That's been bothering me. My lower back, right there. Can you do that some more?"

Kevin's thoughts stumbled over each other, trying to make sense of what was happening. She had to know what she was doing to him. She had to. But he couldn't bring himself to believe that she did. Only days earlier she had made it clear that she thought of him as too good a friend ever to get involved with.

It would be too weird. Those were her exact words.

Now this. He wanted the courage to speak up, to make a move, to kiss her or tell her how he felt.

But the risk was too great. In this moment, in this eyeblink of time, he had her skin under his caress, and he dared not chance losing that.

As best he could, he worked his fingers against her lower back, hauling the waist of her torn Levi's down an inch, then two. Nikki shifted to allow him more room—several times—until finally she arched her back, reached beneath her body and unbuttoned her jeans. He heard the hush of the zipper, and then she turned the top of her jeans down so that he could just see the waistband of her pink panties.

Somehow, his fingers kept moving. His astonishment and his feelings for her mounted, began to overwhelm him. Nikki's skin was pale and a bit chilly to the touch, but soft as silk, with the finest downy hair in a little line that ran down her tailbone.

I love you. The words were on his lips. His stomach churned and his heart performed a mad, hummingbird flutter in his chest. But to speak the words . . . even if she expected them, he was afraid they would sound ridiculous once they left his mouth, hanging out there in the air.

Then a kiss instead, he told himself. On the cheek, while she has her eyes closed. Just one soft kiss upon which all his hopes would be hung. Before he could stop himself, Kevin bent down. He held his breath, every inch of his skin tingling with anticipation and fear and exultation.

The doorbell rang.

Tommy had arrived.

The word "shit" nearly made it to Kevin's lips, but he forced himself to be silent. On the sofa, Nikki had barely stirred.

"Be right back," he mumbled. "That's probably Tommy."

As he went up the stairs to the front door, Kevin's mind suddenly flashed back to the night he and Tommy had almost been run down, had been forced to hustle to avoid being struck by the car that had snuck up on them. The way he felt in those first few seconds, the flush of his skin and the staccato beat of his heart—this was the same.

A surge of anger at Tommy rose within him, but Kevin fought against it. Tommy was right on time. Kevin couldn't blame him for that. But he felt certain that he had been robbed by fate of what might have been the turning point of his young life. He might never get a better moment with Nikki. That knowledge must have shown on his face, for when Kevin opened the screen door for him, Tommy frowned.

"What's up with you?" Tommy asked. "You look like someone just shot your dog."

Before Kevin could reply, Nikki appeared at the bottom of the steps.

"Hey, Tommy," she said.

Kevin turned quickly, and was relieved and disappointed to find that she had made herself presentable again. Nothing had happened, not really, but he'd had her half naked on the sofa in his basement, and it was a moment he knew he would remember for the rest of his life.

"Nikki, what's up? You coming to the movies?" Tommy asked.

He doubted Nikki could tell from Tommy's tone, but to Kevin it was pretty clear the question was asked out of politeness. No way did Tommy want Nikki along for the night.

"No," she said. "I've got plans later. We were just hanging out. Are you guys going to see *Raiders of the Lost Ark* again?"

Kevin smiled. He'd seen *Raiders* five times already. The movie was now one of his favorites, and had confirmed Harrison Ford's place right alongside Clint Eastwood in Kevin's own personal pantheon of heroes. Nikki knew how much he liked the movie, even though she hadn't seen it yet.

"No. That new James Bond is playing," Tommy told her. "Roger Moore is getting a little old for Bond, but I like the gadgets."

"Have fun," Nikki said absently. Then she smiled at Kevin, leaned forward and kissed him on the cheek. "I guess I'll see you when you get back from the Cape."

"Yeah," Kevin agreed, feeling a little awkward, and sad that she was leaving. "See ya."

As he and Tommy stood and watched Nikki go out the door and walk across the yard to the street, Kevin remembered the first time he'd seen her walk off like that, leaving him in awe in the Rosses' driveway nearly three years before. But that was then, as the saying went, and this was now. He felt like one of the most important moments of his life was slipping through his fingers.

It was stupid. Nothing had really happened. He hadn't told Nikki how he really felt, and that was for the best. In twelve days, he'd be fourteen. It wouldn't seem so weird to her then.

Besides, he'd see her on Monday. Maybe even Sunday night.

That was what he told himself, despite the little voice taunting him in the back of his mind, whispering to him that he'd had his shot, and blown it. *Paranoid bullshit,* he thought. *It'll be all right.*

But it wasn't.

Come Monday, everything had changed.

6

The Fourth of July in Chatham was something to behold. There was a parade with antique cars and fire engines and marching bands from at least half a dozen area towns. There were floats and baton twirlers and veteran soldiers on the march. At thirteen, Kevin had spent a lot of hot July celebrations on the main street that ran through the center of town.

There was a candy store that sold the best fudge on earth on one block, and an old movie theatre with velvet drapes and amazing murals and an ornate balcony just a block down. A little ways on was the Mayflower, a kind of country store that had a great selection of the latest comic books.

The street was crammed with people waiting for the parade, and when it came, it did not disappoint. The brothers walked back up the street while the parade went past, and found their mother and grandmother—whom they called Nana—in beach chairs on the side of the road. Nana had a little American flag gripped in her hand. Though it was the anniversary of the death of her husband—and Aileen Murphy's father—both women had broad grins on their faces.

Kevin and Jesse's grandfather had been a very patriotic man, and he infused that nationalism into his family. He had grown up in a time, Nana was fond of saying, when America still remembered what it was all about.

They watched the parade together, the four of them. The boys ate some fudge from the shop on the corner, and clutched their bags from the Mayflower in their hands, and thought of their grandfather. And they wondered, each in his own mind and unaware of his brother's thoughts, where their father was on that day. Kevin even found himself looking for his father in the crowd, and felt stupid when he realized what he'd been doing.

The parade was something they had all enjoyed together, once upon a time.

They ate dinner at a restaurant not far from Ridgevale Beach, which was Kevin's favorite. There was an inlet from the ocean that had cut such a deep path in the sand that you could run along the beach, leap into the air, and plummet into rushing ocean water fifteen feet deep. Mrs. Murphy promised her sons they could go to the beach the next day, right after the memorial service for their grandfather.

After dinner, the four of them drove back down through the center of town and managed to find a parking space only a quarter mile from the bandstand. The music hadn't started yet, but it wouldn't be long. Jesse carried the blankets and Kevin lugged the two beach chairs, and they all made camp right there on the grass not far from the bandstand itself. The boys bought sodas from a vendor, and Kevin spotted a man selling balloons.

You're too old for balloons, he chided himself. But that didn't mean he didn't want one.

There was a small golf course beyond the bandstand, and as darkness began to fall, the brothers ran together up and down the hills, jumped into sand traps as though they were soldiers—or better yet, Spider-Man and Daredevil. They laughed and threw sand at each other. Jesse talked about the werewolf book he was reading, and together they howled at the moon before returning to their blanket for the fireworks.

It wasn't until he was nodding off while reading *Justice League* later that night—he and his brother in twin beds in their grandmother's guest room—that Kevin realized he and Jesse hadn't argued once, all day. Not at all. Miracles did happen, apparently, though he was not foolish enough to think the détente would last.

Still, he smiled to himself as he drifted off, the comic book slipping from his fingers and sliding off the sheets to the floor.

The Murphys got home just before ten o'clock Sunday night. Kevin was anxious to call Nikki, but he knew it was too late. He promised himself he'd call her first thing the next morning, but he never got the chance. Before he was even awake, Jesse walked into Kevin's room, tiredly rubbing his eyes.

"Hey, bro," Jesse said, pleasantly enough for first thing in the morning. "Nikki's on the phone."

Kevin yawned. "Man, what time is it?"

"Dunno. Like nine, I guess."

Nodding, Kevin crawled out of bed and dragged himself to the phone. He was very happy that Nikki had called, but even that wasn't enough to wake him up completely. Going to the beach and running around in the sun the day before had drained him. Still, when he picked up the phone, a little thrill ran through him.

"Hey," he said groggily.

"Hey, babe," she replied. "How was the Cape?"

The word babe perked him up. Nikki had never called Kevin babe before. Definitely a term of endearment. One he decided he liked right on the spot.

"It was cool. A good time, actually. Except for the memorial service, y'know? How was your weekend?"

"Totally fucking fantastic. Hopkinton was unbelievable. What a blast. That's kinda why I'm calling, actually. I met some people there, really cool people. I'm going back today and I figured I'd see if you wanted to come."

Kevin was awake now. He was glad Nikki had had a good time, but he didn't want her to have had *too* good a time. Though she had called to ask him to go with her, and that was a positive sign. Still, the whole "met some people" part bothered him.

She met a guy, he thought. It was Nikki, after all. But she had invited him, and that was the important part.

"What time you wanna go?"

"They're picking me up at eleven," she said. "Come down around then."

"Cool."

Kevin hung up the phone, resisted the temptation to go back to sleep, and headed for the shower. After he had turned the water on, he stripped off his T-shirt and underwear and stretched, waiting for it to get hot enough. There was a little knock at the door.

"Yeah?"

"What time you wanna go?"

With a frown, Kevin wrapped a towel around his waist and opened the door. Jesse leaned against the wall, still half asleep.

"Huh?"

"To the trestle. We're gonna go, right?"

"I'm actually gonna go to Hopkinton with Nikki today," Kevin told him.

Jesse frowned, more awake now. For a second, he looked both angry and disappointed. Then he shrugged and turned away, leaving Kevin feeling guilty. He tried to remind himself that Jesse was the big brother who beat up on him, who teased him mercilessly, who had put dog shit in his hand at the bus stop when they were smaller.

Jesse looked at him, a cynical expression on his face, and laughed. "Have it your way, pussy. I know the trestle scares the shit out of you."

"Fuck you, it does not," Kevin snapped angrily.

"Yeah," Jesse replied doubtfully.

Kevin had thought about telling him what he was feeling with Nikki, what was really going on in his head. But Jesse had shut him out. Things had gone back to the way they always were.

"Don't be such a dick," Kevin muttered.

But he wasn't sure if he was talking to Jesse, or to himself.

As he walked to Nikki's house, a rolled-up beach towel under one arm, Kevin slipped his wallet out of his back pocket. It was leather and worn, and the little plastic sleeve that was supposed to hold pictures had been torn off months ago. He'd have to ask his mom for a new one for his birthday, he thought. Poking it open with a finger, he counted the bills. Sixteen dollars. That was pretty damn good. The last thing he wanted was to end up in line at the food truck and not have any money. But sixteen bucks would carry him for a couple of days, at least.

He rounded the corner of Londonderry and started down the hill. He could see Nikki's house from there, and there were no cars in the driveway. Whoever she had met over the weekend, they either hadn't arrived yet or weren't old enough to drive.

He pushed his wallet back into the pocket of his cut-offs. The Outlaws concert T-shirt he wore was a little big for him, but he liked it that way. It would last longer, he figured. On the back, it bore the legend, "when guitars are outlawed, only The Outlaws will have guitars." It was a cool shirt.

When he stepped into the Frenches' driveway and started up toward the door, Nikki appeared behind the screen. She had a kind of nervous grin on her face that Kevin found unsettling. It wasn't like her. Or, at least, it wasn't at all like she'd been lately. It made her look like a little girl, instead of her usual confident self.

"Hey," he said. "What's up?"

Nikki grinned. "You won't believe it," she said. "I mean, I know you told me so, but it's just weird the way shit happens. So I'm in the water at Hopkinton on Saturday, and this guy—"

The roar of an engine interrupted her. Kevin and Nikki both looked up to see the dark, hulking form of a Dodge Charger tearing down Londonderry, much too fast. The windows were open, and Kevin could hear the music pouring out.

"Oh, shit," Kevin whispered, too low for Nikki to hear. "Oh, fuck."

He recognized that car. In his mind's eye, Kevin saw

Jack throw the rock, saw it arc across the road and through the open driver's window, saw it strike the driver in the side of the face.

Tires squealing, metallic blue paint as dark as night glinting in the sun, the Dodge whipped suddenly into Nikki's driveway. Kevin leaped backward, moving toward Nikki to get her out of the way, to start her toward the house. The Dodge braked, leaving a short black patch behind each tire. Kevin was about to drag Nikki up the steps.

Then he saw her face.

Staring at the Dodge expectantly, smiling broadly.

A tiny breath escaped him, almost like something in his throat had snapped. His chest hurt.

"No way," he whispered.

Nikki glanced at him, saw his expression, and a look of grave concern crossed her features. She said his name, the word a question. Kevin felt like he was connected to her, right then, as though they shared a kind of communication that did not require words.

Then the Dodge's engine grunted and died, and the driver's door opened. Nikki looked away from him, a broad smile on her face again.

The connection was severed.

"Pete!" Nikki cried.

Kevin turned to watch as she rushed to him, that wiry, pale-faced pretty boy with his ice-blue eyes and the long, straight, perfect hair. Nikki threw her arms around him and they hugged, tight. Their lips met, maybe tongues, too. A sickening thought. His hands cupped her ass briefly, and Kevin's entire body felt cold, despite the heat. He had thought, after the way Pete and his friends had acted at the trestle, that he hated them all.

Now he knew that hadn't been hate at all. Hate was more exotic, more personal.

Now he knew.

Pete hadn't even noticed him. Which was okay, in a way. Kevin thought maybe Pete noticing him would be bad. That day at the trestle he had warned them that the fight wasn't over. The odds had been a little better, then. *Fuck that,* he thought. The odds had been piss poor, but they'd been a hell of a lot better than they were now. Four guys who were seventeen, eighteen, maybe nineteen, against one thirteen-year-old who was just tall enough for his age to make them think maybe it was okay to beat the shit out of him.

Lucky me.

What the hell was he doing with her, anyway? Nikki was fifteen, and only just. This guy was some kind of sick bastard. Even if he hadn't run up against Pete before, Kevin would have thought he was a creep.

As he waited to be recognized, as he tried to be scared and angry to avoid dealing with the pain in his chest, the despair in his heart, Kevin glared at Nikki's back, and the guy who had his hands all over her. Suddenly he frowned. There was something wrong with this picture. Other than the obvious. Something that was just out of reach of his thoughts.

In his mind, he saw it again: the rock, sailing across the street, in through the window, thunking into the side of Pete's face.

That was it. There was no scar. No mark at all. He'd seen that rock go in, seen Pete get hit. No way did he get out of that without at least a decent gash on his cheek, if not stitches. But there wasn't a mark on him.

Before he could think about it any further, Nikki broke away from Pete, and turned toward Kevin.

"Pete, this is Kevin Murphy. My best friend."

My best friend. Kevin wanted that, of course. To be her best friend. But it also sounded like the last nail being driven into the coffin of all his hopes where Nikki was concerned. So much for waiting for his birthday. So much for that.

"Kevin, this is Pete Starling."

Pete looked over at him and let out a snort of laughter.

"Well I'll be," he said. He smiled then, but there was nothing warm or kind about that smile. No amusement in it. He turned back to the car with the tinted windows. "Hey, check this out. You guys recognize this kid?"

Nikki looked from Kevin to Pete and back again, confused. "Wait, you guys know each other?"

Before either of them could answer, the other doors on the car opened, and Pete's friends climbed out. Weasel, dough-face and the big kid with orange hair. Curt, Kevin remembered. His name was Curt.

"No shit. Look at this," the weasel said, just a little too happy. "I guess we'll have to flip a coin to see who gets to kick his ass."

The weasel reached into the pocket of his ratty blue jeans and hauled out a few coins. A quarter dropped from his hand as he opened his palm to pick one out. He didn't pay any attention to it. None of the others did, either. Kevin didn't think Nikki even looked at it. But he watched with dull fascination and dread as it fell to the driveway.

The quarter landed on its edge, bounced, and started to roll away. It rolled down the driveway and out into the street, curled to the right along the slope of the road, and kept rolling on down the blacktop. Kevin's eyes widened a little as he watched, expecting it to fall at any moment.

He watched until it had rolled out of sight, still going.

Shit, did you see that? he wanted to say. *That's impossible.*

But now wasn't the time.

"C'mere, Kevin," Pete said. "I want to talk to you."

Kevin swallowed hard and looked at him. "I didn't throw that rock."

"What rock?" Nikki asked. Then understanding dawned on her face. "Wait. The thing at the trestle?" She looked hard at Pete. "You were the guys at the trestle?"

When Pete realized Kevin had told Nikki about the events at the trestle an expression of pure malice swept across his face, flickered in those pale blue eyes that seemed to lose their color, to melt into ice, for just a moment. In that eyeblink Kevin thought Pete might like to kill him, might try and do it right there in the driveway. But then all that tension seemed to drift off on the wind. Pete smiled, genuinely this time, and looked at Nikki.

"Oh, yeah, the trestle," he said, chuckling. "That was fucked up, huh Kevin?"

Kevin looked at the other guys. They didn't seem to agree with Pete on the whole "no hard feelings" thing. But they also didn't look like they were about to argue with him.

Pete threw up his hands. "Hey, we had a misunderstanding. Things got out of hand. I probably deserved to have rocks thrown at me that day, and I guarantee you these assholes did," he said, gesturing at his friends. "But look, any friend of Nikki's is cool by me. Okay?"

Unsure if he really had much choice in the matter, Kevin nodded.

Nikki moved between them, then, and Kevin and Pete both moved closer to her. Kevin hated Pete, and despised his asshole friends, but he shouldn't have been surprised. Nikki had dated a succession of guys, each more obnoxious than the last. Kevin had wanted to change that, but he'd waited too long.

Nikki smiled at him, and Kevin felt both sad and elated. He was her best friend. And she wanted him here, even though she was with her new boyfriend. As hurt and appalled as he was, Kevin knew that counted for something. Nikki might be letting the guy paw her now, maybe she even looked at him with a kind of sparkle in her eye that he'd never seen when she looked at him—except maybe once, on Friday night, before Tommy had interrupted her back rub—but that was all right.

Pete was a jerk. He wouldn't last any longer than the others. And Kevin could wait.

"You guys are cool, then?" Nikki asked.

"Totally," Kevin replied.

"Excellent," Pete said, nodding. Then he turned and gestured at the others, the weasel first. "Kevin, this is my brother, Doug Starling. Curt McQuade." That was the big guy with orange hair. "And that's Hugo."

Just Hugo, Kevin thought, looking at the kid with the doughy face and the sad eyes. *Just Hugo, no last name, like even if he had one, it wouldn't matter.*

"Hey," Kevin said, nodding in their direction.

They just watched him, not looking too pleased with the news that they weren't going to get to kick his ass.

"So!" Pete said happily, clapping his hands together. "We going to Hopkinton, or what?"

Hopkinton State Park was mostly forest, broken up by sprawling green picnic areas and a winding blacktop that led to the parking lot by the lake and a scene of utter chaos.

Like ants on a discarded hamburger, humans swarmed over the lot and the sand and the lake. Ice cream and hot dogs and sodas were consumed by the truckload. Beer sat in coolers in the backseats of cars, or made it surreptitiously to the sand in Dixie cups. On the shore opposite the beach, there were only trees, but on the far side of the lake, an enormous dam rose up in a gray slope, and slabs of concrete that looked like giant steps ran up its right side. It loomed there, strange and ominous, but somehow never questioned. Yet it made for an odd picture, all those people there at the foot of the dam, so vulnerable, somehow.

It was a little before noon when Pete Starling piloted his midnight-blue Charger up the winding drive to the lake parking lot. Nikki sat with the Starling brothers in the front seat. In the back, Kevin was scrunched between Hugo and Curt, the latter of whom turned to grin at him from time to time. It wasn't a friendly grin, but nor was it particularly hostile. Curt was obviously enjoying himself, and there was an insinuation in that grin that Kevin had better be enjoying himself too, or he wouldn't be welcome among them.

Not that being welcome among them was something he necessarily aspired to. They were goons, after all.

Brutal, arrogant thugs who were destined for barroom brawls and jobs that didn't involve any actual thought if they were lucky; prison if they weren't. But Nikki was with them, and if he wanted to be with Nikki . . .

On the other hand, Kevin had come to a surprising conclusion on the car ride from Framingham to Hopkinton: He didn't hate Pete Starling. He wanted to, no doubt about that. Pete was a mean-spirited son of a bitch. But he was having so much fun at it that the twinkle in his eye and the grin on his face made it difficult not to enjoy his company. Much as he hated sitting in the back with Curt and Hugo, much as he wanted to throttle Doug—the little weasel—much as he envied the way Nikki looked at Pete, Kevin couldn't hate him.

In a way, that made him feel worse about the whole situation.

"Damn, look at all that flesh!" Curt cried as they passed the beach area on the right.

"Nice tits!" Doug shouted at a couple of girls who were walking across the parking lot.

Nikki punched him in the arm.

"Don't do that," Doug sneered, glaring as though he might try to bite her.

"Well don't do *that*," she snapped.

Pete shook his head in what was probably mock embarrassment. "No class, Doug."

"You can't ask for miracles," Curt said reasonably.

Kevin glanced out the window. He wasn't going to scream at them as they drove by, but he had to agree with Curt: there were a great many girls on the beach. He grinned, but his expression faltered quickly, as he remembered that the only girl who really interested him at the moment was in the front seat with yet another in a long string of assholes.

Yeah, she doesn't have the sense to stop dating scumbags, and you don't have the sense to realize that's not likely to change, he told himself. *So who's the asshole?*

"Check it out!" Doug said quickly. "There's a space, right there at the end."

There were three cars cruising the lot in front of them, all looking for a parking space. Pete actually looked hopeful after Doug pointed out the open spot, as if it would still be there by the time they went by. It was right by the bathhouse, practically on the sand, and there were cars in front of them. They'd have to be idiots to think it would stay empty.

As Kevin watched, all three of the cars ahead of them cruised by the vacant space as though it weren't there at all. The last one even seemed to veer away from it a little, like there was a school bus parked there with its big yellow ass-end hanging out. A part of him rationalized; must be a motorcycle there. But when they got up to the space, Pete pulled the car right in.

The words came out before he even realized he'd spoken. "I can't believe those people just drove right by this spot."

Pete laughed. "I'm just lucky, I guess. Story of my life."

He looked at Nikki meaningfully as he said it, and Kevin felt a kind of motion in his gut, like there were centipedes crawling around in there. The thought made him want to puke. Instead, he hauled himself out of the backseat after Curt and nearly tumbled to the pavement. When he stood up, Nikki smiled at him. Her expression made it clear that she was glad to have him along.

It gave him hope, just a tiny bit, but enough so that he forced himself to relax and just go with it. He had come with them, and was stuck there until they decided the day was over, or Nikki forced Pete to take them home.

So they ate hot dogs and other assorted crap bought off rusty concession trucks whose proprietors needed some serious hygiene time. They swam. They strolled the beach and ogled women, much to Nikki's chagrin. They passed a joint around right there on the sand. Nikki took a few hits, but Kevin begged off, and was astonished when they didn't razz him for it. Well, Doug did, but the other guys gave him hard looks, as though they were actually defending Kevin.

Around two-thirty, he amazed himself with the sudden realization that he was having a good time. Sure, Doug was a little bastard, but they *all* thought he was a little bastard. Hugo was practically mute, and Curt was intimidating just by his presence, but they were all right. They were the same guys who had almost beaten the crap out of him and his friends that day on the trestle, but now he was seeing things from their side of the fence, and the view was very different.

They were still goons. That hadn't changed. But the sinister intent, the vicious minds he had attributed to them, simply didn't exist. There was another element to his change of heart too, if he was going to be honest. These guys were four, five, even six years older than he was. Hell, Curt had to be nineteen, maybe twenty.

Kevin was just a kid. Despite how he felt about himself, he knew the truth of it. He might look older—and he knew he was smarter than any of them except maybe Pete—but he *was* just a kid. The fact that they accepted him lent him a kind of strength and credibility that was intoxicating.

At three o'clock, he noticed that Pete and Nikki were gone. Hugo and Doug were swimming, hitting on a couple of younger girls, maybe sophomores, in the water. Curt, who sat on a towel next to Kevin, saw him looking around and laughed.

"They went back to the car," he said, grinning. "Pete ain't wastin' no time. Nikki's mom is always around. He's got her to himself right now, and no time like the present, right?"

Kevin nodded, feeling sick. Moments later, Doug and Hugo came up the beach, dripping water. Hugo dropped down on a towel, but Doug looked around.

"My brother take that little pump back to the car?" the weasel asked.

The others laughed. Kevin whipped his head around

to stare at Doug, feeling nauseous and furious at the same time. His jaw and fist were both clenched.

"Lucky bastard," Curt said, not even paying attention, eyes scanning the other girls on the beach. After a moment, he glanced up at Doug. "Nikki's hot. And those titties, man! Not too big, but like Goldilocks said, juuuust right."

Doug chuckled. "No shit."

He seemed to glance at Kevin, quickly, out of the corner of his eye, and Kevin frowned, wondering if all this was for his benefit, just to piss him off. It was working.

"Hell with that," Hugo mumbled. He had been lying on his stomach, eyes closed, completely still, as though he were asleep. Now he responded without even opening his eyes. "Thing about that girl is her ass. Don't know if I ever saw an ass that sweet."

"Hallelujah," Doug chimed in, almost salivating.

Then, slowly, deliberately, he turned to Kevin, a wide grin on his face. "What do you think, Kev?"

A shudder ran through Kevin, a chill that sent icy fingers deep into his flesh, freezing even the burning anger that had been roiling in his gut. It was Doug's eyes that did it. They seemed to slice into him, cutting away the Kevin everyone else saw, stripping off the mask he showed to the world. Nobody else had ever looked at him like that.

Doug's eyes seemed to glow then. Orange fire that might have been just the reflection of the sun. That's what Kevin would tell himself later. And the cold wave that washed over him? An errant breeze.

There was a truth he could not escape, however. When Doug asked the question, and looked at him in that way, Kevin felt dirty. His rage was real, his adoration of Nikki complete. But he could not deny to himself that the things they were saying, which sounded so filthy and demeaning coming from their lips, were things he himself had thought, and more than once. He fantasized about Nikki, dreamed about her even. He cared deeply for her, but that did not erase the dark heart of his lust. The two were inseparable, and though he had never considered it, he would have argued that the one made the other acceptable.

Now it only felt wrong.

"You guys are assholes," Kevin said coldly.

It wasn't a denial. He was incapable of denial. Much as he told himself it couldn't be, he knew that Doug had seen in him all of those hopes and dreams and fantasies, the romantic and the perverse, and Kevin was ashamed.

Curt snorted laughter. "No shit, what was your first clue?"

Doug was more direct. He wasn't going to be turned away. He glared at Kevin. "You trying to tell me you don't want to fuck her, man?"

"Just because your brother can score and you're not even on the board, don't take it out on me," Kevin replied.

With a little growl, Doug dropped down into a crouch in front of him. He whispered, but his voice seemed to carry, so that everyone on the beach should have heard him. But they didn't. Nobody even turned to look.

"You're Nikki's friend. Pete wants her happy right now, so you're his dog at the moment. You don't kick a guy's dog. Especially not Pete's. But there's a line, kid. You piss on the carpet, he'll put you out in the cold. Then you're mine."

Another day, another second, Kevin would have kept his mouth shut. Already, he'd said too much, been too much of a wise guy. But he had been torn open in front of Doug and the others, and they had put a taint on his love for Nikki that might never come off. Doug had him backed into a corner.

"Fuck off."

The weasel's eyes changed again. They seemed to shrink, pupils disappearing, irises turning from brown to bright orange. It was only for a second. Then Doug stood up and turned away, started walking off down the beach, muttering to himself.

Kevin had been holding his breath. Now he let it out. It was as though all the sound at the park had been blocked out while Doug crouched in front of him, and now it came flooding back in. Dogs barked. Kids screamed and splashed.

"Jesus," Kevin whispered.

He glanced at the other guys. Hugo still lay on his chest, eyes closed, dough face getting red from the sun. Curt, though, was sitting up and looking at Kevin with a pitying expression on his face.

"You know better than that, Kevin. You're a smart guy. I don't want to have to hurt you."

Curt got up and went down to the water to cool off. Kevin sat and watched him. A short time later, Pete and Nikki came back to the sand, arms around one another, giggling, their faces flushed. They looked happy. But there was something about Pete's expression, something false in his laugh, that made Kevin believe that he had not gotten what he wanted, and wasn't at all happy about it.

From her expression, it was clear that Nikki had no idea.

Kevin knew that he would have to try to explain it to her, and his stomach did another little flip. He knew how she would respond.

7

If Nikki or Pete noticed the tension that developed between Kevin and the others, neither of them mentioned it. Shortly before five, they piled in the Charger and drove home, radio blaring. Pete and Curt started arguing good-naturedly about who was going to pay for the beer they planned to buy for that night. For the duration of the ride, Kevin kept expecting Doug to turn around and glare at him, but it never happened.

That was worse. A glare would be threatening, of course. But there was greater danger implied in the lack of any overt threat. Kevin watched the back of Doug's head and understood that with great clarity.

When the Charger stopped at the corner of Londonderry and Fox Run, Kevin was both relieved and troubled. It was over, for the moment. That was good. But he had thought they would drop him and Nikki both off at her house, which would have given him a chance to talk to her. Instead, he found himself climbing over Curt and out of the backseat. Doug had gotten out so that his seat could be pushed forward, and even when Kevin was out and he climbed back in, the weasel didn't make eye contact.

"Thanks," Kevin said weakly.

"Hey," Pete replied pleasantly, still up, still oozing charisma. "You had a good time, didn't you?"

Nikki was watching him, smiling. Kevin felt more self-conscious than ever under her gaze.

"Sure."

"There ya go!" Pete cried victoriously. "We're not as

bad as you thought we were." Then he leaned far over
Nikki and reached out a hand. Kevin felt as though he
had no choice but to shake, and Pete gripped his hand
tight and pulled him forward. "Good to have you along,
Kevin. I hope we can hang out more. You're Nikki's
friend, and that's cool. But now you're my friend, too.

"You are my friend, aren't you?"

Kevin was bent over, his face level with the car, his
arm in through the open window, stretched across in
front of Doug's face. His eyes ticked over to glance at
Nikki, who appeared very pleased that her new guy and
her best friend were getting along so well.

"Yeah, sure," Kevin replied.

Pete Starling's eyes were wide and blue, the ghost of
blue, a sheet of ice or a cloud of fog drifting in the
distance.

"We're friends," Kevin added.

"Good deal," Pete said, grinning.

He laid on the accelerator and the Charger's tires left
black patches on the pavement. Kevin barely had a
chance to withdraw his arm before they were tearing
down Londonderry toward Nikki's house. He moved off
to the side of the road, but he waited and watched.

The Charger pulled into the driveway, and Doug
moved aside to let Nikki out. Or so Kevin thought. A
second later, Curt climbed out of the back, and Pete got
out as well. Doug got in the driver's side, Curt got in
front, and then the Charger backed out of the driveway
and tore off down the road.

Nikki and Pete kissed, there in the driveway, and then
she took him into the house.

As he walked home, Kevin tried to force himself not
to picture what might be happening there. It was a losing battle.

It rained on Tuesday, and Kevin was glad. The storm
seemed to reflect the gray mood that had fallen over
him. He woke early, but he lay in bed, rain blowing
hard against the house, spattering in through the screens,

though his windows were only open four or five inches. The sheets felt damp with the moisture in the air.

There were books near to hand. If he wanted to read, all he would have had to do was reach out a hand and turn on the light. But even that held no interest for him.

At eight-thirty, his mother knocked softly and peered in through the slightly open door.

"Hey," she said, pushing the door open further. "I'm surprised you're awake, you were so quiet in here. You feeling all right?"

"Just resting. This weather makes me feel like a slug."

Mrs. Murphy smiled. "I know the feeling. So, your birthday is next week. I thought I'd take you and Jesse out to dinner on the actual night. I guess it's next Wednesday, right? But what about this weekend? Do you want to have a party or anything, even just have some friends over for a cake or something? I could take you and all your buddies to the movies if you want."

All my buddies, Kevin thought cynically. *Yeah, Mom, you'd love Pete Starling and the trolls he hangs out with.* Then there were Tommy and Diana and April. He hadn't even talked to any of them since before the Fourth.

"Maybe we can all just go for pizza or something," Kevin replied. "Let me call around."

His mother smiled. "Whatever you want to do. Just inform the chauffeur when you decide."

"Thanks, Mom." Kevin chuckled at the chauffeur remark. It was the only laugh he had all day.

After Mrs. Murphy left, he pulled on some shorts and went down to the basement to watch television. It was cooler down there, but it was also darker and damper. Kevin slumped across the sofa, huddled down, and felt like he was hiding out. In a way, he was.

A little while later he heard Jesse moving around upstairs, and the banging of cabinet doors. His brother would be having breakfast. Probably Count Chocula. Kevin wrinkled his nose at the thought. Count Chocula tasted like shit.

"Kevin?" Jesse called from upstairs.

"Down here."

His older brother came down with a glass of orange juice and a bowl of cereal near to overflowing. He set them down on the coffee table, which was actually a big, antique-looking colonial-style drum, turned on its side, with a glass top.

"You have breakfast?" Jesse asked, as he sat on the edge of the sofa, shoving Kevin's legs back with his butt.

"Not hungry," Kevin replied. *Not hungry enough to move,* he mentally amended.

Jesse slid back a bit more, then glanced around angrily at his brother. "You mind sitting up? I'm trying to eat."

"Maybe you didn't notice, but I was here first," Kevin spat. "Move to a chair."

Though he grumbled, Jesse didn't move. Nor did Kevin sit up. They sat together and watched *Adam-12,* as they'd done on dozens of rainy mornings.

"This is the one with that guy who fakes heart attacks to get free meals," Jesse pointed out.

"I think that was on *Emergency.*"

"Uh-uh. Definitely *Adam-12.* Malloy just kinda rolls his eyes, but Reed gets all pissed. Watch."

They watched.

"What are you doing today?" he asked Kevin when a commercial came on.

"Nothing. Just hanging out. You?"

"Nothing. I was thinking about trying to get some beers, but I don't want to sit up in the woods and get soaked."

"Maybe tomorrow night."

Jesse grunted his agreement.

They spent the day down there in the basement. About three o'clock, just when the UHF channels were starting their afternoon lineup, the phone rang. The brothers looked at one another.

"You're closer," Jesse told him. "Proximity law."

Kevin sighed. Somehow, the proximity law was only in effect when he was closer to a door that needed closing, a light that needed switching, or a phone that needed answering.

"Hello?"

"Hey."

"Tommy. What's up? You sound pissed?"

"That's one way to put it. I went to Diana's last night. So I'm walking home, out on Pleasant Street, and this car pulls up next to me, tires fucking screeching. Remember those guys from the trestle?"

Kevin closed his eyes. "Yeah?"

"They got out of the car. Well, three of them. The one with the black hair, the pale kid? He wasn't there. But the other three are all over me, giving me shit. The kid with the peach-fuzz buzz cut starts shoving me, so I tell him to fuck off, y'know?"

"Jesus," Kevin sighed.

Behind him, Jesse was frowning. "What happened?"

"What did he do?" Kevin asked Tommy.

"What do you think he did? He fuckin' decked me. I didn't even see it coming, either. For a guy that big, he's really fast. I went down hard on my ass. They would've kept coming, too. I could see the look in that kid's eyes, what's his name, Curt? He was gonna kick the shit out of me. His eyes were . . . it was like . . ."

Tommy didn't finish that thought. He didn't have to. Kevin's mind immediately went to the weird things he had seen in both Pete's and Doug's eyes. He'd blocked those things out, pretty much, tried not to think about them. Tricks of the light, or just some freaky thing he'd never seen before. But that wasn't it.

Has to be drugs. What else could it be?

"Anyway," Tommy went on. "This older guy pulls up in a Lincoln and starts yelling at them. Saved my ass."

"Whoa. You got lucky," Kevin told him.

"I don't feel too lucky," Tommy replied curtly. "Know what else, Kevin? The wiry, freaky one said something to me."

Tommy had sounded angry from the moment Kevin picked up the phone. And Kevin didn't blame him. But suddenly, he felt that anger shift. He wasn't just pissed off at the guys who jumped him. With grim certainty, Kevin realized that Tommy was pissed at him, too.

"What did he say?"

Tommy laughed drily. " 'Maybe we can't fuck Kevin up, but nobody's gonna care if we break *your* legs.' That's what he said, Kevin. Now what the hell do you make of that?"

There was accusation in his tone, but Kevin couldn't blame him. He knew he should tell Tommy about Pete and Nikki, and all of that, but he couldn't. Not then. Tommy was too pissed off. Kevin figured he had to let his friend cool down a bit first. That would be for the best.

"I don't know."

There was silence on the other end of the line.

"Look, Tommy, Jesse and I were just talking about getting some beers for tomorrow night. You up for it?"

"Maybe. My mother's freaked out 'cause I've got a black eye. She thinks I'm hiding something from her, but I'm not. She's seen *West Side Story* too many times. We can talk tomorrow."

"Oh, and my mother wants to take everybody out for pizza Saturday, kind of a thing for my birthday. You and Diana are invited if you want to go."

"I'll talk to her. Unless she's got something going on, I'm sure we'll be there," Tommy said. Then he paused a moment, before continuing. "You know these guys, Kev?"

Kevin stiffened. Put on the spot like that, he couldn't just lie.

"Sort of. The one guy, Pete, who wasn't there? He's going out with Nikki."

"Nikki French? No shit? Another asshole on her list," Tommy said.

"Pete's not that bad," Kevin said quickly. "He wasn't with those guys when they went after you."

"Are you high?" Tommy sneered. "He was at the trestle, wasn't he? He's a jerk, Kev. And what the hell does a guy his age want with a fifteen-year-old? That's pretty perverted. You should remember who your friends are. What are you thinking?"

I have no idea, Kevin thought. But he didn't say that to Tommy. He didn't say anything at all.

"Look," Tommy said, when Kevin had made no reply. "I'll talk to you tomorrow, okay?"

"Sure," Kevin agreed.

When he'd hung up the phone, he went over to the TV and started spinning the UHF dial looking for something worth watching.

"What was that about?" Jesse asked.

Kevin glanced at his brother, and thought about just saying nothing. Then he shook his head and related the whole thing, just as Tommy had told it to him.

"Son of a bitch," Jesse muttered angrily. "And you're hanging out with these guys?" He stared at Kevin incredulously.

"It's not like that," Kevin said hotly. "Nikki's my friend. Pete's her boyfriend. That's all."

Jesse scowled and stared at him in disgust for a few seconds before turning his attention back to the television. Kevin left the room. He didn't feel like watching TV anymore.

Nikki didn't call on Tuesday. Part of Kevin was glad, but mostly he was just jealous as hell. He felt like he'd been so close to telling her about his feelings, and that she had been starting to feel the same things for him. That might have been true, and it might not, but now he might never know.

When she called on Wednesday morning, he was glad to hear her voice. Nikki didn't say anything about Pete, their trip to Hopkinton Monday, or what she'd done the day before. Kevin allowed himself to hope that her silence on those subjects was a sign that Pete had fallen out of favor already.

"What are you doing today?" she asked.

The previous day's storm had given way to a beautiful, cloudless summer day. Outside, it was hot, but not stifling. Jack and Jesse were getting a bunch of people together to play football in the Rosses' backyard. Kevin had said he'd play.

But when Nikki asked, he lied. "Nothing."

"Me either," she said with a sigh. "I'm just hanging out. You want to come over?"

Kevin went.

For a little while, the day seemed perfect. They sat out on Nikki's back deck and listened to music while they talked. She didn't mention Pete. Not once. In fact, she seemed to be avoiding the subject completely. It occurred to Kevin to say something, to ask if she was all right, but he didn't. As long as Nikki didn't seem upset, he'd be an idiot to invite discussion about Pete.

"So, what do you want for your birthday?" she asked him, completely out of the blue, between sips of iced tea that was thick with lemon and sugar.

Kevin chuckled and shot her a sidelong glance. "All sorts of disgusting things come immediately to mind, but I don't want to risk broken limbs."

"Good call," Nikki assured him, arching an eyebrow.

It wasn't like him to flirt with her, and Kevin's heart raced a little bit. He thought he might even have blushed. But Nikki laughed a little, to herself, and then it was all right. Meanwhile, Kevin had an idea.

"Know what? Next month, .38 Special are playing at Westboro Speedway. Tickets are only seven or eight bucks. If you want to get me something for my birthday, you can take me to that. That'd be a blast, I think."

Nikki raised her eyebrows. "I'm not really into them, but I guess, if it's for your birthday . . ."

Kevin grinned. "It'll be cool."

He felt high after that. Even if she was still going out with Pete then, it would be time that was just for them, no boyfriend in sight. If he could steal a little of her time here and there, maybe she'd start to realize how much she enjoyed it.

His thoughts were spinning wildly out of control into fantasies and daydreams, as they often did where Nikki was concerned. He was about two minutes into this round when they heard the roar of a familiar engine from the driveway out front.

Nikki beamed. "Pete's here!"

"Great," Kevin replied, unable to disguise his disappointment.

It didn't matter. Nikki wasn't paying any attention to him. She had already run down off the deck and was starting around the side of the house. Kevin followed. The midnight-blue Charger sat cooling in the driveway. Pete and Nikki stood in front of the car's grill, wrapped in each other's arms. Though it didn't make him any happier to see Pete, Kevin was relieved that he was alone. Doug, especially, was a psycho. Pete might be a jerk, but Kevin didn't feel any real hostility from him.

As he walked over, Pete grinned. "Hey, Kevin. What's up? You makin' time with my girl again?"

There was an edge to the question that was new; an insinuation that worried Kevin. He swallowed hard, but he smiled to cover his anxiety.

"Every chance I get," he said with a laugh that sounded false, even to him.

"I don't blame you," Pete told him. But there was nothing friendly in the words. He focused his attention on Nikki. "Me and the guys are going to hang out with this band we know tonight. They're playing some party and we're gonna just crash. You wanna come?"

Nikki had a smile that could have melted ice. Every time Kevin saw her look at Pete like that, he was crestfallen. Logic told him he should just forget it, give it up completely. If this was the kind of guy she was interested in—older, pretty as a rock star, and definitely trouble— he should surrender any hope of her ever returning his affections and get on with his life. His instincts told him to forget it.

He just couldn't.

I'm such an idiot, he thought. But idiot or not, he refused to give up. Even if Nikki never fell in love with him, even if she never looked at him the way she did

Pete . . . though she had, he reminded himself. That night when he had rubbed her shoulders, and her back. She had looked at him just that way.

But even if she was never to be his girlfriend, he knew that Nikki deserved better than a swaggering thug like Pete Starling. The problem was, he didn't know how to tell her without both of them kicking the crap out of him.

"Sounds cool," Nikki told him. Then she looked at Kevin. "You want to hang with us tonight? Party crashing is always interesting."

Kevin almost said yes. Better to be with her, even with Pete's asshole friends around, than to spend all his time wondering what she was doing with him. But he had made plans with Jesse and Tommy.

"I can't," he said reluctantly.

"Too bad," Pete said in a hollow tone. When he spoke again, he had already moved on. "I need to make a beer run for tonight, though. You guys want to come?"

Though he tried to keep his expression neutral, Kevin couldn't help glaring at Pete just a little. The day had been going so well, and now, without any warning, it had come to a screeching halt. He'd stolen it away without any effort whatsoever.

"Sure," Kevin said dully.

Moments later, they were tearing down Fox Run Drive toward Pleasant Street. Nikki was in the front seat, scooched way over to glue herself up against Pete, who drove poorly enough when he didn't have one arm around his girlfriend. Kevin sat in back and looked out the window, and tried not to think about anything at all. Even the idea of going to the concert with Nikki seemed silly now. With the two of them snuggling so close in the front seat, it seemed pointless.

Pete drove along Pleasant Street, then turned onto Temple and out to Route Nine. There were plenty of liquor stores in Framingham, but Kevin had an idea where Pete was going. West on Route Nine there was a "packy" where they almost never checked ID. Kevin knew a lot of older guys who could buy there. If Pete was headed that way, it probably meant he didn't have ID, which surprised Kevin somewhat.

Not that it mattered. If you could buy, you could buy. Being able to walk into a package store and pick up a case of beer without all the hassle they usually had to go through would be like gold.

"Hey, Pete," he said, breaking the silence in the car. "You think you could buy a couple of six packs for me? I've got some cash."

When there was no answer, Kevin glanced up to see Pete watching him in the Charger's rearview mirror.

"Sure, Kev. No problem," Pete agreed. Then he looked at Nikki, and she beamed.

Kevin felt sick and wished he'd never asked. Okay, so he'd have beer that night, just in case the guys didn't get their hands on any. but he'd given Pete a perfect opportunity to show Nikki what a great guy he was.

Shit, Kevin thought, and stared out the window. He mumbled "thanks," unsure if Pete could hear him, but not caring all that much.

As they bombed up Route Nine, with the reservoir stretching out on the passenger side, Kevin thought again of the fight at the trestle, and Jack throwing the rock that hit Pete in the face. Amazing that he hadn't needed stitches.

Up ahead, the light turned yellow. Instead of slowing down, Pete accelerated. He was too far away, Kevin knew. They'd never make it. He braced himself against the seat, expecting Pete to slam on the brakes any second.

The light changed again.

It turned green.

The Charger tore through the intersection, and Kevin blinked in amazement.

"Holy shit," he said. "Did you see that?"

Nikki turned to look at him, laughing. "No kidding. The light must be broken or something. It went from green to yellow to green." She looked at Pete. "Did you know it was broken? I didn't think you'd make it."

"Just lucky, I guess," Pete said idly, as if it were no big deal. "You gotta have faith, honeybun."

Kevin laughed in disbelief, both at the weird light, and at Pete calling Nikki *honeybun*. She hated that kind of thing. Babe, okay. Darlin', maybe. But when Pete called her that, to Kevin's dismay she just laughed and shook her head.

"My father used to call me that all the time," Nikki replied.

"But not anymore?" Kevin asked her.

"Nah. The few times I've seen him in the last couple years, he doesn't call me much of anything."

Pete grew serious. "That's not right. For a father to act like that."

"I guess it's not," Nikki allowed. "I don't think about it too much."

"Some people shouldn't be parents," Pete added, almost to himself.

With a frown, Kevin studied him. "You're preaching to the converted, man," he told Pete. "My father blew us off two years ago. Nikki's dad had been out of the picture even longer. What about you? Are your parents still together?"

"I don't have any parents."

Pete's voice was cold and guttural, as though he was on the verge of tears or rage. In the rearview mirror, his blue eyes were fading again, to ice blue, and then just ice, nearly clear.

Then he blinked, and the moment had passed.

"You never told me that," Nikki said softly, as she reached out to stroke the back of his head. "I'm sorry, babe."

"Sorry's not worth the effort," Pete told her.

But he didn't say anything more about it, or much else, for that matter. They stopped at the liquor store. Pete picked up beer for himself and his friends for the party they were going to crash that night, and he grabbed half a case of Löwenbrau for Kevin, and wouldn't take the money he offered.

It was damned nice of him.

No parents. Tragic story. Points for good behavior and generosity, all that good shit.

But those eyes. And Doug's eyes, too. And there were other things, like the way Doug and the others had talked about Nikki on Monday at Hopkinton, and what they had done to Tommy.

In the front seat, on the way back home, Pete and Nikki were talking. She tossed her strawberry-blond hair back whenever she laughed. Pete acted like she was his for the taking, like he didn't have to impress her at all. For that, more than anything, Kevin wanted to smack him. But he would never dare.

"Hey, Pete?" he interrupted. "I don't know if you remember Tommy. My friend from the trestle that day."

"The kid with the yellow hair."

"That's him, yeah. Did you know . . ." Kevin paused, not sure he wanted the answer. But then he knew he had to have it. "Did you know Doug, Curt, and Hugo jumped him a couple of days ago?"

"What?" Nikki asked.

She turned to stare at Pete.

He fixed Kevin with a hard look in the mirror.

"I didn't at the time. But, yeah, I know. Can't say I'm all that surprised."

"Why the hell would they do that?" Nikki demanded.

Pete took a turn, his eyes on the road now. He didn't look at either of them as he continued. "You weren't at the trestle that day, Nik. That means it really isn't your business. The only reason we didn't all trounce on Kevin's ass is 'cause I like him, and more to the point, 'cause he's your friend."

"Oh, *that's* nice," Nikki said sarcastically.

"It isn't meant to be nice. It's just the truth."

After that, there was nothing else said in the car until Pete pulled up in front of the Murphys' house to drop Kevin off. There were mumbled good-byes, but nothing more than that. Pete had spelled it out, the way things were, and it was not by any means a comfortable situation.

Kevin was very glad for the beer in the brown paper bag. Oblivion beckoned, and its siren call was quite seductive. As the Charger pulled away, Kevin cut across his front lawn to the door. His mother's car wasn't in the driveway. It was not much after four, and she probably wouldn't be home for at least two more hours. The last thing he'd want would be for her to catch him with beer; after being married to Sean Murphy for sixteen years, she figured any teenager who took a drink was an alcoholic.

In his mind, he had it all worked out. He'd stick the beer in the old fridge they kept in the back basement, then track down Jesse, who was probably already with Jack, to let them know at least some beer had already been scored. He would have bought a case if he'd had the money, or if he'd known that Pete was going to pay for it. But twelve beers for four guys was worth a little buzz, at least.

He was still working that math out in his head when the screen door banged open. Tommy Carlson strode out of the house toward him, with Jack and Jesse not far behind. Not even thinking, Kevin smiled.

"Hey. You're early. Check out the goodies!"

Then he noticed the look on Tommy's face, the wide eyes—one of which was still black and blue—and the way his lip sort of curled up.

"Tell me that wasn't who I think it was!" Tommy demanded.

Kevin blinked, the situation becoming clear to him for the first time.

"Oh, no, Tommy man. Come on. It isn't what you . . . that was just Pete, with Nikki. None of those other guys were—"

"Just Pete? What is Pete, your best buddy now? Kevin, do you even remember the trestle that day? Do you fucking remember that guy? His friend fucking jumped me. In *that* car. What the hell are you doing hanging out with him?"

It felt, in that moment, like Kevin was standing on the deck of a ship, the waves swaying him back and forth. He looked at his brother, but Jesse had a frown on his face. Jack looked pissed, too, and Jack rarely had any facial expression whatsoever, unless it was drug or alcohol induced.

"Guys . . ."

There was no breeze. A little bead of sweat went down the middle of Kevin's back, and he noticed the heat of the day for the first time. He could read the fine print on Jesse's T-shirt, the one that looked like a Jack Daniel's label but said Lynyrd Skynyrd instead. Behind him, Craig Herndon started up his Blazer, the engine roared and music pounded out of ridiculously large speakers.

Kevin glanced away. When he looked back at them, the guys were still waiting.

"I only went with them to get Pete to buy us beer," he lied. "That should count for something."

"It would it if was true," Tommy told him.

Kevin flinched.

"You went 'cause you're chasing after Nikki French like a goddamn puppy. Fuck, man, if I was you, I'd be embarrassed. I'm embarrassed for you, for Christ's sake. You've been ignoring all your friends to spend time with her, like she was your girlfriend or something, but you can't get it through your head that she isn't. She has a boyfriend, Kevin, and he's the weirdo prick who wanted to rip our heads off at the trestle."

Tommy was right, of course. Kevin could see that. But he was too pissed off to admit it.

"Know what?" he said. "Fuck you, man. It's not like I'm hanging out with these guys. So Nikki's my friend. I don't know what your problem is with that. I know she has a boyfriend. Does that mean I can't hang out with her? All right, Pete and those other guys are assholes. Are you happy? I'm sorry they scared you."

"I wasn't scared," Tommy corrected.

"Whatever," Kevin said, exasperated. "I'm sorry, okay. Yeah, I've been making an ass of myself. Yeah, I feel stupid. I know she's with him and I hate it. That what you want to hear? You happy now?"

A dozen expressions crossed Tommy's face. Four or five times, he started to reply, and then stopped. Finally, he shook his head.

"You know what? You guys have a good time tonight. I'll talk to you later," he said. "See ya, Jesse. Jack. Tell April I said hi."

Tommy started around the side of the house.

"Come on, Tommy. Don't be like that," Kevin called after him.

Jesse came up to stand beside his brother. "Forget it, Kev. He's bullshit 'cause those guys beat on him. You can't blame him. Give him a few days."

"He'll be cool," Jack added. "But maybe you wanna stop hanging around with those guys, man."

As Tommy disappeared behind the house, Kevin sighed. Then he nodded.

"This day just sucks."

8

After dark, six-packs in brown paper bags tucked as inconspicuously as possible under their arms, Jack Ross and the Murphy brothers walked up Fox Run Drive to the circle at the top of the hill. Beyond that dead-end turnaround was state forest land, and the woods were thick and dark. There was nothing surreptitious about their movements. They simply walked to the stone wall at the far side of the circle, stepped up, and disappeared into the trees.

Perhaps ten feet from the wall there was a path. Kevin, Jesse and Jack knew the woods up there intimately, the trails almost as frequently worn by their sneakers and boots as the span of dying grass that stretched from the Murphys' front stoop to the Rosses' backyard. Almost.

Unlike the neighborhood, however, the woods were truly theirs in a way the streets and yards never could be. Save for the occasional hiker or horseback rider, the state forest at the top of Fox Run Drive belonged to kids. It stretched seemingly forever in all directions, as far as Ledgewood Road on the one side, Millwood golf course on the other, and straight ahead? None of them could even hazard a guess how deep the forest went.

Far, though. The woods were lovely, dark and deep. Kevin had read that poem in the sixth grade, and thought of the top of his street. The timberland up there might run unbroken to the Sudbury line, for all he knew. Maybe farther.

All of it was theirs to explore. There were a lot of

trails and meadows and such in there. Wide paths and narrow tributaries with stones and roots jutting from the earth that would be covered with a slippery coat of pine needles in the fall. Off of one small path there was a burned out cabin, nothing left but a few blackened timbers and the remains of the chimney. Where the trails led nearer to the golf course there was a farm, and some rusted, turn-of-the-century farm equipment in the deep forest at the edge of its property.

They had played army there, built fire holes out of stones and roasted hot dogs and marshmallows and talked about superheroes and baseball and girls. When a new street went in over near Millwood, they had stolen hundreds of dollars' worth of lumber and built a fort— or rather, three separate forts at three separate times. One of those still stood.

That night they took the main trail off toward Millwood. It was a bit of a walk, but they soon found themselves at the edge of Bud Nixon's farm. A long hill dropped away before them, covered with corn that was already nearly taller than they were and still growing. The weather had been excellent.

On a path that ran along the back boundary of the Nixon farm, between another centuries-old stone wall and the first row of corn, they made camp. In a shallow fire hole, they built a small blaze, not wanting to draw Bud Nixon's attention. It didn't seem likely that he'd see the smoke or fire way up on the hill past the corn, but they'd heard the stories about how protective Bud was about his crops. If you tried to steal corn, or if he even thought you might, he'd call the police, and you might just have a few bruises by the time the cops got there.

For a while, sitting around the fire with lukewarm bottles of beer in their hands, the guys avoided the subject of Tommy Carlson. But as the fire burned low and they all got a bit of a buzz on, it seemed inevitable that it would come back round again. When it did, though, it was more to the point. It was about Nikki.

"I guess I love her," Kevin drunkenly confessed.

They stared at him, there in the dark, faces dappled with orange firelight. Their expressions were grim, eyes narrowed.

"You always did," Jesse remarked.

Kevin's eyes widened. Had it been that obvious? He spent so much time in his own head, just sort of exploring life, that he never paid much attention to whether or not anyone was watching. His brother was an asshole most of the time, but that didn't mean he was blind.

"I got up the guts to ask her out, tell her how I feel—or at least I think I did. I thought if I waited for my birthday, then I'd be fourteen. She's only fifteen months older than me, but until then, it'd *sound* like two years. Then she started dating with Pete, out of the blue, over Fourth of July weekend, and I'm back to just wishful thinking."

"You never left 'wishful thinking,' bro," Jesse mocked him.

"Fuck off," Kevin growled, but only halfheartedly. He had the sense that Jesse was teasing him more out of reflex than anything else.

Jack lit up a smoke, watching them.

"Thing is, this Pete?" Kevin said. "Him and Doug and those two other pricks. They're bad news."

"No shit?" Jesse scoffed. "What was your first fucking clue, genius?"

Kevin felt bile rising in the back of his throat, burning, and he looked down at the ground. Jesse was a dick, but he was also right. He knew he'd been an idiot, hanging out with such assholes just to be around Nikki. Even while it was happening, he'd known it. Just stupid.

"I feel like I should tell her that," he said at length. "That she deserves to know what he's really like. But I don't think she'd listen. Plus, then I couldn't tell her how I feel, 'cause she'd just think I didn't like him 'cause of that."

"Never figured Nikki for stupid," Jack told them. "But she can't see this guy's a lowlife?"

For a moment, Kevin was going to agree. Then he

thought about Pete; the way the guy smiled, the way he laughed and patted you on the back, and included you in whatever cheap magic it was that made him cool. He had charisma, no doubt about that.

"He doesn't seem so bad when you hang with him. I'm not defending him, but it's true. Even now, if it weren't for those other assholes . . . Pete's one of them. That's for sure. But they're worse, somehow. He has some class, at least. They're just . . ."

"Hoods," Jesse finished for him.

Kevin laughed softly, but he nodded. The word brought to mind old episodes of *Happy Days* and reading *The Outsiders,* but it fit well enough. Mr. Orsini, who lived down the street, had called him that one day—a hood—and Kevin had laughed.

The word felt silly in his head most of the time. But when it came to the creeps who hung around with Pete Starling . . . the word fit, but even that was inadequate to describe them.

Kevin told Jesse and Jack about the way Hugo and the others had talked about Nikki that day at Hopkinton. Told them about the way they had threatened him. Of course, they all knew about Tommy being jumped.

"These are just bad guys," Jesse agreed. "But what are you gonna do, Kev? You mess with them, they'll just stomp you."

There it was. A truth that he had been avoiding in his own mind ever since he'd first discovered that Nikki was involved with Pete. He'd been a coward, and he knew it. No one would blame him, not given the odds. But his own fear had prevented him from responding the way he should have when he found out Tommy had been jumped. If he'd allowed himself to be properly enraged, not to rationalize it away, then he would have had to call Doug and Hugo and Curt on what they'd done. They would have hurt him, then, no matter what Pete said.

"I'm a pussy," he said, voice thick with self-loathing.

"Well, yeah," Jesse agreed.

Kevin looked at his older brother, hurt. Jesse just shrugged.

"Those guys'd kill you, Kev. Massacre. There are times you gotta stand up, no matter how scared you are. But fear, nothing wrong with that. It keeps us alive, bro. Anyone who isn't afraid of stuff is just too stupid to think about the consequences."

"One way to avoid 'em," Jack said. He took a long drag on his cigarette, blew out the smoke. "Consequences, I mean. Just stay out of it."

A strong breeze kicked up, and the leaves behind them rustled with it. The corn stalks swayed with a kind of hushed whisper, like a group of people huddled close, telling secrets they don't want you to hear.

"I can't, man," Kevin admitted. "All right, I'm jealous. But I'm scared for Nikki, too. Pete's an asshole, yeah, but he's also way too old for her. He's, like, eighteen, probably nineteen. What's he doing with her in the first place?"

"Could be he likes her," Jesse suggested. Then his expression darkened. "Or it could be he gets his kicks out of using chicks and dumping them, and can't pull it over on girls his age."

Stated so boldly, the idea chilled Kevin. He wanted to cry, and was surprised to find that the tears he would not allow himself to shed would have been for Nikki, not for himself.

"Why does she always pick these bastards?" he asked, but it was a question for the sky and the wind and the trees, and maybe for God, if he was really out there.

"You gotta tell her, man," Jack said suddenly.

When Kevin looked at him, Jack was already sucking on his beer. Almost like he hadn't said the words at all, like they were in Kevin's head. But he knew they weren't. He looked at his brother.

"He's right," Jesse said. "Hey, maybe she's waiting for you to speak up. Maybe she feels the same way. You don't know."

"Maybe she doesn't," Kevin said, forlorn.

"You'll be kicking yourself if you don't find out. Even if she doesn't feel that way, it'll make her have to take a look at the guy she's with," Jesse prodded.

Kevin sighed, took a long swig from his beer. He stared at his brother, wondering if it was the beer making him seem suddenly less obnoxious, less disparaging. Kevin picked up a stick he'd been fiddling with and put one end over the fire, just to watch it blacken. "She doesn't see it, what he's like. He's a charming son of a bitch, and that's all she knows."

"Unless you tell her," Jack repeated.

They all drank after that. For a time, they spoke very little. None of them had worn a watch, but Kevin figured it was near ten when he stood, swaying, and told Jesse and Jack that he had to go see Nikki.

Buzzed as he was, Kevin had the sense to realize it might not be the best way to present his case to her, that if he waited until the next day, when he was sober, he would be better off. But there were advantages to being a little drunk. He might not have the courage to say the things he wanted to say in the morning. And if Nikki laughed at him, or was at all uncomfortable, he could always blame the beer.

It was a cowardly bit of logic, but Jesse and Jack clearly understood it, for neither of them tried to talk him out of going.

"Good luck, bro," Jesse told him.

Kevin nodded, the motion exaggerated by drunkenness.

He waved as he left, heading back along the path they'd used to get there. It was dark in the woods, but the canopy of the trees was open above him, and the moon and stars provided enough illumination to navigate by.

It had been cool, hanging with Jack and Jesse. It was unlike him to let his feelings out like that, to anyone. He had friends, yeah. But ever since he could remember, Kevin had felt like he didn't quite fit in. That might have partially explained why he spent so much time with his nose in a book, or watching TV. Sometimes he felt as though he was more a part of those worlds than the one inhabited by his family and friends. The kids he knew all seemed to just fit in; to know, by instinct, how to deal with one another, whether friends or enemies.

They seemed *occupied* by their lives.

He paused on the path, just for a moment, taking a breath, looking up at the stars. There was no escaping the truth in that thought. Kevin had no way to know if it was illusion or reality, but everyone he had ever known seemed to be fully invested with their lives, completely involved. Yet all his life he had felt an odd, curious detachment, as though he were seeing everything through some kind of filter. In school, Kevin was friendly with a great many people, part of any number of groups, but not inherent to any one. He had interests in things that none of his friends seemed to care about with the same passion he felt.

He was impatient with his life. Impatient for junior high to end so he could get to high school, and he imagined he would feel the same way in high school about college. It was as though he were not living in the now, but gliding above it. His life was the frozen surface of the pond in the woods just a hundred yards from where he stood, and he skated over it without any fear of falling in.

Nikki had shattered the ice beneath him.

For years, she had been an exception, not unlike the books and comic books that he read, and the movies that he loved so much. There was a vibrance to her, and to his passion for her, that occupied him completely. With her, Kevin never found his mind wandering, never felt himself drifting.

Then, that night when she had been waiting on the front stoop, when she had cried and he had held her in his arms and kissed her and inhaled her scent, the filter had been torn away completely, the ice beneath him, separating him from the world, had been completely melted.

With Nikki, he never felt that detachment. But now that she was with Pete he had been drifting again. He needed to talk to her, needed to tell her.

He moved along the path which wound through the trees, more surefooted now. There was a weird clarity in his head instead of the fuzziness that usually accompanied drinking. He felt driven. The wind whispered through the branches above him, like distant applause for his revelation.

Reality was not subjective. But that didn't mean it could not be changed.

Those thoughts moved through his mind in an instant and were now carried off, like fallen leaves on that same breeze. For a moment, it had all made sense to him. Then it was gone, left there on the path behind him as he emerged through the trees at the top of Briarwood Road and started to walk down the hill toward Nikki's house.

Nothing made sense to him after that.

9

Pete's Charger was parked in Nikki's driveway. Kevin stopped as still as his buzz would allow, swaying in the middle of the road as he stared at the vehicle. It was warm out, but he shivered a bit. Mrs. French's car was gone, and he assumed she was either working a late shift or out on a date with the pediatrician she'd been seeing.

The Charger sat there, immobile. No smoke from its exhaust, no rumble from its engine, at least from this distance. And yet, somehow, it didn't seem inert. Kevin felt a kind of anxiety looking at the car, immobile like that, as though at any moment it might burn rubber and aim its broad grill in his direction. As if entranced by it—or perhaps by the knowledge of what might be going on inside the red house—he found himself frozen to the spot.

"Shit," he whispered.

Go home, he told himself. *Just go home.*

His feet began to move forward in spite of his better instincts. He was not only sad and disappointed, but angry. Once more, Pete had interfered with his feelings for Nikki. Though he knew it was wrong to spy, the intention to do exactly that had quickly emerged within him. If they were alone—if they were fooling around— maybe that would be enough to turn him away for good, to make him realize he was only dreaming. But it could be anything, he thought. They might be fighting, or just watching TV. Maybe.

Please.

As he moved toward Nikki's house, a streetlight over

his head flickered and died. With the numb reflexes of the inebriated, Kevin rolled his head back to frown up at it, and nearly lost his balance.

When he turned his attention down the street again, he saw two small animals trotting along the pavement, coming around the corner right in front of Nikki's house, right in the middle of the road. They were the oddest pair of animals Kevin had ever seen; a fat, lumbering raccoon, its bandit mask black as tar on the gray-and-white fur of its face, and beside it, a skinny fox, fur deep red in the glow of the streetlights, its bushy, black tail straight out behind it.

It was all wrong. That was Kevin's first thought on the matter. A fox and a raccoon would be natural enemies. That was part of it, but not all. The way they ambled along side by side was odd enough, but stranger than that, to his mind, was that they were so exposed. The light above him had gone out, but forty yards ahead, where they even now sauntered toward him, the streetlights were bright and threw ample illumination down on the road.

It was almost as though they wanted to be seen. Both fox and raccoon were thieves. Bandit kings of the animal world, they kept to the shadows or near cover as much as possible. And yet here they were like a couple of friendly dogs, bopping on down the road.

Weird. But cool, too. There was a little bit of magic in it, Kevin thought. A small smile began to play at the edges of his mouth. He had realized while stumbling down the hill that he was more drunk than he'd known. Wasted, cocked, shit-faced; no argument there. He hoped he would remember this in the morning.

As if they were following the road, destination clearly in mind, the bizarre animal duo turned right up Londonderry Lane and started moving away from Nikki's house. Kevin shook his head in wonder and, still half watching them, moved to the side of the road and on toward Nikki's house. He was in the front yard of the Lavallees, next door, his view of the house obscured by a line of evergreens, when he heard the engine.

He jumped, thinking, at first, that the Charger had come to life.

It took him a heartbeat to realize the sound was coming from farther down Briarwood. A second later, a rumbling Torino screeched around the corner and then banged a hard right onto Londonderry.

Kevin's eyes widened, and he almost cried out, despite his plan to spy. It would have been too late anyway. The two animals strolling up Londonderry Lane turned toward the sound of the roaring engine. They were pinned in the headlights of the Torino as though a spotlight had found them on stage and they'd forgotten their lines.

The fox escaped.

The raccoon was crushed beneath the Torino's tires. Kevin could hear the crunch from where he swayed. His stomach lurched and he nearly threw up there on the grass at the edge of the pavement. He watched the Torino speed away without slowing at all. Just beyond the edge of the illumination thrown by the streetlight at the T intersection of Briarwood and Londonderry, the raccoon lay still. Out of the corner of his eye, Kevin saw something moving.

The fox. It had slipped beneath the post-and-beam fence in front of the Blairs' house, and now it moved cautiously back out onto the road. It glanced left and right, as though it feared the Torino might return. Then it trotted over to sniff at the raccoon. With a tiny yelp, the fox took a step backward.

The raccoon rose unsteadily to its paws. Its fur stood up at odd tufted angles, and it shook itself all over as though it had been for a swim and now wanted to dry off. The animal glanced at its red-furred partner, and then the two of them set off up Londonderry Lane, continuing on their journey.

Kevin stared after them until they had disappeared into the night. Even then, he was mesmerized by what he had witnessed. He knew he had to be wrong, that his eyes must have been playing tricks on him: no way could the car have run over the raccoon. The tires must have missed it.

But he had been sure. He had *heard* the sickening sound of it being churned under the tires. Had that been all in his head?

Must have been.

Alcohol still affecting his equilibrium, he swayed too far to one side, staggered, and nearly fell into the evergreens. A sudden burst of laughter drew his attention, and he turned too quickly, worried that he'd been seen, drunk as a fool. But no one was watching. The laughter came again, high and cruel. This time he pinpointed its origins—behind Nikki's house, most likely on the deck—and he recognized its source. Doug Starling. The weasel.

Quick as he was able, Kevin stumbled toward the evergreens, keeping as close to their branches as he could without brushing against the trees enough to be noticed. He moved along the line of trees on the Lavallees' property until he was adjacent to the Frenches' deck next door. He could hear their voices clear enough, and when he turned sideways and slid slowly between two of the trees, he could see them as well: Doug, Curt, and Hugo.

"Ssshh," Curt hissed at Doug. "She'll hear you."

Doug laughed. "What the fuck do I care if the bitch hears me?"

Hugo sat on a chaise lounge, drinking a Michelob. Doug and Curt leaned against the railing. The deck was perhaps four feet above the yard, with a cross-hatching underneath to keep out animals, and a little door so Mrs. French could store the lawn mower and a few other things under there. For a second, Kevin considered making a run for that door and slipping under the deck. But only for a second. Drunk as he was, he knew he'd give himself away.

"Maybe you don't care if she hears you," Curt kept

on, "but Pete does. Brother or not, I'm pretty sure he'll fuck you up good."

Doug glowered at him, but when he spoke again, his voice was lower, and unaccompanied by that hyena laugh. "I wish he'd just get over her. She's not even that good looking, and if she won't fuck, what good is she?"

Kevin stiffened, anger suffusing him. But he managed to keep still. He had noticed that Hugo, who was not taking part in the conversation, was nevertheless quite alert. With his doughy face and sad eyes, Kevin had always thought he looked rather stupid. But he didn't think that now. At the moment, Hugo looked more like a massive watchdog than anything else.

"That's not up to you to decide," Curt told Doug.

The weasel cocked his head back and stared Curt in the eye. Not a simple task, given Curt's size.

"Who do you think you are?" Doug said in a ragged voice.

Curt laughed, and in its way, Kevin thought the sound as cruel as the savage titter that had come from Doug's mouth earlier. Then Curt seemed to expand, though it was obvious he was simply taking advantage of his size. He stood tall, spread his shoulders wide, and looked down at Doug from on high, eyes rimmed by those long, unnaturally orange lashes. In that moment, his pale skin and those eyes gave him an almost monstrous countenance.

"We've been here a little while, now, Doug. So maybe you've forgotten why you're still alive. Maybe you're trying to forget," Curt suggested.

His right hand flashed out and clamped around Doug's throat, cutting off the weasel's air almost instantly. From where Kevin stood hidden, he could not see Doug's face, but he could hear the sound of his choking, could see his feet kicking as Curt lifted him off the ground.

Eyes wide with astonishment, Kevin forgot himself a moment. "Jesus," he whispered, in spite of the danger of discovery.

No one heard. Even Hugo's searching eyes did not

turn his way, so occupied were they with the scene unfolding there on the deck.

"Let him go, Curt," Hugo said, his voice a bit higher than Kevin remembered.

Curt ignored him. Instead, he lifted Doug higher.

"You would be dead a hundred times over if Peter wasn't your brother; if we weren't all watching your ass. That you've lived this long is a fucking miracle. Peter ought to kill you himself, but he can't bring himself to do it."

Hugo rose from the chaise. "Curt," he said, voice flat and hard. Kevin could see the kid's sad eyes gleaming in the moonlight, almost as though they had some inner light of their own.

With a snarl, Curt reached down and grabbed Doug in the crotch, lifted him, and tossed him over the edge of the deck. In the trees, Kevin moved back slightly, startled and afraid of being seen, and several branches slipped in front of him.

"Curt, what the fuck?" Hugo snapped.

Vision partially obscured by the branches, Kevin saw Doug tumble through the air, and winced in preparation for the weasel's painful landing. Doug spun in the air. Somehow he managed to turn his body with the momentum and land on his feet. He seemed to barely touch the ground, then he leaped back up to the deck as though the lawn were a springboard.

Doug landed on the railing and crouched there, spider-like, long greasy hair dangling in his face. His eyes seemed impossibly wide.

Hugo moved toward him, one hand raised. "Doug, don't do it."

The weasel launched himself at Curt.

Kevin thought it was the branches obscuring his view. He couldn't really see them hitting one another. Their movements seemed jerky, like they were bathed in strobe lights, so that half of what they were doing was swathed in darkness. But there was no strobe.

Finally, Curt stood completely still. Baring his teeth

like an animal, Doug lunged for him. Curt swung a massive backhand down at the weasel that knocked Doug to the deck and sent blood shooting from his nose. Then he picked up his Michelob and took a long draught; he wiped his hand across his mouth.

"You numbskull," Hugo sighed. "What the hell you gonna tell Pete?"

"Tell him his brother's a fucking retard, and we should never have brought him," Curt said, and took another slug of beer.

Bottle in hand, he turned, crouched, then sprang up off the deck to the low-hanging roof of Nikki's house. Bent over, he scrabbled up the shingles to the peak, then dove off. Kevin's jaw dropped. He had lost track of Curt beyond the treetops, but he waited to hear the sound of the big kid tumbling down the roof on the opposite side, or dropping to the driveway out front.

He heard nothing but Doug's cursing and whining.

As quietly as he could, Kevin backed out of the trees, never more aware of his youth, never more afraid for himself. He hustled along the tree line and poked his head through to peek at Nikki's front yard, and at the silent Charger that waited there, ominously predatory.

There was no sign of Curt.

Baffled, he walked out to the road to get a full view of the front of the house. He looked up Londonderry and both ways along Briarwood. Nothing.

Slowly, he backed away. He was going to turn and go home, thoughts of Nikki put off until he could make some sense of this.

With the whistle of passing air, something plummeted from the sky into the pool of light beneath the streetlamp at the intersection. Kevin saw it fall, and heard it shatter. Glass. It reminded him momentarily of the night he and Tommy had been walking home and he'd broken the streetlight, only to have the bulb fall whole and shatter on the street.

Glass. He frowned.

With a quick glance around to make certain no one

else had heard it, or was coming to check it out, he ran into the street, into that dome of light. Even before he reached the spot, he could see the shards scattered about. Brown glass. And a label.

Michelob.

Barely able to take a breath, he leaned his head back and stared up into the star-filled night. A sudden, unseasonable chill had swept the July night. Kevin watched the sky, but just as his lungs had suddenly refused to breathe, his mind refused to function properly, refused to follow fact with logic.

He turned and ran.

Despite his buzz, he didn't stumble once.

Book Two: What a Fool Believes

1

On Saturday morning, Nikki sat on the deck behind her house in a purple-and-white-striped bikini top and obscenely short cutoffs. Thursday, the temperature had risen to ninety-five. Friday, it had dropped down a few degrees, promising relief. Friday lied. The metal and glass thermometer on the side of the house, near where the bird feeder was hung, read just a hair below one hundred degrees.

Nikki barely felt it. Sweat ran down the back of her neck and on her chest in the hollow between her breasts. She didn't notice. Instead, she lay on the chaise lounge and slowly sipped tart lemonade from a cold, condensation-slick glass. Between sips, she balanced the glass idly on her belly, letting the condensation bead up and run in tiny rivulets down her skin. The circle where the bottom of the glass touched her was growing numb with the cold.

Numb was good.

Nikki thought she was losing Pete. It wouldn't be the first time, of course. She'd been through a lot of boyfriends. Most of them, even the assholes, had been the one to dump her, instead of the other way around. She just didn't know why she couldn't make it work.

Or maybe she did, and she didn't want to think about it. Pete wanted to have sex. *Make love,* he said. But Nikki couldn't be sure he loved her. It wasn't like she was some innocent little girl, afraid of sex. She'd done plenty. But not everything. Not that. Nikki didn't just want to be another notch for Pete; just another fuck.

I don't think I could take that.

Pete kept saying he would be patient, but then he'd turn around and bring it up again. Just as he'd done on Wednesday night. They'd even argued about it. *I thought you loved me,* he'd said. That was the hell of it. She did love him, or she thought she did. As much as Nikki had ever loved anyone. Truth be told—and she didn't like to think about the truth very much, not in her heart— she wasn't quite sure she knew what love was.

One thing she did know; she liked the way Pete made her feel, and didn't want to lose that. In her mind she had gone over the pros and cons of sleeping with Pete a thousand times. It wasn't that she didn't want to do it—she did. After all she'd heard, and all she'd fantasized, she was very curious.

But the first time? She was no romantic. Not really. Not some princess in a fairy tale. Still, she thought the first time should be special and right, that it should be about love, not just sex.

"Face it, Nicole," she whispered to herself. "You're hopeless."

The voice sounded brave, even in a whisper. But she didn't feel brave. To the contrary, she felt fragile and weak and afraid. Mostly she felt alone. Pete had called her twice in the past three days, but he hadn't been by to see her, and when she'd asked when they'd be going out again, he'd been noncommittal. What made it worse was having no one to talk to about it. All of it. Her mom was cool, and all, but it just wasn't a conversation she was ready to have with the woman who'd given birth to her. Plus, since her father was a total asshole, Nikki didn't take her mother's perspective on relationships and romance all that much to heart.

And friends? That was a twisted joke. Nikki had never gotten along with other girls all that well, except maybe Kristen Ross, and she'd run away the year before and never come back There were others, but Nikki knew she couldn't turn to them with the kind of questions she had now. They were potheads and drunks, petty thieves and burnouts. She loved them all, and knew most of them would do anything for her. But they weren't exactly deep thinkers. Most of the girls would have told her to go for it, what difference would it make? The guys were likely to tell her to forget Pete, that they'd be happy to pop her cherry if she wanted.

The thought of it made her smile. Bunch of fucking delinquents, her friends.

Maybe they'd be right.

Problem was, the person she really wanted to talk to about it all was Kevin, and he was nowhere to be found. The last time she'd seen him was Wednesday, after she and Pete had dropped him off. She'd left a couple of messages, one with his mom and one with Jesse, and even gone by the house a few times. Kevin hadn't called her back, hadn't come by to see her. Nikki was convinced he was dodging her, but didn't know why.

That isn't exactly true, she thought.

With a sigh, she put the lemonade down on a glass table, and reached for the box of Marlboros and her lighter. She tapped out a butt, put it to her lips, and lit up, tossing the box back onto the table.

Pete's brother, Doug, and the other guys were jerks. Nikki hated them all, with the possible exception of Curt, whom she couldn't quite get a bead on. Doug looked at her like she was dirt, and she had resisted the urge to slap him any number of times. Slap, or maybe kick. They were assholes of the first order, and they'd been treating Kevin like he was their dog. It hurt Nikki to see it, and she'd complained to Pete a few times— though Kevin had never brought it up, which she thought said a lot for his character.

At least Pete seemed to like him, and though Kevin had been pretty squirmy lately, he didn't seem to have the problem with Pete that he had with the other guys. The whole thing was hard for Nikki.

Nikki cared a great deal about Kevin. There was something so natural about being with him, like all was right with the world. He just *got* her on so many levels.

She wished that she could find a boyfriend who would understand her like that, or that Kevin were a little older, and maybe not quite so . . . good.

That was it, too. He'd be fourteen in a few days, a little more than a year younger than her, and in a lot of ways, he showed it. Nobody in the world got more excited about a book or a movie than Kevin Murphy. He was like a little kid with that stuff, with a grin wide enough to split his face and a sparkle in his eye. Christmas was every other day. But in other ways, he was so much more mature than her other friends, smart and . . . the word that came into her head was *wise,* but it seemed so strange to use that word in connection to a kid. Still, it fit.

Now that she thought about it, Kevin wasn't bad looking, either. Not the cutest guy she knew, but not bad at all. He was tall and broad shouldered for his age. His eyes were a soft brown, and he always met her gaze when she looked at him, made her feel like he was really listening.

Not that she could ever have gone out with him.

Kevin was her best friend. More than that, he was just a little too squeaky-clean for her. There was no sense of danger with him, and the only adventure she was likely to have with Kevin was in a movie theater. In a lot of ways, he was just *too* good.

"Yeah, he's fucking perfect," she whispered, taking another drag on her cigarette. "Asshole."

Nikki was angry that Kevin had been dodging her. She understood, but that didn't mean she wasn't mad. They were friends. He should have come to talk to her about it.

Her heart was aching over Pete, her mind swirling with excitement and guilt and anger over the idea of having sex with him. Who was she supposed to talk to about all of that?

On the radio WAAF played one of her favorites, the Rolling Stones' "Angie," and she sang along, trying to clear her mind. Nikki held her butt out far to the right, so the ash wouldn't fall on her, and leaned her head back, eyes closed, to catch the sun on her face.

"Hey."

Startled, she looked up quickly. For a second, with the glare of the sun in her eyes, she thought it was Pete, and her heart leaped. Then she saw that it was Kevin. Though part of her was disappointed, she also felt glad and relieved.

"Speak of the devil." Nikki sat up and shielded her eyes from the sun. "Where the hell've you been?"

Kevin glanced away, off into the trees behind her house. Nikki thought he'd never looked younger than in that moment, like he was some little kid caught writing on the wall in crayon.

"Hey," she said, concerned. "Kev, what's up? What's wrong?"

With a brief—yet telltale—hesitation, Kevin came around to the steps and walked up onto the deck. He sat down on a metal chair whose rust had been spray painted over but not removed. He wore a green T-shirt with a picture of the Frankenstein monster on it, cutoffs and ratty old Puma sneakers.

Above, the sky was a clear and icy blue, its cool surface belying the oppressive temperature. The sun glared down, unforgiving.

"I got your messages." Kevin held his hands clasped together between his knees. His right leg bounced up and down, always in motion. "I'm sorry I haven't called. Me and Jesse and Jack got drunk Wednesday night, and I was wicked hungover Thursday. Then yesterday . . . I just stayed in and read."

Nikki wasn't about to let him off that easily. "You could have called."

"Yeah." He nodded, eyes darting around, gaze straying to anything but her.

"What's with you?" she demanded suddenly.

Kevin's eyes locked on her, his face pale, as though he were still hungover and might throw up any second.

"Nothing."

"Bullshit. Fuck that, Kevin. You're acting all squir-relly. What's going on?"

It happened, then, all of a sudden. To Nikki, Kevin had always been a kid. But right here in front of her, it seemed to Nikki that Kevin Murphy grew up. He shuddered, as though some kind of ripple were passing through him, and sat up straighter at the edge of the chair. All traces of nervous energy left him. Kevin was perfectly still, his face gravely serious, as he stared at her.

"I think you should dump Pete."

Nikki's stomach lurched. She expelled a breath that made her lungs hurt. Her lips parted in a pout that was more shock than sadness or sensuality.

"What?" she asked, a sense of unreality spreading over her.

"I know you're probably gonna want me to go, and if that's the way it is, fine. But you're my best friend, Nik. I . . . I love you, y'know? And I just don't want you to get badly hurt. Pete and his friends, they're just lowlife shitheads. And . . . they're not normal. They're weird."

"What the hell do you know about weird?" Nikki replied angrily, fighting tears. She wrapped her arms around herself, feeling nauseous. "Pete's always been really nice to you, Kevin."

" 'Cause I'm your friend, and he doesn't want to blow whatever chance he has of getting in your pants."

Nikki blinked. There were little flashes of light beyond Kevin's head, or there seemed to be. Her eyes darted around, looking for something, possibly trying to keep up with her mind, which was whirling, trying to find something to grab on to.

She smelled wintergreen. Like her favorite Life Savers. It was a weird thing, but there it was. It reminded her of going to the pharmacy with her mother. The bald guy at the counter would always give her Life Savers.

"You don't like those guys 'cause of what happened at the trestle. Fine. Okay, maybe Doug and the other guys are assholes. I kinda think so, too. But lumping Pete in with them just isn't fair."

"Those guys beat on Tommy Carlson. They jumped him. You wouldn't believe the shit they say about you behind your back. I've heard them. Shit, they've said it *to me*. Pete's playing you like a two-dollar whore, Nicole. Please don't let him."

Her mouth was open. Nothing came out.

"He's just using you, Nik. Come on, think about it. You're beautiful and smart and funny, but you're fifteen. He's nineteen, easy. Where are the girls his age? He's not even in high school anymore. Never mind robbing the cradle. He figures you're a virgin and wants to get there first. He's Joe Cool, with that car and his own gang of fuckin' hoods."

An inexplicable chill ran through her. Nikki stood up, leaned over Kevin, and screamed in his face. "Get the fuck out of here! Leave! Right now!"

Kevin looked down, swallowed hard.

"He's not a good guy, Nikki. Have you ever even been to his house? Ever done anything with any of his friends other than those guys?"

Furious, Nikki advanced on him. Emotions were raging through her, and she couldn't be sure she was so mad at Kevin because of what he'd said, or because she was afraid he was right. It didn't matter. She just wanted him to go.

"You fucking prick!" she snarled at him, tears she had long held back at last springing to her eyes. "I'm in love with him."

Kevin stood up, face etched with sadness, and backed toward the steps.

"I'm sorry, Nik," he whispered. "I don't think I'm telling you anything you don't know. He doesn't love you. As soon as he gets you to sleep with him, he's gone."

Nikki hit him then. The slap echoed against the trees at the edge of the yard, the sound thrown back to them by the unfeeling sky. There was a bright red mark on

Kevin's cheek that made Nikki feel like sobbing and cheering all at once. Kevin was tearing her apart.

Inside.

Outside, she was steel. Cold and numb and passionless. Her tears still ran, her eyes red, but there was no expression on her face.

"I've already fucked him," she said casually. Lied, casually. "So that shows exactly how smart you are. You don't know shit."

Instantly, she wished she hadn't said it. Kevin went paler than ever, his mouth opening helplessly, a fish gasping for air. Then he scowled.

"You're lying," Kevin said flatly. He stepped off the deck and started walking around toward the front of the house. "I'm not. There's something not right about those guys, and that's aside from the fact that they're assholes. They're on something, and I have no idea what it is. I just . . . I don't want you to get hurt, Nik."

At this last, he turned to face her once again, as if there were some hope of reconciliation. But Nikki needed time, time to take it all in, to make sense of her feelings. She needed him gone.

"If you didn't want me to get hurt, why did you even come down here today?" she asked, her voice weak and raspy.

For a few seconds, he looked at her. Then Kevin turned and walked around the front of the house, and disappeared.

Nikki felt as though she might suffocate, just standing there—like her heart was being squeezed by unseen hands.

She felt totally, utterly lost for the first time in her life.

Nikki was falling, and now there was no one there to catch her.

It rained on Sunday, the heat finally breaking, and the temperature plummeted over the course of the day. By Sunday night, it had dropped to an unseasonably cool sixty-four degrees. Still T-shirt weather, but in the middle of July, a bit of a surprise.

Sweet relief. That afternoon, Tommy Carlson had played basketball in his driveway in the rain. He hadn't had the energy to play hoops for days, with the heat the way it had been. A little rain didn't bother him. His mother thought he was crazy, of course. But his dad had understood. Not a talkative man, his father, but they shared a communication through sports.

It was cool enough when he went in that, after drying off, he put on some sweats and flopped on the dusty sofa to practice on his guitar. A recent purchase, Tommy now spent as much time with the potbellied acoustic as he could. He loved music, and knew a few guys who wanted to start a band.

He was banging out the opening chords of "Lola," by the Kinks, when his mother walked into the room and gave him a look of disapproval.

"Hey, Mom. Too loud?"

"No, Tommy." Her expression was troubled. "I was just wondering if you'd talked to Kevin yet."

Tommy rolled his eyes. Ever since he'd made the mistake of telling her he was pissed off at Kevin, his mom had been after him to call. And he would, too. Kevin was acting like a moron, but girls could have that effect. Tommy knew that. But he didn't feel like calling yet, and it wasn't as though Kevin had made any attempt to apologize.

"I have other friends, Mom," Tommy replied. "Plenty of friends, actually."

His mother offered a tiny shrug, but there was no sincerity in it. "All right. I don't want to make a nuisance of myself. I just think it's too bad you guys have to fight like this. You've known each other almost your whole lives, and most of your other friends from school live too far away to see all the time."

Tommy laughed. "Yeah, but then there's Diana."

"I don't want to know," his mother protested, throwing up her hands. An embarrassed smile played across her features. "I still have cupcakes from yesterday. Would you like one?"

"I could be talked into a cupcake," Tommy agreed.

"I thought you might."

She went out into the kitchen, and Tommy bent over the guitar again, fumbling over the slower parts of "Lola." He was angrier at Kevin than he'd let on, and he knew his mother sensed it. Diana did too, and they'd talked about it a few times.

Kevin was one of his best friends, sure. But he wasn't Tommy's only friend. If he was going to behave like an idiot, Tommy wouldn't stand in his way.

As far as he was concerned, Kevin was on his own until he wised up.

"Where's your brother?"

Jesse looked up. He couldn't speak at the moment; his lungs were filled with pot smoke and he was holding it in. He sat on the back patio of the Rosses' house with Jack and April. When he couldn't hold his breath anymore, he exhaled slowly and passed the joint to Jack.

It was Monday afternoon, and no one else was home. April had ridden her bike all the way over, and they were just hanging out. Jack had put his stereo speakers in the basement window, and the music was echoing through the neighborhood.

"He's home," Jesse said simply. "He's been acting weird for days. Ever since that night we got drunk up at the field. I guess he had some kind of fight with Nikki or something."

"Did he tell her?" Jack asked.

Jesse hesitated. He glanced over at April. Even though she and Kevin were friends, April was still close to Carolyn.

April smiled. Jesse smiled back. She had that effect on people; April might be his best friend's sweetie, but that didn't mean he was going to pretend she wasn't a beautiful girl. Her eyes were unlike anything he'd ever seen, with flecks of gold and silver in them like a kaleidoscope. April in the Sky with Diamonds.

Not like he was lusting for her, though. At least not any more than he did after other girls he knew. Jesse had had plenty of girlfriends for a night or two, but nobody he wanted to be with long term. Which was why he had such a hard time understanding relationships.

"It's okay," April told him. "I know about the whole thing with Kevin and Nikki. Don't really know her, though. What's she like?"

"Kind of a bitch," Jack said, expelling pot smoke with each word, voice hoarse.

"Nah, she's all right. She's not a bitch," Jesse said, looking only at April. "She's just a tough chick. Trouble, y'know?"

April frowned. "Kevin's so straight. It's weird that he'd go all crazy over a girl like that."

"He's a dink," Jesse said curtly. "She's seeing some older guy. She's my age, and he thinks she's gonna be his girlfriend. Not that it couldn't happen, but he shoulda been prepared for the worst, right? Something happened. They had a fight or something and he's just moping around the house. My mother wanted to do all kinds of stuff for his birthday, and Kevin wasn't interested. He's making her crazy, worrying about him. I tried talking to him a couple of times, but he doesn't want to talk."

With a thoughtful look, April took a long hit on the joint, held it, then blew it out. "You think I should try talking to him?"

Jesse nodded. "Couldn't hurt. Though he might be freaked 'cause of Carolyn."

"Carolyn's already seeing someone else," April revealed.

"Really?" Jesse asked, surprised.

"Yeah, she's banging Mike Reagan," Jack added, laughing in disbelief.

"No shit?" Jesse said, perturbed by the news. "She

wouldn't bang my little brother but she'll do it with that skid? I'll never understand girls."

"Hey," April protested.

"Present company excluded," Jesse amended.

April was spooked. She'd been to see Kevin, and now she walked back across the yards to Jack's house. Her cigarettes were on the patio, and she needed one. At first, Kevin had not even come to the door, but she'd called up to him, and finally, he'd answered.

He looked like shit. Tired, eyes all red, and there was no life in his face, like he was a zombie or something. She had tried talking to him, but it hadn't seemed to help at all. Not that he hadn't talked. He had told her about Nikki, and what he felt for her, and about the guy she was dating. About the fight he'd had with her.

"I'm okay. I've just been feeling totally unmotivated," he'd confessed.

"Well you have to get out. Your birthday's in two days," April told him, thinking it would cheer him up.

It had the opposite effect. Mention of his birthday seemed to cause Kevin to shut down even more.

"I'm just depressed. I'll be all right," he promised.

April wasn't so sure. Drastic measures had to be taken. Kevin might not want to do anything for his birthday, but April figured they had to get him to have some fun somehow. He might not want a party, but she figured they had to pull something together for Wednesday.

Anything to get his mind off this girl.

On Monday night, Kevin and Jesse sat in the dimly lit basement, the blue-gray flicker from the television like heat lightning in the gloom. It had been humid, and though it was cool in the basement, the moisture hung in the air, heavy in the lungs, closing around them.

It had taken some time, but Kevin had convinced himself that he'd seen nothing out of the ordinary at Nikki's the previous week. Or, at the least, nothing he could not attribute to beer. The bottle that had shattered in the street had been thrown by Curt, who must have known he was there. That was the only legitimate answer. It also meant that Nikki likely knew he'd been spying.

Despair had set in. He felt helpless to control the changing world around him, as though his best intentions mattered for nothing at all. The worst, though, was the fear. Kevin was afraid that anything he touched would somehow go wrong.

Nikki was with Pete. Kevin knew he had to accept that. The bastard would break her heart, but what could he do about it?

Nothing.

Kevin stole a surreptitious glance at his brother. Jesse had given up asking him what was wrong after the first dozen or so times, and resorted to swearing at him instead. Kevin didn't blame him. But how could he explain to Jesse the things that he felt, the weird things he thought he had seen? His big brother would think he was completely freaking out, and Kevin wasn't sure Jesse would be wrong.

The beer. I was wasted, that's all.

Yet no matter how many times he told himself that, Kevin never completely believed it.

He reached for the blue bag of Chips Ahoy on the big drum table, and his glass of milk. It was just after nine o'clock. On the television, *M*A*S*H* was just starting—a repeat, but one Kevin didn't remember seeing the first time around. It was pretty much always good, but to his mind, hadn't been the same since Radar left.

Choppers were just coming in, and the doctors getting ready for surgery, when the doorbell rang.

Kevin looked at Jesse.

Jesse barely glanced at him. "Proximity law," he said.

With a sigh, Kevin got up from the couch. He went up the stairs to the landing of the split-level, and opened the door.

Doug Starling stood in the front yard, just beyond the light cast by the lantern above the door. Kevin felt a surge of fear, and quieted it down. It was only the weasel; alone. Jesse was right downstairs, his mom was in her room. It was his house, after all. *His* house.

"What do you want?"

The weasel seemed anxious, eyes darting around as though he expected an ambush. His greasy hair shone in the moonlight, and he seemed to sway as he looked at Kevin. It didn't make him look drunk, though. It made him look dangerous, like a snake about to strike. Kevin thought of Kaa in *The Jungle Book,* and knew he'd never think of that movie the same way again.

With a sudden step forward, a cobra strike, Doug moved into the light. His eyes glowed fiercely, reflecting the lantern light; then it was gone.

"Come outside, Kevin." The way Doug spoke, it was a command. "C'mere a second."

Much as he tried to deny it, Kevin felt the fear spreading through him. His stomach roiled and bile rose in the back of his throat. Though he reminded himself that he was not alone, that Doug couldn't really hurt him, the fear continued to grow.

The weasel. The snake. One and the same. Whatever he was, Kevin was certain that Doug was cruel and crazy and very dangerous. A truth presented itself to him: he didn't want Jesse or his mom to come down because he was afraid of what might happen then, what the weasel might do to them. There was more to Doug Starling than just a sadistic little thug.

Kevin just didn't want to know.

He had to play along, to make sure he wouldn't find out.

With one glance over his shoulder—both up and down the stairs from the landing—Kevin pushed open the screen door and stepped onto the slate stoop. Doug had already moved back into the shadows, and now he beckoned Kevin closer.

A breeze rustled the leaves of the oak tree in the front yard. The cobblestoned walk seemed to disappear into the dark. Kevin shivered, but not from fear. It was cold.

It shouldn't be that cold, he knew, but his attention was elsewhere. Out on the street, Mr. and Mrs. Coleman were walking their dog, a collie named Lady. He felt an urge to scream to them for help, but forced himself to remain silent. What the hell would he say? Save me from the weasel? He'd look like a raving lunatic. Doug hadn't done a thing to him.

"Kevin." Doug's voice, only different somehow.

The Colemans walked right on by. Kevin didn't want to meet Doug's gaze, but he couldn't avoid it now. The weasel moved right up close, actually dipped his head to catch Kevin's eye.

"Hello? Murphy, you awake?"

Run, a voice inside him said. *Go back inside, lock the door. Just hide and wait until he goes away.*

Not gonna happen. Kevin couldn't run away. That would be pussy. He'd never hear the end of it, and worse, he'd never forgive himself for it. He forced himself to look up at Doug Starling, to meet the weasel's gaze. *Go on and run,* it seemed to say. *I'll huff and I'll puff and I'll blow your house in.*

Weasel, snake, and now the Big Bad Wolf. Somehow, the thought made it all seem so ridiculous that Kevin felt better. He was able to breathe. To let go of his fear, at least for a moment. Shaking it off, he managed a small smile.

"What's up, Doug? What do you want?"

Instead of moving in farther, crowding Kevin, Doug took a step farther back, into the night. Despite the moonlight, the dark seemed to swallow him. Something about his features didn't look quite right, shadowed like that. But Kevin was focused only on his eyes, which glistened almost as though he were crying.

"I'm not here for me," Doug said, his voice becoming raspy, insinuating, like he knew Kevin's every secret, and would gleefully share them if anyone asked.

"I'm here to give you a message," the weasel rasped. "You should know you're a lucky little shit. If it was up to me, you'd be fucking roadkill right now."

Kevin glared at him. "You and me don't exactly have a love fest going on, Doug. You've made that pretty clear. I guess your message is from Pete, right? So what is it?"

"He's giving you a chance to stay alive."

Any other day, Kevin would have scoffed at the threat. There at the edge of the light that came from his house, he drew into himself protectively, muscles tightening. His mouth opened, tongue prepared for a barbed comeback, but his voice failed him.

Doug grinned broadly. Anyone else seeing that grin would think it friendly as could be, Kevin realized. But he saw something else there: a promise. Whatever came next, whatever the threat was, he knew there would be nothing hollow about it.

"What about it, Kev?" Doug asked amiably. "You want to live?"

Like a burning ember, Kevin felt a tear begin to form at the corner of one eye. He nodded silently. Though he never blinked, Kevin didn't see Doug move, yet the weasel was there beside him, almost dancing on the summer-scorched lawn.

"You said the wrong things about Pete," he whispered. "Stay the fuck away from Nikki."

His head darted in and he regarded Kevin up close. Too close. Close enough to kiss, or to bite.

"Listen, and you'll save your life," the weasel whispered. "But I kinda hope you're not as smart as my brother thinks you are."

The screen door banged open behind them.

"What the hell's going on out here?"

The weasel's eyes ticked past Kevin's face to glower at Jesse. Kevin couldn't turn, instead dropping his gaze to the ground. He bit his lip, urging his brother not to come out any farther, not to get involved. In his heart, he was grateful that Jesse would intervene. But danger shimmered in the air around them, not bothering to hide itself away. It was tangible, as real as the moisture that hung heavy in the air.

"This is none of your business," Doug growled.

Jesse stepped down off the stoop. Kevin didn't have to see him. He felt it, and saw the weasel's eyes move to follow.

"I remember you, shithead," Jesse said pointedly. "And I know you're not here on a social call. You're a punk, a little freak. Maybe you think 'cause you're older than me, you can take me."

With one quick move, Jesse stepped past Kevin and grabbed the weasel around the throat. Doug didn't even try to fight.

"You can't," Jesse fumed. "You come on my yard, giving my brother shit? I'll break you, greaseball. Don't doubt it for a fucking second. Get off my property, and keep away from my brother."

Though he must have been having trouble breathing, Doug grinned. "I wouldn't worry about your brother, Murphy. He'll live long enough to see you bleed."

With a grunt, Jesse shoved the weasel back hard enough that Doug was thrown to the ground, spun away from them. He started to rise up on his hands and knees and Jesse kicked him hard in the ass.

"Get the fuck out of here," Jesse roared. He glanced over at Kevin. "Go inside, bro."

Kevin did as he was told, backing up onto the stoop and then inside the screen door. He didn't turn away, though. He watched as Doug got up, dusted himself off, and calmly walked out to the street where he had left the Charger parked. When the weasel had driven away, Jesse went in. Kevin stepped aside to let him pass. Then he shut the door, and slid the chain lock across.

"Hey, little brother," Jesse said, his voice soft and kind. "What the hell is going on, man? What was that all about?"

Breath hitching in his throat, Kevin turned to Jesse and tried to speak, tried to tell him. His face burned, his eyes wide, and his expression crumbled as tears began to stream down his cheeks, scalding him. Jesse looked shocked, but when Kevin went to him, sobbing quietly, his brother awkwardly enfolded him in his arms and just held him there.

Their mother's voice came from down the hall. "Boys? What's going on? Are you two fighting again?"

Kevin looked up into his brother's eyes, frightened, and shook his head, urging Jesse to silence.

"No, Ma, we're cool," Jesse called up the stairs. "Jack just came by to drop some stuff off. We're just watching TV down here."

"Don't fight," she called.

"We're not fighting."

Jesse started down the stairs into the basement, and Kevin followed, feeling lost and numb. Jesse closed the door, and turned to his brother.

"Maybe it's time you told me what the hell's going on."

2

Jesse sat and listened to his brother's story, and pretty much figured Kevin was out of his mind. The TV droned on in the background, but neither of them really noticed. Though he tried to fight it, Jesse started to get impatient with Kevin about ten minutes into the babbling. The touchy-feely crap wasn't his specialty, and he'd already run through his quota for the month. Not that he wasn't sympathetic, but from his perspective, Kevin was just angsting way too much.

"Stop."

With a hurt look, Kevin blinked and looked at his brother. "Huh?"

"Really, Kev, just shut up a minute, okay?" Jesse pleaded. He held up both hands, as if in surrender, and sat back on the arm of the sofa, facing his brother. "First of all, let's deal with this whacko shit about beer bottles and these idiots moving too fast, all that. Number one, they're morons. Shitheads. Not superheroes."

Kevin laughed softly, then glanced away, a little embarrassed. Jesse figured that was a good start.

"You were drinking, bro. Me and Jack were getting baked, and you inhaled a lot of that smoke. Whatever. You weren't straight, that much I know. So let's just get that shit out of the way up front. Those guys are assholes, and Nikki's not thinking too clearly if she's hanging out with them. Neither are you, by the way. Shit for brains."

"Fuck you," Kevin grunted in reply.

Jesse grinned. That was good. Kevin was starting to think a little more clearly.

"You're out of your league here," Jesse informed him. "Nikki doesn't want to hear it. She's the kind of girl who has to learn this stuff herself. On the other hand, she's your friend, which means there are a couple of things you need to do for her.

"First thing—and I'll go with you for this—you go to Pete's house and you tell him only a pussy sends his little brother to do his dirty work. You also tell him it's illegal in Massachusetts for a guy his age to fuck a fifteen-year-old girl, and that the Murphy family knows plenty of cops."

With a scowl, Kevin shook his head. He slumped down on the sofa and stared at the TV.

"I can't do that, Jesse. Shit, he'll fucking kill me."

"He won't touch you, Kev. Why do you think he sent his greasy little brother? Not only will Nikki never speak to him again, but there's that whole police thing.

"The second thing you have to do is go to Nikki and tell her. Really. You were going to tell her on your birthday, right? That's Wednesday. What's one day early? Tomorrow, find her, and tell her how you feel. How you *really* feel. Then if she's still pissed, and still wants to be with the jerk, at least you had your shot. At least she'll know and you'll never be thinking 'what if?' "

For a minute, Kevin just sat there, eyes roving around, not focusing on anything in particular. Then he glanced up at Jesse, and slowly, he nodded twice.

"You're right. I have to do it. I don't want to be eighteen and thinking, damn I should've said something back then."

"Exactly," Jesse agreed.

Kevin's eyes never left him. "Why are you doing this, Jess? Helping me?"

A familiar expression of anger and frustration spread across Jesse's face. "You're a little puke, Kev, but someone's gotta look out for you. Mom would kill me if I didn't. Doesn't mean I want us to have bunk beds again, all right?"

Kevin dropped his gaze sadly. Normally he would have sworn at his brother, said something bitter and witty, or at least given him the finger. That night he just did not have the strength.

"Well, thanks," Kevin said.

Jesse waved his gratitude away with a flutter of his hand and a sour expression. The brothers each descended into his own thoughts, their attention slowly drifting back to the television.

Pete supposedly lived on Carver Road. Number twenty-something, Kevin had overheard him say. On Tuesday morning, July fourteenth, the day before he would turn fourteen, Kevin and Jesse set off just after eleven for the mile and a half walk. The temperature had already climbed to near ninety, but the humidity had abated somewhat. Coincidentally, and in spite of the heat, the brothers had both chosen full-length Levi's that morning. Kevin figured Jesse had thought the same thing he had: who's going to take someone in shorts seriously?

Kevin wore a Jimi Hendrix T-shirt with Japanese characters that had started black but had faded to a deep charcoal gray over many washings. Jesse had on a deep red T-shirt with the words "Miller's Overland Express" written across the front.

It was quiet outside. Just a Tuesday in the middle of the summer. Most of the adults were at work, most of the kids already busy elsewhere, or still lazing around the house. Nobody mowed his lawn; it was too early for the ice-cream truck or the mailman. Not a single car passed them on the road. The brothers walked in tandem down Fox Run Drive, and Kevin couldn't help but feel a little like he was on the way to the gunfight at the OK Corral.

The spell was broken as they reached the bottom of their hill. It ended at Pleasant Street, a busy road that led into Southboro and Marlboro beyond on the one side, and out to the center of Framingham and Route

Nine on the other. Turning east, they walked along in relative silence, cars buzzing past. A couple of girls in a Mustang honked at them, and the Murphy brothers called after them happily. The girls didn't even slow down; not that the boys were surprised.

At the Brophy School, where both of them had attended kindergarten, they turned in and walked across the ball field in front of the long, two-story brick building. Behind the school, they followed a narrow emergency road to a heavy chain that blocked the way. Beyond that chain was the neighborhood where Pete and his cronies lived.

As they passed the chain, Kevin looked over at Jesse. "You know this is suicide, don't you?"

His brother frowned. "If you think like that, the punk's won."

"Tough guy," Kevin observed.

"Fuck off."

They walked the few blocks to the intersection with Carver Road without another word. At the corner, Kevin went to the right, instinct telling him the lower numbers were that way. He was correct. Though it hadn't occurred to him until now that if Pete weren't home, it was going to be impossible to find his house.

"Any idea which one?" Jesse asked.

"It's not twenty," Kevin replied. That was as much help as he could be.

They walked half a block in either direction from the intersection, covering all the houses in the twenties. There was no sign of Pete's car; at least not without looking in the garages. Without bothering to mention it to Jesse, Kevin started to do just that. He walked up to the garage at number twenty-nine and peered in the side window. An old VW bug sat inside. No midnight-blue Charger.

When he turned around, Jesse was doing the same thing at number twenty-eight.

They'd made it to twenty-three when someone noticed.

"What the hell are you boys doing? I'm gonna call the cops!" a shrill voice cried.

The old woman stood on the steps of number twenty-five Carver Road, where they'd peered in the garage window only moments earlier. She wore a faded blue-and-green floral-patterned housedress, with stockings underneath that had slid down and bunched around her ankles. Despite the heat, a gray cardigan was over her shoulders, perhaps to hide the housedress, Kevin thought. Though there was little chance of hiding anything that ugly.

His first instinct was to run. When Kevin glanced at Jesse, he saw that his brother had the same idea. Even now, Jesse was taking a step back, eyes urging Kevin to take off.

"Book it," Jesse whispered.

Instead, Kevin started walking toward the old lady. "I'm sorry, ma'am," he said. "We're not burglars or anything. I didn't know anyone was home. It's just, I'm looking for a friend's house, 'cause I borrowed ten dollars from him and I want to pay him back."

The lie made his cheeks burn, it felt so obvious and weak. He hoped the flush didn't show, particularly because the old woman was scrutinizing him, eyes narrowed, chin lifted to look down on him like he was some sort of animal digging at her garbage.

"He's your friend, but you don't know which house is his?" she demanded.

"Kevin," Jesse prodded from behind him.

He smiled at the old woman. "Well, I've only been down here once. My mom dropped him off at his house, and it was dark. Doug Starling's his name, ma'am. I guess he lives with his aunt and uncle or something, and his brother, Pete? He's older. Drives a dark blue Dodge?"

The woman looked thoughtful now, and Kevin felt a wave of relief sweep over him.

Then she shook her head. "Nope. No Starlings on Carver Road. You must've misremembered, son."

Kevin blinked. He had not expected that. He knew he had not "misremembered." Twenty-something Carver Road. No doubt about that in his mind. None at all.

"Are you sure, ma'am? I remember—"

"You questioning my memory, son?" she said angrily. "I've lived on this street thirty-seven years. I think I know who my neighbors are."

His mind was in turmoil. Relief that he did not have to face Pete crashed up against his confusion, and his sudden certainty that Pete had lied about his address, both to him and to Nikki, and to anyone else who would listen. Which forced him to wonder what else Pete had lied about. One thing was certain: He had to talk to Nikki, to tell her. Jesse had been more right about that than he had known.

"Let's go," Kevin muttered, even as he turned and walked past Jesse, his back to the old woman.

"Thanks for your help," Jesse called out awkwardly, but the old lady had already started to shut her door.

Nikki didn't know what to do. Just when she'd started to think Pete was going to blow her off completely, he'd come roaring back into her life the day before, more charming than ever. He admitted to having been mad at her, felt like she didn't love him, but he couldn't stay away. Or so he said.

"Promise me you'll just think about it," he'd said. "I want to show you how much I love you."

So she'd promised. And hadn't heard the end of it since.

The usual madness unfolded around her at Hopkinton. Screaming, ice cream melting, water splashing, radios blaring, skin revealing, girl and boy watching. Chaos. The sky was blue and the air was warm but dry, and all should have been right with the world.

Next to her, Pete reclined on an old, faded Star Wars beach towel and gazed at her with that lopsided, beautiful grin, fine hair falling across his eyes in that way that seemed almost girlish. Nikki had no doubts anymore. She knew she loved him.

But that didn't mean she was ready to sleep with him.

Still, just because she wasn't ready, didn't mean he'd wait, no matter what he claimed. She was young, but old enough to know that.

A couple of little kids trudged by, complaining to their mom because she'd made them carry the beach chairs. The boy, maybe seven, accidentally kicked sand at Nikki's back, and she shook it off. When she glanced back at him again, Pete was still looking at her.

"I wish you wouldn't stare at me like that," she confessed, smiling shyly.

He laughed, but just a little. Soft and confident. "You mean with your clothes on?" he asked. "I feel the same way."

Pete reached out a hand, eyes locked on hers, and with the lightest feather touch began to trace the soft skin under her chin. His fingers moved down her throat to the fabric of her bikini top, across the soft lime-green cotton covering her left breast, and over the bump of her nipple. He stroked it, not caring who might see. In the back of her mind, alarm bells went off, but Nikki didn't move. She was mesmerized, staring into his eyes. A sweet warmth spread all through her, and she shivered as though it were a chill instead.

"Tonight, Nikki. Let me show you I love you," he asked, no trace of pleading in his voice. His eyes searched hers.

Barely able to find her voice, she smiled self-consciously. "We'll see," she said quietly.

But she knew as well as he did that those words translated to *yes*.

Nikki was not home. All afternoon Kevin had sat at Four Corners, where Fox Run crossed Londonderry, and watched the cars go by. He and Jesse had walked to McDonald's after trying to find the Starlings' house. They'd have lunch and he could call Nikki, tell her he was coming over, that they needed to talk. It was only another mile away, so it seemed a reasonable plan. But there had been no answer.

Thcy got back a little after two, and Kevin had rung the Frenches' bell. Finding no one at home, Kevin had taken his seat to watch and wait. Jesse had gone off to see if Jack was around and returned a little later to give Kevin some news he didn't need, but which didn't surprise him either. Jesse had called a couple of guys he knew who went to Framingham South High, and another from North. None of them had ever heard of Pete or Doug Starling.

At five-thirty, Nikki's mother pulled into the driveway, but twenty minutes later, she pulled out again, off to meet her doctor boyfriend, Kevin imagined.

He was hungry.

When his mother pulled up in her Ford and started talking about dinner, he couldn't resist. Jesse had left a note saying he was eating at Jack's, so it was just the two of them. Several times, his mother asked if he was feeling all right. Kevin just smiled.

What could he have said? If he tried to explain how he felt, what he was going through, it would be in the simplest of terms. That was the only way he would be comfortable talking about it. But she would have wanted more. He knew that. So he ate his food and smiled, and they talked about his birthday. They were all supposed to go out to dinner for his birthday, and part of Kevin was really looking forward to it.

There would be presents, too.

But none of that seemed very important, or at least their importance paled in comparison to the urgency he felt about Nikki. About what he had to tell her in regard to his own feelings, and Pete's lie.

It was almost dark when he left the house again. He told his mother he was going to walk up to Tommy Carlson's house, since he and Tommy hadn't really talked in a while. Mrs. Murphy thought that was sweet, and the right thing to do. After all, Tommy was his best friend, and it would be too sad if he didn't come to the . . . she almost said party, and Kevin pretended not to notice.

So there was going to be some kind of party for him after all. It was nice, but he didn't feel like he deserved it. He had not been much of a friend to any of them lately, he'd been so wound up about Nikki.

Starting tomorrow, he vowed, all that was going to change. He would tell her how he really felt, she'd probably kick him in the balls, and everything would go back to normal. If he was lucky.

With these thoughts swirling around his head, he walked to the corner and turned down Londonderry, and the first thing he saw was the big Charger sitting in Nikki's driveway.

"Shit," he whispered to himself. It was too late. He'd had a chance, plenty of chances. Times he had glanced at her house and known she was home, and not gone down to talk to her. That once, on Sunday, he had even gone down and tried to tell her, and only ended up pissing her off and not saying what he'd gone there to say in the first place.

Now it was too late.

No way, Kevin thought, gritting his teeth. *No fucking way.* He just was not going to let it be too late. As the sky began to grow dark, he walked boldly down the center of Londonderry Lane.

It was still hot. That kind of summer night where the dark seems to have to fight extra hard, and the sun lingers on the horizon. The pavement was warm beneath the rubber soles of his sneakers. A Datsun went by. The engine noise disappeared too quickly, and Kevin actually turned around to make sure the car hadn't stopped, or just dropped off the edge of the world.

Mrs. French had gone out. For the first time, Kevin found himself hoping to run into Curt and Hugo and Doug. Those guys were goons, but it would mean that Nikki wasn't alone with Pete. Or would it? At least twice before, Pete had sent them off, or taken Nikki elsewhere, so he could have her to himself. Put his hands all over her.

Kevin knew he was going to make an ass out of himself, and he accepted that. Embraced it, really. If Pete wanted to kick his ass, with Nikki right there, he'd screw himself, no matter how mad at Kevin she might already be. Never mind the payback that would come his way.

The more he thought of it, the more he figured this was the best thing. He'd confront them together, and let Pete try to worm his way out of the lie right in front of Nikki. He might sweet talk her if she asked him about it on her own, but with Kevin there to stir things up? Uh-uh.

Maybe he would get his ass kicked. Nikki was worth it.

Jaw clenched, eyes narrowed, Kevin walked into Nikki's driveway, glancing quickly and nervously at the car. It seemed aware of him, somehow. With a quick breath, he started for the front door, determined, angry, and hopelessly in love.

"Don't even fucking think about ringing that bell."

Nikki knew it was going to hurt. All her friends had told her it would. Even her mother had told her. She would probably bleed, too. The smile on her face as Pete touched her felt painted on, so false it might as well have been a mask. But he didn't seem to notice. That was all right. She had made up her mind, and she wanted it to be good for him. After, when the first time was over, and it wasn't such a big deal, she could enjoy it then.

Nikki lay naked in her bed, and Pete was beside her, kissing her all over, his tongue tracing her body. She jumped a little each time he touched her, a delicious thrill running through her body. Her smile was real, then, for a few seconds. She closed her eyes and tried to let herself go, let herself relax. It wasn't the first time he had made her feel this way, but now she knew it was the preamble to something else.

To pain.

Oddly, the pain didn't really bother her. Focusing on it was only her way of avoiding thinking about what was truly haunting her now. Did he really love her, or was Kevin right? Would he use her and then leave? How many girls had he been with? Nikki French had kissed and touched and played with boys with wild abandon since the age of twelve, much too young, according to her mother and a lot of the girls she knew—even some of the guys.

But this was different. This could only happen once, and she had so wanted it to be perfect.

It wasn't going to be. It couldn't be, now. She had realized that earlier in the day; her doubts would not allow it to be perfect. That hope had been cast aside, then, in favor of another, smaller one. If Pete would only stay after, it would be all right. If things weren't perfect the first time, they could make love again and again, and she would understand what all the fuss was about. If he stayed, she knew she wouldn't regret doing what she was about to do.

"Pete," she whispered, her breath coming faster as he slid on top of her, his fingers twining in her hair. "You do love me, don't you?"

"Of course I do," he rasped, kissing her forehead, her eyelids as she closed them.

"Please don't leave me after."

The moment the words were out, she stopped breathing, even believed her heart had stopped beating. She had just handed him all the power in the world, opened herself up to him completely, raw as a wound.

Pete kissed her softly on the mouth as he moved above her, his legs pushing hers apart, his body resting between her thighs. She felt him warm against her.

"After this, we'll never be apart," he promised, his voice a harsh rasp.

Nikki looked into his eyes, searching for the love in that promise, but she saw only sadness there, cold and dark.

* * *

Kevin spun so fast he stumbled over his own feet and nearly fell. At the end of the driveway behind him stood the weasel, Doug Starling, along with Curt and Hugo. Curt had a small grin on his face, and Hugo looked bored, as always.

Where did they come from?

Kevin's gaze darted to the car; but no, he would have heard the doors open. They hadn't been there, hadn't been on the street when he walked down. It just . . .

Impossible. The word came unbidden, but it was exactly right. The bottle crashing from the sky. The coin he dropped, right there on the driveway, which had rolled away and never dropped and might just be rolling still. The raccoon, hit by a car, getting up and walking on. The way the stone Tommy threw that day at the trestle had arced across the highway and gone right through the open window.

Impossible.

His mind went back once more to the streetlight, when he and Tommy had been walking home from Diana's. The stone he'd thrown, flat and sharp, and the way it had cut the end off the bulb. The bulb falling, whole, and shattering on the ground.

Right before the asshole in that car had tried to run him and Tommy over.

Kevin looked again at the Charger in the driveway. It hadn't moved, but there was an energy around it, as though it *could* move. Might do so, at any moment. He looked at that car and he remembered that night, and a horrible certainty came to him.

Maybe Pete was behind the wheel that night, or maybe it had been Doug. More likely the weasel. But it had been *this* car. It might not be true, of course. Anybody could have done it, any asshole nutcase—and there were plenty to go around. But the way that lightbulb had fallen, whole like that? *Impossible.*

And impossible things just seemed to happen around Pete Starling and his friends.

Kevin didn't say anything. Just watched them. For the

second time that day, he thought about the OK Corral. As his gaze shifted from Doug's face to Curt's to Hugo's, something moved up in the sky, in his peripheral vision. Without moving, he glanced up at it.

The largest, whitest owl Kevin had ever seen flew in circles above them.

The light that had burned on the horizon disappeared. It was night now.

Curt broke the silence.

"Kevin. Doug warned you. What are you doing here?"

There was a sympathy in his voice, a sadness, and Kevin felt a tiny spark of hope within him. His eyes locked on Curt now.

"She's my friend," he said, hating the way his voice sounded, the plea inherent in his tone. "I'm visiting, that's all. I just want to see her. She's been calling."

"Not now," Doug spat. "You want to talk to her, come back tomorrow. You can't see her now."

How did you get here? Where did you guys come from? Kevin wanted to ask, but he didn't dare.

"Why not now? Is something . . ."

He wasn't able to finish the question. The grin on Doug's face said it all. Kevin glanced over his shoulder, and his heart sank. In the darkness inside that house, he knew that Nikki was making a terrible mistake.

"You guys are fucking sick," he said, his voice choked.

With a grunt, he turned his back on them, and walked toward Nikki's front steps. Curt reached him first. He felt the huge, orange-haired kid's fingers twine in his hair, and yank his head back, hard. Kevin cried out in pain, but there would be no stopping.

Hugo was next. Curt let Kevin go, but Hugo was there, his sad, dead eyes still showing no emotion as he grabbed Kevin and drove him hard against the metal railing that went up the side of the cement steps. It hurt, and Kevin fought back.

"You asshole!" Kevin shouted, and he swung at Hugo. His hand was slapped away easily, as though he were a mosquito. Hugo grabbed Kevin's shoulders and brought a knee up into his balls. All the air rushed out of his lungs, and Kevin fell there, on the brick steps. Curt loomed above him, a grim expression on his face.

"I thought you were smarter than this, Kevin. Really, I did. Go home, before you really get hurt."

Kevin spat in his face.

Calmly, Curt wiped the spittle from his cheek. His hand came down in a fist. He punched Kevin hard in the jaw, then grabbed him by the shirt and slammed him against the brick. Kevin's skull bounced off the edge of the step, and a moment later, he felt the blood flowing down the back of his neck, getting tacky in his hair.

His lip was bleeding also.

Hugo kicked him in the side, and Kevin leaned over and threw up. He didn't cry, though. Not for them. He wouldn't. The part of him that managed to keep calm, a little primal bit of Kevin Murphy at the back of his brain, wondered why Doug hadn't attacked him. After the previous night on the Murphys' lawn, and all the things Doug had said.

He glanced around. Hugo and Curt had backed off. Doug leaned against the Charger, smoking a cigarette, just watching it all happen. His smile was what did it. Kevin had already surrendered. If they'd just let him go, he had already decided to slink back to his house, and wake up in the morning to rain hell down on these fuckers any way he could manage. Legal or otherwise.

Whatever mistakes Nikki was going to make, it seemed like she'd already made them. Tonight or tomorrow morning, it couldn't make a difference.

But that smile.

Grunting, holding his side and worrying that Hugo had broken his ribs, Kevin got up on his knees on the steps. He reached out for the metal railing and dragged himself to his feet, ignoring the blood on his face and the back of his neck. A little dribble of blood ran down his back, under his T-shirt.

He heard Doug croak, "You've gotta be fucking kidding me."

Then Kevin reached out a finger and pressed the doorbell. He could hear it ring inside.

Doug roared. Kevin turned to see him moving at him, *flying* at him across the lawn. The weasel's feet didn't touch the ground, and he looked more like a weasel than ever. His fingers were hooked into claws and his long, sharp teeth flashed in the moonlight. He barely looked human anymore, and Kevin felt that, somehow, *this* was what Doug really looked like, that he was seeing the weasel for the first time.

"You want to see what's happening?" Doug screeched madly. "You want to know?"

His talons raked Kevin's scalp, then Doug had him by the hair and the leather belt of his jeans. Then he was rising, Doug lifting him up off the ground.

Impossible.

"You want to fucking see?" the creature screamed.

Kevin started to cry. He called out for help from anyone. A car passed, but didn't even slow, as if they couldn't be seen. Impossible. Kevin screamed his throat hoarse.

His face was even with Nikki's window, and he saw her inside, naked, with Pete.

Doug shoved Kevin's face through the glass, then pulled him back so swiftly that he was barely scratched. Small lacerations began to trickle blood. Then Doug dropped him.

Kevin landed on the ground with a grunt of pain. He tried to stand, every fiber of his being screaming at him to run, to get away. But Doug was there beside him, snarling. Doug kicked him in the side of the head, and then Kevin couldn't see anymore.

Where are we going?

The voice is Nikki's. He knows that voice, so sweet, and so familiar. She sounds sleepy, or a little high.

Where are we going?

Second to the right, the other voice responds. *And straight on 'til morning.*

The world came back into focus slowly. Kevin's eyes flickered. The blood was warm on his face, he could taste its copper flavor on his tongue. *How long,* he wondered. *Only a few minutes. Not much more.* The moon was still there, above him, in the same place it had been before.

Not long.

He lay there, bleeding, staring up at the moon. His ears were ringing and the left side of his head was completely numb. He felt like his jaw might be swollen shut. It was almost funny, but his balls barely hurt anymore, there was so much other pain. It had all happened so fast he hadn't been able to hurt, or even hit, any of them. Not one.

The moon stared back at him. Kevin didn't want to move—they might still be there, they might not be done with him—but he had to. Painfully, groaning, he sat up and looked at the driveway. The car was still there, but it had changed. It was still a Charger, but no longer midnight-blue. No longer any color at all, really, if you didn't count the rust and the fire damage.

No tires. Windows smashed. Burned beyond recognition.

Impossible. Only a few minutes had passed.

And the only thought in his head: what if it had always been that way?

Reeling, he lay back again, eyes closed in denial. When he opened them again, there were shadows on the moon. Five of them. Five figures flying across the moon.

One of them was Nikki.

3

A hot, humid breeze billowed the curtains above Kevin's bed. They moved sluggishly, heavy with the moisture saturating the air. The air was oppressive now, though it was still morning, and not much more than eighty. The sun seemed to vow: by noon, you're going to wish you'd never been born.

Unimpressed by the threat of sun and air, birds sat in the ash and oak trees in the Murphys' front yard and sang happily. There were no car sounds outside the window, but somewhere, up the street, a dog barked. There was another distant, yet audible sound: the roll of small wheels on pavement, of ball bearings turning. Andy Cohen was still trying to learn to skateboard, and failing.

Metal popped and banged close by. A couple of sparrows were cooing to one another and romping in the aluminum gutter right above the bedroom window. Eyes still closed, Kevin cursed them. It was important that he stay asleep. As long as he was down there, in the land of dreams, the pain was somewhere else. Not that it had gone away, but it detached from him, somehow, while he slept.

Across the street, Craig Herndon started up his massive truck. The roar of its engine made Kevin wince and narrow his eyes. He was awake, then. Listening. For a moment longer, he was able to pretend to himself that he was still in that dreamworld.

Then the pain came rushing in, and his eyes snapped open.

Kevin lay sprawled across the bed on his stomach,

white sheets wrinkled, one end of the fitted linen popped off a corner and furled back. The red-and-blue spread had been kicked off during the night, as had one of the two pillows he slept on.

There was blood on the sheets.

With a groan, Kevin opened his eyes, tongue roving around his mouth, hoping fruitlessly to be rid of the copper taste he found there. The pain seemed to be everywhere—his back, his side, his face—but mostly in his head. The blood had come from the cut on the back of his head. There were a few stitches there. When he'd slammed his back against the railing, he'd scraped it raw, and that had bled a little, too.

It was perverse, but Kevin welcomed the pain, embraced it, because it was all that kept him from thinking about the events of the previous night. Though he hadn't wanted to frighten his mother, he'd had no choice but to stumble home as best he could. Aileen Murphy had not cried, however; not until she had passed her son into the care of the doctors at Framingham Union Hospital's emergency room. In the face of her son's injuries, she had acted.

When he had come around again, about six in the morning, the stitches in his scalp stinging despite the local anesthetic, the police had been in his room. Nikki's mother had come home from her date to find her daughter gone and a rusted-out hulk of a car mysteriously deposited on her property. At first she had been more annoyed than anything else, and had gone to sleep planning to give Nikki hell in the morning.

But by four a.m., with Nikki still not home, and the car just sitting there . . . the sleepless woman had tried to find a phone number for Peter Starling. Or an address. Or anything at all. And when that had proved impossible, Mrs. French had allowed the fear that had been nipping at the back of her mind to blossom into profound dread and panic.

She had called the police. At first they had insisted she wait twenty-four full hours before filing a missing persons report. But when she had persisted angrily, they had given in just enough to do their own check on the whereabouts of one Peter Starling.

Peter Starling did not exist. Upon the discovery of that particular fact, the police had begun to take Mrs. French's fears more seriously. Of course it was quite possible that Nikki had simply run off with her boyfriend, despite the mystery surrounding his identity.

That was precisely what they had wanted to talk to Kevin about at six o'clock in the morning.

With his mother sitting in a chair in the corner, arms wrapped around her as though she were cold—or simply trying to force herself not to interfere—the two Framingham detectives had questioned him.

Who beat you up?

Where is Nicole French?

What can you tell us about Peter Starling?

That last one had gotten him giggling a little, eyes wide and crazy. Tears had started to spring from his eyes. He could see from the detectives' faces that they knew they were on to something, that he knew more about Nikki's disappearance than he was saying. Kevin had told them that he didn't trust Pete, that he'd gone down to try to talk Nikki into breaking up with him, and that Pete's gang had kicked his ass. He agreed with Nikki's mother, he'd told them. Nikki would never have just left without leaving so much as a note.

You were out the whole time after that? They didn't say anything, or do anything, to give you an idea where they might be headed?

The tears had kept coming, but Kevin had just stared at them, despair and fear flooding his heart. Even though he'd been out, he *had* heard something, hadn't he? Nikki had asked where they were going, and Pete had told her.

The detectives had watched Kevin expectantly, perhaps thinking the sudden change in his behavior meant he'd thought of something that could help. He only shook his head and whispered one word: "Nothing." Shortly thereafter he had asked if he could go home and rest in his own bed. The hospital had discharged him and his mother had driven him. Kevin had slept a few dreamless hours, but that was all he would allow himself.

Now, late Wednesday morning, he let the ache in his body take over. The spike of pain through his head every time he moved helped to blot out the memory of what he'd seen. And he *had* seen it, Kevin had no doubt of that.

Gingerly, he touched his fingers to the stitches on his scalp. As tentatively as he could manage, he stretched. His back popped in half a dozen places, but he could still move. He was alive, and in one piece. An aching piece, but just one. That definitely went into the plus column, considering that the previous night, he'd been half convinced that Doug Starling and the others would kill him.

Out on the street he heard someone swear. Andy falling off his skateboard again, Kevin imagined. He allowed himself a painful half smile. That kid was never going to learn to ride the damn thing. Kevin had given up after his first try. Suicide on wheels, those things. The dog barked. The wind blew through the ash tree, then ruffled the curtains again, and the temperature rose three degrees. It had been a brutal night, and he suspected it was going to be a brutal day.

A tiny knock on his door, not even as loud as the clack of skateboard wheels on pavement outside, told him his mother must have heard him groaning in pain.

"You awake?" she asked, though she must have known the answer or she wouldn't have disturbed him.

Mrs. Murphy pushed the door open, and Kevin gave her a halfhearted smile.

"How are you feeling?" She'd never had much patience with endearments like honey and baby and sweetheart. "I guess it would be a bit ironic to wish you a happy birthday."

Kevin chuckled. "Let's see."

"Happy birthday," his mother said, sympathy etched across her face. "I told you it would be ironic."

She paused after that. He imagined she was waiting for him to ask if the police had caught up to the Starling brothers and their entourage, if they had managed to bring Nikki home. But Kevin wasn't about to ask that. He knew the answer.

"You look a little better," she said, after a long pause.

"It's day," he explained. "Trust me, I still feel like a dump truck ran me over."

Mrs. Murphy winced. That was not what she had wanted to hear. Kevin regretted his words immediately. He had been trying to make light of the situation, but he should have known better. That sort of silliness never worked on his mother. She took everything too much to heart. Even now, she moved to sit at the edge of the bed, looking forlornly at the blood on the sheets.

"So, what about my surprise party?" Kevin asked suddenly.

His mother's eyes went wide. Then she smiled. "I told April you'd know. She said no, that nobody would say anything to you. But I told her. Do you want me to call everyone and tell them not to come?"

Kevin mulled that one over. "Who's everyone?" he asked, frowning painfully.

"Just your best friends," she said. "Tommy and his girlfriend. Dana?"

"Diana," Kevin corrected.

"Why do I always mix her up?" Mrs. Murphy scolded herself. "Anyway, it's the two of them, April and Jack Ross and your brother, of course. Jack was supposed to have—"

She blinked. Swallowed. Smiled sadly. Kevin understood. Jack was supposed to have asked Nikki to come. That statement would undoubtedly have been followed by some comment about the questionable reliability of Jack Ross. But now his mother said nothing, merely looked down at the wood floor.

When she looked up, she was biting her lip. "They'll find her. She'll be okay."

Kevin grunted in response. He knew better than to

argue. Then he'd have to explain why he knew that the cops were not going to find Nikki or Pete or any of the others. And he couldn't do that. Not to his mother.

"I'd like it if they could all still come," Kevin said. "Let me guess? Pizza from the Union House?"

"That was the plan," Mrs. Murphy said happily. "What about now, though? You must be hungry. I have the day off, so take advantage. Do you want eggs?"

"That'd be great, mom," Kevin lied. He wasn't very hungry, but he knew she would feel better if she could think she was doing something for him. He watched as his mother turned to leave the room. Then he called her back. "Mom? Is Jesse home?"

The smile disappeared from her face. "He's still sleeping," she said. "He must have stayed out very late."

"Can you wake him up?" Kevin asked. "I need to talk to him."

Mrs. Murphy frowned. It was an odd request for Kevin to make. Jesse would be up soon. Certainly he should be able to wait. There was more to it than that, however. His mother was pretty smart. She would no doubt consider the possibility that Kevin had kept some information to himself so that he and his brother and their friends could pay Pete Starling and the others back for the beating Kevin had received.

But then her frown disappeared. Just as Kevin had known she would, Mrs. Murphy realized that Kevin would never have withheld information that could have helped Nikki. If it were just that he'd been beaten up, sure. But Nikki had been abducted. That changed everything.

"I might have to splash some cold water on his face," she joked, her tone bittersweet.

"Thanks, mom," Kevin replied.

Jesse dragged himself out of bed at his mother's prodding. His bedroom was opposite the family room in the basement, a hard-won bit of real estate, but Jesse was the oldest, and that alone had given him the victory.

When he was eighteen, he'd move out, and then Kevin could have the basement bedroom for a couple of years if he wanted.

He yawned and scratched his head, then trudged into the bathroom to relieve himself. The phone rang, and he heard his mom answer it upstairs. It might have been related to what happened to Kevin, but it could just as easily be work.

After he'd pulled on some ragged shorts made from sweatpants he'd cut the legs off of, Jesse went upstairs and down the hall to his brother's room. His mouth tasted like aluminum foil and cotton, and the smell of beer lingered in his nose. Too much beer.

His mouth opened and he had actually begun to greet his brother; then Jesse got a good look at Kevin, and stopped short. His smile, and the teasing that would normally have come next, withered and dropped away.

"Hey Jess," Kevin said. His smile was pained. "You look like shit. Late night?"

A deep frown grew slowly on Jesse Murphy's face. It was a look of profound anger. He glanced down the hall behind him, heard his mother still on the phone, and closed Kevin's door. Jesse went over to stand closer to his brother's bed.

"This was that asshole and his buddies?" Jesse demanded.

"They're all pretty much assholes," Kevin pointed out. "But yeah."

"Holy shit," Jesse whispered to himself, shaking his head. "Bro, I'm sorry. I should've stuck around last night."

Kevin shrugged, then winced. Jesse noticed and grew angrier.

"We're gonna fuck 'em up, Kevin. Don't doubt that for a second. Bastards. I'm gonna call Jack right now. There are plenty of guys we can get. We'll figure out where they've taken off to, don't worry."

"They flew."

Jesse blinked. He looked at his brother strangely.

"Yeah, listen, are you sure she didn't just run off with him? I know it's gotta be killing you, but are you—"

"They took her. Away."

"The cops are looking for them, Mom said. We're gonna look for them, too. She'll be okay, Kevin. She'll—"

"They flew."

"What the fuck does that mean, they flew?" Jesse demanded, starting to get irked at his little brother. He knew Kevin was upset, that he was in love with Nikki. He'd gotten the shit kicked out of him for it, and they'd taken her away anyway. But he was just being too bizarre. "Are you sure the doctors should have let you come home? Maybe you've got a concussion or something."

Kevin's expression became grim. Jesse was startled by it, so different was that look from what he'd expected. Anger, yes. Fear for Nikki, sure. But Kevin's features were dark and severe. Almost dangerous.

"I do have a concussion," he told Jesse. "A mild one. And you're not listening, bro. Maybe you don't want to. I understand that. Tell me this much. If I thought I could find her, would you come with me? Would you help?"

"The cops—"

"Will think I'm crazy. And couldn't find her anyway."

Jesse opened his mouth to speak, but only let out a short breath. After a moment, he nodded.

"Of course I'd come with you, you stupid shit," he said, almost embarrassed by the sentiment. "What the hell do you even ask for?"

Suddenly energized, Kevin sat up in bed. As he moved, Jesse noticed the blood on his sheets for the first time. It was upsetting. Too real. His assurances up until that point had been mainly bluster. Not that he wouldn't have gathered up a bunch of people to kick the crap out of Pete Starling, but he didn't have the first clue how to start looking for the guy. Now, though, seeing the blood . . . he thought the look on his face was an exact mirror of his brother's.

As Jesse watched him, Kevin looked out the window. His head dipped down a bit so he could look up at the sky. He was a pretty pitiful sight, sitting there in an Incredible Hulk T-shirt and his Fruit of the Looms. A little kid, still, at least in that outfit. But Jesse knew that Kevin wasn't a little kid anymore.

"Oh, shit, little brother, I'm sorry. I forgot to say 'happy birthday.' "

Kevin laughed. He slid his legs over one side of the bed, then bent and reached for his blue jeans.

"You supposed to be getting up?" Jesse asked with concern. "Your head—"

With a furious scowl, Kevin glared at Jesse. "Just shut up and listen a minute, will you?"

"Hey, what the fuck, Kev? I'm just trying to—"

"They flew. That's what I'm telling you. Whatever the fuck Pete and Doug and those other two goons are, they aren't normal. Not people. Not . . . I don't know if they're even human. They move wrong. Weird things happen when they're around. Impossible things. *And they can fly.*"

Jesse raised his eyebrows. "Uh-huh."

"Just listen," Kevin snapped.

So Jesse listened with growing wonder and astonishment, not merely at the insane ramblings of his brother, but at the total conviction in Kevin's voice. The kid believed it all, without the smallest doubt. And though all of the things that Kevin was saying were impossible, when he was done talking, it was that conviction that made Jesse pause, for just a moment, before allowing himself to remember that it was all bullshit.

"Gimme a fuckin' break," Jesse spat. "Come on, man. When Ma gets off the phone, I think you should go back to the—"

"Where are they, then?"

Jesse stared at Kevin.

"Where are they, Jesse? Pete doesn't have a home. Not that place he told us he lived, and not anywhere else, either. The cops would have found him by now. Or one of them. That's the only reason they're even taking this seriously instead of just thinking like you did, that she ran off with him. They tried to find Pete, and he's like a ghost. Mrs. French is their worst nightmare right now, kicking ass and taking names. I know her. There's no public record anywhere of any of these guys, and they're not going to find one."

"You don't know that," Jesse said, trying to reason with his brother.

"Yeah," Kevin replied flatly. "I do. 'Cause I saw them take her. Remember the car? I told you what happened to it, when they were gone. It looked like it hadn't been driven in ten years, rusted, burned out completely. You can check with the police on that, Jess. Or ask Mom. Or Mrs. French. Explain the car."

Jesse was about to continue the argument, when Kevin came up and stood right in front of him.

"Look at me, man. I know what your brain is trying to tell you. I hurt my head. I was unconscious. All the shit I've read and seen on TV and at the movies," Kevin said, his voice firm yet containing within it the most intimate of pleas.

"Look into my eyes," Kevin demanded.

Jesse did. There were tear streaks on Kevin's cheeks. His face was swollen. But there was no trace of humor, nothing but the deepest sincerity and regret in his eyes, and his voice. Jesse Murphy stared into his little brother's eyes, and his world fell apart.

"Oh, fuck," he whispered, and he sat down on the bed. He glanced up at Kevin, prepared to beg his brother to tell him it was a joke. But those eyes were staring at him, and he knew.

Kevin sat down beside him. He was crying again, but only a bit. With a sniffle, he drew the back of his hand across his eyes.

"She asked him where he was taking her," Kevin said.

Jesse looked up. "You didn't tell me that before."

"Yeah," Kevin replied with a crazy laugh. "I figured if I told you what he said, you'd think I was nuts."

"You are nuts," Jesse confirmed, but they both knew he didn't mean it. "What did he say?"

Kevin glanced down at his hands where they lay curled into helpless fists in his lap. Jesse was suddenly sure he didn't want the answer, didn't want to know.

"Second to the right, and straight on 'til morning," Kevin said, his voice low. "I don't know if you remember, but it's from—"

"*Peter Pan,*" Jesse finished for him. "It's just a book, Kevin."

"A fairy tale," Kevin agreed, nodding. "I know. But do you remember that book about vampires I read last year? It said all legends have their origin somewhere. Not that vampires are real, but that the legends were created as a way for people to explain something else. There may not be vampires or werewolves in the world, or UFOs or Bigfoot either, but any legend that's so widespread, and been believed by so many people, has to have some truth. It has to have started somewhere.

"Maybe the guy who wrote *Peter Pan* knew something, and he wrote this children's story based on it. Maybe it was the only way he could talk about what he knew without people thinking he was nuts. His name is Peter. And what's Starling? Child of the stars or some shit like that, right?"

Jesse shook his head. "No, Kevin. Come on. Fuck you." It was too much. Too much to hear, too much to think, too much to know. Not possible. "No fucking way," he whispered.

Kevin stood up and went to the window, looked up at the sky. At length, he turned to face his brother again.

"No way, huh? Maybe you should tell Nikki that. I need your help, Jesse. I need to know if I can count on you."

April shook her head, offered a short, guttural laugh. "I love you, Kevin. You're one of the best friends I've ever had. But you're out of your mind."

She was all set to laugh again, but there was something in the way he winced, the hurt look in his eyes, that made her stop. She'd halfway believed it was a joke, a complex gag for him to play on his friends on his birthday. Kevin had always been a little odd, so it wouldn't be the biggest surprise in the world.

But it was no joke. She could see that now.

April turned to look at Jack. He noticed her in his peripheral vision, she could see that he did. But he didn't look at her. Just watched the Murphy brothers without expression or comment or judgment. At least, there was no judgment on his face. They'd been dating almost nine months, and yet she didn't really feel like she knew him that well. Everything happened behind those cool blue eyes. But she knew this much: He wasn't going to let it go by without any response at all. Not this . . . insanity.

Tommy Carlson spoke up next. "Jesse, come on, man. Don't tell me you believe this. Somebody's nuts or high, I think, or it's a joke. Not funny, but a joke."

Jesse looked grim. "It's no joke. I went down there to look at the car. The cops had been all through it, but the tow truck hadn't come to take it away yet. I think it's that same Charger, all right. Impossible, but there it is. Me and Kevin went through it. There was a tape in the tape deck. *Get the Knack.* Nikki loved that 'My Sharona' song."

"It was her tape," Kevin told them, every word heavy with emphasis.

April drew a deep breath, completely stumped as to what to do or say next. This get-together, for Kevin's birthday, had been her idea. She had wanted to distract him from his mooning over Nikki. And the party, such as it was, had gone just fine. Tommy and Diana had been a little late, but that was no big deal. April had thought both Kevin and Jesse had been acting a bit weird, but after the cake—after their mother had decided to stop treating it like a fifth-grade birthday, and leave them all alone—things had gotten really bizarre.

While Kevin had gone to make sure Mrs. Murphy wasn't around, Jesse had asked them all to gather around the wrought-iron table on the patio. It was a nice night. Some of those stinky candles were burning to keep the bugs away. It was late, but the sun was just now going down.

Kevin had started to talk. A few times, Jesse looked embarrassed, but he didn't speak up, didn't argue. If it wasn't a game, that left only a few unhappy options.

She shook her head, not even wanting to think about any of those. Her resolve crumbled in seconds as she continued to analyze what Kevin had said. If Nikki was really gone, that would be easy to check. Still . . .

"You're just freaked 'cause you're into her and she took off with that asshole," Tommy said. "I don't want to be a jerk, Kevin, but it happens. I think you've been reading too many comic books, or something."

April bit her lip. She knew how Tommy's words must have hurt Kevin, but she also couldn't really argue with them. Diana, who had sat quietly through the whole thing, reached out for Tommy's hand, her gaze ticking back and forth between Kevin and Jesse.

"It isn't funny," Diana said suddenly.

"It isn't meant to be funny," Kevin replied, face pale and drawn.

"Just stop it!" Diana snapped. "Jesus, you guys have the weirdest sense of humor. If you're right, and she didn't go willingly, this girl could be in serious trouble. She could get raped, even killed. If you really cared about her, it wouldn't be a joke to you."

"It's not a fucking joke!" Kevin cried.

Jesse hushed him. For a few seconds, they all sat in silence, waiting for Mrs. Murphy to come to the door. When there was no sign of her, Kevin let out a long breath, as if he were deflating, and turned to look at them again.

"It isn't a joke, you guys. I'm serious."

April was about to speak up again, but Jack cut her off, finally speaking up.

"What're you gonna do?" he drawled.

Everyone stared at him.

"Jack, what are you thinking? You're not buying this?" Tommy demanded.

With a grin, Jack shrugged and slid a cigarette from the box of Marlboros on the table. "Naw. I think they're both tripping. Or I would, if I thought Kevin would come within a mile of acid. But let's just pretend for a second. You think these guys are, like, vampires or ghouls or something? They took Nikki over the rainbow, right?"

He paused long enough to light the butt; then his grin disappeared. "I've known Nikki longer than anyone here, and I'm pretty sure she'd be happy to go over the rainbow with that asshole. Wouldn't be the first time. But I'm not gonna argue that right now. I just have a question. You really believe this shit, then what are you gonna do about it?"

Jack took a long drag and let the smoke out through his nostrils. While he'd been speaking, he had everyone's attention. April, particularly, was amazed. She figured it was the most she'd ever heard him say at one time. Now, though, her attention went back to Kevin and Jesse. The brothers were looking at each other, as if in confirmation. Kevin had been sitting back from them a bit, arms crossed defiantly. Now he seemed to relax, and pulled the wrought-iron chair forward. He leaned over the table, his expression intense.

"I'm going after her," he said simply.

Diana laughed, sounding a little crazy herself. "How are you planning to do that?"

Jesse sat on the table's edge. "Much as I can't even fucking believe I'm saying this, we think we can follow them."

"But they flew," April said, barely recognizing the sound of her own voice as she engaged in that surreal debate. "You can't do that. You'd have to walk."

Jesse nodded grimly. "We talked about that. Maybe it won't work. But you're right about one thing. We sure as hell can't fly. If it is real, and you have no idea how much I hate that I believe it is, walking's our only shot.

If it doesn't work, if it's all really bullshit, I'll beat the piss out of Kevin myself. But I know I don't have an explanation for any of this. Hell, I'd be happy if one of you does."

Nobody said a word.

Jesse sighed in disappointment. "Jesus. All right, look, we were—"

"Wait," Kevin interrupted, holding up a hand. "It should be me."

With a nod, Jesse stepped away from the table again, taking up a position slightly behind his little brother.

"Tom," Kevin said gravely, staring at his best friend before looking at the others. "Jack. You were there at the trestle that day. Pete said something about us being lucky it happened during the day. They're more dangerous at night. I don't know how or why or what that means, exactly, but I know it's true. They're older. Stronger. Not necessarily human."

He allowed himself a little laugh at that, but there was no amusement in it.

That laugh was what convinced April. It was the same old Kevin. Whether it was real or just fantasy, that didn't matter. It was clear to her in that moment that Kevin, at least, really did believe it all.

"Oh my God," she whispered. April felt like she might cry and brought a hand up to her face just in case. No tears came, but she felt that her cheeks were warm, as though she were blushing, or frightened.

Which she was.

"I need help," Kevin said at last. Then, as though he'd just finished a job, he leaned back in the chair and sprawled there, waiting for a reply.

Tommy swatted at a mosquito on his neck. He looked at Jesse. "You're not really going to do this?"

To April's surprise, Jesse got mad.

"Of course I am," he snapped. "Don't be a dick. You think he's crazy, fine. I'm not sure he isn't. But I really don't know, Tommy, and neither do you. But there's enough here that doesn't make sense that I'm willing to give him the benefit of the doubt. And if he's wrong, if it's just my brother turning psycho, I'll know in the morning, won't I?"

Jesse glared around the table at them. "We'll all know in the morning."

"You mean you're going tonight?" April asked.

Beside her, Jack shifted. Tapped the ash from his butt onto the concrete patio floor. "Gotta go tonight. They've got too much of a head start already."

Slack jawed, April stared at him. But even as she formulated a protest in her mind, something else was happening inside her. She turned to look at Kevin's bruised face and split lip. April had known him since the first grade. When she was fighting with her sisters, or her parents, or sad about a guy, she could always talk to Kevin. He just always seemed to know the right thing to say; he understood people. Sure, he was odd, but in other ways he was the most normal person she knew. He was her closest guy friend, but on top of that, she'd had a little crush on him here and there all through junior high, just as she suspected he'd had on her. It was part of their friendship.

April loved him. Jesse had made it clear he didn't necessarily believe Kevin's story, but he wasn't ready to ignore it either. And Jack . . . what was going on in Jack's head?

"You're going with them?" she asked, a tiny smile on her face.

Jack grinned. "Shit, yeah. If Kevin's psycho, fine. But what if he's not?"

What if he's not? The words reverberated in April's mind. So simple.

Tommy scowled and rose from the table. "You're all psycho." He turned to Diana. "I need to get home. You coming?"

She nodded, and stood to join him. Kevin watched them, his sadness painful to see.

"Hey," he said, voice almost a whisper.

With a sigh, Tommy turned to regard him again.

"Kevin, I'm sorry, man. It's obvious you really believe this shit. We've been friends a long time, so I'm not just gonna say you're out of your mind. But I can see where this is going. It's gonna get crazy from here on out. One way or another, there's going to be trouble. More than likely the kind where you turn out to be a lunatic and everyone gets busted for going AWOL overnight."

"Is that asking so much?" Kevin said, frowning. "You could tell your mother you were gonna sleep here."

"I could," Tommy agreed. Then he shrugged. "But I won't. When you were into Nikki, there wasn't another person on earth as far as you were concerned. Now you need help. All the fucked-up stuff you've read, and you never heard the story of Peter and the Wolf?"

They stared at each other a moment longer. Then Tommy shrugged again, and started across the back lawn to the gap in the trees where he and Kevin had been cutting through to get to each other's houses ever since their moms would let them.

"Sorry," Diana said, her gaze taking in everyone there on the patio. Finally, she looked at Kevin. "I know you're scared for your friend, but I think you need help. I hope you get it."

"I do need help," he told her. "Just not the kind you mean."

A flash of regret crossed her face, then Diana turned and hurried to catch up with her boyfriend. She and Tommy disappeared into the trees. For a minute, no one spoke. April could feel the climate out there, the atmosphere among them changing. It had hurt Kevin to have Tommy walk away like that. But from the looks on Jack and Jesse's faces, it had also damaged the inertia they'd had going.

April jumped up, went over to give Kevin a quick kiss on the cheek. Then she ran after Tommy and Diana, sprinting for the stretch of trees behind the Murphys' house. She wondered, for a moment, if Jack would call out after her, wondering what she was doing. He didn't, of course, and she realized she ought to have known better.

"Diana!" she called as she dashed through the trees and into the backyard that was parallel to the Murphys' on the next street. She thought the family was named Brennan.

"Hey," Diana said as she and Tommy stopped there on the burned-out grass.

The last of the sun had faded away on the horizon, and they stood together in the dark, the shadows only diminished by the purple light of the bug zapper hanging from the Brennans' back porch. They spoke for just a minute, the three of them. Tommy scowled, rolled his eyes, and started to move away. Both girls scolded him for it, and he stood impatiently while they completed their pact.

Moments later, April ran back through the trees and into the Murphys' yard. Kevin, Jesse and Jack were sitting together on the patio, talking quietly. Jack noticed her first, and only nodded toward her to indicate to the others that she was approaching.

"I thought you'd taken off," Kevin told her, obviously pleased to be wrong.

"Here's the deal," April replied. She spoke quickly, not giving herself the chance to change her mind. "Jack, tell your mother you're sleeping here tonight. Jesse, Kev, you guys tell your mom you're staying over at Jack's. Diana just said she'd try to cover for me, so I'm gonna tell my mom I'm sleeping at her house."

"What?" Jack asked, incredulous, his usual cool falling apart. "You can't . . . you should go home."

" 'Cause I don't have a penis?" she demanded, her attention all on Jack now. "Kevin's my friend, Jack. He needs help. Okay, I think Diana's probably right. He's probably beyond our help. But you guys are going, risking getting bagged to see if there's any truth to this shit? Then so am I."

April turned on Jesse and Kevin, finished with Jack but expecting an argument from them as well. Instead,

Kevin looked as though he might cry. He wrapped his arms around her and held her tight.

"Thanks, April. Thank you. I can't promise you won't get in trouble. You probably will. But I swear to you it's all true."

Jesse sighed and shook his head. "Like I said, we'll find out in the morning." He glanced up at the sky, where the stars were beginning to come out en masse.

"If we're gonna do this, we'd better get moving."

4

It was astonishingly easy for them to arrange it. A lie is only difficult to construct when you intend for it to endure. Kevin knew that—warned the others of it, even. None of them had any illusions about what they were doing. It would require a miracle for their deception to go undiscovered. And when it was revealed . . . well, the gravity of their punishment would vary according to the nature of their parents, and how long they remained away from home.

The Murphy brothers would be grounded. Their mother had been through enough heartache with their father that they hated to create more, but it wouldn't be the first time. For Jack Ross, the idea of being grounded—a near certainty—held no particular power. April was not so blasé. The idea of their fourteen-year-old daughter going off on an overnight in the woods with her boyfriend would not sit at all well with her parents.

Kevin and Jesse had rummaged through their closets for backpacks. If they kept walking until morning—even if they called Jesse's friend Greg Esper for a ride home—the soonest they'd be back was midmorning. That meant they would need some supplies, at least for breakfast. While their mother was sitting in her bedroom going through bills with a cigarette in one hand and a Diet Coke on the nightstand, they raided the refrigerator: Chef Boyardee meals and a can opener, a small pot, long wooden matches, half a loaf of bread, a can of Spam and a bag of Oreos. It was not exactly the breakfast of champions, but none of them addressed the possibility that it would not be breakfast at all, but the only food they would have in whatever place awaited them when the sun came up.

All the food went into one backpack. Into the other, they jammed a pair of metal flashlights, clean T-shirts, socks and underwear. Jack made a quick run back to his house for a change of clothes. If they were gone long enough, April would have to deal with dirty clothes, or wear the spares they packed for her. Four sweatshirts went in, just in case it got cold. And a bar of soap.

Just after nine p.m., heavy with the knowledge of the likely repercussions, the four of them walked together up Fox Run Drive to the wooded circle at the top. They paused there for a moment. Kevin leaned his head back and looked at the darkened sky. It was so clear that he saw not only the bright stars, but the tiny pinpricks beyond them, and the distant flickers past even those. The sky was filled with stars; too many, as if those which usually lurked on the far horizon of space had come out to look down upon them in morbid curiosity.

At least, that was how it seemed to Kevin. A rare night, warm and electric.

As he stared up at that beautifully adorned sky, Kevin sensed his brother coming up beside him.

"Know what this reminds me of?" Jesse asked.

Kevin answered without turning. "The night dad left. When I ran away."

It was a private exchange, the sort of thing the two boys would never have said to one another with anyone else around under normal circumstances. But these circumstances were hardly normal. Jack and April were standing just behind them.

"You ran away?" April asked, surprised.

Jack chuckled. "To the tree fort."

A bit embarrassed at how silly it sounded, Kevin smiled. "Yeah. Didn't get very far. I was pretty upset. I don't even really remember much about it, except him leaving, and just taking off." He paused a moment, glanced down at the ground. "Jesse came to find me."

They were all quiet then. Finally, Jesse spoke up.

"Guess we better get a move on, bro."

Kevin nodded.

"How do we know which way to go, Kevin? I mean, what do those directions really mean? Second what to the right?" April asked.

He was self-conscious responding to the question. He knew how foolish it all sounded, particularly when spoken aloud. Peter Pan words; the directions to Neverland.

Then he thought of Nikki. Pictured her in his mind's eye, with her strawberry-blond hair splashing around her shoulders and the way her green eyes seemed to laugh even when she was angry. The perpetual, sardonic lines at the corners of her lips; lips he wanted so much to kiss.

Her tears. Nikki crying on his shoulder, sobbing with the pain of her broken heart. How she had felt in his arms. Maybe it was crazy. He was starting to doubt it himself. They would know in the morning.

"Star," he finally said, clearing his throat and meeting April's inquiring gaze. "Second star to the right. I'm pretty sure that's right."

"The right of what?"

The question had come from Jack. Kevin looked over at him, standing there in the dark at the top of the circle, the moon and stars the only light. He looked almost bored, somehow, standing there waiting for the world to turn, for the adventure to begin. For a fight. Many times, Kevin's mind had pulled an image of Jack into the novels he read. He was the gunfighter, the laconic hero, cool and dangerous. Never had the image been more appropriate than in that moment.

"To the right of what?" Kevin repeated. "God I never even—"

"The moon," Jesse suggested. "Gotta be the moon. It's the biggest thing up there."

"Not the moon," Kevin replied, suddenly sure. "The north star."

They all looked up then at the gleaming beacon of the north star, shining so close it seemed almost unnatural, as if it had been hung there, or shot into space from the earth.

Kevin's eyes drifted to the right. There were an infinite number of stars there. The longer he stared, the more he could see. But it had to be a star bright enough to navigate by. He was sure of that. One. Two.

"That one," he said, and lifted his arm to point.

There was a long pause. At last, Jesse withdrew the two flashlights from his pack. He clicked one on, and handed the other to Jack. Then he hefted his pack and started for the stone wall separating the circle from the thick woods of the state forest. Kevin glanced at Jack and April, saw that they were holding hands, and that Jack had leaned down to kiss her, quickly, and without prompting. It wasn't like him, and the only proof that beneath that cool exterior he was nervous.

Not a gunslinger, but a kid like the rest of them.

"Haul ass," Jack muttered and inclined his head.

Kevin set off after his brother, with Jack and April following. They went up over the short wall and through the trees to the well-worn path they had traveled hundreds of times. Only then did it occur to Kevin that he did not have a compass. He paused, glanced back at April, her big blue eyes watching him expectantly, looking to him for guidance. She had placed herself in his hands, and he'd been stupid enough not even to bring a compass.

"We going?" Jesse asked from up ahead.

He sounded annoyed, on edge. Kevin was used to it. That was how Jesse dealt with feeling anxious or afraid. But his brother's prodding snapped him out of his hesitation. No way was he about to point out the lack of a compass, something they all had likely realized already.

On the wide path, they strained to look up through the trees, and with some effort, found the second star. As if it knew which way they needed to travel, the path curved round to the northeast, leading in that general direction. But there would be times, he knew, when they wouldn't be able to see the sky. When not having a compass would come to be a big deal.

Without another word, he walked on, avoiding rocks and tree roots that were imbedded in the dirt path. The path was wide enough for two, and soon Kevin had caught up to his brother, and they walked side by side, with April and Jack following.

It was their woods. Familiar paths, twists and turns, stone walls and fallen trees. Despite the dark, cut only by the bobbing illumination thrown from the two flash-lights and the stars which dotted the opening in the can-opy above, this was their territory. Kevin was reminded of the fight at the trestle that day, and the way he had felt upon reaching the neighborhood after they had run all the way home. This was sort of like that.

Sort of, but not exactly—this was the opposite. They weren't moving into familiar territory, but out of it, and that unnerved him, that sense of the unknown stretching out before them.

They stopped from time to time, in a field, in a clear-ing with a clumsy stone fire circle built up in its center, on a ridge where the path was wide and the trees not so dense above. Yet they managed to stay on existing trails, paths most of them had walked at least once or twice before.

Soon enough, all that changed. The path they knew curved due west, and a narrower trail went off in an easterly direction. It was barely north, but the only other choice was walking through the trees. They had agreed early on to hold off on that as long as possible. Kevin was reassured when, only a few minutes after branching off, the new trail turned north again. A break in the trees above confirmed it; they were headed in the right direction again.

Some time later, as they stopped to piss for the second time, and even April had gone a ways into the woods to relieve herself, Jesse came up next to Kevin.

"You're an asshole," he said, his voice low.

"Yeah. I'm getting that feeling myself," Kevin agreed.

Then, worriedly, he'd looked up at Jesse's face, hauntingly illuminated from below by the flashlight's glow. "You don't want to turn around, do you?"

"Thought about it a hundred times, but that's not what I meant, Kevin. You're not the only asshole. We didn't bring any water."

Kevin stared at his brother wide-eyed. "Shit."

"Yeah."

April came back to the trail then, and Jesse set off again. Jack looked at Kevin oddly, apparently wondering what the brothers had talked about, but Kevin said nothing. He looked at April.

"You all right?" he asked her.

She laughed. "Fucking crazy. But yeah, I'm okay. It's weird, but its kinda cool, too."

Jesse started to whistle the theme from *The Andy Griffith Show,* and Kevin and Jack joined right in. But a moment later, Kevin stopped whistling.

Cool, April had said. He wanted to let himself think of it that way, but he couldn't. Nikki was in trouble he didn't even dare try to imagine. It shouldn't be fun, what they were doing. They might laugh to assuage their fear, or to hear their own voices, or in disbelief at the lunacy of their journey. But it shouldn't be fun.

They went up a long hill, and across wide open fields. They came to several unfamiliar back roads, and crossed them. Fortunately, and despite Jesse's fears, they crossed two narrow streams, both with small bridges. There, they were able to drink water.

Eventually, inevitably, they ran out of path. Fortunately, the woods had become less dense where they were—*somewhere near the Sudbury line,* Kevin thought—and it wasn't quite as hard as he'd imagined to walk through. But after an hour of that more rugged terrain, Jack called for them to stop. April had to rest.

The guys were glad. All three of them needed to rest as well, but none had wanted to be the first to suggest it. Kevin had lifted his wrist for Jesse to shine the flashlight on, and they were all startled to discover that it was after two o'clock in the morning.

"Only a few more hours," Kevin said, surprised that his voice was hoarse from not speaking. "I guess pretty soon we should stop and eat something."

It was nearly twenty minutes before they stumbled out into a clearing, with a new set of three paths leading away from it. They gathered stones to build a small fire circle—it wouldn't do to set the forest aflame—and kindled a blaze. There, in the little pot they'd brought, they heated two cans of the Chef Boyardee ravioli and shared it around.

As they sat on the hard ground, riddled with rocks and upthrust roots, the fire making them too warm, Kevin began to feel drowsy. Nikki's predicament had previously combined with the adrenaline rush of what they were doing and how much trouble they might get in to keep him awake and alert. But now, he felt his eyes begin to droop. His body tingled lightly all over, in that way it did before he fell asleep, a little bit of novocaine spreading all through him. Kevin glanced over at April, and saw that she was snuggled up to Jack with her eyes closed.

"No!" he snapped suddenly.

April didn't respond.

Kevin got up. "Shit, guys come on. Stay awake. We've got to keep going."

At last, she opened her eyes. Jesse had already stood up and started kicking dirt on the fire. Jack was looking at Kevin without expression.

"Maybe we *should* take a break," Jack suggested. "April's exhausted, man."

"So am I," Kevin replied. He knew that Jack didn't care, that he was only speaking up for April's sake. But he was still a bit angry. "You knew what the deal was when you agreed to come, Jack. We have to go on. Straight on until the sun comes up. I don't know if we should even have stopped, but I guess that's okay, right?

All travelers stop to rest and eat and stuff, right? But we've gotta keep going until it's light."

Kevin knew he was babbling, but he didn't care. His words had the desired effect. April nodded and got up. She kissed Jack on the cheek and started walking after Jesse.

"Let's go," she said. "I'll feel better if we just keep moving. When the sun comes up, I'll get my second wind."

By four thirty, they had stopped twice more to rest, but didn't take the time to build a fire. White-skinned birch trees grew at odd angles, leaning over to lattice themselves into oaks and maples all around. Breaks in the canopy above were few and far between, but they had managed to follow the star with only the occasional unintended detour. Now, though, the stars were beginning to lose their sparkle, the darkness not yet abating, but blurring somehow.

Dawn was not far off, and the thrill was gone. Whatever excitement and trepidation and magic had driven them throughout their long trek to a distant, wooded place, it had dissipated as the night wore on. They spoke less, grumbled more, and laughed not at all as dawn began to approach.

April sensed it very clearly; felt it within herself. Kevin was disheartened, Jack just looked bored. But none of them seemed more affected than Jesse. When he stopped to glance back at them all, she caught a glimpse of his furrowed brow and sour expression. She was almost amused; would have been, if her feet and her back didn't ache so badly, if she couldn't smell the stale aroma of her body, a thin layer of dried sweat built up on her skin.

Much as she liked all three of the guys she was with, April felt strange. She knew she looked like shit. Her hair was in a tangle, her face was a bit grimy, and she'd worn the same clothes for nearly a full day. Not to mention the times she'd had to go off the path and into the trees a ways to pee. It was embarrassing as hell. During the night, when everything had seemed somewhat surreal, and the idea, the possibility, that Kevin might not be out of his mind on this thing made everything crackle with a queer energy, it hadn't bothered her as much.

Now that it was almost over and April felt the urge again, it was too awkward. They had maybe an hour before dawn. She'd hold it if she could. Much as she loved Kevin, she had begun to realize she had been an idiot to insist upon coming along. Particularly because, once he realized how absurd his theory was, he'd be crushed, and none of them would be able to console him.

April wasn't looking forward to it.

Jack wondered how they were going to get home. Right now, though none of them were ready to talk about it. They were pretty fucking lost. No doubt if they kept on the way they were going, or even turned back, it wouldn't be very long before they came upon another road. But even if they did, it was not as though they could call their parents. They would have to hitchhike, or try to track down a friend with a car, which wasn't completely impossible, even first thing in the morning.

Not that he planned to bring it up until day broke and nobody could argue that their quest had failed. If Jack suggested it now, Kevin would be pissed. Another hour wouldn't kill him. He had nothing better to do. Still, he was tired. Jack felt hollow, eyes a little droopy and skin too slack. He'd only had a couple of cigarettes during their trek, but as soon as the sun came up, he planned to light up. It would be over then.

Hands stuffed deep in his pockets, Jack walked a bit more quickly. Beside him, April picked up the pace to keep up. Ahead, Jesse pushed through a low-lying clutch of branches. One of them was shorter than the others, and it whipped loose and struck him in the face.

"Shit!" Jesse hissed.

"You okay?" Kevin asked his brother.

Jesse laughed. "Yeah. Great. Why wouldn't I be?" He turned around to face them, a thin scratch on his cheek. "How the fuck did we let you talk us into this, Kev?"

With the glow of the flashlights flickering as batteries weakened, and the sky beginning to lighten, the brothers looked eerily pale and two-dimensional. The whole forest looked ghostly.

"What?" Kevin replied angrily. "Come on, Jesse. I'm just as tired as you guys. It's not much longer. Morning can't be more than—"

"Oh, enough of that crap," Jesse snapped. "Let's just get it over with. We'll keep going till we find a road, then walk until we find a phone. I think Greg'll come pick us up if I call. You've always been a little freak. Don't know what the fuck I was thinking going along with this shit."

With a grunt, Jesse started moving again. Jack followed, his arm around April, supporting her as much as he could with the branches all around them. She was limping a bit, though she made no complaint about hurting her foot. He wondered if she had even noticed.

Kevin was a good guy, but this whole Peter Pan thing was fucking nuts. Jack had gone along with it because Jesse seemed willing. So much for that now. He had to admit, though, that there had also been a small part of him that was curious. There were a lot of unanswered questions, even impossibilities, about Nikki's taking off with that asshole Starling, and—

April tugged on the back of his dark green T-shirt. Jack stopped and glanced back to see that Kevin hadn't moved. He appeared much the same as he had during the weeks after Mr. Murphy had left the house for good, Jack thought.

"Kevin, come on," April pleaded. "I just . . . I'm so tired. Please."

"You guys?" His voice was small.

"Come on, Kevin!" Jesse called from ahead.

But he kept standing there. Then his eyes ticked over to Jack, who flinched as if Kevin had spat at him.

"Jack, you too? I mean, we're all tired, but what about Nikki?"

Before Jack could respond, Jesse came back through the trees and pushed past him.

"For Christ's sake, Kevin, let's go!" he shouted. "We did what you wanted, okay? We're here. We're assholes for being here, lost in the goddamn woods, but we're here."

"Jesse, don't—"

"Shit, Kevin, I *don't* know what got into me, but I know what got into you. You spent the last two years daydreaming about Nikki's titties and whether or not her bush is just as red as the hair on her head, and now you can't believe she took off with some greaseball and didn't realize how much she was missing even though you never bothered to tell her you were fucking in love with her. You and your drunken fucking hallucinations."

With a growl, Kevin stepped in close, grabbed the front of Jesse's shirt, and threw a wild punch that glanced off Jesse's skull. He went to hit his brother again, but by then, Jesse was reacting. The two of them went down hard amidst the brush and roots. Fists swung and connected with sickening thuds as they rolled around, trying to get the upper hand.

April screamed at them.

Jack waded in. He dropped to his knees and grabbed Kevin by the shoulders, hauling him backward.

"Cut the shit, you guys," he said, voice as flat and cool as ever.

With Jack holding Kevin at bay, Jesse swung and hit Kevin hard in the gut. Kevin cried out. Jack let go of Kevin, reached out and shoved Jesse, who had just come up on his knees, back over on his ass in the brush.

"I said cut the shit!" Jack roared.

That was it. Jack stood up, brushed off his pants, and let his gaze wander out into the woods. He didn't want to look at them. Didn't want to think about any of it. Finally, he went back to April.

"Let's just go," he said. "It'll be light soon."

Above them, the sky was finally beginning to lighten.

*   *   *

Kevin's lip was bleeding and his nose felt swollen. His chest hurt where Jesse had punched him. But he didn't feel any of it. The despair inside him was worse by far. He knelt on the ground for a moment, catching his breath. A hand appeared before him, and he glanced up to see that Jesse was offering to help him up.

"Bro, I'm sorry. I said I'd come. That I'd help you. It's just . . . I feel really stupid now, y'know? Let's just go, all right?"

He sounded so reasonable. Kevin batted his hand away and spat the words "fuck you" with a rasp and a little bit of bloody spittle.

Jesse shook his head, looking guilty and sad and angry and exhausted. Flashlight held in front of him, he turned to follow Jack and April. After a moment, Kevin stood and went after them. He tried his best to prevent it, but couldn't stop the tears that welled in the corners of his eyes. Not one of them fell, however. He wiped them away, took a deep breath, and simply kept on.

It wasn't the fight that had bothered him so much, or even the fact that none of them seemed to believe him at all. He'd half expected that; had considered it next to miraculous that they'd come with him at all. What filled him with such sorrow was that even he didn't believe it anymore. Doug and Hugo and Curt had beat the crap out of him. He'd been delirious when he'd seen them, flying.

"Flying," he whispered. *What the hell was I thinking?*

Even if it were real, he had studiously avoided the knowledge that Starling and the others were following those directions in flight, and walking all night through the woods wasn't likely to do the trick.

The night before, it all seemed so possible to him; so much so, that he had managed to convince the others that he wasn't out of his mind. With all that had happened leading up to his birthday, all he'd seen and suspected . . .

But his birthday was over. All of that seemed so far away.

Embarrassed, aching, missing Nikki so bad it hurt, Kevin trudged after his brother and two friends, who cared for him enough to have done something stupid and dangerous. In his heart, he knew what he had seen and heard was real, as was the shiver that went through him when he thought about the beer bottle falling from the sky, or the way Pete's eyes changed when struck by a certain slant of light. But that was his heart, and even at thirteen—*no, fourteen now*—Kevin knew that human hearts were often blind and stupid.

The woods thinned out a bit. They crossed a short stone wall marking the outer edge of some long ago farmer's property, and then a small stream where they stopped to drink. It was still growing lighter. In the sky, most of the stars were no longer visible, but the north star remained. Still, Kevin had been glancing up at one spot in the sky so long that he felt sure they were on course. Not that it mattered anymore. The first road they came to, it would all be over. Part of him didn't even care, longing only for sleep and an end to things.

April dropped back to walk beside him, now that they could move more easily through the trees. Kevin glanced up once, saw her watching him from beneath her long eyelashes, and the fine brown hair that hung like a veil across them. He studied her eyes in that half-light and was disappointed that it was not yet bright enough for him to see the flecks of silver and gold in them. He had always thought there was something magical about those kaleidoscope eyes, always so far away.

Oddly enough, as he studied her now, Kevin realized that it was the first time he had ever looked at April's eyes and not seen that distant, haunted aspect in them. Tired as she was, April seemed fully *there,* not dreaming about a place she'd rather be, for the first time in as long as he could remember.

"You okay?" she asked, in that rasp that was so pleasing and familiar.

With a grimace, Kevin shrugged, forgetting about her

eyes as he was overwhelmed by his guilt for putting her
in this jam to begin with. "I'm sorry," was all he said.

He felt her fingers touching his, and he slipped his
hand into hers and squeezed.

"Don't be," she said. "Something happened. I believe
that much. Something impossible and too weird for us
to ever understand. I believe you saw the things you
saw, or something just as strange. But we're just people,
Kevin. We're just kids. If those guys were more than
that, I think wherever they are now, it isn't a place we
can just walk to. I don't think I'd feel like this, then."

"Feel like what?" Kevin asked, his heart swelling with
her warmth. He had thought she might hate him for this
awful night.

"Like shit," she said and laughed. "Like I've spent
the last seven hours walking, off and on, through mud
and woods and fields."

"All for some girl you don't even know," Kevin
added somberly.

"I didn't do it for her," April said, her tone implying
that Kevin wasn't all that bright. "I did it for you.
'Course I'm gonna kill you later, but it'll be all right."

Kevin paused, looked up at April breathlessly, his
chest contracting, retreating from the pain that filled
him.

"You don't think I'm crazy, then. You don't think she
just took off with him, like Jesse does?"

"Jesse *doesn't* think that. He's mad now, and tired,
but he wouldn't have come out here if he didn't believe
you at least a little bit. He's your brother. Jack and I
are your friends. We know you, Kevin. You may live in
weird books and stuff, but you know the difference between that and real life."

Kevin sighed, and nodded thankfully, though in truth,
he wasn't as certain of that as April seemed to be.
Slowly, her fingers slipped from his grasp. They walked
on together.

"Thanks, April. Guess I should've fallen in love with
you instead, huh?"

She laughed. "Nah. I just would've broken your heart. It's what I do."

Kevin chuckled drily, but he glanced ahead through the trees at Jesse and Jack, who were perhaps twenty feet ahead of them. April was right. Breaking hearts was what she did. Kevin thought that maybe that was why he had never really tried to get her to go out with him. When you were with a girl you wanted to love you, and she always seemed as if she was somewhere else . . . no wonder she had never kept a boyfriend more than a month before Jack. It made Kevin realize that April's relationship with Jack was doomed too, and he was sad for both of them.

The land began to slope upward, and a few minutes later, Kevin looked through the trees ahead and saw a field. Its crop was green and low to the ground, but he couldn't have said what it was, particularly not in the dim predawn light. The four of them emerged from the woods and started up the slope. A dirt path left by a tractor went up the center of the field, and they followed it to the crest of the hill.

"Finally," Jesse said.

Kevin stepped up beside him. Beneath them, down the other side of the hill, was a rambling old farmhouse with lights already burning inside. Beyond that was a narrow road. As they watched, a pickup truck rumbled by on the pavement. The windows were open, and they could hear Kenny Rogers crooning on the radio, the music drifting up to them.

The four of them stood side by side, there on the crest of the hill, with the heavens quickly brightening. On the eastern horizon, off to their right, the sky had turned bright pink, burning. In minutes, the sun would peek over the trees. Dawn had come.

It was morning.

"I guess that's it," Kevin said, his voice breaking. "I'm sorry, you guys."

The very top edge of the sun seared the treetops, and

Kevin brought a hand up to shield his eyes, and maybe to hide them from the others. Jesse patted him on the back.

"Come on, bro," he said. "Let's go home."

Kevin nodded. He looked up at the sun one more time.

It disappeared. Blinked out as if it had never been there. Blotted out by a solid wall of black ink that filled the sky and then began to sweep across it in a crashing wave of darkness.

"Oh my God," Jesse whispered.

April clutched Jack tightly. "What is it?" she asked.

But that wasn't all that was changing. In the sky, the darkness swept toward them. Beneath it, the field changed as well. What had been some kind of harmless-looking green crop became windblown, ravaged-looking land.

"Run!" April screamed. "We've got to run."

"Where would we go?" Kevin asked quietly.

More than that, though, he knew they *couldn't* run. This was why they had come, after all.

A cold, arctic wind splashed against their faces. Kevin shuddered, gooseflesh rising on his arms, and hugged himself against the cold. The dark spilled across the sky like an oil slick. Soon it was right above them. The land beneath their feet changed without a sound, without even a ripple or rumble that wasn't caused by the wind. It was impossible, of course.

Like magic.

"Guys. Look," Jack said.

They followed his gaze. He was staring down the hill. The truck and the farmhouse and the road were gone. Even the land was gone. The hill dropped away to a stone cliff face, and the cliffs dropped away to an ocean crashing with whitecaps. Rock formations jutted from the water, some of them so tall they were nearly even with the hill. Kevin could see ice on the stone towers out there on the water.

On the western horizon, the last of the dawn was swept away, swept back into night and darkness, into the world that was all they had ever known before now.

In his brother's face, Kevin saw horror and disbelief,

but also a kind of readiness. Jesse was prepared to do something to fix it, to make it go away, to make it over. Beside him, Jack's eyes were wide and haunted.

Of all of them, it was April who surprised Kevin. Her expression was serene and filled with wonder. She glanced around just as rapidly as the others, but there was a kind of frisson of excitement in the air about her. "It's real," she whispered. "You can smell the ocean. The wind . . . oh my God . . ."

She laughed brightly. Kevin wanted to think there was a little madness in that laugh, but he sensed none. April was entranced by their new surroundings. With an awed shake of her head she moved to Kevin and put a friendly arm around him.

"You got what you wanted, Kevin," she said airily. " 'Cause we sure as hell aren't in Kansas anymore."

Jesse snorted derisively. "No shit. So what do we do now?" His voice was hollow, and as cold as the wind that threatened to sweep them all off the land's end, or to freeze them blue where they stood.

"Kevin?" he prodded.

"Now we find Nikki, and we bring her home," Kevin said, as though it were the simplest thing in the world.

He glanced at Jack, but Jack wasn't looking at him anymore. He was staring east, toward the tree line where the darkness had first blotted out the sun. Kevin turned to see what had claimed his attention. At first, he saw nothing, just shadows on top of shadows.

Then it moved.

A rider on horseback, a huge man, to judge by his silhouette. Suddenly, he wasn't alone. There were three, then five, then eight. Kevin took a step backward, suddenly feeling all the exhaustion of their night's long trek catch up to him at once.

"Do we run?" April whispered.

"Fuck yes," Kevin croaked.

The lead rider screamed something unintelligible and began to gallop toward them with the others falling in behind.

Book Three:
Over the Hills and Far Away

1

The fire was wrong.

Nikki had noticed that right away, yet instead of growing more used to it, the simple wrongness of it bothered her more and more as the hours passed.

It would have been easy for her to pretend the world around her was her own. Despite its grandeur, the house was normal enough. On the walls were hung paintings of haunted seascapes and dark, mounted hunters. The home itself was built of stone, but not the rough-hewn rock she might have imagined. Instead, this was a structure of great artistry, with high, arched windows of thick, clear glass. There were finely spun carpets on the cold, wide-pine floor—though set far enough from the fire so as to avoid an errant spark—and an extraordinary tapestry on one wall, depicting a human form in flight, silhouetted against a blue moon.

Her bed was luxurious, crafted of mahogany, with four tapered posts and a canopy of fine lace. The spread and pillows were stuffed thick with down. Her chamber might have been a young girl's fantasy, a vacation to a far off, exotic region she and her mother would never visit, save for the fact that the thick pine door with its iron hinges and straps was locked.

Nikki was a prisoner.

Even then, it might have been the world of her birth, the world she knew as reality . . . if not for the fire.

She was sleepy again. It was hard for her to know

when to rest and when to rise. The sun had peeked
through only once for a few scant seconds since she had
been locked away in that room. Her heart now dulled,
her eyes now exhausted of tears, she lay on her belly on
the bed and watched the fire. Orange and green and
blue and candy apple red, the fire burned, the embers
danced and twirled about one another in the enormous
cave of a fireplace set into the wall of her chamber.

Alive. Each little tongue of flame was a creature unto
itself. A fire sprite or some other simple being, together
forming a blaze. Impossible, of course, and she could
make out no detail that made truth of her fancy, but
nor would she rule it out.

Nor *could* she rule it out. Not after having seen the
things that stoked the fire, and brought her meals. Low
to the ground, with skin like leather, glowing black in
the flickering firelight, they moved in and out of her
room with only the simplest noises, a grunt, a snuffle, a
tiny growl. They were shaped like men, but men whose
features and forms had been scrawled on paper by
angry children.

Cruel things, they were. That was obvious just to look
at them.

Worse, though, was the shadow in the hall.

Even now, with the warmth of her fire, and the plush
bed beneath her, Nikki shivered and almost whimpered
at the thought of the thing beyond her door. A thing
she had never seen, save for its eyes. It whispered, there
in the hall, but she couldn't be sure if that was its voice
or the sound of its moving. Each time her door opened,
she saw it only as a shape, a ghastly haunt, there in the
dark of the corridor beyond her door, with its mirrors
and ornate furnishings.

It loved her.

That was the worst of it, really. Nikki felt it watching
her, but not with lust or cruel intent. In some way, she
knew that those eyes coveted her, the way they might
one of the fine paintings or tapestries or vases in this

home. But it would destroy her in an instant if she tried to leave.

Not once since her arrival had Pete come to see her. Nor had she had a visit from any of the others. Alone, with only the horrid little creatures she had come to think of as goblins for company, and the dancing fire.

Nikki thought of her mother, and regretted the fear she knew her disappearance must be causing. She thought of Kevin, and wanted badly to tell him she was sorry. That he had been right. The simple thought that she would never see him again caused her an acute pain like nothing she had ever known. Part of it was that she missed him, yes, but another was the knowledge that she had hurt him. It grieved her.

Mostly, she wondered if she were crazy. It might be as simple as that.

Suddenly, she didn't want to fall asleep anymore. She stood and walked to one of the high, arched windows. Drawing back the iron latch, she pulled the windows open and felt the icy breeze rush in. The fire crackled behind her, attempting to fight off this intrusion, perhaps even a bit angry with her.

The cold was bracing, exhilarating. Nikki was instantly more awake than she'd been all during that long, terrifying night. As she surveyed the landscape beneath the window, her eyes widened. The enormous estate sat upon a tumble of rock too cold and raw to be called an island. Starling's home protruded from the water as though it had been placed there by giant hands, the ocean crashing against its cliffs.

With the bright, ice-blue moon shining above, the black water below, the islands that thrust from the sea beyond her window—little more than massive stone pillars—reminded her of parts of Arizona she'd seen once on a family trip, back when her father had still loved them enough to stay. Red Rocks, she thought it was called. But here it was as if that harsh landscape had been flooded by the ocean, and then flash frozen.

Flash frozen. Despite the fire blazing in her chamber,

Nikki could see her breath outside the window. On the cliffs below, ice draped the rocks like wet sand dripped down onto a child's clumsy sand castle. Her gaze ranged across the choppy water to the shore . . . what shore there was. The mainland rose up from the sea just as violently as the pillars did, as though a blade much sharper than mere erosion had dropped from the heavens to cleave off the edge of the land, leaving only harsh cliffs and ledges behind.

And the ice. Plenty of ice.

Snow would have made it easier to look at, Nikki thought. Even pretty. But this frozen, dead view elicited only despair as she stared out at the night, her breath fogging, her eyelashes beginning to stick together when she blinked.

It might have been tears, turning to ice.

The cold had done its work, however. For the first time since the nightmare had begun, Nikki felt truly awake and aware. Her fear and sorrow were matched only by her rage at Pete for using her so badly, and for bringing her here.

Wherever *here* was.

Though she did not know if it had been his doing, or simply her own mental defense mechanism, Nikki had been nearly delirious while they traveled here.

While they flew.

A numbness unrelated to the cold outside the window spread through her as the memory of flying filtered into her mind. The lightness of her body, the cold firmness of Pete's fingers twined in her own. The lights of Framingham disappearing behind her, wind tossing her red hair wildly around her face. The stars above guiding the way. Flying.

"Now what's this?"

With a ragged intake of breath, Nikki snapped from the near paralysis she had sunken into, and spun to see Doug standing just inside the door to her chamber. Her stomach churned and tightened.

"You don't wanna jump, believe me," he told her, feigning concern. "It's a loooong way down."

Her expression hardened. Nostrils flared. "I wasn't going to jump."

"No? Pity. Well, then, you should get away from the window before you catch your death. The fire inside, the cold outside. Fuckin' pneumonia, y'know?"

Nikki moved to her left, putting her canopied bed between herself and Doug, trying to make it seem as non-chalant as possible. The flash of anger in his eyes told her she had failed. His hair was greasier than ever, but there was more to it than that.

He didn't look human.

Oh, he still looked like himself, pretty much. That straight, thin nose, the tiny, insinuating eyes. The false smile that poorly hid the malice in his heart. But his teeth were longer, his face more savage somehow. Subtle differences, but they identified him as something *else*.

Surprising herself, Nikki had gotten used to that thought. Once she had slept with Pete . . . *and the memory of him was fresh and clear, the warmth of him, his hands on her, him moving inside her, the tenderness in his eyes, the sweet lie of it all . . .* they had stolen her away. Before she had been locked up here, she had gotten a good look at all four of them, seen that they were different.

Nikki had stripped off her dirty clothes when they'd first locked her in that room and dressed in a thick cotton nightgown with a light flower pattern sewn into it. It had crossed her mind that she might wash her clothes in the water provided for her bath and dry them out by the fire. Now, with Doug eyeing her so openly, lascivious grin on his face, she wished she had done exactly that. She wanted clothes, blue jeans and a shirt and sneakers under her feet. Not that she was naked, but she might as well be.

"You know, you're not exactly being very hospitable. I mean, here you're living like a princess, and you can't even invite a visitor in. Maybe give me a little thank-you," Doug said, adding that last almost as an after-thought.

He laughed a little, apparently amused by what he considered his own cleverness.

Nikki flinched at the sound. So many responses came into her head, some of them angry, some of them pleading, others defensive, using Pete's interest in her as some kind of shield. What came out was none of those things. Nikki French wasn't going to be intimidated by whatever the hell Doug was. They might have her, but they'd never get her.

"Fuck you, you little cocksucker," she snarled.

With a growl, Doug came for her. He tore through the lace around the bed, clambering over it. Nikki thought to outrun him, to race around the other side and maybe even make it out into the hallway. The shadow thing out there might have let down its guard, with Doug coming in. She ran past the open windows, the chill breeze ruffling her nightgown, then the fire.

Doug caught her before she got any farther. His talons sliced the fabric and the skin beneath as he grabbed her and spun her to face him. Nikki recoiled at the stench of his breath, barely responding to the pain of the scratches on her upper arms.

"Get off me!" she screamed at him.

Doug, the greasy little darkling creature that he was, only smiled.

"My brother touched you. More than touched. But I'm not worthy, is that it?" he sneered, lips curling back from sharp yellow teeth.

"That's it," she agreed, refusing to be cowed.

Without a sound, and yet with uncanny speed, he drew back his right hand with its tapered claws and gave her a savage backhand across the face. Nikki went down hard on the wide-pine floor, and all her courage left her. It poured out of her as though bleeding from a wound in her soul. She shivered, whimpered, bit her lip to fight back the tears that threatened to spill down her cheeks.

An upward glance, and she was looking into the fire

once more. It had grown dark, reflecting her fear and the hostility in the room. The violence. The little spurts of flame she had thought alive no longer seemed to be dancing, but lashing out, cinders tearing one another to smoke and ash.

Doug pounced on her from behind, drove her against the floor. Her cheek hit the wood hard, bounced. The pain drove the tears away, somehow; perhaps the shock. His hands, too strong to be human, tore at her nightgown, hauling it up, his fingers probing.

Nikki screamed. Ashamed, she cried out for help.

The heavy wooden door crashed open as though a gale were driving it. Doug looked up, furious, then scrambled back away from Nikki—or more likely from the door—in fear.

For just a moment, she glimpsed the shadow thing in the hall, her keeper, slithering into the room. Then, abruptly, the fire died, snuffed in an instant. The room was plunged into darkness broken not even by the light of the moon through the open window.

Sitting upright, Nikki held her hands out in front of her, trying to feel something, anything in the dark. She heard Doug scream, and she slid her butt backward across the floor, away from him, until her back was pressed against the warm stone of the fireplace.

There came to her ears the sounds of a struggle. Of boots stamping the wooden floor. Of muffled shouts for mercy. The open windows swung in the wind, banging, glass rattling. Despite the warmth at her back, Nikki felt the icy wind cut her deeply.

Something was dragged across the floor. The door slammed, and then there was only silence.

Yet, still, she was not alone. She sensed it, could almost see the shape of someone else moving in the darkness, and prayed that somehow it would be neither Doug nor the shadow thing that had come to her aid.

"Hello?" she put forth, tentatively, into the gloom.

He was right beside her then. She could hear him

breathing, though the room was cast in pitch so dark she could not even make out the twinkle of his eyes.

"Come now, my friends. Don't be afraid. Our guest needs you," he whispered.

His voice was so soft and kind and familiar, it made her want to cry.

A single ember began to burn in the fireplace. Then another, and another, and soon a blaze of dancing sprites roared and crackled. In the firelight, trembling like an anxious heart, she looked up into the face of her lover, Peter Starling, now forever changed. As with his brother, whatever glamour had masked Pete's true features had fallen away. His teeth were savagely sharp, his eyes blazed, his ears were slightly pointed at the tips, and his fingers ended in sharp claws.

"Nikki," he said, greeting her with the eyes and voice of her lover.

With a cry of grief and rage, she balled her fist and knocked him on his ass.

Nikki tried to shake the pain out of her knuckles, even as Pete rose up quickly, teeth bared, eyes narrowed with fury. She thought he might kill her. When she blinked, the moment had passed. Pete stood and walked slowly to the window, where the wintry breeze was still swirling in. He grabbed both sides of the open window and swung them shut again, latching them carefully.

Pete turned and looked at Nikki, no emotion at all on his face.

"Doug is going to be punished for coming here. You should know that," he said.

Though she made no response, Nikki was glad.

"He's never done anything like that before," Pete continued, almost talking to himself. "That kind of behavior just can't be tolerated." His gaze moved to her face, her eyes. "You must have so many questions. I know that."

"Where is this?" she demanded.

"Yes. I thought that would be the first one."

"You're not talking the same. Like you have a weird

accent or something. Who are you? *What* the hell are you?"

Pete nodded slowly. "That's why I'm here. To tell you all of that."

As the fire burned, and Nikki became drowsy with the heat, her eyelids heavy as her heart, Pete did exactly that.

For the first time in recent memory, Kevin wasn't thinking about Nikki. Not at all. He was not thinking about the extraordinary nature of his surroundings, and the way the landscape had transformed in a wave across the sky and beneath his feet—the incredible, impossible way the world had changed.

Mainly, he was thinking about staying alive.

April stumbled and fell. Kevin hesitated, tempted to keep running. But he couldn't just leave her there. Jack had stopped immediately, reaching down for April and hauling her to her feet again. Kevin grabbed her other arm, and then the two of them were running with her between them.

Jack was silent, his face grimly stoic.

April sobbed, all the sense of wonder she had exhibited upon their arrival in this world burned away by fear. "I . . . can't. You guys, I can't run. My legs—"

"Run!" Jack snapped furiously.

"You've got to run, April," Kevin told her.

"Maybe," she said breathlessly, "maybe they're not going to hurt us. How do we . . ."

Her words trailed off. Her lower lip quivered and then stiffened, her chin dimpling. She ran between them and no longer needed their support. Kevin was glad. He didn't think he could make her run if she decided she couldn't, but he knew he would not have been able to live with himself if he left her behind.

And he didn't want to die.

Kevin smelled the salt in the air, and other things as well. Smoke from a fire, somewhere far off, and the stench of manure nearby. He glanced down as the smell became stronger, watching for mounds of dung he reasoned had probably been left behind by the horses that now pursued them.

The sound of the surf seemed omnipresent, inescapable, and it kept drawing his gaze out to the ocean. On several of the stone towers that thrust out from the water, he could see houses. Huge, rambling mansions, with lights in some of the windows. Before he could spare a second on curiosity, however, he heard the cries and screams of the hunters behind him. They were closer.

Gaining.

Hooves clattered on frozen ground.

He didn't dare look back, for fear of falling. But there was more to his reluctance than that. If he had to see them in that moment, with their heavy leather garments and the helmets adorned with antlers, and the way their eyes burned red in the darkness—it was not a trick of the light; he wasn't foolish enough to believe that—if he had to look, he knew that he might just surrender. Just stop and let them catch him.

Just die.

He could hear them shouting to one another, the barking commands and triumphant cries of the hunter. They were close enough now that the grunts and snorts of the horses carried to Kevin and the others as well.

The wind picked up off the ocean, blowing up over the cliffs and cutting through him in an instant. It had been there all along, of course, but running, adrenaline flowing, he had blocked it out. And just as the cold hit him suddenly, touching him, grabbing hold and refusing to be ignored, so did his fear.

It was *his* fault. That was what tore at his mind now. Whatever happened to them, it was his fault.

Kevin's foot slipped into a hole and he stumbled, fell and hit the frozen ground hard, scraping his hands and tearing his pants. Momentum carried him into a somersault, and then, incredibly, he was on his feet again.

The screams behind him, savage and filled with blood lust, were closer.

"Kevin!" Jack yelled off to his left. "This way!"

Jesse had made a turn for the woods off to the west. Initially, fear had driven them toward the distant southern edge of the clearing, as it was directly opposite the hunters. Kevin cursed himself and the others for their stupidity. Jesse was nearly at the western tree line, with Jack and April close behind. With his fall, Kevin had lost ground.

Now he turned to run after the others. Ahead, he heard April cry out in alarm and he glanced about, trying to find his friends in the darkness of the forest, the tree line only a few yards distant.

Horses thundered up behind him, too close.

"Hold there, boy! Stand fast, or I'll have your head!" roared a voice.

Kevin turned and stared up at them gathered there. Six. No, seven. They were horrid creatures, huge and yet somehow withered, with skin like worn, mottled leather, and twisted features. Their mouths were too wide, teeth far too numerous, stretched into hyena grins. Boar tusks jutted up on either side of their long snouts. Their arms were too long by far, their hands disproportionately large. In a fist, they would be able to crush a human head.

"Ha!" barked one of the hunters, a creature whose chin glistened with drool. It watched Kevin with great amusement, one eye drooping slightly. "You'll have his head whatever he does, Farragher. And his guts for garters besides."

There was a snuffling that Kevin knew must be laughter. The hunters nudged their horses toward him slowly. He backed up toward the trees. His bladder ached, and he discovered he needed to pee quite badly. The huge hunter who had first spoken, Farragher, dismounted with a grunt like the snort of a bull. He was the largest of them, with massive, quivering jowls. The tip of one of his tusks was snapped off near the top.

Kevin's eyes darted from hunter to hunter like a cornered fox. In his mind, in his heart, he had given up. They had him. There was nowhere left to run. The best he could hope for was that the others had gotten away.

At which thought, he was startled by a hand clamping on his shoulder from behind. He turned quickly and saw that Jesse had emerged from the trees, looking wild and furious.

"What the fuck you waiting for?" he snapped.

Then Jesse hauled on his arm, and Kevin found himself stumbling into the trees, tripping on undergrowth, branches slapping and scratching at his face. He heard the bellow of rage from behind, as Farragher crashed into the trees after them. The other hunters would not be able to enter the wood on their horses, and it would cost them precious seconds to dismount. But Kevin didn't think Farragher was going to need their help.

"Jesse, you should have kept going. We're both dead now," Kevin huffed as he ran.

"Shut up," Jesse snapped. "Just run."

A moment later, Kevin felt himself tugged off to the right. Jesse yelled "Here!" and shoved him onto his knees in the dirt among the trees. At first, Kevin didn't know what he was supposed to do. Then he noticed that the huge tree before him had a hole in its trunk, barely big enough for Jesse to squeeze through, and certainly not large enough for Farragher.

On the other hand, Farragher had an axe.

"Go!" Jesse shouted.

Kevin scrambled through the hole, headfirst, and realized too late that it was not meant to be entered in that fashion. Rather than climbing up into the tree, he found himself moving down into a hole in the ground. A passage in dirt that gave way quickly to smooth stone.

He was sliding.

Screaming.

It was a short trip. Kevin tumbled out of the narrow passage into a rocky tunnel, scraping his chin and cheek on the stone floor. He bit his tongue as his chin banged the ground, and he tasted coppery blood in his mouth. But he was alive down there, while Farragher was still above. With Jesse.

Alarmed, Kevin turned, but only in time to see his brother drop, feetfirst, from the hole in the wall a few feet above the ground. Dirt slid down the hole after Jesse, and Kevin could hear Farragher howling above them. He imagined the slobber on the beast's quivering jowls and shuddered in revulsion and relief.

Kevin glanced around the tunnel, which he thought might actually be a fissure torn in the rock around them by some violent tremor. The thought was disturbing, because it implied that the fissure could be closed up just as quickly and violently. Unnatural light shone from somewhere down the north end of the tunnel.

"Don't worry," Jesse said. "They can't get down here. They're too big."

Kevin nodded anxiously. "Just the same, is there a way out of here?"

"That way," Jesse said, and pointed down the tunnel in the direction from which the light was weakly emanating. "Follow Toska."

"Toska?" Kevin asked, frowning, distracted by the roaring of the hunters up above.

Then he narrowed his eyes and gazed along the tunnel, and the hunters were forgotten. The thing that crouched in the tunnel was gray, and had blended almost completely with the stone, such that Kevin had not seen it at first. Its legs were short and bent into haunches like those of a dog or wolf. Its arms, if they were arms rather than forelegs, were long and thin almost like an orangutan's. A fine coat of fur gave off a dull sheen. If not for the glint of devious intelligence in its eyes, then its black eyes, snout, and bared, glistening teeth would have reminded Kevin somewhat unsettlingly of a seal or walrus.

Now it blinked and scrabbled at the stone as if urging them to follow.

"Toska?" Kevin asked.

"Yeah," the creature barked, the sound reinforcing the mental image of a seal. "What of it?"

It turned and went down the tunnel, sliding on its belly on the stone. Now that it was moving, Kevin caught the creature's damp odor, a mixture of gasoline and the ocean at low tide. Bewildered, Kevin turned to look at Jesse, who urged him on. More dirt slid down the hole in the tree above them, and Kevin could only imagine the hunters were still trying to dig their way in.

Toska had moved on quickly, and Kevin and Jesse had to hurry to catch up.

2

Toska led them along the underground passage, with its mysterious illumination. Kevin studied the rock formations around him and began to think the tunnel was probably part of a warren of caves. There were signs all around that others had passed that way. He thought, for a moment, of the cartoon version of *Journey to the Center of the Earth* that he'd always loved, the one with a duck named Gertrude. The memory struck him oddly, out of place as it was, and he felt keenly the distance, real or imagined, from the comfortably musty basement where he'd watched those old cartoons.

He shook himself out of that melancholy and followed Toska down the tunnel, Jesse bringing up the rear. In less than a minute, they reached a junction where the source of the weird underground luminescence was revealed. Veins of mineral deposits which gave off their own light striated the walls, stretching on down the tunnel from the junction, as far ahead as they could see.

"Wow," Kevin muttered.

"Yeah, cool isn't it?" said a familiar female voice.

He glanced up and, with a sigh of relief, saw April and Jack standing together against the far wall, hand in hand. They both looked nervous, even scared, but had been silent until they knew it was their friends coming down the tunnel, and not those damned hunters. One of the backpacks lay open at Jack's feet, and he and April had put on two of the sweatshirts they had brought. Jack tossed one each to Kevin and Jesse, who slipped them on quickly, though it was warmer below than above.

"God, I can't believe we're all okay," Kevin said, incredulous. Hc felt as though he should hug April, but she and Jack were holding on to each other tight as a lifeline, and he didn't want to break that.

"You guys weren't that far ahead of me," he said, glancing at Toska. "How did—"

"Toska met us at the edge of the woods," Jesse explained. "Led us to the tree. He wanted me to go down with them, but . . ."

Jesse did not finish, but he didn't have to. Kevin understood. His brother had come back for him, even though the hunters were there, only feet away. Monsters in the flesh, but Jesse had come back for him.

"Thanks, bro," Kevin said gently.

Jesse looked away, nodding, uncomfortable with the intimacy.

"He brought us down here, 'cause there was light," April continued. "Then he went back for you guys."

Toska barked again. "Didn't think you'd make it."

Kevin studied him again. In the brighter light, the bizarre wrongness of his body was even more pronounced. It was as though some mad doctor had genetically merged a seal, a dog and a monkey. And, looking at Toska's mouth, Kevin had no clue how the thing was able to speak.

"I have a question," Jack said suddenly, his tone flat and cold. "Why'd you help us? Your spot down here's pretty safe. Why'd you risk it?"

Toska shook his head, and his whole body shook with it. "You'd be dead otherwise. And they weren't after you, anyway. They're hunting me, and my people. I was out in the field when the Trows came, and they would have caught me, but they saw you. Chased you. You got them off my trail. I returned the favor, yeah?"

"Yeah," Kevin gratefully agreed.

Before he could continue, Toska turned and started to amble down the tunnel away from them.

"Wait!" Kevin called, his voice too loud in the cavern. "Please. We need your help."

Toska turned slowly, his fleshy eyebrows narrowing to a crease. "More help?" he asked.

"Yes, more help," Kevin replied. He hesitated for a moment, watching Toska's wide black eyes and the way his little snout twitched, like he was sniffing them. Kevin felt like crying, not because he was frightened—though he was—but because he felt so lost. None of them had discussed, nor did he think any of the others had imagined what they might do once they had passed over into this world. Perhaps because none of them had truly believed it existed.

Now here they were, already hunted, exhausted and scared, and this creature looked to be the only source of aid or information they might encounter. Kevin felt overwhelmed. He looked at his brother and their friends, and then sat down, cross-legged on the cold stone, so that Toska would not have to look up at him.

"Look, Toska, we're not from around here," he said, and heard Jesse laugh softly behind him. "I guess that's pretty obvious. This is all kind of unreal to us. Or maybe a little too real."

Toska's black eyes narrowed. He looked distracted, kept glancing up the tunnel back the way they had come, as if the things he called Trows might come down after them, though Kevin thought that pretty damned unlikely given their size.

"A friend of ours has been taken," Kevin continued. "She was stolen from her house by this guy, Peter Starling. I think he's from this . . . near here. You don't know us, and I know you don't have any reason to help us, but I need to find my friend. I just want to bring her home."

The seal-face seemed to smile. Toska tilted his head slightly to one side, and then he barked laughter and rolled around on the ground on his back, slapping at his belly with those long monkey paws. Finally, he got control of himself and managed to sit up on his haunches again, snuffling laughter even still.

"You four soft things against the Tuatha de Danann?

They are not strong anymore, certainly. But still a powerful race. I don't know what you are, or where you came from, but you should go back there. Leave your friend, she is already lost."

"What do you mean, lost?" Kevin demanded.

Jesse squatted down beside Kevin and glared at Toska. "Who are the Tuatha whatevers?"

With a grunt, Toska's snuffling laughter stopped. He rose up on his haunches, long hands coming up to stroke his chin, slick gray fur ruffling in the queer mineral illumination.

"You know nothing, eh?" he asked, a bit of disbelief and disgust in his tone. "Where do you come from, then? How can you not know of the Tuatha de Danann? You must be quite far from home."

"Quite far," April whispered softly, though her words carried in the stone tunnel. "Too far."

Toska cocked his head again. He had only little holes in the side of his head to hear with, but he seemed to be listening particularly closely to her. April seemed uncomfortable with his attention and looked away. Still, the pain in her voice seemed to have gotten his attention and, at least for the moment, his cooperation.

"Settle down then, creatures—"

"Humans. We're humans," Jack said in that low drawl.

From anyone else, it would have sounded absurd, Kevin thought. But from Jack, it was only blunt and true.

"Humans. I've heard about the likes of you, though I've never met one before. Well, welcome then, humans. I've told you to go, and it doesn't look like you'll be paying any attention to that. So I'll tell you all you need know of the Tuatha de Danann, and your man Peter Starling."

With a conspiratorial air about him, Toska glanced back up the tunnel. He dipped his head a little as he spoke again.

"But not here. Let's move along now, shall we? And we'll have a little chat where it's a bit safer."

Kevin frowned. "You think the hunters are going to be able to get down into the tunnel?"

"Not likely. But it's best to be careful, ain't it?"

Toska turned and ambled his way along the tunnel toward the north. Kevin glanced at Jack and April, who were looking at him for an answer, and then he turned to Jesse.

"We can't go back the way we came," Jesse muttered, as if that said it all.

And, actually, it did.

The four of them followed Toska, but Kevin watched the creature closely and asked Jack to keep an eye on the tunnel behind them, just in case.

It only took a few minutes for Kevin to realize that while they were moving north, in what, above ground, would have been the general direction of the ocean, they were also descending. Several times, the guys had to duck their heads to get through a section of tunnel, and at other times, it widened so that it became almost a cavern, large enough for them all to make camp—if any of them had been willing to sleep underground.

Sleep *was* becoming an issue, though. Kevin felt it, and he knew the others must as well. He felt jittery, as though a current of electricity were running just under his skin. His eyes burned, and the phosphorescent light emanating from the veins of ore in the walls made it even worse somehow.

The group was silent, save for a curse now and again when the tunnel floor would become slanted or steeper, or the ceiling too low. From time to time, the humans had to put their hands out, trailing their palms along the rough walls. Kevin tried to keep his hands on the solid granite, avoiding the glowing mineral deposits, though he didn't really know why.

"The walls are warm," April observed at one point.

Kevin grew thoughtful. He had noticed how much warmer it was below the ground than above, but had attributed it mainly to the lack of wind. But it was more than that, he began to realize. Out in the open in just their T-shirts and jeans, they had all been frcczing. Had they stayed out there, dressed as they were, he imagined they would have ended up with frostbite or worse, even with the sweatshirts they had pulled out of the backpacks. But down below, it couldn't have been less than fifty degrees.

"It must be the stuff in the walls," Kevin replied. "It gives off light, maybe it gives off some heat, too."

Toska shushed them. From his strange mouth, it sounded more like a growl. For fifteen more minutes, they kept on behind him, dutifully, yet with great caution as well. There were several junctions in thc cave system, but despite several turns, Kevin had a feeling that their overall direction had not changed. Gradually, the atmosphere around them began to alter. April noticed it first.

"There's a breeze," she said. "I can smell the ocean."

"Yeah," Kevin agreed. "And it's getting colder."

Jesse tapped Kevin on the shoulder and gestured to the walls ahead, where the tunnel became even more narrow. "Darker, too," he observed.

Kevin focused on the mineral deposits in the walls. Jesse was right. As the tunnel narrowed ahead, the phosphorescent veins grew smaller. The cave narrowed to a thin crevice that might be too small for them to fit through. Beyond that crevice, there was very little light.

"Toska, what's going on?" Jesse asked.

The little creature didn't answer. He only shushed them and continued moving down the tunnel on his haunches and long monkey arms and belly.

Then they could hear the ocean as well. The crashing of the surf and the howl of the wind in the caves grew louder as they moved toward the crevice. Kevin had a momentary image of the tunnel as a huge, stone body, and the crevice as the throat. It was disturbing, and he shook his head to rid himself of the mental picture.

The floor of the tunnel, if it could be called that, became a jagged incline. Toska moved up the jagged slope with a sureness that came from great familiarity, despite the gathering gloom. It was dark enough now that Kevin had to strain to make out the figure of Toska slipping into the crevice. Suddenly nervous that they would be left behind, he moved faster, lost his footing and banged his knee on the jagged stone, drawing blood. He cursed, but not loudly. Just in case. There was no telling what else might be down in the dark with them.

All his life, his mother had told them the dark was not to be feared, that there was nothing in the shadows that wasn't there when the lights were on. He had grown to believe her, over time. But his mother had never been here. When the dark moved and whispered in this world, it would be smart to be afraid. To run.

"You okay?" April asked softly.

Jack steadied Kevin as he got up.

"I'm good," he said, nodding at Jack in thanks.

Jesse had moved ahead, but stopped when his brother fell. Kevin stared at the darkness beyond that open crevice. He did not want to lose Toska. But even if they did, the ocean was near. At least they would have their bearings and be away from the hunters.

When they resumed traveling, Kevin went first, Jesse following close behind in case his brother had any trouble walking. Kevin was fine, actually, in spite of the little bit of blood. They had already been through an ordeal, and if he could manage it with the bruises and cuts from the beating a day and a half before, he could handle a little fall.

Jack and April whispered to each other behind him, but Kevin wasn't listening. His focus was on the total darkness beyond the crevice in front of him.

"Toska?" he whispered.

As he turned sideways and slipped through, Kevin thought he heard a wet slither on stone on the other side. Toska was just ahead. He emerged into the darkness and reached out for the wall, hoping to get a hand hold until Jack came through with the Bic lighter he always carried. His right foot probed the floor ahead, careful not to trip.

With a shock, he drew back his hand. For it had not touched stone, but cold, damp fur. Fur which had recoiled from his touch.

"Toska?" he asked again.

Long thin fingers tangled in his hair from behind and yanked his head back. Another hand was clasped over his mouth, just as he tried to shout a warning. Then they were on him, all over him. Kevin was punched, kicked, slapped and scratched, driven to the stone floor. His head struck granite hard enough to bounce, and for a few seconds, he was disoriented.

His heart raced and his muscles tensed, both to protect himself and in the instinctive yet hopeless desire to retaliate. Eyes wide, Kevin desperately tried to get a look at what was attacking him. Sharp teeth nipped his forearm, drawing blood. He felt claws on his back, felt his sweatshirt catch and tear. He struggled, freed his mouth, and cried out for his brother.

The things were all over him, strong and wiry. Soft and slick and wet. He knew what they were, if not what they were called. Toska's people, his race. They slipped between his legs and tripped him up and Kevin went down hard on the stone floor of the cavern. The smell and sound of the ocean was even nearer than before.

"Get off me!" Kevin roared. He tore an arm free and rammed his elbow backward. It struck dark fur with a satisfying crack, as something beneath the creature's skin gave way.

Then they were rolling him. His forehead was bleeding from where he had struck the floor. Blood got in his eyes. He began to lose his sense of direction.

The ground fell away beneath him, and Kevin felt his stomach lurch, as every molecule in his body tried to hold on to its place, tried not to fall. He had seen Pete Starling and the others fly. He was sure now that it was no illusion. But he was only a human, and a kid at that, and he knew that gravity could not be conquered.

Scrabbling at the air in terror, Kevin fell. He struck one of the beasts, and realized they were diving with him, after him. The sounds of the surf rushed up to him, and then he hit the frigid water with a slap. His heart hesitated a moment at the sudden drop in temperature, and then resumed beating.

But Kevin could not breathe. Still disoriented, he opened his eyes against the salt water—something he hated to do—and tried to get his bearings, but there was only darkness surrounding him. Darkness and cold and monsters in the water.

Monsters, that was what they were.

They swam so fast he felt the water surge against him as they went by. They battered him; one rammed him in the belly, and what little air he'd held was pushed from his lungs. He sucked water in to replace it, choking.

Kevin began to drown.

April screamed. One of them was on her back, pulling at her hair, and she felt its breath on her neck. They were reaching for her, touching her all over, dragging her down.

"Jack!" She cried his name, tried to look around in the dark. She'd been holding his hand but when the creatures attacked, they'd been separated. Long, thin fingers wrapped around her neck and began choking her. One of them licked her face.

April got angry.

"Let me go, you little freaks!" she screamed.

Though it was dark, she had a general sense of where the wall behind her had been. One of the creatures had its arms around her legs, but she kicked out, hard, caught it in the jaw, and then her legs were free. With several of them trying to bring her down, she leaned forward and used their joint weight and momentum to propel herself toward the wall. Her head was sideways when she hit, and her skull made a dull thump on the stone, but she'd been tensed for it, and she was all right.

One of the things that had been holding on to her fell away, dead weight. Something in it had snapped. Several of the others screamed, and the screaming was the same sound Toska had made before, that seal-like bark, only much louder. Angrier.

From somewhere nearby, Jack bellowed her name.

April looked up, blinked, and realized that she could see, just a little.

They were in an enormous cavern filled with warrens and remnants of lives, like one of her mom's garage sales. Pots and pans, clothing, things that had been stolen or scavenged at one time or another, were scattered around in disparate and yet orderly groups. At the center of the cavern was a wide hole in the floor. She wasn't sure what was down there, and didn't want to know.

Jesse was on the stone floor near the edge of the hole, being beaten by the creatures. He wasn't moving. April feared he was dead, and prayed he was only unconscious.

She couldn't see Jack or Kevin anywhere.

The light came from the moon and stars. The far end of the cavern was open to the sea. There were clouds in the sky that had blotted out the light from above for a time, but now they were clearing off. For the moment. At any time, they could be plunged into darkness again.

"Stop!" she screamed at the beasts. They had faces now, not just claws and wet fur and snuffling snouts. Toska could talk, which must mean they could do so as well.

"Please, why are you doing this?" she cried.

"You think your disguise will fool us, girl? A little glamour and we'll be none the wiser?" one of them roared, spittle flying from its dark lips.

"What disguise?"

It ran at her, leaped up, drove her down. "We know what you are!" it screamed, then dipped its snarling jaws at her throat.

April didn't even see Jack coming, but suddenly, he was there. He kicked out a tan work boot and caught the beast in its throat, driving it away from her.

In the dim light, she caught sight of his face, of the grim set of his mouth and the cool, emotionless blue of his eyes. He must have gotten back through the crevice, she thought. That was why she hadn't seen him.

With a snarl, he kicked another of the creatures pawing at her, and then reached down to help her up. Several of them attacked him, but Jack moved too fast, now that there was light to see by. He grabbed one by its long arms and swung it against the wall. One of them clawed his belly, cutting him deep, and he held a hand to his bleeding abdomen and used the other to choke the thing, then shove it backward at the others.

Across the cavern, the beasts left Jesse's still form alone, and started to move on Jack and April. In seconds, they were surrounded.

There were just too many.

"Reveal yourself!"

Kevin's eyes fluttered open even as he vomited sea water. He blinked, vision coming back into focus. A long-fingered hand slapped his face, and his eyes shot wide open. He was completely awake now.

"Shed your disguise! Admit what you are!"

"Toska?" Kevin croaked, throat raw from swallowing water and then throwing it up. "Please . . . why are you doing this? You helped us."

"Your kind never come to us, except in secret. You hate us that much, don't you, Tuatha de Danaan?"

As if the force of the creature's fury had propelled him away, Kevin felt his back strike stone, the wall of the chamber, or well, into which he had fallen. Like the walls of the cavern above, it was warm, and the chill he had felt at first now abated. He blinked water from his eyes, tried to focus on the creatures that bobbed in the water before him, eyes glowing yellow in the dark. There were five of them, if he could judge by their eyes. Four kept back a bit, but the fifth was there, only a few feet away.

"Reveal yourself," it barked.

"Toska," Kevin said, trying to be calm. "I swear I

don't know what you're talking about. We're human. I told you."

It snorted, then ducked under the water. With a single massive shake of its body, Toska surged toward him. The creature rammed Kevin's abdomen with crushing force. He was thrust against the stone. Disoriented, he dry heaved from the pain, but managed to produce only stomach acid.

Eyes fluttering, Kevin looked up again. All five were moving toward him now.

"Please," he groaned. "I'm just me. My name is Kevin Murphy and I'm not from . . ." he coughed, his throat raw. "I just came to find my friend and bring her home."

They surrounded him again, eyes on him, intent upon hurting him. Or so he thought. Then, suddenly, they began to sniff. Their steel-gray fur and cold snouts snuffled at his hair, prodded his body, poked at his face. Kevin would have tried to bat them away, to fight this intrusion, but he had already surrendered. He could not fight them, and if they would not listen . . .

The creatures started to bark, all together. It was a mournful sound. They were joined a moment later by a chorus from above, in the cave, where Kevin knew April and Jack and Jesse might well already be dead.

Toska slapped a pair of the others aside. His head hung low, so that his snout was in the water, and his eyes were downcast. He lifted his head only so that he could speak unimpeded.

"We have made a grave error," the creature confessed.

"Yeah, no shit," Kevin mumbled.

Then he passed out.

3

In his dream, Kevin is flying. Far below, his mother stands on the slate stoop in front of their house, smoking a cigarette and glancing expectantly up and down Fox Run Drive.

He realizes, quite suddenly, that the fingers of his outstretched right hand are twined with another's. Before he even looks that way, he knows it is Nikki.

Beneath them, the landscape changes, suburbia gives way to hard-packed earth and rocky cliffs, crashing ocean waves and towers of stone. He clutches at Nikki's fingers more tightly, and sees her clearly for the first time: her green eyes twinkle as she smiles at him, her red hair flowing as though part of the wind itself.

Side by side, they fly. There is magic in it.

Suddenly, informed by his subconscious, Kevin snorts derisively. Shit, he thinks. This is just like in Superman, *when he takes Lois flying. Another glance to his right, and the person clutching his hand is Margot Kidder, the actress who played Lois Lane. She's naked.*

In the dream, Kevin grimaces at the absurdity of it. Even so, he tries to focus and get a better look. Then the dream falls apart.

When he woke, warmth all around him, Kevin knew he had been dreaming. Precisely what the dream was, he had no idea. His eyes opened to slits, and he saw that the walls had begun to glow once more. Memory returned to him, and he stiffened, expecting pain. Even before, he'd had stitches on the back of his head and bruises on his face and ribs. After this beating, though . . . Slowly, surprised, he relaxed into the realization that he was not at all hurt.

His body was draped with heavy material, soft and warm and thick as leather. Fur, or animal skin of some kind. Abruptly, he realized that he was naked beneath it. That knowledge brought him fully awake. Frantic, he tried to sit up, held the skins tight to cover himself, and looked around.

A low, guttural voice responded to his movements. "He wakes."

The cavern was much smaller than the one they had been in before. In the phosphorescent light, he saw April sitting with Jack on the other side of the chamber, their backs to the warmth of the wall. Jack held a cigarette between his lips; it had been lit, and partially smoked, but was out now and just dangled there. They glanced at Kevin, but said nothing, eyes dead and lost.

He noticed right away that they had their clothes on.

Nearer to him, and also wrapped in what he now understood to be animal pelts of some sort, Jesse sat straight up with his legs crossed. He smiled at Kevin.

"How's it goin' there, naked boy?"

Kevin flushed. "Go to hell."

A look colored Jesse's features; one that Kevin didn't want to interpret. He knew how it would translate: *I'm in hell now, little brother, and it's your fault.*

"Where are my clothes?" Kevin asked.

Jesse pointed across the cavern, and Kevin was surprised he had not noticed before. They were spread out on the stone floor on a particularly bright section of glowing rock. A bit of steam was rising from the cavern floor there.

"They were wet." Jesse shrugged.

With a moan more of pain expected than actually experienced, Kevin rose and moved to his clothes. He was pleased to discover that they were not merely no longer wet, but warm and crisp and soft as if they had just been pulled from the dryer.

While he dressed, making every attempt to hide his body from April, he noticed that she and Jack bent to whisper to one another from time to time. Jesse seemed to notice it as well, but he said nothing. Once he had his clothes back on, the vulnerability of his nakedness erased, Kevin crouched down beside his brother and gazed steadily at Jack and April.

"What's the story?" he asked. "What's going on?"

April looked away, her silence awkward. Jack held up the half-smoked butt between two fingers.

"They wouldn't let me smoke," he said, as if that explained everything. "Fuckers."

Kevin shook his head in confusion, then turned his attention to April once again. "April?"

A tiny shiver passed through her before she looked up to regard him. "You should be dead. You and Jesse both. They beat the shit out of you guys. When the light came up again and Toska dragged you up out of that water hole, you looked drowned. Never mind the blood, and the bruises and cuts on your face. But you're both just fine now."

She was right, of course. Kevin glanced down at himself, though now that he was dressed there wasn't much to see to confirm her words. But they felt right. He remembered the pain, the fall, the attack. Maybe dead was too strong a word, but he should definitely have been more severely wounded. From what they said, so should Jesse. He didn't know what to make of it.

"Is that a bad thing? Us being okay, I mean."

"Don't be stupid," April snapped, her face a grimace. "It's all wrong. None of it is real, don't you get it? We're not even here. I don't know what it is, but this isn't the world."

Jesse laughed. "No shit, really? What was your first clue, the trolls?"

After that, April just crossed her arms, leaned back and glared at the brothers.

Kevin shot a questioning glance at Jack, who offered the tiniest shrug in response. A knot in his stomach,

Kevin moved to April's side. He could see that her mouth was pinched tight in indignation, but he also knew her well enough to realize it might just be the only thing keeping the tears from falling.

"April."

"I thought you were dead." Her voice was a whisper. "You and Jesse both. They cut Jack's stomach open. He should probably be dead, too. And wherever this is, Kevin, you got us here. I'm pretty sure if you die, none of us is going anywhere."

"That doesn't make sense. Hell, I don't—" Kevin cut himself off so abruptly his teeth clicked together. He'd been about to tell April that he wasn't sure if they'd get back, or how they'd go about doing it. That, he knew, would have been a dreadful mistake.

Instead, he crouched beside April and forced her to meet his gaze. He glanced at Jack, and now saw only the clear blue gunslinger eyes. Kevin took heart in that; if nothing else, he could count on Jack. Even Jesse seemed a bit unhinged by everything, but Jack was just steady on, get it done.

"April," Kevin said again, his tone softer this time. "Do I have to pinch you to prove this is real?"

Her brow furrowed and she looked at him with real anger. At length she glanced away, shaking her head. Kevin reached out and laid a hand on her bicep, and April covered it with one of her own.

Jack broke the silence. "They have healers."

"That explains a lot." Kevin studied Jack's face again. He was more perceptive than Kevin had ever given him credit for. While April was freaking out, Jack had waited patiently for Kevin to come around and to connect with her, to ground her, in a way that he had intuitively known he could not do himself. Until then, he hadn't wanted to speak of things April didn't want to hear. Now, though . . .

"It's a whole system of caves and tunnels," Jack explained, gesturing with the extinguished cigarette. "Whatever that shit is that runs through the walls gives them both heat and light. Don't know if they really need it, though. They're water animals of some kind. Like mutant seals or something."

Kevin nodded. Jack's words reflected much of his own thinking.

Jesse shifted, throwing off the pelts he'd wrapped around him. "Why attack us, though? We didn't do anything."

"They thought we were somebody else. Something else," Kevin said. "Maybe they've really never seen a human being before. When Doug and the others attacked me, they looked different. Still like themselves, but not normal. Not human. Like the faces we saw were, I don't know, edited versions of their real faces. Toska and his people thought we were like that. Wearing some kind of magical disguise or something. That we were, what did he call them? Tuatha de Danaan."

"I can't even believe we're having this conversation." April shuddered and wrapped herself in Jack's embrace. "I just want to go home."

Before Kevin could respond, Jesse spoke up.

"We all want to go home, April. A couple of problems with that. One, we need to find out if Nikki is here, and if we can help her. Two, we need to figure out how the hell to go about getting home. Before we can do either of those things, we need information and a way out of here. Let's not even talk about the trolls or Trows, or whatever the fuck they're called."

Jack slid the half-smoked cigarette behind his ear. "How are we supposed to do all that?"

With a grin, Jesse shrugged. "Hell if I know. Ask my little brother. He's the one with the imagination."

They all looked at Kevin, who suddenly felt quite small. He really didn't have any answers. All of the things they thought of him, what they expected of him, Jesse's crack about imagination, all felt like a fake to him. A facade about to crumble, revealing only a stupid fourteen-year-old kid who'd stumbled onto something wonderful and horrible and brought his friends with him.

"First let's eat," Kevin said.

The creatures had brought their backpacks in as well. Inside, they found what was left of their food—a crushed loaf of bread, a can of Spam, and a bag of Oreos. The Spam was cold, and disgusting, but they ate it anyway. When they were done, April looked at him closely.

"So what now?"

Kevin swallowed hard. Opened his mouth to tell them all this, to admit they were lost. Possibly doomed. But something stopped him. Instead, Kevin sighed deeply and stood up.

"Let's go," he told them, and went to the cavern's narrow entrance.

"Where?" April asked.

"To find what we're looking for."

The tunnels were alight with that odd glow. It cast all their faces in an odd pallor reminiscent of figures in a wax museum. In the tunnel outside the cavern where they had been brought so that the brothers might recover, Kevin paused and listened intently.

"This way," he said.

Jack frowned. "Why?"

"The ocean," April said. "I hear it too."

For the first time since he'd awoken, Kevin thought she sounded better, more stable, as if the simple act of moving, of doing something, was enough. He understood, for he felt it too.

After several minutes, they had turned twice, continuing to follow the sound of the ocean. Jesse was the first to notice that the phosphorescent mineral veins in the walls were thinning out, and the glow dimming. They were getting nearer to the main cave, Kevin thought, for he remembered that the walls had not been as thickly laced with the shining mineral where they had first arrived, before Toska and his clan attacked.

He might have said just that, but a sudden bark came to them from just ahead. It was joined by a chorus of them, a cacophony of hoarse cries that Kevin could only imagine was some kind of warning system.

They rounded a narrow corner in the tunnel, and were immediately confronted by half a dozen of the creatures, their slick gray fur matted against their bodies. Yellow eyes blazed, even with the dim light. Their barking eased.

"We need help," Kevin explained, before he could allow his fear to stop him. "All we want to do is find our friend and go home. If you know anything about Peter Starling and his friends, whatever they are, please tell us. Help us."

Yellow eyes stared.

Behind Kevin, the others began to stir. Jesse grabbed his little brother's elbow and leaned over to whisper in his ear. "Let's just go. We'll find out what we need some other way."

Kevin sighed and his shoulders slumped. April, Jack and Jesse began to back along the tunnel the way they'd come, eyes on the bizarre creatures before them. Then, from the shadows down along the tunnel, another of them appeared. Kevin knew it was Toska. There was something about the slant of his eyes that made him recognizable.

"Humans. Is that really what you are?" Toska said. "You're a myth to us, you see. A part of the history, but long enough ago that none of us have ever seen one."

"Join the club," Jack grunted.

Toska started as if at the sound of a gunshot. His nostrils flared as he looked at Jack. "We wish you no harm."

"Yeah. We can tell." Jesse turned and put his back to the tunnel wall, so he could see both ways.

Kevin was surpised to see that Toska looked almost sad. He began to shuffle backward, as if to make room for them to go. But that would mean starting all over again, with no idea where Nikki was or how to get home. He was not about to let it end like that.

"So you know what we are. What are you?" Kevin

studied Toska closely. He imagined he had begun to be able to interpret some of the emotions he saw on the thing's seal-like face.

Toska stared at him with large almond eyes and then nodded slowly, snuffling a bit. "Come into our home. There is much you will need to know."

Kevin stiffened. He expected his brother, or one of the others, to make some protest. But they must have sensed, as he did, that this might be their only chance, their only potential ally, and they could not afford to waste that. He stood aside to let Toska pass, then the four of them followed the creature into the large, semi-darkened cavern in which they had been ambushed earlier. How much earlier, he could not say, and did not want to imagine, considering what could have befallen Nikki in that time.

There were dozens of the gray beasts in the cavern. Now, with the half-light there, he could see more of what appeared to be a communal living space. Individual dens, with fire circles and pelts and other objects whose purpose escaped him were spread all around. The far wall was open at its center, and beyond, the moon and stars shone in the sky. Kevin walked to the floor-to-ceiling opening and looked down at the waves crashing perhaps twenty feet below, then across the water at the stone columns that thrust from the sea. The cold from the ocean swept over him, and he shivered and pulled back inside.

At the center of the room was the deep hole in the floor, at the bottom of which ocean water sloshed. A lower cave, open to the ocean, he surmised. Though why they should leave it open in that way he did not know. Unless it was for fishing. He suspected fish to be the main source of nourishment for them. That, and whatever they could forage from the hard lands above.

The creatures had gathered around the hole at the center of the cavern in a rough circle. One, much larger than the others, remained outside the circle with two smaller beasts on either side. Kevin imagined this must be their leader, but he said nothing. It was Toska's turn to speak, and the little creature, with his twitching snout, glanced around the circle before settling his gaze on Kevin.

"We are the Roane. These caves and the sea, and the jagged stone breakers are all that remain to us now. That was not always the way. Once we moved across the land without fear of the Kunal Trows, the hunters you ran from this morning."

The mention of the morning struck Kevin as odd. The world around him and his friends had changed, become night, and they had not seen a single moment of daylight since their arrival here.

"The Trows are the lords of the world above, ever since the Long Night began. They are spread far and wide across the land, but the Kunal tribe are closest. And cruelest."

"What is the Long Night?" Kevin asked.

"Upon a time, in the far times past, day and night fell in equal portion upon the land. In those days, the Tuatha de Danaan ruled the land, and only the richest and most powerful of them lived in the manses upon the stone breakers out among the waves. They were never a friendly people, but the fey races just aren't. Still and all, they let us be.

"The Long Night came from nowhere, dark forever, the pass of the day marked by an eyeblink of morn, and no more. We blame the Kunal Trows, for they cannot bear the light or they'll turn to stone. But with the Long Night, the Trows left their lair under the mountain, and slaughtered the Tuatha de Danaan. Once the land was green and strong, but it was drowned in the blood of the fey. My people, the Roane, were caught between the two sides of this war."

Toska paused, looked around at the Roane, all of whom shuddered. Several of them barked or whimpered. Then he brought his stubby legs beneath him and stood up straighter, chin proudly held high.

"They eat us, you know."

April sucked in a breath, cursed low in words Kevin couldn't hear, but knew he would agree with.

"What caused this war?" he asked, trying not to dwell on what he'd just been told. "The Trows and the Tuatha de Danaan. Why do they hate each other so much? These Kunal Trows, they're just evil?"

The enormous Roane beyond the edge of the circle barked, a long, quavering rasp. They all looked at him, human and inhuman alike. "The Roane have never cared for their war, or their purpose. We wish only to live, and to feed our children, and to swim."

Silence followed. For half a minute, no one spoke. Finally, Toska returned his attention to Kevin. "This one you seek, Starling? He is the closest to a lord the remaining Tuatha de Danaan have. They're dying out there, on the rocks, the last of their breed. The Kunal Trows have won, and they don't even know it yet."

Mind reeling, thoughts skittering about his head, Kevin walked to the opening in the wall again. Salt water splashed up from far below. The wind pushed against him, but he leaned into it, narrowed his eyes and peered out into the night at the stone columns and the large rambling homes atop them. Lights burned in several of them, but not all.

"So Nikki . . . she's out there?"

"If Starling has taken her, yes." Toska ambled closer to Kevin and the others. He stopped in front of them and stared up, head cocked to one side as if making his mind up about something.

"You may die, I think, if you go out there," he said. "But if you still mean to go, I'll take you."

Kevin looked at Jack and April. They did not encourage him, but nor did they shake their heads, or beg him to say no. Before he even turned to look at his brother, Jesse laid a hand on Kevin's shoulder.

"It's what we came here for, bro. Besides, if anybody knows how to get us home, it's Starling."

"He'll probably kill us, Jesse. No way is he going to help us," Kevin warned.

Jesse's expression was grim. "We go. We don't have any other choice."

On the precipice of the plateau island upon which his home had been built centuries before, Peter Starling stared grimly out across the ocean. The mansion stood sentinel behind him, overlooking the other stone columns which jutted from the water and the homes built upon them. Some were dark, but others burned brightly from within. An unknowing observer might have thought families lived therein, or that some form of merriment was under way.

The idea disturbed Starling greatly, for both were grievously far from the truth. He glanced over his shoulder and frowned as he studied the face of his own home, a mere stone's throw from the edge. There was light within, but only just a little, orange fire burning somewhere in the core of the manse. It gave the place a haunted look, not unlike the candle flickering ghoulishly within a jack-o'-lantern.

He stood atop the rocky ledge, one hundred and seventy-nine feet above the crashing waves, sheer stone face falling away in front of him, and yet he had no urge to fall, nor even to fly. A sound from far off, the blast of a hunter's horn, brought his attention back to the south. The sky was clear above, the moon and stars enough to illuminate the mainland well enough. Squinting, he could just make out a clutch of hunters on horseback.

The urge to kill them was powerful; to break and bleed the Kunals. His lip curled, revealing the double row of razor teeth within.

Starling's icy eyes lost their last trace of color, clear and frozen and filled with hate. The chill wind tore across the lonely plateau. His long leather coat flapped about his legs and his straight black hair was whipped across his face. The leader of the Tuatha de Danaan tucked his hair behind the peaks of his ears, only to have it blow loose a moment later. He ignored it then, lost in thought.

The smell of salt from the ocean was strong and welcome to him. The crash of the surf drew his attention once more, and Starling glanced down. At the tips of his leather boots, a bit of stone crumbled away and dropped the long way to the ocean.

Once upon a time, the manse, his ancestral home, had been fronted by an enormous estate. Most of that property had long since fallen away into the ocean. One day, the entire house would follow.

Peter Starling dearly hoped he would not live to see that day. And he had faith that hope would be fulfilled.

Something flapped in the breeze above him, and Starling glanced up quickly. Seabirds were plentiful, even now, but the Kunals had been known to sway the creatures, even use them as spies or weapons. Little more than an annoyance, usually, but one must be careful.

But it wasn't a bird. "Doug," Starling said.

"Hello brother." Doug Starling flew the way he walked, the way he moved: like a predator. Not a lion or a tiger, or even a Trow, but like a hyena or some other skulking savage.

Pete did not like his brother very much, but brothers they were.

Doug did not set foot upon the plateau, not even the ledge. The wind buffeting him, he slipped back and forth upon the air, seeming to hover several feet away from the cliff, face-to-face with Pete.

"Where've you been?" Starling demanded.

With a laugh, Doug pretended to fall backward in shock. "You mean you missed me?" He cackled—a false sound, worn like a mask. "You know very well where I've been, Pete. To the grave of our mother. It looks the same, in case you wondered."

"You forget yourself, Douglas."

"Not at all, Peter. It is you who forget, not yourself, but your mother."

"I will see her stone when I can walk or fly there

without fear of discovery, when the land she is buried beneath belongs to us once more."

For several moments, the two stared at one another, a furious energy passing between them. It had ever been so. At length, Doug moved, just a bit, as though allowing that energy to pass him by.

"Curt and I went through Duncan's house earlier. Turned the place upside down. No sign that the Kunals have been there. You still want me to move out there, I guess."

Starling narrowed his gaze, studied his brother's face. For a moment, he thought he might have heard regret in Doug's voice. It would be odd, an emotion he didn't think he'd ever heard his brother express before. But Doug only stared at him. Pete glanced back at their father's house, of which he was now master.

"Duncan was the last of his line. His family home is empty. I don't want the damned Trows in there out of principal, but there's more to it than that."

"Yeah," Doug said, with a derisive snort that propelled him back several inches, where he wavered on the wind, so far above the water. "You want me gone."

"What I want is for the Kunals to think our numbers are greater than they are. We're barely more than a hundred now, Doug, not including staff. And what are a few shadows and goblin servants? Lot of good they'll do in a fight." Starling scowled and turned his back on his brother. "I shouldn't have to explain this to you, Doug. But that's always been the problem, hasn't it? You're always trying to figure out how things relate to you, even when they don't."

No response. Pete shook his head slightly and laid a long, thin finger against his temple, wishing the conversation had never happened. He wanted it to be over.

Doug likely sensed that desire, but he ignored it completely.

"So, have you had her again?" he asked, tone insinuating and hurtful. "Or are you still waiting for the little whore to love you?"

Pete froze. As if in a dream, he turned to regard his brother, who floated there, just out of arm's reach, over the edge of the abyss.

"I've killed and I've deceived when necessary, but I won't take her," he said through gritted teeth. "No matter what the cost, I won't just take her. Not to have her bear sons that would hate me for it. I've told her what's at stake—"

Doug's eyes went wide with surprise, such that he looked the perfect fool for a moment. Then he laughed again, and it was Pete who felt the fool. His younger sibling's cynical amusement took an uncomfortable length of time to exhaust itself. When it had, Doug wiped the back of his hand across his mouth, still grinning.

"It has to be done, brother. Fuck, Pete, you don't want to do it, give her to me. I'll split the bitch in two going in, and my pups'll do the same on the way out. Wipe that snotty look off her face, that's for—"

Starling was in the air before even he knew it. His feet left the rocky ledge with the first breeze, and not even the twitch of a muscle. Flight was like that. His fingers locked around his brother's throat, and Pete drove him back and down. Down and down, toward the thrashing seas below, toward the rocks.

Doug fought him, of course, talons scrabbling at his brother's hands. But Pete was stronger.

Just above the waves, he stopped, released his hold. They hung there, above the water, glaring at one another, heaving for breath. Doug struck him once, and Pete's head rocked backward with the force of the blow. The elder Starling tasted blood in his mouth.

"Nikki did nothing to you. She's just a girl, Douglas. Just a human girl." Numb and grieving, Pete pointed across the water to the mainland. "*They* are the animals, little brother. You forget yourself. I may not visit the grave of our mother, but at least I don't shame her memory."

The words were bitter in his mouth, mixed with the

copper taste of his own blood, but Pete did not regret them, nor did he take them back. Doug glared at him a long moment, then flew off in silence, disappearing into the dark sky above.

Lost in the stars.

In the lair of the Roane, April stood at the edge of the water hole in the center of the cavern, frozen.

"Just jump," Kevin told her. "It'll be okay."

Kevin and Jesse stood across from her, on the other side of the gaping hole. She wanted to say something snide, even mean, but she couldn't. Her fear was her own responsibility. She couldn't blame it on anyone else.

Not that she didn't have reason to be afraid.

This was real, she now understood. Somewhere, by now, her mother and father would be searching for her, terrified for her. She wanted to think they would be furious that she'd run off, but her parents knew her better. Or thought they did. They would fear for her.

It hurt April to know how much.

Somehow, Kevin and Jesse didn't seem to be dwelling on home that much. Well, except for trying to figure out how to get back there. And Jack—she glanced quickly at him now, and found the severe cast of his features unchanged—it was as though he had known this place existed his whole life. April knew that wasn't so, but it still bothered her. Irritated her. Humbled her, in a way.

He was afraid, though he would not show it. But his fear propelled him forward, ready to face whatever came.

I'll have to be like that, she realized. *Just like Jack. Whatever comes, just beat the shit out of it, get it out of the way, and get home.*

"You sure about this?" Jesse asked.

Around them, the Roane that had gathered shifted, almost as though they had taken insult at the question. Toska snorted and ambled forward. The little Roane stood on his stumpy rear legs and beckoned for Jesse to bend down. The creatures had given them cloaks made of Roane-skin, pelts sewn together with rawhide, which could be tied at the throat. Toska checked the knot at Jesse's throat.

"You wear the skins of our fathers, Jesse Murphy. Do not doubt the spirits of our ancestors," he sniffed.

"Hey, no offense." Jesse shrugged. "It's just . . . the water's cold, and it's far to swim. We don't have any other clothes, and we can't afford to get pneumonia right now."

April nodded slightly in agreement, but said nothing. Toska lowered his head, obviously perturbed. He sighed, if a Roane could sigh.

Kevin squatted in front of Toska. "It isn't that we don't appreciate the help," he said. "We're just—"

"Afraid."

Surprised to hear the word from Jack's lips, April looked over at him. He was touching the knot at his own throat, almost as if he had not spoken that word aloud. But he had.

"As you should be," Toska said thoughtfully. "But set your fears to rest at least on this. Wearing the skins of our fathers, the ocean will believe you four truly are Roane."

Kevin stood up. "We're ready."

April blinked. She did not feel ready. Wasn't even sure what they were talking about. Though she was grateful no one had suggested they leap from the gap in the wall and fall to the crashing ocean below. It looked dangerous enough jumping into the seawater in the hole at the center of the cave.

While everyone else hesitated, Jack stepped forward and dropped down through the hole. Mineral veins lit the water's surface, but Jack plunged down into the water, past the reach of the light. The splash below seemed to echo around the cavern endlessly. She waited for him to emerge, to call out, but there came not a word from the dark water. Nothing stirred below.

"You must trust me," Toska insisted.

Then he changed. With what seemed a completely

fluid alteration, his fur ruffled and his arms and legs seemed to shrink, drawing in, metamorphosing. In the blink of an eye, Toska had gone from awkward, peculiar beast, to a more familiar creature.

Whatever he had been, Toska now appeared in every way to be nothing more than a common seal.

He barked and dove into the water hole.

Forcing herself not to dwell, April leaped into the water after him, even as Jesse and Kevin prepared to do the same. They left the backpacks behind. They couldn't very well swim with them, and if what they were about to do got them killed, it wasn't as though a change of socks would do them any good.

The ocean will believe you four truly are Roane, Toska had said. The instant April hit the water, she understood what he'd meant.

The cloak of pelts around her seemed to envelop her, and yet her limbs were free to swim. When April glanced around in the water, she saw something impossible. The Roane hide seemed to have grafted itself to her body. No longer did it flow like a cloak around her, but had become almost a second skin on arms, legs . . . all over her body.

April could barely feel the water as it swirled around her. She started to swim, and was startled at the speed with which she moved. It was almost as though the water itself were helping to propel her along. Though she held her breath, there was no panic in it, no sense that she might drown. For the first time since she could remember, perhaps since she had been born, April felt completely content with her surroundings. Her fear had been sloughed off like a layer of dead skin. It was as though this world embraced her, and she felt oddly at home with it.

The others were with her as she sped through an underwater tunnel. Moments later they were out in open ocean with the moon and stars above and April was dancing on the waves. It was glorious, so perfect she felt she might cry.

With Toska guiding them, she and the boys swam likc Roane across the stretch of ocean that separated the mainland from the columns of stone upon which the Tuatha de Danaan made their homes. When they had come to the rocky base of the towering island upon which the mansion of Peter Starling sat, it was far too soon for April.

From delight, they were moving toward danger, even death.

As they crawled onto the rocks at the base of the craggy cliffs, she looked longingly at the water. The Roane cloak slipped off and hung behind her once again, dripping what little water had not simply slid off the pelts.

Jack came and stood beside her, placed a hand on her arm. His eyes in that moment reminded her of a seal's, soft and piercing, soulful and insistent. "You all right?"

She realized, just then, that she had never really loved him before. Perhaps, with the niggling sense of unease that had been almost a constant in her life, she had never had the focus to be able to truly love anyone. And now, like throwing a switch, she did. Oh, she did.

April offered him a small smile that she could tell only puzzled him. She stared longingly at the sea as Toska emerged. The Roane transformed once again, arms and legs returning. He moved to stand between Kevin and Jesse, but the brothers barely noticed. Their attention was on the cliff face, and the plateau high above, and the stars and the moon in the infinite darkness beyond.

Toska shook himself, almost a fearful shudder. "Look hard enough amongst the rocks here, you'll find a small cave. Inside the cave, you'll find a set of stairs meant to be used by the goblins and sprites and whatnot that have served the Tuatha de Danaan since memory began. A long way up, so I'm told, but at the top, you'll find what you're looking for, ready or not. It's Peter Starling's home up there. I wish you luck."

"You're leaving?" April asked, alarmed.

Toska snorted. "I'd be a fool to stay. The skins you

can keep with the blessing and friendship of the Roane, and our sorrow for the error we made in judging you. If you should live, we'd be grateful to have them back. But if you die, I've no plans to come back here and look for them, that's certain."

April found that she was relieved that they were to be allowed to keep the Roane cloaks, but still concerned with Toska's departure. There was a measure of comfort in having someone along who knew what was what in that bizarre place, and no small amount of anxiety in the knowledge that he knew enough to leave them there as fast as he could swim.

"Before you go, a question," Kevin said, a hesitation in his tone.

Toska barked low and tilted his head to listen.

"These cloaks. They're magic. In our world, the Tuatha de Danaan were able to do things that seemed magical. More than that, though. Magical, impossible things seemed to just happen around them."

"Aye, I know what you mean," Toska rasped. "There's magic in the world, true enough. You're wearing some of it. The Tuatha de Danaan have a bit of it, but not much really. Not the way you mean. The legends speak of it, though, the way that those of our world were more powerful, and filled with magic when they crossed to the realm of humans. Some say there were humans who could do the same here. The worlds met around those folks, changing what's real and what ain't. Possible, impossible. When you've got two realms touching, mixing about with one another, I figure anything can happen.

"The Trows, though, they never had taste nor talent for magic. Not the Kunals, nor any of the tribes further inland."

"You mentioned that before. Are there a lot of other tribes?" April asked in horror.

"Oh, aye. Many more tribes. But we've seen nothing of them for generations. I wish you luck, humans."

"Thank you for everything," Kevin told Toska. "And you'll get the skins back. We'll see you again."

Before Toska could offer a response April was certain she would rather not hear, Jesse swore under his breath.

"What's up?" Jack snapped.

They all glanced at Jesse, but he was still staring straight up. It was Kevin, though, who actually spoke the words.

"The sun's coming up."

And it did. In the space of no more than a minute, the stars and moon faded away as the sky went from black to deep blue to orange to yellow to white, and began to drift into a soft powder blue. The sun peeked above the horizon to the east, which they could barely see around the side of the towering island above.

Even the wind had seemed to fade with the dawn.

Then darkness swept across the sky from east to west in a tidal wave of shadow, a pool of indigo that drowned the sky in oily night. The stars and moon faded back in, as if they'd never been gone.

"My God," Kevin whispered. "What the hell was that."

"The morning," Toska replied. "All the morning we've got around here."

When April tore her gaze away from the light-swallowing darkness above and glanced at Toska, he had changed again. The seal that stood there on the rocks cocked its head to regard her for a moment, then barked and slipped off into the water.

They were on their own again.

4

Haunted by that glimpse of morning, Kevin stumbled as they searched for the cave entrance. The rocks were slick with sea spray, but he quickly righted himself.

Once he had found his footing, it didn't take long for them to find the cave opening Toska had talked about. The wind buffeted his back, trying to push him over again, but Kevin stood fast.

"Jesse," he called.

His brother was at his side in a moment. Jack was there with April as well. She held on to her boyfriend's hand tightly, staring at the waves as though she feared she might fall in. With the cloaks, that wasn't a concern, but April's expression of anxiety told Kevin she wasn't quite as confident about it.

The cliff face towered above them, seeming to lean over as if it might tumble down on top of them. Kevin craned his neck to look up, but saw nothing but the cliff and the sparkling night sky beyond. The crashing of the ocean seemed suddenly louder to him in that moment. For a second, he closed his eyes and tried to picture Nikki's face. He had the hair, and the eyes, they were easy. Even the slightly upturned nose, the mischievous grin. But when he tried to put those elements all together, to really see her in his mind, the image dissipated. It had been only a few days since he'd seen her, and he couldn't form a complete picture of her in his head.

It hurt.

A bit dizzy, he opened his eyes and waited for his

equilibrium to come back. Then he turned to face the others.

"Nikki's up there," he said, with a confidence he did not feel. It was what made sense, of course. This was Starling's place. But they couldn't be absolutely certain it was where Nikki was being held until he saw her with his own eyes.

For the first time, it occurred to him that when they found her, it was possible she would not want to come along. He pushed the thought away. She'd been stolen away. Her own home, her own world was waiting for her. Kevin meant to bring her back.

"Last chance to turn back." Kevin swallowed hard, studying first April's eyes, then Jack's. Finally, he looked at his brother.

Jesse returned the look with a bit of a sneer, familiar to Kevin from thousands of fights. Then his older brother laid a hand on his shoulder, gripped it firmly.

"You're a little shit," Jesse told him. "We had our last chance to turn back at the top of our street, night before last. When we get home, you're a dead man."

Then Jesse laughed, and Kevin laughed with him. If they all made it home in one piece, and Jesse wanted to beat on him some, he doubted he would mind all that much.

With one last look at their faces, Kevin stepped into the cave, ducking his head to avoid the overhanging rock. It was a rough-hewn tunnel that looked as though it had been blown out of the rock wall. Less than twenty feet into the cave, they found the stairs.

Jack grunted, impressed.

Kevin nodded. "I don't know what I was expecting—"

"But it wasn't this. No shit, huh?" Jesse agreed.

April glanced back along the cave toward the entrance and then started forward. She was the first of them to mount the bottom step. The staircase was built of wooden timbers, supported at odd intervals by stone out-croppings in the cave wall. Twenty feet above, the stairs disappeared into the ceiling.

"Looks pretty dark," Kevin said, then felt stupid for stating the obvious.

He could not help himself. The extraordinary nature of the Roane and their swim here had lost its ability to fascinate him. Or that fascination had been stolen away the moment they had entered the tunnel. In his mind he saw the odd way Pete Starling's eyes looked when he was angry, remembered the savage glee Doug and the others had shown when they attacked him.

Kevin's throat was dry, his heart pumping too fast. A chill went through him and he could barely continue. This was a world ruled by the same impossibility that made Peter and the others so frightening. In the dark, venturing into the bowels of Starling's home, he saw with greater clarity than ever exactly what he had done. Risked his life, all of their lives, for Nikki's.

Kevin felt like crying, or throwing up, or both. There was an odor like burning rubber that lingered in the air, and the moldy smell of stones slick with the moisture of the sea. He tried not to think what sort of creatures might be hiding down there in the tunnel. Instead, he tried to focus on the other end of their journey, on going home.

It was not easy. Home had never seemed so far away.

At the first stone landing, he touched April on the shoulder, and she paused to let him pass carefully on the stairs. From there, Kevin led the way again. When the stairwell closed up around them, the tunnel now barely big enough to accommodate them, Kevin paused, waiting for his eyes to adjust to the dark. When they did, he noticed that it wasn't completely dark after all.

"Light," Jack said behind him.

"Not sure how happy that makes me," Kevin replied. "If there are torches or whatever, there's gotta be somebody around, right?"

"What, you thought you were just gonna walk in, grab Nikki and go without anybody noticing?" April asked, her voice carrying up to him in the dark.

"Seemed like a wicked good plan to me," Kevin said,

shrugging sheepishly, though he didn't think the others could see the gesture. "Not likely to actually happen, but what the hell?"

Jesse was the first to laugh. Jack and April followed suit, and soon all four of them were snickering and shaking their heads. Kevin was dimly aware, in the back of his mind, that what they were doing was akin to whistling in the dark, trying to comfort themselves in the imminent presence of danger. He didn't care.

At length, they came to a subbasement, where the rough-hewn walls were replaced by wood and stone masonry that had been arranged at least to pass as a room. Candles burned in glass sconces on the walls. A large door fashioned from wooden planks with iron straps stood at the opposite end of the large basement, but there was no lock on the door.

The room was used mainly for storage, but there were also wine racks against one wall. Once, they must have held hundreds of bottles, but the supply had been severely depleted. Less than a dozen bottles filled the odd slot now.

Jesse went to the door and opened it; peered quietly out into the corridor beyond. He went out, and the others followed, with Kevin bringing up the rear. It was only as he went out, passing close to a sconce on the wall right beside the door, that Kevin chanced to look at the flame sputtering within the glass.

It moved.

He blinked, cocked his head back and looked at it more closely. For a moment, the candle burned as candles do. But just as he started to look away, thinking he must be even more exhausted than he knew, it sputtered again and began to dance about. Not just in one way, but several, as if there were four or five separate flames, all kind of boogying together in there.

He opened his mouth, looked out into the corridor beyond the door and saw the others waiting for him expectantly. His brother wore a frown, a question there. Kevin knew Jesse had seen something in his face and wanted an explanation. He simply wasn't prepared to offer one.

Kevin shrugged and followed them out into the hall, stone construction with wooden timber supports. After a moment, Jesse stopped watching him and went down the corridor to the bottom of a second stairwell that went steeply up toward what Kevin hoped was the main house.

As he went, though, Kevin looked at everything more carefully.

Which was how he came to notice the passages in the wall on either side of the stairs.

"Look at this," he said.

The others stopped and clustered on the steps above him. Kevin bent to peer into the opening on his left, a three-foot-square box tunnel that might have been a vent of some kind in any modern house. When his face was no more than a few inches away—staring into what seemed to be complete darkness—he heard something move within.

April was at his side. "What was—"

Kevin shushed her and wished for one of the candles from the wall sconces. Wondered, in that moment, who changed the candles when they burned low, as they must often have done.

The rustling noise came again, like bat wings, he thought, and a shiver ran through him. He thought he saw something move, just a little. Black on black. When he blinked, he thought, in the afterimage burned on his eyelids, that he might have seen it move.

A tiny hand flashed from the vent and slashed his cheek.

"Ah, shit!" Kevin stumbled back, nearly lost his footing, and then bent to peer into the crawl space once more, keeping well back this time.

"What the fuck was that?" Jesse asked, moving down beside his little brother.

They both saw the eyes, glowing red in the dark of the crawl space. Two pair. They heard the breathing, too, a kind of hissing that might have been sinister glee. It was the laugh that did it, the laugh that froze thc blood in his veins. For whatever had scratched Kevin's face was no simple animal. It was cruel and evil and it thought the fact that Kevin was bleeding was pretty damn funny.

"Shit," Kevin whispered, dabbing at the scratches with the dirty collar of his burgundy University of Paris at Sorbonne sweatshirt. He glanced down at the blood it left behind, and was relieved to realize the wounds were superficial. Still, his revulsion was overwhelming. Who knew what filthy taint the evil little beast might pass to him?

Jack flicked his lighter on and whipped the flame toward the crawl space on the other side of the stairwell. The creature there cringed, holding up its hands against the light. Its skin was like cracked leather and it was shaped like a man, an old and angry man. Its eyes were red pinpricks and its teeth like a shark's.

"Intruders!" it cried, and its voice was like the screech of an angry cat. It turned and fled down the crawl space, bent slightly to keep from whacking its head on the ceiling.

Jack stuck a Marlboro between his lips and lit up. The flame from the lighter roared a little too high and singed his eyelashes, and he snapped his head back with a curse and a grin.

"What are you doing?" Kevin asked, startled.

"Come on, Kevin. Not like they don't fuckin' know we're here," he muttered.

Kevin would have argued, mainly as a way to vent his own fear, but for the first time he saw the terror that lingered in Jack's eyes. He was afraid after all, just better at hiding it. His eyes were a little too wide, his teeth clamped on his cigarette just a little too tightly.

The lighter went out and they were in darkness again, save for what illumination came up from the subbasement below, and the glow of the burning ash at the end of Jack's cigarette.

Kevin felt numb. Determined still, but afraid. It was Jesse who moved first. He stretched, and some of the joints in his back popped. Then he took a long, deep breath, and faced them.

"Fuck it. Let's go. The clock's ticking now."

"Oh, excellent," Jack said drily, but he didn't hesitate to follow Jesse's lead up the stairs.

April put a hand on Kevin's shoulder. He could barely make out her soft eyes, so serious.

"It'll work out. You'll see." She went up after them.

Kevin didn't know how he had ended up so lucky as to have such people in his life, but he wasn't going to question that good fortune now.

"We're coming," he whispered, the words for no one but himself.

In the walls, though, there were listeners. He thought he heard them laughing softly.

There was a door at the top. Once again, it had no lock. They emerged into a wide corridor in Peter Starling's home. It was extraordinary. There was no other word for it. Kevin stood with the others and they stared up at the chandelier in the hallway, at the tapestries that hung from the walls, at the plants and paintings and brass and glass and gold. Could it be gold? Kevin thought it just might.

It wasn't a palace; not by a long shot. Nor even a castle. But it was a mansion unlike anything he had seen except in old movies. The ceiling was twelve feet above their heads, maybe more. The stone staircase off to their left wound up and around to disappear in on itself, like a tower in a fortress somewhere. The glass in the windows was thick and warped.

They stood at the back of the first floor, though Kevin suspected the kitchen was farther back still, and whatever quarters the servants might use. Or have used, once upon a time. For there was dust here, and spiderwebs. Not so much as to prove the house empty, but enough to show that it had tarnished since the days of its real glory.

Tarnished, also, were the two full coats of armor

which seemed to stand at attention on either side of the hall. Unlike any other armor Kevin had ever seen, even in a museum, they had jutting fins of iron all about the helm, and spikes at the knees and elbows. Both were scored and dented, as though fresh from battle.

On either side of the corridor there were rooms upon rooms. Through the open archways they could see a long dining table and elegant furniture on one side, and what must have been a library on the other.

Kevin wanted to look at those books, knowing he would wonder about what was in them for the rest of his life. But there was no time. At the far end of the corridor, opposite the spot where they had emerged, was an enormous pair of wooden doors, each of a single piece, so that they must have come from the biggest trees in the world.

On the walls amidst the paintings and the tapestries and the sconces which gave enough light for them to see it all, there were other displays.

Weapons.

Crossed swords and hanging shields, maces and morningstars, huge double-headed war-axes with grooves and knicks in each blade.

Jesse went instantly to a thick mace on the wall and lifted it from its hooks. Kevin noticed that he had chosen the more practical weapon instead of the morningstar— a spiked ball on a long chain—and was glad. A weapon they didn't know how to use was a toy, and toys were no good to them now.

"Jackpot," Jesse said, hefting the iron mace in his hands.

Quite suddenly, and unsettlingly, Kevin felt as though the world around him had begun to tilt. The climate in the mansion changed. There was a queer energy, as though the door might open at any moment and suck them headlong out onto the grounds, perhaps pound them against the trees around the house or toss them screaming over the cliff and down to the roaring ocean below.

"Kevin?"

It was April's voice, pulling him back to reality. He

was stunned to find that he was supporting himself against the stone wall with both hands, his legs not quite enough to hold him up.

"I'm okay," he lied, though it was quickly becoming true.

With a shake of his head that carried all the way through him, he looked at the two heavy, ugly broadswords that were crossed on the wall above his head. His glance went to the stone stairwell that wound up and out of sight.

If Nikki was really here . . . but no, he told himself. No if.

He took the sword down off the wall before he was even aware he had done it.

"Let's hurry," he said. "I don't think he's here now, but I think he's coming back."

April and Jack looked at him strangely, but Jesse only nodded. An unspoken communication passed between them. Maybe they wanted to kill each other half the time, but they were brothers. If Kevin said they were running out of time, Jesse wasn't going to question him.

Jack took the axe, and April the other sword, though it dragged heavily in her grasp. Kevin wasn't concerned. If she needed to use it to save herself or someone else, April would do that. The time when they could pretend their circumstances were anything but dire had passed.

Together, they ran toward the stairs, their sneakers loud on the stone, then softly muted on the finely woven carpets.

"No further!" came a booming voice.

Kevin didn't stop running, but he looked around to find the source of the voice. The creatures tumbled as if from nowhere, from other rooms and the stairs above, from behind tapestries and furniture, from spots on the high ceiling where those same vents must have run through the stone walls. There were dozens of them, creatures like those in the crawl spaces below. Goblins, or whatever they might be—they looked dangerous despite their size, and gleeful at the prospect of a fight.

They screamed as they came on, leaping and showing their teeth.

Jesse was in front, and they got to him first. A goblin whose left eye was open wide and completely white fell upon his shoulders from above. Another tore its claws through his jeans, while a third landed on his back. Jesse didn't even hesitate. With one sweeping strike of the mace, he cracked open the skull of the creature at his legs, knocking it to the stone floor like a ragged old doll, porcelain head shattered. The one on his back could not tear through the Roane cloak he wore. The half-blind, scarred goblin screeched and went to rip Jesse's eyes out.

Kevin was there. With one hand, he gripped the thing's neck and pulled it away, then turned and hurled it at a window. The glass shattered and the cold wind swept in on the sound of the ocean and the agonizing cries of the one-eyed goblin.

When he turned, Kevin saw that the others were fighting as well. April and Jack were back to back; just as he'd thought, she had no trouble using the sword now that she was forced to it. And Jack . . . blood was spattered in a line up his clothes and across his face like war paint.

The axe fell.

Kevin felt claws rake his arm, just above the wrist. Sword gripped in both hands, heavy and awkward, he spun and hacked downward at the goblin who'd done it, a wrinkled, cruel-looking thing. The blade sliced deeply into the joint of bones where its head met its neck, then slid cleanly from the cut.

He wanted to throw up.

But they kept coming. And dying. He ran one through and pinned it to the floor.

"It's our house," the thing sighed, mewling like a cat.

Startled, Kevin froze, still leaning on the sword. The hilt felt hot and slippery to him, and he let it go, taking a step back and bumping into the wall, only feet from the shattered window. Though most of the broken glass littered the ground outside the window, some had been blown inward by the wind, and it crunched beneath his feet.

"Stop." It sounded almost like a whisper to him.

The second time, he screamed it.

Even the goblins froze, staring at him. Jesse's right arm was covered with blood. He took a step back, almost as though he were drunk.

"They really are just the servants," Kevin said, his voice loud in the sudden silence. His eyes darted around at the goblins, all of whom he now saw were terrified. "Jesus," he croaked. He glanced at Jesse. "Go for the stairs."

Instantly, Jesse responded, backing toward the stairwell, sneaker squeaking on a smooth stone. One of the goblins moved to go after him.

"Don't," Kevin said.

The thing looked at him.

"I know," he said. "It's your house. I'm sorry all this . . . I'm sorry. But our friend is upstairs. We're taking her home."

The goblin who had moved glanced at Jesse, then at April and Jack as they started to follow, and then his red eyes burned down on Kevin again. With sword hanging at his side, Kevin moved to follow the others.

"The Master's guest cannot leave. He will kill us if we allow it."

"You'll die if you try to stop us," Jesse snapped from the stairs.

As a wave, the goblins moved, but toward one another rather than the stairs. They whispered together, the sounds uniting into a loud hiss. After a moment, they split up again, spreading out at the bottom of the steps.

"We will not suffer. The Shade will kill you. The Master will see that we have sacrificed for him, and not punish us. You will be dead."

Its voice was almost singsong now, like a taunting child. Kevin ignored the tone, if not the words. As he rounded the curve in the staircase, he nearly bumped into April, who had held back, waiting for him.

"What's this Shade?" she asked.

Kevin would have shrugged, but Jesse shouted from above, and he found himself running up the last dozen steps to the second floor. Jack was in front of him, but Kevin pushed him aside.

He screamed his brother's name.

The hall was not unlike the one below, but darker, less ornate, the ceiling lower and more confining. Candles had burned low in their sconces; only four were left flickering.

A creature made of pure darkness, a shadow sprung to life from the wall, wavering in and out of reality in the dance of the candle flames, lifted Jesse Murphy above its head and slammed him hard to the stone floor. Jesse cried out in pain, but Kevin promised himself he hadn't heard anything break.

As if to prove it, Jesse went on his belly in an instant, trying to scramble away. At some point he'd dropped the mace and it lay only inches from him now. He reached, grasped it just before the thing had his legs again. It dragged him back. Jesse swung the mace at it.

The weapon passed through nothing, through shadow, through a whisper of the dark.

April screamed something Kevin barely heard. Jack was moving in, swinging the axe. Kevin thought even he must have known it would do no good. The axe sliced through air and sparks flew from the blade as it glanced off the wall.

"Fuck," Kevin whispered.

The Shade shoved Jack hard into the wall. His skull hit stone with a hollow sound, and he staggered, dazed, barely able to hold the axe. Jesse, still on the ground, looked over at Kevin.

"For Christ's sake, do something!"

April turned to stare at him, eyes pleading.

His brother, his friends, he himself might well be about to die.

Kevin froze.

*   *   *

Hugo flew in from the east, his own manse having been built by an ancestor near two thousand years before on an island plateau. Once upon a time, there had been no islands, or so the story went. Then the land had collapsed into the sea, and only the magick of those homes, built by the Tuatha de Danaan to last till the end of time, held the stone around them, kept the integrity of those rock and soil columns so that the houses didn't go tumbling down into the waves.

Over the ages, the homes had become strongholds, the isolation of the towers and the ocean splashing below all that had saved their kind from dying out altogether.

Hugo hated it. More than once, he'd suggested to Pete that they give up, leave the lands and go into the human world, live there amongst them. They could pass, he'd insisted. Have a good life there.

"The humans are fools," Pete had told him, time and again. "Without magick, they've managed to create everything they might want, and they're destroying it all, day after day. *This* is our home, our world. I mean to take it back. We are kings of this world, Hugo. I'll not live as a fugitive in another."

Hugo could not argue with that, though part of him wanted to. Instead, he would capitulate. Starling wanted to fight, to bring an end to it, one way or the other. Hugo would fight at his side.

They had no choice now.

Fight, or die.

These were his thoughts as he flew low, wind buffeting his body, long jacket flapping behind him, over the thick stretch of woods behind Peter Starling's house. The salt smell of the ocean came to him, just as the roar of its surf reached his ears.

And another sound as well.

Shouting. A crash of something shattering. A scream of terror.

With a frown, his heart beginning to race, Hugo picked up speed, racing through the air toward the home of his leader, his friend, Peter Starling. If the Kunal

Trows had attacked Starling unawares, all their hopes would be destroyed.

"The candles!" Kevin shouted. "Put out the candles!"

He rushed forward, not waiting for the others to respond. Hands tight on the hilt of the sword, he swung it around and shattered the glass globe around a wall sconce. The candle fell to the ground, but the flame continued to burn.

Even dance.

"They're alive," he said, shooting a glance at April, who shattered another sconce as he watched. "Find a way to snuff them."

"Kevin, what—?" she began.

"Do it!"

The Shade knew. It ran at Kevin, huge, thick shadow hands raised above its head. Waves of cold emanated from the creature, and he felt its awareness of him, its hatred. A chill rippled through him as he stamped on the candle, sneaker smearing melted wax, burying the wick. From beneath his foot came tiny cries of anguish.

With a grunt, Kevin dove out of the Shade's path. April extinguished a second light. Farther down the hall, Jack shattered a sconce with his axe. He shoved the tip of the still burning candle into a niche in the stone wall.

One remained. Jesse was there, blood from a scalp wound running down his face. He seemed to be limping just a bit. The mace was clutched in his hands, and he lifted it.

In a grotesque pantomime, the Shade loosed a silent scream and lunged. Jesse brought the mace down, destroying glass, candle and flame in one stroke.

The corridor was plunged into darkness. The window at the end of the hall provided only moonlight, not even enough to throw a shadow. Kevin ran to his older brother in the dark, let Jesse rest on him a moment. He moved his fingers gently through Jesse's hair to make sure the scalp wound was nothing more than a cut, sighed with relief to find that it was merely that.

"That's a lot of blood," he said. "You gonna die?"

"Yeah. But not today." Jesse smiled weakly.

"Good. Be kinda hard to explain to Ma."

A pop resounded in the darkened hall. One of the fallen candles flickered to life, flames dancing about its wick. Then another. The other two remained dead, whatever magickal life was in them snuffed forever. Kevin was sorry, but not very much.

The Shade also did not return. Which was what mattered.

April reached out to touch Jesse on the arm lightly, letting him know she was glad he was okay. Though he'd noticed it before, Kevin pondered for the first time how quiet she'd been ever since they'd left the lair of the Roanes. He studied her face, wanted to ask her about her silence, but now was not the time.

Then, as if in answer to his thoughts, she spoke. "How did you know?"

Kevin shrugged. "Shadows can't exist without the light."

For a moment, none of them spoke. Then Jesse stood up, stretched again, and let out a breath. There were no more smiles, no more whistling in the dark, no more pretense to hide their fear. Now there was only dread. It seemed miraculous that they were still alive, and fruitless to think they might all continue to survive in a world where such horrors lurked around every corner.

April's voice was a whisper. "Nikki."

Kevin looked around, winced at a sharp pain in his neck. Then the pain was gone. One of the heavy wood and iron doors along the hall had opened, just slightly. A pale white face poked out between door and frame, lush red hair in a tangle over her shoulders.

Her green eyes were wide, and they gleamed in the dim light of the two surviving candles.

"Kevin?"

5

To her shame, Nikki had cowered in the far corner of her chamber, hiding away even from the glow of her fire. The window was wide open, the breeze feeding the flames, making the bedclothes sway. She shivered, but shivering was good. It meant she was awake, alive.

Then she'd heard a voice. A human voice, and a familiar one.

Nikki knew about the Kunal Trows. She knew a great deal she wished she had never been told, for most of it horrified or frightened her or made her deeply sad.

So at first, she didn't open the door. There was shouting. Glass shattering. A dark wind that she felt in her heart, like a spirit passing through her. Then nothing. All was quiet again.

The memory of that voice in her head—though her mind was already trying to force her to think she had imagined it—she rose at last and went to the door. Forced herself to look out into the hallway, though she knew the Shade would be there to lunge at her, make her shrink back into her room.

But the Shade was gone.

"Kevin?"

"Oh, Jesus, Nikki."

He ran toward her, but Nikki didn't really believe, couldn't really believe it was him until she felt herself enfolded in his arms. Kevin had been in her thoughts so much since Pete had taken her here. Her best friend, the only one who really knew her heart.

He had tried to tell her, and she had been furious.

"You're all right," he said, voice desperate as he held her close. "You *are* all right? Did he—"

"I'm okay," she confirmed. No more than that.

For in that moment, their embrace ended, they parted, and she looked up into his eyes. Searched them for answers to all the questions she knew she needed to ask. His face held almost no expression, but in his eyes there was fear and sorrow and so much more.

"You came after me." The words sounded so foolish once she'd said them, so obvious.

Kevin nodded. Gestured to the others. "We all did."

Nikki felt tears threaten the edges of her eyes, but she wouldn't allow herself to cry. All that she had felt for him, and Nikki had ignored it for no reason other than that he was too innocent, too good. Now she knew what a fool she had been. For no one else in the world would have come for her save perhaps her mother, and the poor woman would never have had the imagination to know where to begin.

She asked a question she already knew the answer to: "Why?"

"You're my best friend," he whispered.

Their faces were close now. She felt his breath on her cheek.

"Kevin, for fuck's sake!" Jesse growled.

"You really are," Kevin insisted, ignoring his brother. He glanced down at the stone floor, swallowed hard. "I love you."

Before he could look up, Nikki kissed him, long and deep, her breath frozen in her chest.

When the kiss ended, reluctantly, she laid her forehead against his. "I'm sorry I missed your birthday," she whispered.

Kevin laughed a little.

She stared at him, still barely able to believe he was there. "I can't believe you came for me."

Jesse roared. "Jesus, neither can I! Can. We. Fucking. Go?"

Nikki looked at him. Smiled. "Thanks, Jesse." She

looked around. "All of you. But yeah, we should go. If Pete comes back and you're here—"

"He'll fucking kill you."

The voice came from the doorway to the chamber where Nikki had been held captive. Hugo stood there, glaring at her, eyes blazing with fury, lips stretched back over his sharp teeth in a snarl.

"Hugo." Nikki stepped in front of Kevin, took two steps toward the Tuatha de Danaan. "Don't do this."

"You're not leaving," he told her in a snarl. Then he looked past her, at Kevin. "And you're dying."

Nikki lunged at him. "Bastard, I'll kill *you*."

"Wait!" Kevin shouted.

Hugo's huge fist drove her staggering back to crumple to the stone floor in a heap. Dazed, she rolled onto her back and looked up.

Kevin stood with his sword in both hands. "Come on, then. You want to kill me, kill me. Pussy."

Nikki blinked, trying to shake her disorientation. She wanted to shout at him, tell him to stop taunting Hugo. The creature would kill Kevin without a second thought. She couldn't let that happen.

Then Kevin was moving backward, away from her. Nikki thought that was strange, but good.

"Come on, pussy," he taunted. "Or can't you do anything without Peter fucking Pan?"

Hugo stepped past Nikki, giving her a little kick as he went. She whimpered, then started to rise.

"Kevin, what are you doing?" she asked.

He ignored her. She studied his face, the twinkle in his eyes. It didn't make any sense. Jesse and April were behind him, but neither even raised their weapon or said a word to stop Kevin from inviting his death.

"You guys passed pretty good in our world," Kevin said. "The look, the clothes, but mostly it was the way you talked. The slang. You got that down. That's good. So you understand what I mean when I call you a fucking pussy."

Hugo flinched as though the word were an arrow that

had punctured his flesh. Then he roared, and charged headlong down the corridor, his hands hooked into long talons. Kevin held his sword at the ready. Nikki's heart hammered in her chest. If he could just wound Hugo, at least, they might still get out alive. But the Tuatha de Danaan weren't even human. Their strength was incredible. Without the guise of false humanity, they were savages.

Hugo snarled. "Little prick, Murphy. I'll take your head off." He thundered down the corridor, leather soles slapping stone, and passed an open doorway.

From out of the doorway came Jack Ross, with a hideous, bloodstained double-edged axe. He swung it with all his might, a look of sheer determination on his face, teeth bared. With a wet crunch, the axe buried itself in Hugo's back. The Tuatha de Danaan screamed shrilly, then fell onto his chest on the floor.

Twitching.

Blood ran from his mouth and the wound in his back, spreading quickly into a large pool on the floor, little rivulets running through the gutters made by the mortar between stones.

They all stared at Jack.

"Let's get out of here," he said, voice wavering. "Fast."

When they descended to the first floor, the goblins were nowhere to be seen. The ocean wind blew in through the shattered window, and Kevin shuddered, even with the Roane cloak over his shoulders. They had left a Tuatha de Danaan dead upstairs, killed some of Pete Starling's servants, destroyed his property, stolen Nikki back; there would be repercussions. Kevin knew it, and though none of them had said a single word, he knew the others did too. They had no time to waste.

The descent along the servants' stairs would take time. There was nothing they could do about that.

Except hurry.

It was dark on the stairs going down from the first

floor to the cellar. Kevin reached back and took Nikki's hand in his own, unable to stop himself from thinking how wonderful it felt, how amazing, to just touch her like that. Not only had he told her the secret of his heart, that he loved her, but she felt the same. There hadn't even really been time for him to take that in before Hugo attacked. And now they were running.

They had found Nikki, yes. But that didn't constitute a rescue. Not yet. Not until they all got home, back to Fox Run Drive.

When they passed the shafts on either side of the stairs where they'd first seen the goblins, they moved with great caution. There was no sign of the little creatures, however. After that, they moved quickly, hustling down the rest of the stairs and running for the cellar door. Jesse was in front. When he hauled the door open, the goblins were there.

One of them leaped at Jesse, its claws snagging on the Roane cloak. He batted it away with a crack of breaking bone. By then, others were flooding out of the cellar to block their path.

"The girl is the Master's prisoner," one of them whined. "We will not let you take her."

Kevin and Jack moved up beside Jesse, keeping April and Nikki behind them. The goblins shuffled around a bit, as though waiting for the right moment to attack.

"We don't have time for this," Kevin muttered.

One of the goblins screamed and rushed at Jack. He had retrieved his axe from Hugo's back—had to put his foot on the dead man's back to work it free—and now he swung it in a downward arc that split the goblin in two. Kevin had a moment of wishful thinking when he imagined the others might turn and run, but they screamed as if they had been the ones cut by the axe, and began to swarm in toward the guys.

Kevin swung his sword, wounding one. He lifted the blade again, but from behind Nikki caught his arm.

"Wait," she said.

Her green eyes, overwhelmed with hope and love and

relief only moments before, now flashed with a fire forged through endurance and determination, a facet of her personality that Kevin had always admired. Though he paused immediately, the others kept on with the skirmish.

"Stop it!" Nikki shouted.

Even the goblins paused, startled by her ferocity. Nikki pushed past Kevin and Jack to stand beside Jesse, though all three of them stood ready to leap into the fray once more.

"You!" Nikki snapped, then crouched in front of one particular goblin, whose face was even more cracked and leathery than the others. It glared at her. "You're the one who brought my meals," she said.

There was no trace of a question in her voice, but the goblin only watched her defiantly.

"You will not be allowed to leave," croaked the one Kevin had wounded, as it cupped a hand to the bleeding gash in its shoulder. "Even if you get past us, you won't get far. The Master hears everything that transpires within the walls of his home. Everything."

Nikki stood up, sighing as though merely exasperated. Then she kicked the goblin in front of her. It shrieked in pain as it slammed back into the stone wall, and then slumped to the floor, heaving for breath.

"Get out of the way," she growled. "We're going. Try to stop us, and we'll kill you all, I swear to God. I am going home today."

Kevin tried to hide his grin. Much as he wanted to be the hero, to rescue her and play that whole role, he'd known from the start that despite her predicament, Nikki was no damsel in distress. If he'd even suggested such a thing, she probably would have hurt him.

Similarly cowed, the goblins stared back at her, then looked at the weapons the others were holding, and finally began to move aside.

"You'll never escape," the wounded one muttered.

"That's my problem, you little shit," Nikki purred.

"Now why don't you go upstairs? I think you've got a pretty big mess to clean up."

The goblins stood aside while they went into the cellar, where the last few bottles of wine were still undisturbed. Candles burned in sconces, but this time the flames did not dance nor waver at all. In a far corner, in a pair of large baskets filled with dirty clothing, Nikki found the clothes she'd been wearing upon her arrival. They were dirty, but nobody else was going to complain. By then, they were all wearing filthy clothes.

Moments later, they started down the steps. This time, it was Nikki who reached back and took Kevin's hand. They continued for several minutes, until April broke the silence.

"I can't believe we killed him," she said.

In the soft glow of candles, they all slowed on the stairs and exchanged glances.

"The goblins, or whatever, that's one thing. But I can't help remembering what he was. I mean, on the trestle and after, we thought he was human." April didn't look at any of them, just kept moving down the stairs, speaking quietly, as though to the shadows.

"He wasn't human," Jesse said bluntly.

Jack grunted softly. " 'Sides, you didn't kill him. I did."

"It's the same thing," April protested.

Nikki shook her head. "I'm sorry if I can't be more sympathetic, but if you hadn't killed him, Kevin would be dead. I'd be dead. Maybe the rest of you, too."

Kevin felt her squeeze his hand and he squeezed back.

Jesse cleared his throat before speaking up. "We've got to get home. Whatever that means, whatever it takes . . ." he paused, turning it over in his head. He went down a half dozen more stairs before continuing. "They won't think a second before killing us. We've got to deal with them the same way. You mentioned the trestle. They threatened us even then. Pete took advantage of Nikki; then he kidnapped her, for Christ's sake.

Took her here. Who knows what he had planned for her?"

That seemed to satisfy April. But now Nikki was silent. In the light from a wall sconce, he saw that she was chewing on her lower lip.

"Nik? You okay?" he whispered.

"I know what he had planned," she said aloud.

"Are you going to tell us, or should we guess?" Jack drawled.

From anybody else, Nikki might have been offended by those words. But she'd known Jack a long time, knew what he was like. She laughed softly, sadly, and kept on down the steps.

"I don't have a real solid grasp of the timing here, but I think we're talking in thousands of years. Even one like Pete, who looks young, has been around for centuries, at least. We're talking about fairies, I guess. Other things. A lot of myths and legends we have in our world are wrapped up in the Tuatha de Danaan, and in the Trows. The Trows were here first. They were the originals. Along with a lot of the other weird species around, the goblins, sprites, all of that. Pete . . ."

Her voice caught, revealing a painful truth: part of Nikki was still in love with Pete Starling. Kevin tried to pretend he didn't notice.

"We might have to get past those Trows again," Jesse interrupted. "We know they can't go out in the daylight. The Roane told us it would turn them to stone. But since it's almost never daylight, that's no friggin' help. Did you learn anything about them we could use?"

Nikki was thoughtful as she touched the stone wall to steady her on the stairs.

"The only thing I can think of is that they hate loud noises. All of the family estates of the Tuatha de Danaan have bell towers. Besides the fact that they're across the water and so exposed and the Trows don't want to risk the sun coming up, even for a second, he said they tend to stay away because of the bells."

"Huh." Kevin held tight to Nikki's hand. "Maybe I'm

missing something, but this is a war, right? When they go to fight the Trows, why don't they just bring the bells with them?"

"They're too big, I guess. If something smaller would do the job, I figure they'd have tried that already," Nikki replied. "Like I said, the Trows were here first. But at some point, I don't know if it was from war or some kind of disease or what, all the females became sterile. The way to pass into the human world had not been discovered, but once in a while, a human being would stumble into this world by mistake, get trapped in a fairy circle, disappear in the Bermuda Triangle or whatever and end up here.

"The Trows wanted offspring. They used some kind of magick to hide the way they looked, and they got the human women to have sex with them. Some didn't bother with the magick, and just raped them instead. After a while, there were families here. The human women died, of course. They'd grow old and be gone so fast, the Trows would have to take new wives. Eventually they started really taking them, going into our world and coming back with women they'd seduced."

Jesse glanced around anxiously. "Not to rush you, Nikki, but can we save this for later? History is good, but it's not going to help us right now."

"You're missing the point," Nikki told them. "Pete and the others? Their fathers were Trows."

Kevin was befuddled. "Why are they at war, then?"

"There was a kind of uprising. The Trows started to see humans as diseased, and anything from our world as tainting this one. There were some who actually loved the women they'd abducted, and argued the point. They were murdered. So were all of the human women."

"Their mothers," April whispered, actually stopping for a moment to stare back at Nikki on the stairs. "Pete and the others, the Tuatha de Danaan, their fathers murdered their mothers?"

"The ones who hadn't already died of old age. The mixing had been going on for ages by then," Nikki replied. "But yeah, Pete and Doug's mother was one of them. That was when the war started. The Tuatha de Danaan against their fathers and brothers and uncles. Pete's father was pretty well respected. They made him the leader, pretty much. At first, he was afraid that not having humans around would do the opposite of what the others feared, that without their mothers, they would turn out to be like their fathers after all.

"For a while, they went to our world and pleaded with women to be their mothers, to take care of them."

Now it was Kevin's turn to freeze. He stared at Nikki, fingers slipping away from hers. Then he turned and looked for Jesse, finding in the gloom that his brother's expression matched his own.

"Peter Pan," Jesse muttered. "Holy shit."

"Yeah," Kevin agreed.

As they all took that in, they started walking again. Faster, it seemed to Kevin, as if the urge to leave had grown even greater in those few seconds.

"You had sex with him," April said, her tone apologetic. "He didn't want you to be his mother, Nikki."

Nikki nodded. "That's true. They gave that up after a while. The Trows would kill the women if they saw them. And there was already another problem. There are no females among the Tuatha de Danaan. None were ever born. Or . . . Pete figures they may have been born, but killed by the Trows because they thought girls were too weak to be warriors.

"The war went on, and the Tuatha de Danaan were losing. They are losing. Period. No more Trows will be born. Not ever, unless they interbreed again, and they won't. But no more Tuatha de Danaan either. And Pete's people are just outnumbered, plain and simple. They decided they had no choice but to start again, to find human girls who would stay, who would have children."

"Just to send them to war and watch them die," April said, horrified.

Kevin stared at Nikki from behind as they emerged

into the cavern near the bottom of the island. Another eighty steps or so and they'd be at the tunnel, and then out on the rocks, the crashing waves threatening to wash them away.

"You were the first one?" he asked.

Nikki nodded.

With a sick feeling in his stomach, Kevin laughed. "Unbelievable," he said. "You almost had me feeling sorry for them. That's pretty sad shit. Fucking tragic." He could hear the snarl in his own voice; didn't like it, but could not to erase it. "But when it comes right down to it, Pete and the boys did exactly what they were afraid of the most. They turned out just like their fathers, doing the same damn thing."

"Not quite the same," Nikki said, her voice tight. "He never raped me. Doug . . . Doug tried, and Pete stopped him. He never touched me after he brought me here. He said he wanted me to make up my own mind."

Jack chuckled softly. "What a prince."

"He still pretended to be something he wasn't," April argued. "God, Nikki, he kidnapped you. And what would he have done if you just told him to screw. Sure, that was your choice, but was he going to send you home, or just kill you?"

Nikki shrugged. "We'll never know. And it wouldn't matter. I'd rather die than stay here. This isn't real. It isn't home. I won't lie, I feel bad for them, but I'm not going to trade my life for that."

They reached the bottom of the steps. In the cavern, Nikki turned to Kevin. Her eyes were wide as she regarded him gravely.

"I want to go home." There was a plea in her voice that almost broke his heart. Despite the strength she exhibited, her hard shell, she was just as lost and afraid as the rest of them.

"Me too," Kevin agreed. "It's going to be tricky, but I think I have at least part of it worked out. As long as I don't drown."

*　　*　　*

Peter Starling had extraordinary eyesight. Even from so far above, he could see the outcropping of rocks where the servants' entrance to his ancestral island home was tucked away.

High above the house of his forefathers, the freezing wind whipping around him, he seemed to dance on air. Flying was the only way he knew to really let his mind go, let the thoughts come, and the knowledge of what he must do enter him.

From there, he could see the dead goblin amidst the shattered glass outside one of the windows of his estate. He had heard it all, of course, with the magick that allowed him to hear everything that transpired in his home; but he had been too far away to return before now.

He had heard them invading his home, fighting his servants, freeing his captive. Only moments before he had made it back to the estate, he had heard Hugo die.

Hugo had never been very bright.

Nikki, Kevin, and the others had made it past the goblins, as he imagined they would. They'd outwitted the Shade, destroyed it. Now Starling waited patiently as they descended the inner stairwell in the house.

At length, his patience was rewarded. When Nikki emerged with Kevin, Starling could see, even from so far above, that their hands were entwined. The others came out after them, and for an instant—only an instant—he thought of killing them all. Swooping down from the frozen night and tearing them open, strewing their entrails across the waves.

They turned out just like their fathers, Murphy had said, his words resonating in Starling's ears, no matter that they were deep within the earth and he so far above it.

It was the truth, and it made him ashamed, and feeling that way made him want to hurt them. That was the last thing in the world he had wanted, and yet, Nikki herself was proof of it. It was a truth that Pete had managed to hide from himself until he found his little brother attacking Nikki, ready to just take her, no better than a monster.

No better than a Trow.

Starling closed his eyes and breathed deeply, and let the power of the wind lull him until he was in control again.

For a brief moment, he wondered how they were going to make the swim back, given that they had Roane pelts only for four of them. Then Murphy gave his to the girl, to Nikki. Starling grinned, but it didn't feel like smiling. Of course he'd given it to her. He loved her. Always had. Hell, Pete had seen that much right off. He'd known Kevin was trouble, and done everything he could to avoid it.

Managed it pretty well, too. How was he to know the kid would actually try to follow . . . no, not just try, but actually follow them back home, straight on 'til morning. Once in a while, humans wandered in, or found the way after years of trying.

Eventually, Neverland killed them all.

Cloaked in Roane skin, they dove into the ocean from the rocks. A moment later, Kevin jumped in after them. The frozen water would kill him if he was in it long enough. Or it would, if he was going to be in it that long. Two of the false Roanes grabbed him beneath his arms and, propelling him along, they swam for the mainland.

Pete let them go.

They made the mainland in no time. April's heart soared. Though she had never let herself think about dying, never in her wildest dreams had she imagined they would succeed.

As she climbed out of the ocean onto the rocks beneath the open cliff face where the Roane had their lair, she let the cloak slip down around her sides again. She tasted salt water on her tongue. A sense of melancholy filled her, and she looked at the ocean again, remembered the way the water had sluiced off her, the power she felt as she sliced through the waves.

"You all right, April?" Nikki stood there on the rocks, stretching, looking at her fingers as though she had never seen them before.

April understood. The first time she had worn the pelts into the water and felt the transformation their magic had induced in her, she had felt herself redefined by both ocean and magic. To her, it had been a pleasure, an exhilaration unlike any she had ever known. But she understood how it could be disconcerting for others. The expression on Nikki's face made it clear the girl was in no rush to don the pelts again.

Then Jack and Jesse were there, climbing up out of the water. For the first time, April saw the transformation clearly. She watched in amazement as the creatures stood up on the rocks, humans with dark, oily scalskin for flesh. Then the illusion—a glamour so strong it fooled the sea itself—fell away with a ripple and the pelts once more hung as cloaks around the guys' necks. Jack and Jesse blinked, both glancing down to be certain they had indeed returned to normal, and then turned to haul Kevin out of the water and up onto the rocks. He was not moving.

"Kevin!" Jesse shouted at his brother's still form. "Open your eyes, Kev!"

Nikki went to him, crouched there, and April watched her. She was surprised to see the love in the other girl's face. Kevin loved her, they all knew that. But none of them, April thought, had really expected Nikki to love him back. She hoped it wasn't just that they had come to rescue her. Hoped that it was real love.

Kevin coughed, water spilling from his mouth. He shook his head with a groan, and his eyes opened. Slowly, he sat up.

"Goddamn, I'm cold," he cursed, then shivered.

Jesse slipped a Roane cloak over his shoulders. "You'll be warmer up in the Roane cave," he told his brother. "We all will. Now if we can just figure out how to get home—"

"I've been thinking about that," Kevin interrupted. "We came through the woods at dawn. I think maybe if we go back the same way, we'll be able to find the trail home. We can ask the Roane to tell us when it's almost dawn, and stay away from the Kunal Trows. Once the sun comes up, we're on the way home."

"Let's hope so," Nikki said. "It isn't how I got here, so I hope you guys are right."

"We have to be right," Kevin said, coughing a bit more. "I don't think anybody who knows how to get us home is going to help us at this point."

April glanced at the ocean again. She closed her eyes as the salt spray spattered her face, waves crashing so close by. With a sigh, she pulled the Roane cloak around her again. Then she shook her head to clear the bizarre thoughts that were intruding upon her mind. Every time she thought about going home, she felt all turned around, like she had walked into a room to search for something and then forgotten what she had been looking for.

Home. What is that? All her life she had felt awkward and out of place, without any sense of belonging. "Somewhere Over the Rainbow" had never been a pretty song from a movie to her, but a private anthem, a dream of finding her place in the world, knowing that she belonged.

Ever since they had arrived here in this Neverland April had been by turns horrified and amazed to realize that for the first time in her life she *did* feel at home, despite the danger and the madness. It baffled and frightened her, and the logical part of her mind kept pushing to the fore and reminding her that she had a home and a family, and they were likely stricken with grief by now.

Though she had always had friends, people who loved her and made her laugh, April had too often thought the world around her gray and drab. This world was vibrant, intense.

But it's not home, she reminded herself insistently. Home had her family and friends and school and malls and movies, and it had Jack.

He stood behind her and touched her elbow. With a sigh she turned to regard him.

"You okay?" he asked, frowning with concern.

April nodded. She took one more glance at the sea, then reached out and twined her fingers into his. "Come on," she said. "We don't know how much time we have until morning. I don't want to miss it."

Jack slipped his arms behind her back, and pushed her tangled hair away from her face. He stroked her cheek, his blue eyes no longer so icy and clear.

They kissed. Only for a moment, but it was sweet. As they began to move, side by side, toward the rudimentary steps that led from the crumbled rocks to the hole in the cliff where the Roane had their lair, Jack kept his arm around her waist. The pull of the ocean and this bizarre world was still there, but that easy familiarity, silent and yet so full, gave her the strength to hide her regrets, even from herself.

Besides, as long as Trows were here, it was not as though she could stay, even if she were crazy enough to really want to. Nor would she do that to her family. It wouldn't be right.

Content, relieved, and suddenly feeling all the exhaustion of the previous days, she bent over and used her hands to maintain balance as they climbed the wall. The wind wrapped icy fingers around her and tried to pull her off the cliff face, but they didn't have far to climb, less than twenty feet from rocks to the opening in the cliff. Jack moved more quickly, and so was the first to reach the cave.

"Kevin. You've gotta see this," Jack said, the wind carrying his voice away almost too quickly for April to hear.

She moved faster. When she had finally pulled herself

into the cave, she stood up beside him and looked around. The heat of the Roane lair touched her instantly, but it did not warm her. The phosphorescent mineral veins in the walls lit the chamber well, but April wished she could not see what was illuminated.

"Oh, God," Jesse muttered behind her.

April didn't even realize she was crying until Jack reached over to wipe a tear from her eye.

"They're all dead," Kevin whispered.

Lost, all the excitement over rescuing Nikki and their own escape bleeding out of them, the five of them wandered the large chamber, with its water hole at the center.

"God, poor things," Nikki whispered.

Kevin dropped to his knees and threw up, the sounds of his retching making April's own stomach lurch. A moment later, he stood up, embarrassed, and wiped the back of his hand across his mouth.

"Its . . . it's Toska," he said, gesturing at a tiny corpse which lay not far from the gaping water hole.

Toska had been torn open. As April moved even closer, tears coming stronger now, she saw that wasn't the worst of it. From the condition of the Roane's viscera, and marks on the bones of his arm, it was clear that something had been eating Toska, gnawing at him.

"That hole," Kevin said. Nikki put a hand on his bicep, trying to comfort him in her way. "They couldn't fit down it, though."

"Once they figured out where it was, though, they must have started looking for another way in," Jesse added, his eyes sad, his face slack with the shock of it.

Jack frowned, gaze darting about the room. "And they found one," he said, voice dropping to a hoarse whisper. "Which means they could still be—"

He was interrupted by a low grunt that sounded to April like a pig snuffling in the dirt. She looked across the chamber at the narrow exit that led into the tunnel. It was blocked by three Kunal Trows, and there was movement behind them. More coming.

With a roar unlike anything April had ever heard, from him or anywhere else, Jack ripped the sword from Jesse's hands. He screamed as he ran at the Trows.

"Motherfuckers!"

He brought the blade down on the first one he came to. The monster's leather armor turned the edge of the sword away. Jack tried to bring it up again. Kunal Trows were slow, but not that slow.

The one he had attacked clutched Jack's throat in its left hand, lifted him off the ground, then punched through his rib cage with its other hand, and ripped his spine right out through his chest.

It made the most horrible noise.

April barely heard it over her own screams.

6

The goblins had piled the wood high in the enormous fireplace in Peter's private chambers. The warmth was welcome, soothing, in light of the battle to come. After Hugo's body had been put to the fire and the ashes scattered to the sea below, a war council had been held. The others had gone to gather their men and prepare for the attack, and Pete had returned to his quarters to ruminate one last time, to make absolutely certain that he had considered everything. There was a great deal left to chance, and no guarantee that even if all went as he hoped it would, they would emerge victorious. But it was the only chance they had.

Curt sat with him in silence. They had each had a small snifter of brandy, set ablaze for warmth and then swallowed only seconds after the fire had been snuffed.

Pete had a mission for him, one equal parts whimsy and cleverness. It would put his most trusted warrior away from the battle for a time, but if all went well, it would gain them a moment or two of confusion that they would sorely need.

In huge, high-backed wooden chairs carved with the images of sprites and nyads, they sat before the fireplace. Pete watched the flames through the amber liquid in his snifter, the blazing light refracted within the glass, diffused in the brandy.

When Doug came in, throwing the door open with such force that it banged against the wall, Curt jumped. Pete didn't. Rather, he was surprised that it had taken so long for his brother to confront him.

"You're a coward, Peter. And a fool." Doug stood at the center of the room and glared defiantly at the back of his older brother's chair.

Curt started to rise.

"Sit down," Pete ordered.

After a moment's pause, Curt settled back into the chair and turned his attention to the fire. Pete Starling was lord of the Tuatha de Danaan, and he had given a command. From that point on, whatever was said in his chambers, it would be as though Curt were not even there.

Pete remained seated, his back to Doug. "You have something to say?" he asked.

"I've said it," Doug growled, nostrils flaring as though he were truly the savage beast he sometimes seemed.

"Then you should go."

"I will not go. This is the house of my father, damn you. You're the oldest, yes, but it's still my home, no matter where you send me to live or what reason you—" Doug roared. "Look at me, you bastard!"

He grabbed Pete's shoulder from behind and hauled back on him so hard that the chair toppled to the ground. Testament to the craftsmanship of its maker, it did not break. Doug lunged out at his brother with his talons.

Pete rolled out of the way, sprang to his feet, and kicked his brother in the chest. Doug slammed back against a shelf of leather-bound volumes, and then Pete was on him. Faster, stronger, he pinned his brother to the bookshelf.

Nose to nose, he snarled at Doug. "You forget yourself, Douglas, for the second time in as many days."

"You intend to set the humans free. That girl, the bitch you coddled so well, she and her friends killed Hugo, and you're going to let them go."

Almost without realizing he was doing it, Pete released his brother. Doug's chest rose and fell with his rage, but that dwindled as they faced one another.

"I don't care one whit about the humans. Live or die,

their lives are in fate's hands. But they did not kill Hugo. *I* did," Pete said, voice low. "We all did."

Curt twitched in the chair by the fireplace, but did not turn. Though Pete would not have blamed him if he did.

"What the fuck are you talking about?" Doug said, his disgust obvious.

Pete turned away. He walked to the fire and leaned on the mantel, watching the dance of the cinder sprites.

"Maybe you were too small to see it, Douglas. Or it's been so long, these hundreds of years, that you've forgotten. Or it may be that you just don't want to remember how sad our mother was, most of the time. She loved us. You especially, her little one. But she had been stolen away from the world that she knew. Father took her and told her there was no way back, and then, when she knew it was hopeless, he seduced her."

From behind him, Pete could hear Doug's labored breathing cease, just for a moment.

"If not for that, we wouldn't have been born," Doug said, voice tight with emotion.

Pete watched the fire dance. "Perhaps that would have been best."

"How can you say that?" Doug snapped. "Lore Starling was kinder to his wife, our mother, than any Kunal Trow ever was. He didn't rape her, Peter, she loved him."

"She had no choice. What else was there for her to do, but love him, or die lost and alone, a prisoner in this world? All along, I've been against this. The memory of her eyes haunts me. But for the good of our people, I've gone along with it. I know what you'll say: the Tuatha de Danaan will be extinct without human women to bear our sons. Well I say so be it. If we give them the truth, and they are willing to come here, to stay here, that's one thing. Anything else—will never succeed."

Finally, Curt did stir. He didn't rise, but he looked up at Pete, their gazes locking in the flickering firelight.

"You told Nikki about us. Everything. She left, Pete."

"Aye," Pete said, unconsciously drifting into an older

speech pattern. "Which may mean there's no hope for us."

He turned to face Doug once more. "I seduced her. I brought her here against her will and made her a prisoner. Her friends came to rescue her, Hugo got in the way, and they killed him. I'd never have imagined them capable of such a thing. They're humans, and children besides. I'd forgotten, though, the way the very world around us reacts to the presence of human beings. Just as the impossible becomes possible for us in their world, the same is true for them in ours.

"That's beside the point, however. Hugo is dead, and wouldn't be if we hadn't started all of this. If Nikki and her friends are still alive, they'll be trying to get home. The humans may be weak, but our mother was one of them. For her sake, I'm not going to stop them and neither are you. This war is ours to finish."

"You're a coward and a fool," Doug said again. "She's here already. Just take her and be done with it. How you became lord of the Tuatha de Danaan I'll never understand. And if you want to blame yourself for Hugo's death, that's your business. For my part, I'll have blood in payment for his."

Pete glowered at him. "The Trows are monsters. I won't be that. We'll let them go if they survive that long. Then, if we are victorious in the coming battle, we will attend once more to the question of extinction. As for you, brother, you'll obey me, or I'll kill you myself."

With a snort of impatience, Doug turned and left the room. After he'd gone, Curt spoke softly from his chair. "Watch him carefully, Lord Peter."

It wasn't a dream anymore.

The Kunal Trow stronghold was little more than a mountain that had been carved to look like a castle. From far enough away, it might even have carried off the intended appearance. But close up, it was nothing of the sort. Crude, rough-hewn, and carrying a repugnant stench, the Trow lair reflected its denizens perfectly.

Enormous rats scurried about as if busy on errands vital to the encampment. There were spiders, too, so enormous that the rats were their primary source of food. Narrow tunnels carried air from the mountain's surface down into its bowels, bored through as much as hundreds, perhaps thousands of feet of rock. Kevin had no idea how those holes had been made, but he suspected that the stronghold was only livable thanks to the air they brought down from the surface.

The four of them had been dragged from the Roane den by warrior trolls, perhaps even the same ones they had escaped upon first arriving in this land. Once out into the night air, the Trows had bound their wrists with thick rope and marched them across the dead, frozen land, withered scrub crunching beneath their feet. Nikki had screamed and fought, slapping and clawing at the huge, snorting things. Their piglike faces seemed almost pleased with her struggles, until one of them struck her across the back of the head, and Nikki dropped to the ground in a heap.

She was not unconscious, but quite disoriented. Kevin feared brain damage. But he also wished for all of them the oblivion such an injury would have brought. Almost anything would have been better than the bitter truth they were left with now.

It wasn't a dream anymore.

With Nikki tossed unceremoniously across the hindquarters of a huge horse, the Trows linked Jesse, Kevin and April with chains and alternately marched and dragged them across the frozen land. During that time, Kevin nearly froze to death. He had given his Roane cloak to Nikki, and the cotton sweatshirt he wore was not enough protection against the elements. For a time, his mind ceased functioning.

He relished it. If he stopped thinking, he would not have to remember the fourth cloak, the one that could have kept him warm. The one that was still on Jack's corpse, back in the lair of the Roane.

Not a dream.

Kevin was numb, part of him more frightened than he had ever been before, and the rest of him just weak and exhausted and sick with grief. He had surrendered himself. His mind flashed back to years before, when his father had still lived at home and had sparred drunkenly with his mother on a regular basis. Kevin remembered how tiny and powerless and insignificant he had felt then, how like a child.

His fate was in other hands now. Throughout their ordeal he had manufactured a kind of pretense that whatever happened in Neverland would not affect his own world. His brain knew better, but his heart had somehow convinced him that this place was not real.

In a single, bloody, devastating moment, he had learned better.

Jack was dead.

Kevin lay on the cold stone floor of a dungeon, chained to the wall alongside his brother and Nikki and April. Kevin could not even look at them, so heavy was the guilt in his heart. He was too numb even to cry.

"Oh, Jesus," he whispered to himself. "Oh, God."

Jesse moved closer to him, leaned in, stretching his chains to their limit. "Kevin. Don't, bro. Come on."

"But it's my—"

"Don't even say that shit. He's . . . he was my best friend. My head's so fucked up right now I don't know what to do about anything. But we've gotta hold it together. Wishing, or blaming it on yourself, won't make Jack any more alive. You didn't force him to come.

"And I gotta tell you, little brother, I'm fucking scared. I didn't want Jack to die, but right now, all I want to do is figure out how to keep the rest of us from following him. So stop fuckin' whining about it being your fault, and help me figure out how to get out of this."

Kevin felt like throwing up. Bile rose in the back of his throat and he had to breathe through his nose. He fought it, though, and in a moment, it had passed. Tears burned the corners of his eyes, and he bit his lip. He

had felt so cold and hollow since the Trows killed Jack
that he hadn't stopped to wonder why they were still
alive. According to what Peter had told Nikki, the things
hated anything human. They had started a civil war to
expunge any trace of the mortal world from their own.

So why?

With supreme effort, Kevin closed his eyes, took a
few long breaths, and pushed his fear away as best he
could. For the first time since the Trows had chained
him there, he stood up and looked at the others. Nikki
had a cut on her forehead, but the blood had dried and
he thought she would be okay. April watched him, her
eyes glazed with shock. Jesse was bruised, his lip split,
his face ragged with light stubble. But he was okay.

"Nikki, I want you to think," Kevin said. "Try to remember if Pete said anything that would give us an idea
why they're keeping us alive."

She nodded, but before she could so much as roll the
question around in her head, April snorted. Her eyes
still gazed off into nothing, but a sickening grin now
etched her features.

"Oh, shit, is that all? That's easy," she said, her voice
high and wild. "When we were being marched over here,
one of the Trows whispered it in my ear, while he was
grabbing my tits and pawing my ass. Maybe you guys
noticed, but there aren't a lot of growing things around
out there. Not a lot of animals either. And the big fuckers don't look like much by way of fishermen to me."

April focused at last, staring hard at Kevin.

"They're going to eat us."

They were horrified, and April was glad. A part of
her, the bitter, terrified girl who took up so much of the
space in her head now, wanted them to hurt. Her whole
body felt cold, as if she were as dead as Jack, and her
mind seemed to move slowly, registering everything
around her just a bit after it happened.

The Trow had ripped through him, torn out his spine.
She'd seen it all. Much as it sickened her, it left April

with the perverse desire to hurt someone. Kevin in particular. It wasn't his fault, not really. But she wanted it to be, just so there would be someone to blame whom it would be within her power to hurt.

"I wish we knew how much time we had," Jesse said.

April watched as Nikki pulled herself up by her chains and turned to the wall.

"I guess that means we ought to assume we don't have any time at all," the other girl said. Hanging by her chains, she put her sneakers against the stone and pulled, trying to tear out the iron hook that kept her there.

"Oh, that'll work," April said coldly.

"April, please," Kevin said. "Don't do this. I know . . . I mean, I understand that you're just trying to deal, but we've got to work together on this."

"We've done so well up till now," April retorted, her tone earnest enough for the sarcasm to really cut him deep.

Kevin lowered his eyes.

Nikki had stopped trying to tear the moorings of her chain from the wall. Her expression was filled with pain and fear enough that those emotions erased any sympathy she might otherwise have had.

"I've known Jack five years," Nikki said bluntly. "His older sister was my best friend, right up until she took off. You're not going to want to hear this, April, but that's never stopped me before. I know you're hurting. If there's a God and heaven and all that shit, I'm pretty sure Jack's pissed off right now. But I know Jack, and he wouldn't be blaming me, or Kevin, or even Pete. He'd be blaming the motherfucker who killed him."

April winced, dropping her eyes under the intensity of Nikki's words.

"And if he was still alive, and you'd been the one murdered, I can guarantee you he wouldn't say word one about who to blame, or how hopeless it all is. He'd be figuring out how to get the fuck out, to stay alive, and keep alive the people who survived.

"When Jack was ten, an older kid on the bus gave

him a wicked beating. The kid wanted him to say his sister was a slut. Other shit no little boy should ever say about his sister. Even if it's true. That kid and his buddies beat on Jack every chance they got for a month. It ended with Jack getting his wrist broken, and the kids getting expelled. I'll tell you what, though, he never said it. And he never would.

"You want to blame someone, fine. Blame me. Blame Kevin. Blame fuckin' Jack, while you're at it. He's the asshole who agreed to come along. None of you should be here. You shouldn't have come after me, and I shouldn't have fallen for Pete. Even if he wasn't . . . whatever he is, I knew he was trouble, and I liked it.

"But deal with the blame when we're all out of here and home."

"Home," April whispered. In her mind's eye, for just an instant, she saw the ocean, felt it around her as she swam, a Roane hunting fish. Then the image shifted, and she could picture her house on Applewood Road, and her sisters, and her parents . . . and Jack.

But the picture shouldn't have had Jack in it anymore. He was gone.

The tears came suddenly, sprang from her eyes between one breath, one blink, and the next. They coursed down her cheeks, hot and salty, and she looked at Kevin and Jesse, her hands raised helplessly. Nikki was next to her, the only one close enough for her to touch. Though the two girls didn't know each other that well, when April reached to steady herself, Nikki held out a hand. April collapsed into her and sobbed. Nikki held on.

"I don't even know what home is anymore," she whispered.

With a sniffle, she wiped her eyes and ran her hands through her stringy, days-unwashed hair. Kevin was watching her warily, as though she might explode.

"Don't look at me," she said grimly, gaze shifting from Kevin to Jesse. "Figure out how to get us out of here."

7

In the silence of their cell, Nikki sat cross-legged on the floor, back stiff and straight against the rough stone wall. The chains were long enough that she could have stretched full out, but she couldn't have stayed awake then. She needed to be awake.

The others were all sleeping. Just a little. A couple of hours, they had all agreed. Nikki had been able to sleep off and on while a prisoner in Starling's estate, but the others were physically and emotionally exhausted. Fear and adrenaline had driven them all for going on two days, with only a catnap or two in the lair of the Roane.

A tiny voice whispered at the back of Nikki's mind, a voice that told her it was all just procrastinating, putting off the acknowledgment that they had nothing; no way to escape. They were dead, and just hadn't accepted it yet. Each time the voice spoke, a louder one—more recognizable as her own—shouted it down inside her head. She was stronger than that. She'd been stupid, yes, but that wasn't going to keep her from getting out of there. Kevin and his friends had come after her. Jack had died to rescue her.

They would find a way.

But every time she managed to convince herself of that, she would be forced to breathe, to inhale, to keep her lungs working, her body functioning. And when she breathed in, she could smell them. The stink of the Kunal Trows permeated everything around her. The mountain above and around them seemed somehow saturated with the stench. Nikki had tried breathing through her mouth, but even that made her want to retch and left the taste of them in her mouth.

It was in her clothes. On her skin where their huge, filthy hands had touched her when they had knocked her out and brought her here. It was in her hair. Not far away from her house in Framingham, just a few miles of back road into Southboro, there was an old farm where they kept a herd of buffalo. Kids were allowed to feed them. On a hot August day, when the animals were sweating, and the odor of the dung-strewn field carried downwind on the breeze, it smelled something like this.

But the stench of the Trows was worse.

Everything about them was worse. Not the goblins nor the Shade, nor the Tuatha de Danaan themselves had frightened her like this. The Trows were huge and dark, tusked and leathery as rhinoceroses, scarred and crude and stupidly cruel. One or two she had seen, mostly being berated and pummeled by others, were literally stooped and drooling, dangerous as brain-damaged grizzly bears. The thought made her smile, but only for a moment. Then it made her sick.

The stink.

While the others slept, Nikki watched the door to their cell with a hot ache in her belly that perfectly balanced the cold fingers that trailed across her scalp. Quite purposely, she avoided looking at Kevin. He was so good; too good. Innocent, in that way. The opposite of all the guys she'd dated. She wondered what all of this would do to him, what it would cost him. It felt so good to love him, and to recognize that. But in other ways, she had never been more miserable.

As she sat there, so alone while the others slept, there was a sudden grinding noise, like car tires on gravel. In the center of the cell, a hole formed, stone crumbling around it. A long serpentine creature burrowed up through the floor. Its body was segmented and looked like it was made entirely of stone, but there seemed to be a kind of skin on it that rippled as it ground across the floor with that gravelly sound. Despite the noise, none of the others moved.

"God, what now?" Nikki whispered in horror. "What are you?" Even as she spoke those words, part of the answer came to her. Creatures like that rock snake, she reasoned, must have been responsible for the matrix of narrow tunnels that brought air down into the stronghold.

The snake sped up suddenly. It bored a hole into the wall not far from the door and was gone. Though she was relieved it was gone, Nikki frowned, curious as to what had made it move so fast. There was a torch burning just outside the cell, and their only light came from the barred window set high in the door. The corners of the cell were filled with shadows. Nikki squinted, staring around at the darkest places. Her heart began to race.

When she swallowed, her throat was dry.

There was a sound. With the noises out in the corridor, clanging and shouts from elsewhere within the Trows' underground den, she hadn't really noticed it before. Jesse was snoring, and that was part of it, too. The other sound seemed to match it, lingering insinuatingly beneath it.

A scratching sound.

In the gathered dark in the corner of the cell farthest from the door, something shifted. Flowing, skittering.

Nikki held her breath. She peered into the dark, not really wanting, but needing, to see. It crawled forward, unnatural and sinister, and approached the edge of the light that sprayed through the bars.

When they'd been brought to the stronghold, Nikki had been slipping in and out of consciousness. Kevin and Jesse had told her about some of the things they'd seen on the way in. Horrid little things like goblins, but smaller and more crooked. Enormous snapping lizards on chains. Like Komodo dragons, Kevin had said, only larger. Spiders as big as puppies.

Nikki's eyes were wide. Her body felt still and cold,

but oddly, her scalp and spine tingled with heat. She had to pee.

It was not a spider. She might not have been as frightened if it had been. It walked with the unnatural, impossible gait of a spider, true, and it had the same predatory awareness. But its trunk was longer, more antlike, and its body was covered with a carapace edged with jagged spines. The shell gleamed in the dim light, as though it were made of ebony glass or some kind of mineral. The pincers at what must have been its face opened and closed reflexively, and what it revealed each time was a maw like the fresh wound from a blade. Something with a needle tip darted out of that maw like a frog's tongue, and then pulled back. The pincers snapped together with a clack like the break at the beginning of a game of pool.

It came at her, skittering. The needle whip from inside its maw flashed out again.

Nikki couldn't help herself. She screamed.

The others awoke instantly. Jesse was the first to see it. He roared something she didn't hear at his brother, and both guys started hauling hard on their chains, trying to free themselves. Jesse pulled so hard that his wrists began to bleed, red lines running down his forearms.

"What the fuck is that?" Kevin looked at Nikki, eyes hard, jaw set. Thinking. "Try to use your chains to climb the wall, Nik. Do it!"

Even as she scrambled to try it, she knew it was useless. The needle whip shot from its mouth and nearly reached her, though it was still a few feet away.

"Kill it!" April shouted wildly. She danced madly around for a minute, liké a boxer ready to brawl. Her head shook, and her shoulders followed suit.

Nikki thought she had lost it.

April started kicking at the spider-thing, and got in one good blow that resounded with a crack. Then the needle whip shot from its mouth and April shrieked her pain as it sliced across her left leg.

"Oh, shit, April," Kevin muttered.

"You've got to get away from it, Nikki!" Jesse warned.

"No shit!" she snapped angrily.

With a surge of adrenaline, she turned, grabbed the iron ring through which her chains were run, and pulled herself up. The ring was moored to the wall, and it held. All that time she'd been wanting it to pull loose, and now she prayed for the opposite. Her muscles already aching, she held her legs up to one side in a gymnast's pose, but she hadn't done gymnastics since the fourth grade, and she knew she could not hold it very long.

If it mattered. She thought the thing might be able to get her, even there.

But it wasn't after her now. It moved back and forth in front of April, who cried out in pain and fear. The thing lashed out at her again, but April lunged to one side, as far as her chains would allow her. The thing still grazed her shoulder, cutting skin.

Kevin and Jesse started to shout, to scream, even. It was their only chance. Her muscles weakening, Nikki screamed as well. She slid down the wall. The spider-thing was waiting for her. The needle whip shot from its maw, and she dodged it. The tip sank into the wall, chipping stone away.

With a sudden crash, the door swung in, banging against the interior of the cell. A Trow guard stood just inside the cell, his massive frame silhouetted by a flood of light from the torch in the corridor. His eyes flared with hellish torchlight.

"Stop that!" the Trow growled.

Nikki let out a stream of filth and curses at the guard. Kevin and Jesse tried to draw the guard's attention to the spider. Finally, the Trow noticed the creature and, with a snort, took three long strides across the cell and crushed it underfoot with one heavy stomp. It broke into jagged shards.

Watching the Trow wipe its boot on the floor, all four of them tried to catch their breath. Nikki's chest rose and fell, and she tried to shake her hair out of her face.

Sweat beaded up on her forehead, despite the cool temperature in the cell. The Roane cloak Kevin had given her was too much now.

"April, talk to me. You okay?" Kevin asked. "April?"

"Good," she said, with a bleary smile. But she did not stand up, and from the way in which she swayed, ever so slightly, Nikki was not sure if she would ever do so.

While the guys were relieved, and mostly concerned about April being wounded, and whether or not the spider-creature was poisonous, Nikki kept her eyes on the Trow. It was too close to her. The stink too much. Her stomach lurched and she almost threw up on the shards of spider in the dust.

Then it looked at her and grinned. One of its tusks was snapped in half. A scar ran across its snout and in a vertical line down its throat. The leather of its armor was worn and shifted noisily as it came toward her. Nikki winced. She did not want to show this thing her fear, but she couldn't help herself. Pain shot through her lip where she bit it, and her breaths came short and ragged.

"Hey! Get the fuck away from her!" Kevin snapped.

Jesse shouted at the thing, too.

The Trow paid no attention. It snorted out clouds of fetid air. When it smiled, Nikki could see the green rot on its teeth. It was a stupid beast, but there was something sparkling in its eyes, a kind of savage intelligence, that terrified her more than its appearance. Something seemed to scurry insectlike inside its mouth. Dozens of tiny somethings. She closed her eyes and turned away and stopped breathing.

The stink was in her nose and mouth and in her brain, even though she held her breath.

"Hey!" Kevin screamed, railing against his chains, trying to get to her. "Hey, you ugly motherfucker. Leave her alone, you hear me?"

The Trow flinched and glared at the two guys for a moment, but then his smile returned. The four-fingered troll reached up to play with Nikki's hair, examining it closely. It sniffed her.

Then it touched her. Rough, thick hands with jagged nails pawed her breasts, tweaked her nipples, began to reach up under her shirt, tearing the fabric in the process.

Eyes squeezed tightly shut, Nikki stopped holding her breath only to scream at it, to deny it. Her eyes popped open and she pounded on the thing. It snorted laughter and shoved her head against the stone wall with one massive hand. Its laugh sounded like pigs rooting in their own waste.

The Trow leaned in and licked her, from throat to eyes, the rough hot scrape of its tongue sending her into a fit of screams. Something skittered across the bridge of her nose. Something else crawled on her neck. Parasites, she thought. From inside the troll.

"No!" she screamed. "No more. Just fucking kill me."

With all her might she shook free and started beating at the Trow with her comparatively small fists. Shackles and chains tore the tough hide on its face, and it snarled and hit her. Nikki's head thunked against the stone wall, and the world began to swim away from her.

It clamped a monster hand between her legs, and she came around fast.

"Jesus, no!"

The entire time, Kevin and Jesse had been screaming at it, but she had dropped into a kind of fugue state, hardly aware of anything going on around her. Now she heard them again.

"You son of a *bitch*, leave her alone! You want to hurt someone, you dumb ugly fucker, come over here! Don't fucking touch her again!" Kevin was raving, out of control.

Jesse tried to kick the Trow, but missed and nearly fell on his ass. While he was righting himself, Kevin continued to scream.

"The Tuatha de Danaan are right. You're a bunch of

cowards. Rapists and murderers without the brainpower to do anything but kill anything you don't control."

Kevin spat a huge gob of mucus onto the Trow's cheek.

It dropped Nikki. Turned toward him. When it walked, it boots were loud as slamming doors. Its chest rose and fell and the putrid stench of its breath, worse even than the odor of its body, preceded it.

Nikki was covered in both smells, but for that moment, they were forgotten.

The Trow drew its sword, the crude blade dull in the torchlight. It grabbed Kevin by the hair with one hand and hauled him up, nearly off his feet. Nikki saw the pain on his face and cried out. The Trow held the sword back, and its intention was clear. It meant to behead him.

"Jesse, help me!" Kevin screamed.

Nikki thought he might have been crying.

Wild, face red with fury and fear, tears on his own face, Jesse lunged at the Trow. It had stepped between the brothers in order to get a grip on Kevin's hair. Stepped in too close.

Jesse threw his chains around the monster's neck and dropped, hauling it back and choking it. Its sword clattered to the ground. The Trow was much stronger than Jesse, and its neck thick as an oak tree. But Jesse just hung there, beyond its reach. In a moment, it would have him, crush him.

Kevin reached to the hideous troll's belt and snatched away its dagger. Both hands over his head, chains rattling as he swung them, he drove the dagger with all of his strength—not down, into its chest, where the armor might have stopped the blade, but up into the Trow's throat, which tore like rawhide.

Blood surged from its neck. Jesse let go as the Trow fell to the ground, clutching its throat. Kevin dropped the dagger, staring at his hands in horror.

"I killed it," he whispered.

"No shit," Jesse said, panting, amazed. "You fucking did it, Kevin, you saved us."

But Kevin wasn't listening. He turned away and vomited up what little there was in his stomach.

"Hey," Nikki whispered his name. When Kevin looked up, she only gazed at him. He had saved them, though neither of them knew for how long. But he had also saved her from whatever the Trow had intended.

Kevin nodded, understanding without her having to speak the words. He wiped the back of his hand across his mouth, then spit several times. Jesse reached out and grabbed his brother's forearm, the closest he could get. Something passed between them. Nikki would not presume to have really known what it was, but she thought that, for as long as they had left, the brothers would be closer than they ever had been before.

On the floor, April stirred. Her eyes were open, and she began to get weakly to her feet.

"I need a doctor, I think," she said, a wan smile on her face. "Maybe we should go now?"

Jesse held up his shackled wrists. "Chains?"

April pointed at the dead Trow, under which a pool of black-red blood had started to form.

"Keys."

The corridors of the Trow lair were crudely excavated, but they were vast. Jesse had used the dead guard's keys to release them, and they wandered about, searching for an exit. Slowly, quietly, they looked around every corner. Thus far, they had not seen any Trows, though they'd heard one or two along side corridors and hurried on quickly.

Nikki had the guard's dagger, Jesse its sword. Kevin was weaponless, but he was more concerned with supporting April than anything. Whatever the spider-thing was, its darting tongue had definitely been poisoned. April was able to walk with his support, but she was fading fast, and he feared he might have to carry her before long.

Gently, as they moved, Kevin leaned his head in and kissed her hair. "I love you, A. You were always one of my best friends. I'm . . . I'm so sorry about . . ."

"I know," she said weakly, her whisper even lower than his own.

"It's just this place. We're so far from home."

"Are we?" she asked. A strange light shone in her eyes "The Trows are evil fuckers, yeah. But there's . . . there's magic here, isn't there?"

Kevin was surprised, but pleased by her response. "I guess there is. But there's magic at home, too."

"You know what?" she said, standing straighter. "I think I'm feeling better."

April pulled away from Kevin and stood up straight. He couldn't deny that, even the way the torchlight made them all look like corpses, April looked better. There was a rosy flush to her skin, as though she'd been laughing. Her voice had gotten louder, and now Nikki and Jesse stopped to look at her.

"Hey, keep it down," Jesse whispered.

"I feel better," April repeated, voice filled with the wonder of a Christmas morning. "Really I do. And look."

She pointed to her left leg, where her jeans were slashed open. The skin beneath was unbroken, without cut or blemish.

"What the fuck?" Jesse said, forgetting now himself to keep his voice low. "How can that be?"

Nikki crouched to take a closer look. "That's impossible," she said.

But Kevin's mind was racing. "Maybe not." They looked at him. "Remember what Toska said? When they were in our world, all kinds of weird shit would happen. Nothing big, no real magic like monkeys raining from the sky or people turning into frogs or whatever. But impossible things. Toska said that was possible for humans in *this* world."

" 'Cause we're not supposed to be here," Nikki finished for him.

There was a roar. Caught off guard, they stumbled back and away from the sound, trying to escape the Trow that charged down the corridor toward them with a heavy axe in hand.

"Oh, God, not now!" April shouted.

She knelt, picked up a large rock and threw it with all her strength at the Trow. The stone struck its face, the Trow stumbled and went down, slamming heavily onto the stone floor on its ample gut. The pig-faced monster rose up, snorting angrily, and hefted the axe again. Too late, however. Jesse put all his weight behind the sword and drove the blade deep into the Trow's chest with a crunch of bone and armor.

Kevin turned to look at April, eyes wide, astonished by what he had just seen. But they had no time for questions. He went to take the war-axe from the Trow's dying grip and had to pry it loose.

Even as he lifted the heavy weapon up and tested its weight, they heard a piercing cry coming from somewhere far away. It was a terrible sound, like animals fighting to the death. Almost immediately, a great ruckus could be heard throughout the mountain stronghold. Shouts and barks, roars and the clamor of weapons. The elephantine, booted feet of dozens, maybe hundreds of Trows as they hit the ground running. It felt as though the entire mountain was shaking.

Kevin, at a loss for anything else, spoke two words. "Oh, shit."

"I think we've run out of time for being sneaky," Nikki whispered.

They ran headlong down a corridor, fast as they could manage. April kept up with them easily, and Kevin forced himself not to think about it for the moment. Up ahead there was a junction, but before they reached it, five huge Trows, scarred and ugly and reeking to high heaven, rounded the corner in front of them. The monsters went in the opposite direction, not even noticing that their prisoners had escaped.

"Wait, they're not coming for us?" April asked, confused.

"Don't jinx us," Jesse grunted.

"Can we *be* more jinxed?" Kevin snarled. "Just move."

They let the Trows get a bit ahead, then picked up speed again. At the next junction, they were forced to stop. There were simply too many Trows. A flood of them. From the corner where he stood, Kevin could see a window of sorts, bored down through the mountain. Some kind of light streamed in. Around the corner, large numbers of Trows were leaving the fortress, prepared for battle. Others gathered, conversed in low, guttural tones.

"They're under attack," he whispered back to Jesse and the girls.

"Good," April sniffed. "So how do we get past them?"

Kevin looked at her. "I don't know if we can."

Suddenly, another clamorous noise arose, this one completely different. Kevin frowned in disbelief.

"Is that . . ." Nikki asked.

"Birds," April said. "It sounds like birds."

Jesse shook his head. "What the hell is happening *now*?" he demanded, voice quavering with panic.

It grew louder, accompanied now by the sound of wings. A great many wings. The first of the birds—huge black crows—appeared back along the corridor the way they'd come. Moments later, two Trows without armor came charging at them.

No, Kevin thought. Not at them.

"They're running away," he said.

For even as the Trows approached, a dozen more crows were behind them.

"Fuck that, they're running *this* way," Jesse said. "We've gotta move."

"We've got nowhere to go," Nikki replied grimly. "We'll have to kill these two."

Kevin raised his axe. "Marvelous."

Without warning, chunks of stone rained from the ceiling. A large rock struck his shoulder and he shouted, nearly dropping the axe. The first of the crows flew over their heads and the Trows pounded toward them, hands over their ears, eyes not really seeing anything.

"It's the noise, remember?" Nikki cried, having to shout over the cawing of the crows. "They can't stand loud noise."

Another stone hit Kevin, and he grabbed Nikki and threw her against the wall, pressing himself against her to keep her from harm. He shouted for April and Jesse to move.

Then a five foot wide section of the corridor's ceiling gave way in a shower of rock and burning embers. Something was on fire. The crows flew right by, and the Trows kept on, obviously determined to find the exit.

Nikki held Kevin tight. She kissed him softly on the cheek, incongruous but sweet. It gave him the strength to turn and face the Trows again, Nikki beside him with nothing but a dull-bladed dagger.

From the hole in the ceiling came a huge creature, tall as the tallest of the Kunal Trows. Nothing they had seen thus far in Neverland had prepared Kevin for this creature, like a demon carved of burning darkness. It was shaped like a man, but its body seemed made of coal, burning inside like the final embers of a dying fire. Its eyes, though, were blazing cinders. And it saw them.

"Oh my God," Kevin whispered, heart pounding, frozen with fear despite the heat that blazed off the monster. "Oh, Jesus, what is it?"

He reached for Nikki to protect her from the creature's burning touch. But it did not want them.

The coal-monster turned on the Trows, grabbed them, and incinerated them where they stood, leaving sooty black stains on the stone.

From the hole the charcoal creature had melted through the ceiling came another flock of crows to join the first, the cawing growing even louder. Jesse swore and covered his ears and ran, and the others followed suit.

All except April. She was smiling, and cawing in tune with the birds, floating along happily.

Floating . . . along. Though April was running, Kevin squinted hard to look at her feet, and he was fairly certain they were not touching the ground. He didn't even bother thinking it was impossible.

The crows drove the Kunal Trows from their stronghold. In the madness that ensued, Kevin and the others were forced out into the open as well. There were Trows in front of them, and Trows running up behind them, and only the starlight above to see by.

"The woods!" Jesse snapped. "We've gotta get some cover."

So they followed the exodus of the Trows up the slope into the woods. But there were so many Trows—hundreds of them, far more than Kevin had imagined—that it was impossible to find a safe place to hide. They were forced to keep running amidst the chaos of the beasts, frightened by the noise of the crows and furious at their own fear.

It was not far at all through the woods before they came out into the open clearing where they had first emerged into this wondrous, hideous world. The roar of the ocean just beyond the cliffs could be heard even above the cawing of the crows. Two hundred yards back, the Trow fortress was empty, save for the madly cawing birds who barred their return.

The noise would keep them out.

The sky was lit by fire sprites who hung in the air like eternal flares, and the clearing had become a battlefield. For above, in the dark of night beyond the sprites, the Tuatha de Danaan warriors waited.

With a battle cry older than human memory, they soared down from the sky and attacked.

8

The world was ablaze, or so it seemed. The illumination provided by the fire sprites cast the clearing atop the sea cliffs in a flickering glow that would have been warm at home before the hearth, but was merely sickening and sinister with battle in the offing and monsters afoot.

Shifting on their currents, Peter Starling observed it all with cold calculation. The odds were so terribly against the Tuatha de Danaan that timing was everything. The burning beasts called Manx had tunneled into the mountain, preparing the way for the crows, whose cawing drove the Kunal Trows out into the open, then up the slope through the tree line and into the clearing.

Outnumbered three or four to one, and by an enemy with greater strength and better arms, Starling's warriors flew down upon the Trows with great wails of fury. He smiled as he watched them. Many of the great ogres had left their weapons inside when the crows had come. Now, as they looked into the sky and saw the Tuatha de Danaan descending, the crows were no longer needed to draw them on.

The Kunal Trows saw what had been done. They understood that it was an attack, and they rejoiced in it. Thundering shouts of rage and battle rang through the skies along with the clang of armor. Merely the sight of their enemies descending upon them was enough now to draw the Trows farther into the clearing.

All of them.

Starling raised his left hand. From the darkness beyond the limits of the light thrown by the fire sprites, five quartets of Tuatha de Danaan warriors plunged from the sky, weary from their burdens. For even though many of their kind had inordinate physical strength, the weight of what they carried was staggering. Each set of four warriors was ringed around a massive wooden frame. Within each of the five frames was a huge iron bell.

As the twenty warriors spread out across the clearing, the bells began to clang, the noise reverberating across the land and out over the ocean. One bell was lowered on the western edge, three along the southern forest line, and one to the east, between the Trows and their mountain fortress. To the north, where the land fell away to the ocean far below, there were no bells. There was no need.

The Trows screamed. Many clapped their hands to their ears as they rushed away from the clamor of the bells. Once the warriors alighted, bells in place, they began to ring them by hand, and what had been a jumble of noise now became a riot of sound. The huge, piggish hunters, the ancient fathers of the Tuatha de Danaan, congregated near the middle of the clearing, even as they fought off the flying warriors who attacked from above.

Starling saw two of his own followers—friends since his childhood—die beneath the blade of a Kunal sword. With a loud curse, he dropped from the sky above the ocean and let the updraft at the cliffs catch him and bear him up once more. He raised his right hand, then brought it down.

Ranged all along the ocean cliffs, more than two dozen Roane emerged from behind scrub brush. Their gray pelts had hidden the seal-creatures well enough amidst the chaos, but now they were out in the open. They stood as tall as they were able. Their leader screamed out orders in their language, reminding them of the slaughter of the Roane pack that had lived in the caves below their feet.

Each of the Roane had a bow; all were nocked with arrows made by Gobhan the armorer, whose magic was imbued in his work.

"Let fly!" Starling cried in fury.

Weapons made by Gobhan never missed their mark. The arrows cut through leather armor, even split the metal armor some of the Trows wore. Their tips thunked into flesh, spilling blood and bringing a collective roar of pain and rage from the monsters. At least a dozen Trows fell dead that Pete could see, and many more were wounded.

The Roane had already nocked another round of arrows, and they were let loose to similarly devastating effect. That was the extent of their part in the battle, however. From stupidity or courage, the Trows were fearless. With their swords and axes and war hammers swinging, dozens of them cut through Tuatha de Danaan warriors and went after the Roane. The seal-people were vulnerable to attack from close range, as the bows were their only weapons.

"Go!" Starling shouted to them. "You've done enough!"

One by one, the Roane turned and leaped from the high cliff, more than a hundred feet above the ocean. On the way down, they shapeshifted, taking on their natural form before slicing into the waves and swimming off. Some of the Trows were carried too far by rage and momentum and went over as well, falling to their death on the rocks below or drowning when they hit the water.

Pete surveyed the clearing. The bells rang, keeping the fighting limited to a small area. The dead earth on that stretch of ground had begun to darken with the black-red ichor of Trows and the gloriously bright crimson blood of the Tuatha de Danaan. The clanging of blades could be heard, even amidst the clamor of the bells and the cawing of the crows, who continued to dart in and out amidst the warriors, distracting the enemy at pivotal moments.

Grunts and howls and cries of agony rose up into the air.

The trap had been sprung. Every advantage he could imagine had been put into play. The odds were better now, but still dangerously uneven. The war between the two races, fathers and sons, was coming to a bloody close. It wouldn't be long now before the victor would be decided.

Kevin's chest hurt. Panic surged through him, adrenaline spiking painfully in his head and heart. The Trows were all around, snorting and roaring, thundering like an elephant herd.

That's what they are. A herd of elephants. And we'll be trampled underfoot.

They'd been driven into the clearing along with the Trows. In the glimmer of light from the sprites, he looked fearfully around to find one of the monsters bearing down on him.

"Human!" it roared. "You brought this on us!"

The thing's piggish snout was furled back at the lips to reveal long fangs. Foamy drool slid over its teeth. Its eyes were red, but the pupils had dilated so wide they seemed like embers. The beast's tusks had blood on them already, and Kevin didn't want to know where from.

It held an axe above its head.

He froze.

With a scream—his name, Kevin realized—Jesse lunged in from the side, sword flashing, and skewered the Trow through the middle. The thing gaped almost comically, its stench growing suddenly worse, and then crumbled to the ground in a heap of flesh and leather.

"Oh God," Kevin whispered, and stared at it.

Eyes wide but emotionless, feeling numb all over, he turned to his brother. Jesse slapped him.

"Wake up, you asshole!"

Slap!

For the first time, Kevin really focused on his brother. He shoved Jesse back with both hands, frowning angrily. "Get the fuck away from me!"

Jesse glowered. "I can't protect your ass while I'm

trying to keep myself alive, Kevin. Pick up the god-damn axe.''

Around them, arrows flew. One of them sang right past Jesse's ear, and he ducked down, in case there were more. Kevin only stood there. He saw the troop of Roane bowmen over at the edge of the cliff.

An arrow flew above his head, feather whistling on the air. There was a meaty pop, and he turned to see a Trow, sword raised, staggering toward him with an arrow jutting from its chest. The thing fell, the weight of its flesh forcing the arrow up through its body. The tip poked out through its back with a wet tearing sound.

"Holy shit.'' Finally breaking from the terrified trance that had overcome him, Kevin dropped to the ground and reached for the axe that had fallen from the grasp of the Trow his brother had killed.

From above, Tuatha de Danaan warriors flew down, swords slashing air and Trow flesh. It was only this at-tack from above, he believed, that had allowed them to live as long as they had. The monstrous creatures' atten-tion was directed skyward, and Kevin had been beneath their notice for the most part.

No more.

A Trow had its back to him, fighting off an attack from above. For half a second it occurred to Kevin to get its attention, to fight it face on. That was fair.

Fair was suicide.

He buried his axe in the back of the Trow's skull. Above, the Tuatha de Danaan warrior grinned at him, blood across the flying man's face, then moved on to another enemy.

Kevin spun around, searching for his brother. He saw Jesse only a few feet away, his sword up. The Trow attacking him had no weapon, but it didn't need one. It quickly overcame Jesse and forced him to the ground. Kevin ran to help, but before he could even get there, a Tuatha de Danaan with long, straight raven hair and tapered ears cut off the Trow's head.

Jesse was up in a second. Cautiously, Kevin moved toward him.

"Where are the girls?" he shouted.

It earned him only a confused look from his brother. Jesse couldn't make out the words above the clanging of the bells and the screams of the crows.

"What?" he shouted back.

With a scream of fear and fury, Kevin gave up any semblance of reticence. The only way they were going to survive was to fight for their lives, to kill for them. He hacked at another Trow. It staggered, but would have turned on him, likely torn him apart, if Jesse hadn't come to his aid.

Together, they killed the tusked beast.

"Where are the girls?" Kevin asked again, frantic.

Jesse's expression was cold and hard. "I don't know. Just concentrate on staying alive. We'll find them when we can."

But Kevin couldn't do that. He had looked around and seen no trace of Nikki or April. Jack was dead. Kevin couldn't take that back, and he'd be a long time crucifying himself for it if he lived to do that. But if anything happened to Nikki or April, he figured he might as well just stop fighting and die. He could not survive that guilt.

The ground was hard beneath the rubber soles of his blue Puma sneakers. Around him, the wind was cold, and he shivered, half frozen, the only one among them who no longer had a Roane cloak to keep him warm. A Trow off to his right nearly tripped over the monster whose skull Kevin had split with the axe, and the newcomer spotted them.

"Fuck," Jesse whispered.

Kevin laughed without humor. "I'm with ya on that."

With a howl and a savage grin that stretched around its tusks, the hideous, drooling thing advanced on them. It snapped orders to a few others and they converged around the brothers. Several more stepped in to cover them from the attacking Tuatha de Danaan.

One of them was Farragher, the hunter who had nearly killed them upon their arrival.

"Filthy humans," the Trow snarled. "You made a fool of me, not long ago."

Farragher glowered at Kevin, focusing on him, and came forward with utter confidence. Blood was spattered across the Trow hunter's face already, and he wanted more. He wanted Kevin's. Farragher's eyes were wide and furious, his chest rising in angry rasps of breath.

"I'll gnaw the marrow from your bones," the hunter said, his tone intimate, almost a whisper.

A promise.

"Jess," Kevin muttered. "If I die—"

"Shut up," Jesse barked.

They both backed up a step. Kevin's right foot slipped in black Trow blood. Somewhere, he heard Nikki shout his name. Her voice was like a vise, locking him in place. He wasn't going to back up anymore.

He shifted the heavy axe, gripping its long handle with both hands. The stink of the beasts was in his nostrils, churning his stomach right along with the fear.

"Come on, then," he whispered.

Then, though Farragher and the other Trows were still advancing slowly, Kevin bellowed as loud as he could, swung the axe up and lunged at them. The Trows were taken so off guard by him, likely astonished that the scrawny human boy would dare attack them, that they flinched.

Only a second, but it was all the hesitation Kevin needed. He buried the axe in the chest of the nearest one. The thing staggered backward, the axe lodged in its rib cage. The weapon was torn from his hands, and he was left to stand there in front of the other two without any way to defend himself.

Farragher reached out and grabbed Kevin's throat, roaring in fury. Jesse brought his blade down, whickering through the air, and hacked off the hunter's arm halfway to the wrist. Blood spurting from its stump, the Trow hissed in pain.

Suddenly, they had become the center of attention. Around them, five, six, now seven Trows moved into a circle, weapons raised.

Then, in what seemed like a single instant, the Tuatha de Danaan dropped from the sky like blood-soaked angels, fresh from Lucifer's rebellion. Their own blades flashed in the glimmering light shining from the weakening fire sprites, now dimming. Farragher and the other Trows around them were cut down in an instant.

Kevin felt a hand grip his shoulder, spin him around. Without a weapon, he raised his fist.

Pete Starling glared at him.

"You shouldn't be here," Starling growled.

With a fresh surge of panic, Kevin stared at Starling's face, at the sharpness of his teeth and the tapered ears. The Tuatha de Danaan leader's pupils were so enlarged that his eyes were almost clear, like frosted glass. Cold as ice.

There was nothing but death there.

"I didn't want to be here," Kevin whispered, his voice a plea, nearly lost in the clamor of the melee going on around them. "You took her. You shouldn't have done that. I only wanted to bring her home."

"And so you shall," Pete said, pupils shrinking. "If you live long enough."

"Kevin, run!"

Jesse rushed at them, sword high, face etched with determination. "Keep your hands off him, you bastard!" he screamed.

But Kevin had seen something in Pete's cold eyes. Heard something in his tone.

"Jesse, no!" he cried.

The sword fell.

Nikki ran. The only thing she could think to do was get away. She had a sword, but that would not be enough. She did not know if Kevin and the others were alive, and she tried not to let herself think about it. There were Trows everywhere, killing everything.

One spotted her, ran at her with a huge hammer. It screamed, eyes bulging, drool slipping over its chin. The thing was in a frenzy. Nikki could only run faster, trying to escape. She turned to look at the tree line, perhaps sixty yards away.

Another Trow stepped into her path.

The bell at the edge of the tree line clanged, and the Trow winced in pain. She rammed the sword into it, but only managed to pierce its lower right side. It doubled over in pain and she dodged around it, leaving the sword stuck in its wound. The one with the hammer had to slow to avoid crashing into it. But then the two of them were after her, even more furious.

Sweat ran down her back beneath the Roane cloak. Once upon a time, she had felt so in control. Back home, she'd known who she was, what her life was about. This was just insanity.

Without Nikki even realizing it, tears began to course down her face. It was over. Kevin had come to bring her home, to end what she had been pretending was just some long nightmare. Jack had his spine ripped from his body. Kevin and Jesse and April might be dead as well. Pete was a monster, but these Trows were worse.

"Oh, God, please help me," she sobbed. Or she thought she did. The words might not have made it to her lips. *I love you, Mom. Sorry I went away,* she thought, hoping that somehow her mother might hear her.

Nikki ran, sneakers pounding the cold, hard ground, heart drumrolling in her chest, green eyes wide with terror. Her hair flew, and she ran so fast she stumbled, arms pinwheeling at her sides, barely keeping her feet beneath her.

But she did.

The bells clanged louder than ever.

The bells.

With a thought, her head snapped up, and Nikki glanced behind her. The Trows had stopped. The one she'd stabbed attempted to fight off an aerial attack, but the other glared at her, hands over its ears.

The bells.

Tears coursing through the grime on her cheeks, Nikki collapsed to her knees on the ground, laughing. Then, an instant after she knew she had reached temporary safety, she thought of Kevin. Eyes narrowed, she searched the clearing desperately for some sign of him.

She shouted his name, but there was no answer.

Nikki had never felt so alone.

9

Jesse brought his sword down at Pete Starling's neck, roaring in rage and fear for his brother's life, and despair that it had all come to this. Jesse expected to die. Kevin could see in his eyes that his brother thought this to be his final act.

Pete darted a hand out and grabbed Jesse by the wrist, then slipped behind him and shook the sword free.

"Son of a bitch!" Jesse screamed.

"Stop," Kevin snapped. He crouched before his brother, looking up at him. "Jesse, wait, he's not trying to hurt us."

With a grunt, Jesse shoved him away. "What the fuck are you talking about, bro?" he wailed. "It's his fault we're here in the first place. All of this . . . it's his fault!"

Pete lashed out and slapped Jesse so hard that he went down on his knees, blood dripping from his nose. With a shout of protest, Kevin turned to Starling, but before he could say anything at all, the Tuatha de Danaan had grabbed him by the throat and pulled him forward. They were eye to eye, nose to nose, and Kevin's toes barely reached the ground.

"If you live, I'll help put you back where you belong. Until then, stay the fuck out of my way."

Before Kevin could react, several more Tuatha de Danaan warriors alighted nearby, and nearly a dozen Trows began to converge on them. Blades flashed and clanged, crows cawed above, blood flowed.

Pete dropped him and then dashed away to hack at the nearest Trow.

Kevin turned to his brother, head down, hoping the Trows didn't get any closer. "Well?" he cried, voice rising with his anxiety.

Jesse grimly lifted his sword. "Do we have a goddamn choice?"

The wind swept across the blood-soaked land, and April felt herself lifted from the ground. Several of the Trows moved to attack her, and she was astounded to find herself floating, shifting on the breeze, toes pointed with the physical memory of elementary school ballet lessons. The laces of her left sneaker were untied, and they dangled beneath her.

Distantly, she recognized that she ought to be afraid. But there was no fear in her at all. Not now that she was above them.

In her right hand, she gripped the pommel of a dull Kunal sword. When she had first hefted it, the weapon had felt heavy. Too heavy. Now she swung it with ease. A kind of song began to race through her, a melody that played in the throb of her temples and the rush of blood through her veins.

From below, a Trow howled in frustration, seeing her there, suspended in the air. With a grunt, it hurled a double-bladed axe at her. The axe turned over and over in the air, and April's mind split in half. Part of her felt terror, panic, and surrender to the agony that was to come. The other felt none of those things. With the slightest whisper of the wind, April glided to one side and plucked the axe from the air as it spun.

The Trow was silent, staring up in astonishment. For just a moment, its eyes widened even further, as though it had seen something beyond her that alarmed it all the more. Angry at the fear the beast had caused, April swept down toward it from the sky.

The monster reached out to tear her from the sky, arrogant and brutal. April swiped the axe down and lopped its arm off at the elbow. With a single thrust, she ran the sword through its leathery throat, and then withdrew it just as cleanly.

"That was for Jack," April spat.

She swore at the dead Trow as it hit the ground, and then she rose up into the air again. In the back of her mind she knew it was all wrong, knew that it wasn't her doing these things. And yet somehow she knew that was only partially true. In some ways, this was more her than she had ever felt before.

Here, the impossible was possible.

Bells continued to toll, the sound rolling across the clearing. The salty scent of the ocean mixed with an acrid odor she realized must come from the fire sprites. Crows darted about. A pair of burning black charcoal-creatures, like the one they'd seen in the Trow fortress, lumbered about, frying the ugly trolls where they stood. At least one of the charcoal monsters was dead, smolder-ing in a heap on the dead grass, which was even now starting to burn.

Kevin. April glanced around, spinning in the air, searching for her friends. They had been separated only minutes before, but minutes were an eternity. Death came in an instant.

She spotted Nikki on the outer southern edge of the clearing. The Trows would not go after her because of the bells. That was one of them safe. If she could round up Kevin and Jesse, then they could . . . leave. Right as it was, the thought made April frown.

Below, several Trows had brought down one of the Tuatha de Danaan, and were beating him. April's ex-pression turned hard, and she darted down from above and swung the axe, decapitating a Trow so swiftly that its fists fell one, two, three times more before its body slumped aside. Her sword whickered through the air and blood splashed her clothes as she cut the others down.

The warrior who had been the subject of their attack climbed wearily to his feet, face bloody, hand on his abdomen. He limped as he took three steps toward her, and then rose ever so slowly into the air.

The warrior stared at her. "You're one of us?" he muttered. "How can that be?"

"No, I'm . . ." her words trailed off as she gazed into the eyes of the Tuatha de Danaan. At length, she blinked and shook her head. "I don't know."

"I must find Lord Peter," the warrior said, and then shot up into the sky.

April craned her neck to watch him. She didn't see the Trow approaching from behind. Her feet dangled too close to the ground, and it reached up and grabbed her left ankle.

"Arrows," the Trow growled.

In its hand it held one of the razor-tipped shafts that had been used to cut down the Trow numbers at the onset of the conflict. With a grunt, the Trow jammed the arrow into her. April twisted at the last second, and it passed through her right side, just above her pelvis. Her untied left sneaker slipped off as she screamed and tried to escape, and then she was rising into the air, bereft of one shoe, blood seeping from the wound in her side.

Then she fell.

It was a slow fall, the air currents wrapped around her, cradling her as best they could. But she had lost her concentration and the ground rushed up to meet her. She struck hard, and the tip of the arrow snapped off beneath her, tearing her flesh a bit more.

For a second, she blacked out.

In that dark unconscious moment, she felt the huge, thick, cold hands of a Trow wrap around her arms and haul her to her feet. The stench of it, now that she was so close, filled her nose and her stomach convulsed. It was so strong, she forgot about the pain for a moment. Her eyes flickered open.

It glared down at her with one burning red eye. The other had been removed long since, a ragged scar running down the side of its face. Thick, syrupy drool slid over its ropy lips, past the tusks that thrust up from its lower jaw, and slopped across her face. April winced, tried to wipe the stuff away, but then the beast grabbed her throat and began to squeeze.

April was going to die.

A terrible sadness filled her as she thought of the Roane cloak over her body, and the open ocean, and what it felt like to fly over this strange land. But then she thought of Jack's gunslinger eyes, and his soft words and his simple love for her, and it was all right. She could tell him what he meant to her, then.

The one-eyed Trow leaned in, sneering at her.

"I am Ganfer Drow, lord of the Kunal tribe. I don't know what *you* are, girl. You stink like a human, but you fly like one of my bastard sons."

April went rigid, despite that her breath was growing short.

"*I* stink?" she croaked, barely able to hear herself.

Her right hand whipped around, almost of its own accord. Her fingers sank into Ganfer's empty eye socket, and she *pulled*. Something tore, cartilage, muscle . . . something. The Trow roared and dropped her.

"You think *I* stink, you ugly, rancid fuck?" she screamed, past any kind of rationality, and past caring.

She attacked it then, while it was still reeling. But too late. Two more Trows came at her, and she tried to fly off, but they grabbed her and dragged her down.

Crows cawed, swooped down at them, and they batted at the birds, trying to protect their ears at the same time. April had a moment where she thought the birds might actually save her life, but they flew off a moment later, after other prey, she suspected.

The sound of bells was too far, and she wished that she were at the edge of the clearing with Nikki. The bells. The ocean. The crows. And a thumping, pumping sound that seemed to erupt suddenly from nowhere.

With a chorus of grunts, the Trows turned to see what the noise was. Ganfer Drow, blinded, turned his head in that direction as well. But April recognized it right away. She didn't believe it, of course. Her mind refused to accept the sound, so incongruous was its sudden addition to the weird world around them.

But there it was, just the same.

With a roar of its engine, Pete Starling's Dodge Charger crashed through the trees to the south of the clearing. Impossible, given that it had last been a rusted-out hulk in a police impound lot somewhere in Framingham. But what, after all, was really impossible?

Whoever was behind the Charger's wheel laid on the horn a few times as the car swerved around Nikki, throwing dirt as it fishtailed. The thumping wasn't just thumping. There was wailing in there as well, and screeching guitar. The Charger turned again, back tires slewing across the frozen ground. Led Zeppelin pumped out the open windows. The song was "Kashmir," and it had been one of Jack's favorites.

The Trows screamed and ran from the car, both in terror of the metal beast—unlike anything they had ever seen—and from the merciless pounding of the music. The Tuatha de Danaan took advantage of the confusion to renew their attack. But there were still so many Trows. Too many.

Ganfer clapped his hands over his ears and roared in pain. She hadn't blinded his single good eye after all. April shook loose the other Trows, sword whisking out to punch through the abdomen of the nearest. The third one ran, though she thought more from Led Zeppelin than from her.

But the scarred monster, Ganfer Drow, lord of the Kunal tribe, would not run. Though she could see blood running from its ears as the car approached, the Trow reached for her again. April swung the sword, but it was batted from her hand. The Trow reached down and grabbed the arrow that jutted from her belly, and shoved it deeper.

April screamed.

Behind her, the Charger laid on its horn.

Ganfer's eyes went wide.

Pain driving her as much as fear, April kicked loose

and flew into the air, able to focus only long enough to break free. Then she began to fall once more.

As she fell, the Charger tore across the barren ground and slammed into the one-eyed Trow. She heard its bones shatter as she alighted nearby, saw it crash through the Dodge's windshield.

The music still played.

The other Trows stayed away from the car as it rumbled to a halt. April staggered over to it, hand pressed to her belly just above the arrow. As the dust settled, she saw one of the Tuatha de Danaan step out of the car. He had long, flowing orange hair, a ragged beard, and orange eyes, and he was pale as an albino. After a moment, she blinked. April knew him, recognized him as one of Pete Starling's cronies from the train trestle that day. It seemed so long ago. At first she didn't know him, for he'd had a crewcut then, and no beard.

"Curt?" she said aloud, as she approached. "Your name is Curt, right?"

He had moved around to stare down at Ganfer, dead and broken on the hood of the car. The music was loud enough that it made April's head hurt. Curt seemed not to notice.

"You saved my life," she told him, fully aware that it had likely not been his intention, that he and Starling and the other Tuatha de Danaan might kill her and her friends just as quickly as the Trows would have.

But Curt didn't kill her.

When he turned to her, there were tears in his eyes. He went to April and he reached for her, and wept on her shoulder, and she let him.

"You're crying for a Trow?"

"Funny, isn't it?" he said, choking on the words. Then he stood up straight and wiped a sleeve across his face and turned to look at the dead, scarred beast again.

"He was my father. I killed my father."

The full weight of the tragedy of this war fell upon April's heart, and she found herself unable to speak, barely to breathe.

Around them, chaos still reigned. She only hoped it would be over soon.

Nikki stood frozen, watching the melee. From her vantage point, it did not look good. When Curt had arrived in the car, she had thought the tide would turn, but it had only postponed the inevitable. The odds were simply too great. The field ran black with Trow blood, but there were still too many, and a lot of Tuatha de Danaan had died as well.

"Kevin, where are you?" she whispered to herself.

"If he's not dead," came the answer, "he soon will be."

Nikki spun to see Doug slipping out of the sky from between the branches of two large trees. The nearest bell was thirty feet west, and there were Tuatha de Danaan there, but they didn't so much as glance Doug's way.

"Keep away from me," Nikki snapped at him.

The weasel grinned, stood up straight and pushed his hair behind his ears.

"I don't think so. My brother was willing to let you go home. Do you believe it? And I guess there's nothing I can do about that. But it doesn't mean I have to let you go without having the pleasure of your company first."

A shudder ran through her. "What the hell are you talking about?" she asked, though she knew.

"Don't be obtuse," Doug barked. Then his grin returned. "You wanna go home? Fine. We win, you get to leave. But not until I've taken my ride."

Nikki turned to run west, hoping to stay between the Trows and the woods. But Doug caught her by the hair and hauled her, screaming, to the ground.

"Kevin!" she shrieked.

Doug laughed. "Oh, yeah, call for Murphy. What the hell is he gonna do, the little pussy? You're mine, Nikki. You've had your nose in the air too long, stuck up bitch. We might just have to break that little pug thing while we're at this, ya think?"

She cried out for Kevin again.

* * *

The Trow that drove Kevin to the ground was bleeding from a shoulder wound. The black ichor poured onto his filthy shirt and blue jeans. He was disgusted, but shivering as he was, he at least registered the fact that the blood was warm.

It held a heavy hammer in its right fist and his throat with its left. The hammer rose.

Kevin screamed for Jesse.

Out of the corner of his eye, he saw Starling in the midst of a sword battle. The Tuatha de Danaan's sword broke, and his Trow enemy thundered laughter.

Where was Jesse? Kevin wondered.

The Trow whose stink was all over him now, whose blood soaked his clothes, brought the hammer down toward his head. Kevin bucked against the creature, but was pinned in place. He winced, and closed his eyes.

The hammer never fell.

Kevin blinked, opened his eyes. In the glow from the sprites, he could see the Trow perfectly— not to mention the hammer that was mere inches from his face.

Frozen.

Forever lodged in place in the grip of a statue.

As he crawled out from beneath the Trow, he looked around and realized that the fire sprites were gone. The dim light in the sky was that of the oncoming dawn. It was perhaps a minute away, not much more.

Every Trow in the clearing had turned to stone.

The bells stopped ringing.

The crows stopped cawing, settling into the trees.

The Tuatha de Danaan did not cheer, for it was as painful a victory as war had ever achieved.

With April in the passenger seat, Curt drove the Dodge across the rutted ground toward Lord Peter.

Kevin and Jesse stood side by side, leaning on one another as Pete walked over to them. Curt got out of the car and stood beside it as April rushed to embrace the

Murphy brothers, tears on her cheeks. Neither of them noticed that her feet sometimes did not touch the ground.

"This was the plan, wasn't it?" Kevin asked. "To keep them occupied until dawn?"

The sun flashed on the horizon. Then the oily black of the magical night swept across the sky once more.

Pete nodded. "It was."

He might have said more, but a scream split the air. Kevin looked in the direction from which the cry had come, but it was truly dark now for the first time in an hour. Nevertheless, he began to run. He knew who that scream had to have come from.

"Nikki!" he shouted.

"Candlewicks, burn!" Pete roared.

Many of the sprites had left, but others were near enough to come burning to life at his command. They swept across the clearing in the same direction that both Pete and Kevin were running. Jesse, Curt and April were not far behind.

Suddenly, in the flickering light of the exhausted sprites, Kevin could see them. Nikki was on the ground. Doug was on top of her, one hand covering her mouth. With the other, he tore at her clothes.

Kevin shouted her name again and sped up. Somehow, miraculously, he made it there before Pete. He dove, tore Doug off Nikki, and began to pummel him.

Doug laughed, and Kevin struck him so hard in the mouth that he felt a knuckle give way in his hand and cried out in pain, even as he hit the weasel again.

Afraid to stop hitting, Kevin hauled back his fist again. Pete caught his hand before another blow could fall. As Jesse and the others ran up, shouting, Doug lunged at Kevin, slavering like an animal.

Pete lashed out and drove his brother back with a single blow.

Kevin tried to move forward. Jesse came up beside him and did the same. With both hands, Pete held them back. He met their gaze with his own, then glanced at

Nikki, who had risen painfully and stared hatefully at Doug.

"He's my brother," Pete said, voice harsh and low, filled with loathing and sadness. "You presume too much."

With an air of power unlike anything Kevin had ever seen, Pete Starling turned to regard his younger sibling.

"My greatest fears I see mirrored in you, Douglas. You are not Lore Starling's son. He did things that were wrong, yes, but he would have killed you himself had he seen what you've become. I won't do that. It's their way." He gestured around him at the statues that had once been their ancestors. "It isn't our way."

The lord of the Tuatha de Danaan signaled to several of his warriors, and they wrestled with Doug until he was under control. He spat and swore and charged at his brother, but he was overpowered.

"Put him in a cell. If he insists upon behaving like an animal, then from this day forth, he will live like one," Starling commanded.

They rose from the clearing, their captive firmly restrained, and flew out over the ocean toward the tallest and grandest of the plateau island estates. Starling's own. Pete gazed after them until they could no longer be seen in the dark, not even with the starlight to silhouette them against the night.

"So, what now?" Kevin said.

"At the dawn, you go home," Pete replied, without turning.

Kevin cleared his throat. Shuffled his feet. He slipped an arm around Nikki and held her close at his side. They shared a glance that held a great deal of understanding, of relief, and of love. Then he turned back to Starling.

"I meant for *you*. All of you," Kevin said.

With a thin smile, containing only a trace of humor, Pete looked at him. Looked at all of them, Kevin, Nikki, Jesse and April. The rest of the warriors had fallen back to a respectful distance, leaving only Curt there of his people. Starling glanced at the red-haired warrior and shook his head sadly.

"We will try to discover what magick the Trows used to create the Long Night, and to bring day back to the world. After that, I don't know. Extinction, perhaps."

"I'm sorry," Kevin told him, and was surprised to find that it was true. "Here you've got a chance to start over, to make it right, and it's going to be taken away."

"Not necessarily."

They all looked at April, who had the tiniest smile on her face. She was floating.

Flying.

Starling's face was etched with amazement. "What . . . *how* are you doing that?"

"Couldn't tell you."

The amazement disappeared, to be replaced by dawning understanding. Pete turned to Curt, ignoring the others as if they weren't there at all.

"Only sons were born to our kind here. But I remember my father telling of Trows and Tuatha de Danaan who would fall in love with a human woman, and sometimes find themselves lost in the human realm for all time."

"Wait," April said doubtfully. "Are you trying to suggest that my father was one of you? Please. You'd have to meet him to know how funny that is. He's a little league coach, for God's sake."

Nikki moved up next to April and pointed at the space between her feet and the ground.

"Then how do you explain that?" she asked.

April shrugged. "I can't."

Curt moved to stand by April, looking at her gravely. "If there are female Tuatha de Danaan in the human world . . ."

Nikki held up a hand. "She gets it, Curt. Back off. Just because she might be like you, doesn't mean she's gonna hang around and churn out babies."

Pete crossed his arms. "No one is suggesting that. Not now, anyway. And not against her will. But if she could help us find other women of our breed in your world, and explain to them—"

"Hey!" April snapped. "I'm standing right here."

Kevin studied her. "You're not really thinking about this, are you?"

April looked around. Kevin noticed that her gaze kept wandering off toward the ocean. She pulled the Roane cloak tightly around her. After a moment, she drifted up into the sky rather aimlessly.

"I need to think," she told them.

Moments later, she was out of sight.

"I can't believe this," Jesse said, mostly to himself. "After everything that happened, with Jack and all . . . how can she not go home?"

"She didn't say that. Not yet," Nikki countered.

But Kevin thought he knew what April's decision would be. He looked at his brother and smiled wanly. "Maybe she *is* home, Jess. Did you ever think of that?"

Jesse scowled. "Bullshit. You always think you know everything."

Kevin punched him lightly on the shoulder "Don't be such a dick."

"Don't fuckin' hit me," Jesse snapped. "I'll take your head off."

They were, after all, brothers.

Epilogue

In the hour before that briefest of mornings would come to Neverland, Kevin, Jesse, Nikki, and April stood at the edge of the clearing, at roughly the same spot where they had entered that world days before.

Their wounds had begun to heal. They had had a great deal of sleep since the previous morning's battle, though Kevin and Nikki had less than the others. April's wounds, to no one's surprise, had disappeared almost completely.

Peter and Curt stood perhaps fifty feet away, with a handful of other Tuatha de Danaan. There were other Trow clans, farther inland. But now that they turned the tide of battle, the Tuatha de Danaan were prepared to take back the land.

Jesse stood just over Kevin's shoulder, silently urging him to hurry. At his other side, Nikki held tightly to his hand. April faced them, and from her posture alone, Kevin knew what her decision had been.

"I'll miss you," he said.

April frowned. "I hope you understand, Kevin. I'm not staying for them. And I'm sure as hell not going to become some breeder for them. But if I can help find females of their race in our world . . ."

Kevin studied her. "There's more to it than that, isn't there?" he asked. "Somehow you fit here. Ever since I've known you, April, you've looked like you were about to fly off somewhere. I guess now we know where."

She smiled, more beautiful than he'd ever seen her.

"It feels like home," she said, so softly that none of the others could have heard.

Kevin touched her face, leaned forward, and kissed her forehead, hugged her briefly.

"You'll see me," she promised. "I'm going to have to travel back and forth, hunting for others like me. Plus I have to talk to my parents. Chances are at least one of them knows more than they ever told me."

She fell silent then. Kevin thought she looked troubled.

Reluctantly, she glanced over at Jesse. Kevin turned to see that his brother was surprised to be singled out.

April's voice quavered as she spoke. "Jess. What do you think Jack would say?"

Jesse's expression was grim, but he managed the tiniest smile at the edges of his mouth. "Not a damn thing," he said. "But he'd back your play all the way."

April smiled gratefully, and hugged him.

Pete had come up while they were speaking. He stood before Kevin and regarded him grimly.

"Do not speak of this," he instructed.

"Who the hell would we tell?" Kevin replied. "Who would believe us?"

Pete nodded slowly. "I appreciate what you did," he said.

"Me? I stayed alive and not much else."

"The bells." Pete explained. "I heard you wondering why we'd never used them, and it made me feel foolish. But it also helped us to take back our land, to win the war."

"How did you . . ." Kevin began to ask. "Wait, the goblins said something. You hear everything that happens in your house."

"True," Pete agreed.

Nikki laughed, a bit embarrassed.

"Are you going to blush?" Kevin asked her.

She gave him a dubious look. "You know me well enough by now, Murphy. I'm not the kind of girl who blushes."

Then she looked at April. The two girls had nev
known one another well, but there was a closeness be
tween them now that Kevin only partially understood.

"Good luck," Nikki said. "And thank you."

With a nod, April leaned in and whispered to her.
Kevin thought he wasn't supposed to hear what she said,
but he did.

"Don't hurt him."

"Never," Nikki replied.

April looked wistful as she spoke.

"Never's an awful long time."

They said their good-byes, and then the three of them
set off into the woods, due south, as best they could tell.
Pete had told them that the path would be clear, if they
only looked for it. As is almost always the case, the trip
home seemed far shorter than the journey they had
taken to get there.

Still, they walked all day, south and south again, until
the light drained from the sky, and the night came on.

With the night, the world changed. Dusk stole over
the forest, and moments after the dark had come, they
stepped out into the circle at the top of Fox Run Drive.

They stank of sweat and blood. Their clothes were
torn and ragged. But the smells of their own place in
the world, their own neighborhood, pulled them on. Together, Kevin, Nikki, and Jesse trudged down the hill in
silence. Not one among them bothered to ask what they
would say when the inevitable questions began, for they
had already agreed upon it the night before.

Nikki had called to say she was in trouble, that she'd
been abducted by Pete and the others, but had escaped.
The four of them had gone to meet her in Sudbury and
attempted to walk through the forest to get home.
They'd gotten lost. Now they were back. Of Jack and
April they knew nothing save that the two had talked
about running off somewhere, even getting married
down south, where they'd heard it was legal in spite of
their age.

Nobody believed them, of course. The popular opinion among the parents was that they'd all just run away, but that Kevin, Jesse, and Nikki had grown homesick and returned. None of them ever changed their story, however.

Things settled into a new rhythm after that. Kevin and Jesse still fought, but there was always an undercurrent to their conflicts, the bitter acknowledgment that what they had been through together made their petty squabblings absurd and childish. They played at still being kids, but when Kevin looked into his brother's eyes, they both knew better.

Where once upon a time their group had been inseparable, it barely existed in later years. Kevin and Nikki would sometimes get together with Tommy Carlson and Diana Abbott to go to the movies or the beach. Sometimes Jesse would come along. Invariably, the subject of Jack and April would come up. Though Kevin tried to hold it all together, remembering what it had felt like to be surrounded by a group of friends who would always back him up, eventually even he began to let go, to stop making the effort.

He knew that it was natural, that this was what happened when kids got older, passed through high school's trial by fire and beyond. But somehow Kevin had naively believed that what he and Jesse and Nikki had been through together would bind them more tightly to one another. Instead, as though it were a hideous secret, what they had shared became a subject never spoken of by any of them.

And eventually entropy, the most fundamental law of the universe, took effect. Things fall apart.

From time to time, Kevin would think about how different things might have been if he had just said something sooner, told Nikki he loved her. He had no way to know, of course, how the information would have been received under different circumstances. But it haunted him to think that if he'd had the courage to just tell her, Starling and his friends might never have brought Nikki under their influence, spirited her away. April might never have known her true self.

Jack might still be alive.

Years later, those thoughts lay especially heavy on him whenever he thought of Nikki.

It might have been different in Neverland, of course.

But this is the real world.

And never is an awful long time.

Please read on for a
bonus short story
by Christopher Golden

RUNAWAY

Kevin ran.

Hot tears cut a shameful path down his cheeks as his legs pumped beneath him, his Pumas slapping the pavement of Fox Run Drive. In some primal part of him, he felt the urge to vomit, but he couldn't. His belly was just ice, a cold counterpoint to the prickly heat flushing his ears and face.

Kevin ran, and the scene that had played out only moments before came back to him in sharp detail. His father had come home late again. Drunk again, or at least with the smell of alcohol on his breath. Sean Murphy wasn't around much. Never had been. He was an attorney who spent too much time with female "clients," and the rest of his time in a bar. He was around for vacations, for the fun stuff, and Kevin could remember a time when he'd been around a lot more, playing ball on weekends or cutting the grass. But it had been a while since then.

It was October 1978 now, and Kevin was eleven. He didn't think he'd played basketball or even thrown a football with his father since the summer of seventy-six. He remembered, 'cause that was the big Bicentennial year. Everything was red, white and blue, and fireworks, and the Tall Ships came into Boston harbor. He thought his father loved him, then. And he'd loved his dad more than anything.

The hell of it was, he still loved his father. Even now. Kevin and Jesse had been watching TV on the floor in their parents' room when the fight had begun. Their mom, Aileen, was just tired of it all. The screaming started; accusations flew and were barely denied. Kevin had never heard so much swearing. Jesse, who had turned thirteen only two days before, went into the hall and told Kevin to stay put.

The tears had already started, though, and Kevin was fighting so hard against them that he couldn't respond. Moments later, when the screaming had reached a fevered pitch, and he heard the argument start to move outside, he left his room, went down the hall and stood at the top of the stairs. Just outside the storm door, he saw his world falling apart.

His mother's face was etched with pain and fury and desperation. His father cursed her so loudly and angrily that spittle flew from his mouth. Jesse stood on the slate stoop just beyond the door, pleading with their dad to stop it. Just to stop it.

But it didn't stop. It exploded. Kevin's dad started to walk away, reaching into his pocket for his keys. His mom reached out to try to stop him and grabbed hold of his arm, and he shook her off so violently that she stumbled and fell over a bush along the stone walk.

Jesse snapped. He screamed something unintelligible. He leaped onto their father's back, trying to stop him from leaving, or stop him from hurting their mother any more, just to stop him. Just to stop it. But their dad bucked Jesse off his back and swore at him. He didn't even pause as he strode to the battered old Pontiac in the driveway, pulled out and tore off down the road.

Kevin went down the stairs slowly, almost as if he were sleepwalking. He'd stopped fighting the tears by then. He pushed the storm door open and stepped out onto the slate stoop, and watched as Jesse helped their mother up off the ground. They were all crying, but she was hurting the worst. Her tears came in huge gasps and sobs, as if everything inside her had suddenly come unhinged. Kevin supposed that was close enough to the truth.

His mother looked at him. Kevin tried to speak to her, but what came out was a wail of pain and sorrow.

Then he ran. Away from it all. Away from the home and the room and the faces that would remind him of the pain that was tearing him apart. He wanted it behind him, all of it. Didn't want to think, ever again. Not at all. Thinking about anything would lead right back home, right back to the wounds in his heart and soul. It was always bad at home, with them. Always had been. But he could handle it.

This, though. This was something else.

The moon and stars shone brightly above—the night sky not that eternal, universal black, but a warm and textured indigo. It was warm for late October, but cold enough that he should have had a jacket over his Captain America T-shirt. There were nine houses on either side of the road going up the hill. At the top, Fox Run Drive dead-ended in a small circle, where teenagers sometimes parked to make out or drink or both.

Beyond the circle, there was only the woods. It was a state forest, actually, but that made little impression on the Murphy brothers and their friends. To them, it was a world apart from school and family, a reality all their own. It was winding paths that went on forever through the trees, and hidden gulleys, and huge rocks to climb on. They played army and hide-and-seek, but more often than not, they just explored.

Unless they were building.

Kevin and Jesse and their friends had built three forts in the past two years. The latest and greatest was over a small rise about a hundred feet from one of the secondary paths. It was a tree fort, built in and around four huge oaks, expertly patched together with wood stolen from the new houses being built at the edge of the forest. The fort was twelve feet from the ground and sturdy as anything, with four solid walls and no entrance save for the trapdoor in the floor.

It was there Kevin fled now, forcing his mind to stay numb. He ran half the distance to the top of Fox Run

Drive, and then he began to lose steam. At the circle, he slowed to a walk, wiping the tears from his face angrily, embarrassed by them. Yet still they came. Not quite so copiously, but there just the same. As if he'd truly begun to leak, and it was now beyond his power to make the necessary repairs.

He wondered if that, too, might not be close enough to the truth.

A single glance back down the hill sent him on his way. It might have been harder if he could have seen his house from there, but there was a curve in the hill and trees as well. If he could have seen the end of his driveway, even, he might have hesitated longer, thought about it more.

Kevin walked to the edge of the circle and entered the dark woods, put off only momentarily by the sounds there, and the way the trees seemed more ominous and closer together at night, and the sense that there was a presence there, some malevolent and grinning entity that was part of the air itself inside the forest.

But that was baby stuff. Kevin knew that.

Eyes front, he plunged into the trees, brushing branches away from his face and careful not to trip over roots and such. Moments later, he broke through onto the main path. It led away to right and left, but Kevin could see very little of it, now that the canopy above blocked out all but the narrowest swath of illumination from the moon and stars. His eyes compensated as best they could, and Kevin turned right, shivering now that the rage and fear had worn off.

All that remained to him was the ache in his heart, the lost, hollow feeling inside of him, and the unformed certainty that at the fort, he could stop. At the fort, he could make the rest of the world disappear. Kevin felt as though he had once been part of something larger but had been torn away, the way some of the shingles had been ripped right off the roof in the tropical storm that had swept through New England the month before. They'd never found those shingles. The storm had carried them away, just as another storm was now carrying him away, off to another place, the world within that forest.

He trudged along in silence, his feet moving along almost without instruction from his brain. A ways along the main path, he turned left. Perhaps sixty yards down that way, and he turned off, blue Puma sneakers buried in wet, fallen leaves as he stepped over a downed tree and then started up the small hill. The forest was dense there, but he had picked his way through dozens, maybe hundreds of times.

At the top of the hill, he could see the fort.

Though the pain was still there, he didn't feel lost anymore. With a longing he could never have named, Kevin tromped down the hill and stood under the fort, next to the widest of the four oaks. To its trunk they had nailed slats of wood, which could be used as a ladder when necessary. There was a rope as well, thick and strong, and strung from a branch above the fort. It hung down through a hole in the roof, and then further down, through the trapdoor. They could use the rope to haul themselves up, and the slats as footholds to aid in the climb. But when they left, the last one always hauled the rope up and dropped down or climbed the "ladder." Likewise, whoever got there first had to climb up and drop the rope down.

The slats weren't very sturdy. Jesse had said he didn't think they'd hold a grown-up. Not a full-grown man, anyway. That setup—with the rope and all—made the fort feel even more special.

Kevin's expression was grim as he climbed the makeshift ladder. He shivered a little, and his fingers were cold. But he didn't care. Inside the fort, he was sure he would feel warmer. At least the walls would keep out the wind that shook the bare branches all around.

When he reached the top, he boosted himself up into the darkened fort, with only the slightest light coming in through the square windows cut out of each wall. A deep sigh escaped him.

He was there, alone and safe. Everything else was far, far away, and he wanted to keep it that way forever.

At which thought, fresh tears began to burn the corners of his eyes. Their warmth felt good on his reddened cheeks. Not just the warmth, either. The tears themselves felt good. The pain inside was his pain, and being alone with it felt inexplicably good. Kevin felt the sob building in his chest. It would break like a wave on the shore, and spill out of him. But that was all right. He needed that.

He drew a long, shuddering breath, about to cry out.

"You can't make me go back."

The voice, barely above a whisper, came from a shadowy corner of the fort, and Kevin shouted out in fright and scrabbled back into the opposite corner. He narrowed his eyes, trying to make out the figure that sat across from him in the meager moonlight.

"Did you hear me? I won't go back to my parents. You'll have to kill me first."

Kevin could barely make her out. Her eyes glinted in the shadows, reflecting what little light there was as though they sucked it from the air. Wild black hair fell in a tangle over her shoulders and covered part of her face. Her skin, as well as he could make it out there in the huddle of the fort, looked brown.

He hadn't said a word, stunned into silence by her presence and her venomous tone. Now he realized he had to say something. What came out was not what he intended.

"This is our fort," he told her sternly, sniffling away his now-forgotten tears. "You can't be here."

The fort was the solace he had so looked forward to. It had been invaded. Though there were endless questions flashing across his mind, that territorial instinct had come quickly to the fore. Instantly, he regretted it.

For the girl had a knife. He hadn't seen it before, but now the blade twisted in the air in front of her, flashing starlight as it turned in her grasp.

"Who are you?" she demanded.

"You're asking me?" Kevin snapped, growing angry now. Or, at least, covering his fear of that blade by pretending anger. "This is our place, I said. We built it. Me and my brother and our friends. Nobody said you could be in here."

The girl seemed to relax, quite suddenly, sinking back in upon herself, almost disappearing in the corner again.

Kevin heard her crying. His heart went to her, as it would to any girl he heard weeping. He was eleven, but he wasn't one of those boys who thought girls were gross. Not even close. Still, though, the sound of her quiet sobs was like salt in his own fresh wounds, and so his sympathy was dulled quite a lot.

"I'm sorry," she said, at great length. "I thought you were someone else. You're right. This isn't my place. I was running, just running through the wood. And I came upon this place, and I was so tired. I thought I could hide here, just 'til morning, and then I might be safe, or at least not afraid to find my way."

He wanted to tell her to get out. He truly did. But she'd been crying. And she sounded so lost. Lost and empty, just the way he felt. There'd been that knife, sure, but who knew what she was running from. Maybe she thought she needed that knife. What was that she'd said at the beginning anyway? If he wanted to take her back, he'd have to kill her.

That was serious. Much worse than what had happened to Kevin. Hell, his mom and Jesse were home waiting for him. They loved him at least. But this girl would rather die than go back home.

"All right, take it easy," he said softly. "You can stay. I just . . . You scared me—that's all. I didn't expect anyone to be up here, and I'm . . ."

His words trailed off, but somehow, she sensed what they would be.

"You've run away, too, haven't you?"

Kevin only nodded, but she must have seen him in spite of the dark, for she slid forward a little, into the moonlight, and looked at him so gently with large, round eyes the color of milk chocolate. He could see now that she looked a little older than he. Though she was smaller, she certainly seemed more mature. In spite of the dark clothes she wore wrapped around her almost like a cloak, he could not help but notice the swell of her breasts.

"Then we have each other, I guess," she said. "I never imagined I'd find a friend in the wood. If we can be friends? My name is Laurel."

"I'm Kevin," he said, automatically.

Everything about her distracted him now. Her name was beautiful. She was beautiful, or as much as he could see there in the gloom. Something else, too. It wasn't "the woods" to her. Or even "the forest." *The wood*, she'd called it, and more than once. Otherwise, she spoke pretty much like other kids he knew, but that was sort of peculiar. Not that he minded. It was kind of nice. It had an odd ring to it, a kind of magic quality that only added to the idea that lingered in his mind that the forest and the fort were a world away from home.

"Kevin," she repeated. "What are you running from?"

Though he knew he would never tell any of his friends, and that he and Jesse might never discuss it more than superficially, he found himself telling Laurel about his family, the pain in his heart, the way his father had thrown his mother and Jesse aside and just gone away. Just left. Before he could stop himself, Kevin found himself crying, and quickly wiped the tears away.

He had never cried in front of a girl before, and he was embarrassed.

"What about you?" he asked, mostly to change the subject, but also because he wanted to know. Wanted to help, if he could. Talking helped a lot. His mom had always told him that, and he'd found it to be one of the truest things she'd taught him.

Laurel laughed, then. It was an ugly laugh.

"My mother treats me like a dog, and my father treats me like a whore. They eat like royalty, and I eat slop. I'm a servant in my own home." She paused then, to wipe at her eyes. But then she lifted her chin high. Her hair fell away from her face a bit, and Kevin saw long golden strands dangling from her ears.

He frowned. Her ears looked almost pointed.

"Well, no more," she said dangerously. "No more."

"Jesus," Kevin whispered. "I guess . . . I mean, it was bad, and my father's an asshole, but nothing like . . . aw, hell, I'm sorry."

For just a moment, he thought that Laurel might have smiled a bit.

Then the howling began. Kevin flinched, looking around nervously, so that at first he didn't notice her reaction. Then he heard her whimper, and he looked to see that Laurel sat rigid, blade out in front of her once more, eyes darting from side to side as if someone might be sneaking up on her. Which was impossible, of course. She had the walls of the fort behind her, and just the trees beyond. They were twelve feet up.

"They're coming," she whispered. "I thought I'd be safe here."

Kevin frowned. "Come on. What are you talking about? Your parents have bloodhounds or something?"

It was absurd. But the thing was, it didn't feel absurd. Not sitting up there in the fort in the dark in the middle of the woods—the *wood*—and Laurel looking like the devil himself were coming for her.

"Go," she said suddenly.

Laurel scrabbled across the wood and pushed him toward the trap door. "They won't dare hurt me, but they'll kill you, Kevin. I don't think I could live with that."

"What?" he scoffed. "Come on, Laurel. You have any idea how that sounds? Who's going to kill me? Your parents?"

She gave him a hard look, then shook her head. "Then I'll go," she said. "It's the only way."

With that, she slid to the edge of the hole in the floor, and then simply pushed off into space.

"Laurel!" Kevin shouted, and stuck his head over the hole to look down.

The girl landed on her feet, knees slightly bent. He blinked, peering into the night, but he didn't think she fell down. At all. Kevin was astounded. He couldn't have done that, and he was bigger than she was. If he wanted to get down without the rope, he'd have held on to the lip of the hole, dangled down and let himself go, and even then, he probably would have had to tumble into a roll when he hit the ground.

With a quick glance up at him, Laurel whispered. "Goodbye, Kevin."

"Wait," he called.

At the sound of his voice, the howling began again. Much closer this time. Kevin shivered, and suddenly needed to pee quite badly. It was like nothing he'd ever heard before, not even the howl of werewolves in old movies on *Creature Feature*. They sounded almost as if they were calling out to someone. To one another, maybe, or to Laurel? He didn't know, but that was how it sounded.

And they sounded angry.

"Oh, fuck," Kevin groaned, truly afraid now.

For half a second, he'd thought that he could stay up there, in the fort. But they were coming this way, and if Laurel was going to run, he was going to run, too. If he could catch up to her, they could run to his house. Surely his mom would let her in, at least to get away from the hounds, or whatever. If they could get out of the wood, they could even go to the Levensons, right there at the top of the street. Mrs. Levenson knew him; she wouldn't turn them away. They could call the police.

Fast as he was able, Kevin threw the heavy coil of rope through the trapdoor and slipped down it, burning his hands a little and dropping the last few feet. He managed to keep his balance, but only barely. Then he was sprinting up the hill and into the trees, branches slapping his face, scratching him deep. He caught his arm on a splintered tree branch and got a good scrape that would leave a thin white scar for the rest of his life.

Still he ran on. The sound was coming from behind him now, and closer. Back there in the dense forest beyond the fort, he could hear them crashing through branches, whatever they were. They growled now, and seemed to roar instead of howling, as though they smelled something good to eat.

"Jesus," Kevin whimpered.

There was something else, too. Something with them. Something big and lumbering. It was a man, he thought. When he glanced behind him, he could just make out a human shape back there. But it moved fast, slamming through the trees, snapping off branches as it went.

Despite the cold, Kevin was sweating. His bladder cramped up, and he wanted badly to stop, but didn't dare. His heart thudded in his chest, and he felt it reverberating all over his body, starting at his ribs, then moving through him like an echo.

He ran. He stumbled over a root. Slipped in fallen leaves. He peered through the branches ahead.

Where's the path?

He should have come to it by now. Before now. Terrified, Kevin knew he had to get his bearings or he might get lost in the wood forever. Those dogs would get him. The man . . . the man who wanted Laurel back would get him.

They'll kill you, she had said. Suddenly, he believed her completely.

Kevin stopped short, desperate to find his way. He looked back, eyes searching for the hill, trying to place the path in relation to where the ground rose up in front of the fort.

It was there.

So were they.

Through a break in the trees, he saw them, standing at the crest of the hill in the moonlight, which streamed down through an opening in the canopy above. For a heartbeat, they were silhouetted there. The hounds weren't hounds at all. But what they were, he couldn't have said. They walked on all fours and were covered with fur, but they were the size of ponies, their snouts dangling low to the ground.

What stood between them could hardly be called a man. It was half again as tall as Kevin, a good two feet taller than his dad. It was naked, and its skin looked like leather. It was as broad across as a barn door, and its arms were the thick as a telephone pole, fists the size of a Christmas turkey. It was bald and scarred, and it had a pair of stumpy tusks that stuck up from its lower jaw like a walrus.

That last was what did it. That last was what made Kevin realize that it couldn't be a human being, not even in a circus sideshow.

In that moment, he couldn't breathe. Only that fact kept him from screaming. He was frozen in the dark, and thanking God that he hadn't screamed, when the beasts sniffed him. His silence no longer mattered. They started down after him.

Now Kevin did scream. He turned and fled in the direction he thought the path should be.

It still wasn't there.

He cried—it felt like he'd been crying for days, like there should be no tears left to fall—and he called for his mother, and he felt like his head would split or he might just fall down there and wait for them to get him. A branch gouged his cheek. He held his arms up to protect his face, but still, there was no path.

No path. It was impossible. He should have come upon it way before this.

"Kevin!"

A strong hand clamped upon his arm, and he cried out again, afraid it might break.

"Be quiet, please," Laurel begged, voice hushed.

He turned to look at her, desperate with terror. Her eyes locked on his. She kissed him, quickly, on the lips— the first kiss he'd ever had from a girl, really.

"You were kind to me, Kevin. I won't forget you. But go home, now. Your mother's waiting for you."

No shit, he wanted to say. *What do you think I'm trying to do?*

What came out was "Come with me."

"We'd never escape together," she told him. "They only want me back. I'll be punished, but I'll live. You won't. You have to run, now!"

He tried to find the words, though he could hear the man—the thing—crashing through the wood. He couldn't hear the hounds, though, and that worried him even more. They were there, but silent. Maybe too close already.

"Run!" she snarled, and gave him a shove.

Kevin let the momentum carry him, and he ran. Shame built up inside him, and he wanted to stop. She was a girl. He couldn't leave her behind. Even if they didn't kill her, if what she'd told him was true, her life was horrible enough. He had to find a way to save her.

We'd never escape together. I'll live. You won't.

Kevin kept running. He heard the hounds start growling, too close behind him. Heard a thundering laugh that he knew had come from the hunter. That was what he was, too. Some kind of hunter.

If he heard Laurel scream, he'd go back. He promised himself that. If it sounded like she was being hurt, he'd . . .

I'll live. You won't.

"Oh, God," he whispered.

She had stayed behind to make sure he got away. And all he could do was run. For the second time that night, he wanted to throw up.

Then, suddenly, he burst out of the trees onto the main path, tripped on a stone jutting from the ground, and fell hard to his knees. Kevin's gaze darted down the path to his left, and he knew it immediately. It was the main path at the top of his street. Impossible, of course, 'cause he couldn't have gotten there without crossing

that secondary path first. Unless he'd been so scared that
he had crossed right through without even noticing.

Ready to get up and run, he peered into the trees for
some sign of Laurel, or her pursuers. But there was no
sign. No sign, no trace, and even stranger, no sound. He
could not hear the hounds. He could not hear the
hunter. No branches snapped. Just the wind whistling
through the naked trees, and the sound of a dog—a real
dog, a house pet—barking somewhere down on Fox
Run Drive.

"Kevin!"

His head snapped to the right, heart thundering in his
chest. Then he saw his brother, Jesse, coming along the
path in the gloom. As he got closer, Kevin saw the jean
jacket in his brother's hand, and he shivered, longing
for it.

"Jess," he said, his voice a croak.

Jesse walked up to him, the pain in his eyes almost
unbearable, even in the near dark. Kevin looked away
from them. Then he threw his arms around his brother
and held him tight, in a way he hadn't done since they
were just little boys.

"Mom sent me to find you," Jesse said. "I figured
you'd be up here. You go to the fort?"

Kevin nodded. He didn't know what to say. He
glanced into the wood several times, but saw nothing.

"Hey," Jesse said, looking hard at his cheek, and his
arms. "What the hell happened to you?"

If he'd heard anything at all, then, even the snapping
of a twig, Kevin probably would have spilled the whole
story, frantic and fearful, even dragging Jesse back into
the wood to try to help Laurel. Already, though, what
had happened at the fort had begun to seem less important. The girl had a horrible life—that was true. But in
that moment, in the here and now, what was happening
between them was more important.

"I was running," Kevin replied. "Got a little lost, I
guess. I was afraid."

"You're okay now, bro," Jesse said and threw an arm around his brother.

Together, they started back along the path. Kevin glanced over his shoulder several times, the story right on the tip of his tongue. But somehow, he never shared it. Not with Jesse, or with anyone. He kept it to himself, just as he never told his friends the story of what had happened with his father that night.

When he and Jesse emerged into the circle at the top of Fox Run Drive, Kevin hesitated one last time, thinking of Laurel. He wanted to cry for her, and for himself, but he could find no more tears. They had stopped at last.

"Come on, Kev. Let's go home. Mom's worried about you," Jesse said.

Kevin nodded, and they walked on together. He didn't know what else to do. Laurel's life sucked—that was for sure. But with each step, the things he had thought he'd seen seemed all the more ridiculous. The dogs were just dogs.

Of course they were.

And the hunter was just a man. A big bastard, no doubt. Maybe he'd been wearing a leather jacket with the collar turned up, and Kevin had seen . . . no, what he'd seen was just ridiculous. It was probably her father. If so, then he figured he was the lucky one. Better to have his father gone than to have a father like that.

Better. Only it didn't feel better.

The ache inside him had been temporarily edged out by fear, and whatever weird hallucinations being in the wood at night had brought about. But it was back now.

Even wearing the jean jacket his brother had brought him, he was cold. Kevin shivered.

"He's really gone, isn't he, Kev?" Jesse asked.

Kevin looked at him in surprise. Jesse was supposed to be the strong one, not him. He was the big brother, after all. But now he saw that pain in Jesse's eyes again, and he knew his brother was waiting for the answer. Waiting for the truth.

"Yeah, Jess. I really think so."

"Do me a favor, Kevin?"

Kevin shrugged.

"Don't run away again."

His heart tightened. There was a tiny chunk of ice in his stomach. Kevin shook his head, vigorously.

"I won't. Not ever. And if I do, I'll take you with me."

At that, Jesse smiled.

The Murphy brothers walked side by side down Fox Run Drive. When they came in sight of their house, it might have been that they walked a little faster.